Falling Shadows

A Harry's Game Story

Falling Shadows

A Harry's Game Story

Karl Jackson

Alpaca & Goose
2025

Book design & Illustration by Karl Jackson

First published – November 2025

First Edition

ISBN: 979-8-2691508-8-8

www.harrysgame.com

'Friends'

Dedicated to those who lived in the shadows,
so others could live in the light.

The life that I have
Is all that I have
And the life that I have is yours

The love that I have
Of the life that I have
Is yours, and yours, and yours

A sleep I shall have
A rest I shall have
Yet death will be but a pause

For the peace of my years
In the long green grass
Will be yours, and yours, and yours.

Leo Marks, 1943.

Chapter 1

Leap of Faith

It was a grey and damp day in London, the type of late autumn misery that heralded the approach of winter, and all the cold and darkness that brought with it. Businessmen shuffled by with their collars pulled up, and umbrellas floating above them, while women came and went, some in smart overcoats and hats, others in less fine clothes. Nobody was smiling, despite the country somehow surviving the Battle of Britain just a few months earlier. There'd been much to cheer about when the pilots of the RAF crisscrossed the sky over London with white vapour trails and black smoke, as they held off, and eventually pushed back the might of the Luftwaffe, the German air force that had vowed to sweep the skies above England clean as a prelude to invasion. It was a scary time to be alive, especially with bombs being rained down all over the country, and at the same time it was warm, it was summer, and the radio and newspapers excitedly told of the RAF's many victories. Then it all stopped. By the end of October, the battle was over, and the Germans only ever came at night. The threat of invasion had been postponed until the following spring, and the country could breathe a sigh of relief. Though without the good news, or the warmth, the country was left with the bleakness of late autumn, a closing winter, and thoughts of what would come next.

"Good morning, Ma'am," a grizzled RAF Corporal barked from under his peaked cap as he stood in his long, heavy wool greatcoat by the sandbagged side entrance to the Air Ministry building.

"Good morning." Emily's reply was firm, yet warm, as her well spoken words with the softest of Scottish accents drifted through the Rain. "I'm told I can talk to somebody here about joining up?" She tilted her umbrella back as she talked, and looked him in the eyes. "Yes, Ma'am." He pulled the door open for her after looking her up and down for a while, and stood tight against the sandbags as she walked past and gave him a nod and smile of thanks, while collapsing her umbrella and giving it a spin to shake off the drops as she did. Inside the room were a few men sitting on chairs along the far wall,

all wearing suits, with a desk against the opposite wall, behind which sat a tall, barrel chested Sergeant with thinning silver hair.

"Excuse me, I'd like to talk with somebody about joining the RAF," she said as she stood in front of the desk.

"Ma'am?" He looked up at her from the notes he was writing.

"I'd like to talk with somebody about joining the RAF." She gave him a firm·stare; one she'd perfected in the years she'd worked as a nurse.

"Sorry, Ma'am." His face warmed as he stood and smiled at her. "I didn't hear you right at first. I'm a bit mutton on account of an artillery shell going off right next to me in the last war."

"Mutton?" She narrowed her eyes slightly as she looked at him, trying to work out what the big Londoner was talking about.

"Mutt 'n Jeff. Deaf," he laughed. I got a limp and a lifelong ringing in my ears for my troubles, and it stops me hearing quite as well at times. Quite the souvenir."

"Quite…" She let herself smile. "So, am I in the right place to talk about joining the RAF?"

"We can help you join the WAAF, Ma'am. That shouldn't be a problem." He turned to his filing cabinet and started rummaging in the paperwork. "I'll get you some forms to fill in."

"I'm sorry, you must have misheard. I said RAF, not WAAF."

"Ma'am?" He looked over his shoulder and frowned at her in confusion.

"Royal Air Force, not the Women's Auxiliary Air Force." He looked at her for a moment, then turned and returned to his desk holding in his hand the papers he'd retrieved from the cabinet. "If it's not too

2

much trouble." She smiled while her firm words cut through the air, as though she'd just ordered him to take his medicine.

"You see, Ma'am. The RAF doesn't have women, only men. Any women wanting to serve join the WAAF." He looked a little sheepish as he explained, as though he was embarrassed to tell her.

"Well, that's not on at all. I want to join the RAF."

"Sorry, Ma'am..." He shrugged while half offering the papers. "It's the rules."

"I see... I'd like to speak with your commanding officer." She gave him a slight wave of her hand as she gestured him towards the door. "I'm assuming he's through there?"

"Ma'am?"

"Sergeant, I've come all the way to London to join the RAF, and I'm not leaving until somebody's talked with me about it." She smiled in a fierce way that would send ice through the most fearsome of enemies. As they stared at each other, the men across the room muttered and laughed to each other, and she spun on her heel to face them. "Can I help either of you?" she demanded, and got some embarrassed looks and shaking of heads before she turned back to the Sergeant. "Come now, Sergeant, we don't have all day. I'll wait here." She gave him a firm nod, getting one in return before he put down the papers and headed through the door.

She stood in her place and waited in silence, hearing the men whispering behind her, but not bothering to say anything. She'd dealt with soldiers in her hospital after the Dunkirk evacuation. Some were in a terrible way, but others, mostly young officers who'd taken shrapnel or a bullet, and were moving around after a while, could be a handful if they weren't managed, and as a Senior Sister in the hospital, she'd developed a bark fierce enough that the person on the receiving end wouldn't even want to think about her bite. She never raised her voice, though. She was always composed, and always calm

3

and well spoken, choosing her words carefully to make sure her meaning wasn't missed, and it was a brave patient who challenged her. Dettol was always her go to when proving a point. Wounds and bodies needed to be cleaned, and Dettol antiseptic liquid could leave quite a sting if applied liberally instead of soap and water. Patients learned very quickly who was in charge, and she wasn't one for suffering anybody's nonsense.

"Good morning," an RAF Flight Lieutenant said as he followed the Sergeant into the room. He had medal ribbons across his left chest pocket, and pilot wings above them. "Miss…?" He held out his hand as he walked over to Emily.

"Strachan…" She took his hand and shook it firmly as she looked at him with a degree of curiosity. He was Asian in appearance, and his English had the slightest hint of an accent not of the British Isles.

"A pleasure to meet you, Miss Strachan. My name is Flight Lieutenant O'Kara." He bowed his head smartly. "Sergeant Baker tells me you would like to join the Royal Air Force?" He had a pleasant and relaxing demeanour, and Emily instantly felt comfortable with him.

"That's right. However, your Sergeant tells me that because I'm a woman, I can only join the WAAF."

"Which is correct," he smiled.

"Yet a young lady who I cared for in my hospital some months ago would say otherwise."

"Is that so?" He frowned at her with curiosity, while still smiling.

"She flew with the RAF in France, and was shot down over the beaches at Dunkirk, then went on to fly Spitfires in the Battle of Britain." There was a snigger from the young men behind her, but she didn't turn, but the officer looked over her shoulder at them, and stared for a moment before turning his gaze back to Emily.

4

"Harriet Cornwall…" He said as his smile broadened.

"How would you know that?" Emily's head tilted a little as her eyes narrowed.

"Miss Cornwall and I are acquainted, and I'd liked to think we are friends." He looked over her shoulder again at the young men before continuing. "At the height of the battle, just a few months ago, she'd run out of ammunition while flying in combat over London, and went on to ram a German bomber out of the sky before it could bomb Buckingham Palace while the Royal Family were at home…" The smiles fell from the men's faces as he talked. "I believe she was awarded the Distinguished Service Order by the King himself for such bravery." he looked back to Emily as the men looked down at their shoes. "You cared for her in hospital?"

"Yes…" Emily felt herself smiling as she heard of Harriet's exploits. Even had her name not been mentioned, she would know who he was talking about. The girl who threw a vase of flowers over the Senior Sister's head, and was nothing less than a mischievous live wire from the minute she'd regained consciousness after floating burned and wounded in the English Channel, to the day she walked out of hospital in a borrowed skirt suit heading for home. Only she could ram a German out of the air. She was the only person Emily knew to be dedicated enough, not to mention stubborn enough to do it.

"Tea?" he asked.

"Excuse me?"

"Would you like a cup of tea? It looks like you've been out in the cold and rain. You would be most welcome to join me in having a cup?"

"That would be wonderful, thank you."

"Tea is always wonderful, at least we Japanese think so. Shall we?" He gestured to the door, and with a nod and a smile, she joined him heading through it, while Sergeant Baker looked on in surprise.

5

"Thank you," Emily said as she took a sip of the delicate tasting tea that actually tested more like tea than much else she'd tasted since the rationing started. "This tea is..."

"Wonderful?" he replied with a knowing smile as he sat facing her in his small office, having moved his chair around so the desk wasn't between them. "So, tell me about why you want to join the RAF?"

"I want to do my bit, I suppose..." she replied thoughtfully. "Things got very busy when Harriet left the hospital, but she stayed with me at the same time. Her words did, at least. She talked with such spirit about how she'd managed to fly with the RAF, and she was so passionate about getting back to her squadron so she could keep fighting. It was... Well, it was inspirational. Even before she left, I'd decided that I want to do something more for the war effort, and it's only now that I've had the opportunity."

"Because you had so many patients?"

"Yes... We were only a small hospital, and received quite a few officers and senior ranks, but the flow just didn't stop. Finally, when everyone was home from France, and we'd done what we could, things started to ease a little bit, but then we got casualties from the Battle of Britain. Some pilots who'd been shot down, and civilians who'd been hurt in bombing raids. It was a busy time, and we needed every nurse we had. Then, in November it started to return to normal, and when it didn't pick up again, I knew that it was time before something else happened, and I ended up staying. A now or never moment, I suppose."

"You said you were a Senior Sister?"

"Yes, I had my own ward to look after, and my own nurses. Actually, it was Harriet that got me the promotion, believe it or not?" She smiled to herself and almost let out a laugh while O'Kara leaned forward with interest. "My predecessor was leaving for a while, and the Matron was looking for a replacement. She told me that she gave

6

me Harriet as a test. If I could handle her, I could handle anyone." She let out the laugh, as did he.

"You must be a good nurse if you managed to take her from such a desperate place, to being able to fly so bravely over London."

"I try," she quickly took a sip of tea to try and hide her blush at the compliment.

"Then why leave to join us? Surely you would serve the country best by using your skills as a nurse to get more pilots like Harriet back in the fight?"

"Yes…" she replied. "You'd think that would be enough, wouldn't you?" She forced a hard smile as she stared into space for a moment. "It's not, though. I know I sound ridiculous, but I want to do more. I want to be on the front lines…" She frowned as she spoke, becoming a little distant for a moment.

"I assume that you're not a pilot, as well as a nurse?"

"I'm not…" Her eyes refocused as she looked at him. "I've only ever been in an aeroplane once, in fact, and that was when Harriet took me for a joy ride in a Tiger Moth. At least, that's what I think she called it."

"Indeed," he smiled as he nodded. "Unfortunately, the only females serving in the Royal Air Force are pilots in the Volunteer Reserve, and there aren't many of them at all. All others serve in the Women's Auxiliary Air Force, the WAAF…" Her frown returned at the news. "The Air Ministry bent the rules for our mutual friend, and that was because there were people in very high places supporting her. I'm not sure we would have much chance of twisting their arms a second time, I'm afraid."

"So, what you're telling me is, despite my best efforts, there's no way I'll serve in the Royal Air Force, unless I join the WAAF?"

"Unfortunately." He smiled politely, though his eyes suggested that he understood her frustration and pain. "The WAAF need confident and intelligent women in their ranks, and they do a number of very important jobs in the service such as clerks, drivers, parachute packers…"

"Clerks, drivers, and parachute packers?" She sat back in her chair and gave him a firm stare. "I said I wanted to do my bit, to do something more!" Her tone had a polite force that brought out her soft Scottish accent all the more. "Is that the best the RAF, or WAAF, can do?"

"If I may continue?" he asked politely, before she went any further. She took a sip of her tea, then gave him a composed nod. "The WAAF do important work, however, the RAF chooses how best to use the skills of those joining, and I have no doubt that you would not be sent to any of those jobs, instead I fear you would be employed as a nurse, specifically in the Princess Mary's Royal Air Force Nursing Service."

"They'd make me a nurse?"

"I'm afraid so."

"I'd refuse!"

"Sadly, once you are in the service, you cannot. You must obey orders like anybody else."

"You're telling me that I can leave my post as a nurse, only to join the RAF as a nurse?" The annoyance at the rigidity and inflexibility of the system frustrated her, and despite having experience of similar in the nursing profession, she was desperately struggling to believe it was the same in the organisations apparently desperate for people to help defend the country. It made her sit rigid in her seat, back straight, shoulders pulled back, and head held high as she fought not to let out her frustration at the polite officer who'd brought her to his office for tea.

8

"Alas, it's how the organisation is…"

"Thank you for taking the time to explain it to me," she said with a firm smile as she put her cup down on the table and stood. "Some years ago, I'd be inclined to accept that my role as a nurse is how I can best serve my country in a time of war, but we grow, and we change, and I'm just not prepared to accept that anymore. If other women are putting themselves in harm's way for our country, one way or another I'll be doing the same, and if the RAF can't help, I'll find somebody who will. The Army, or Royal Navy, perhaps. Or I'll just make my own way back to France and kick the Germans out before they come here!" She headed for the door, carrying herself as confidently as always, while trying not to let the emotion that was rising inside her be seen. From day one of nurse training, she'd been told in no uncertain terms that emotions of all sorts were to be managed out of sight of others, and buried deep down inside until such a time to deal with them privately presented itself. The slightest public display of emotion was frowned upon, and she knew why. Emotions got in the way of doing a difficult job. There was no place for crying when peeling burned skin from the body of a pilot, or being elbows deep in blood and guts while trying to stop a soldier's stomach wound from rupturing entirely. The patients were already in enough distress, and they needed to know that their nurse knew what they were doing, and would make everything alright. They didn't need their nurses crying, or struggling to contain their emotions. "Thank you again, I'll see myself out. Goodbye."

"One moment, please," he said as he stood. "Miss Strachan."

"Yes?" She half turned to face him, glancing around the room to make sure she hadn't left something. She looked him in the eyes after confirming she had her belongings, and a slow half smile spread across his face. "What is it?"

"You said you'd go back to France?"

"What of it?"

"Back? You were already there? In France, I mean?"

"Not for a while, but I spent some of my summers in Paris when I was young. Why"

"I have an idea," he replied. "Please, sit a moment." He gestured to the chair she'd vacated, and after a moment she did as he asked, feeling a little intrigued as to what was going on. She put her bags down again and picked up her cup to finish her tea, while wondering if it had all been some sort of test, and her firmness had somehow got her through to a job in the RAF. He stood by his desk and picked up the phone, then asked for a number and waited, while smiling at her warmly. She let her mind wander a little, and thought of Harriet. She was stubborn, and determined, and maybe that's what it took to get into the boy's club of the RAF. For a moment she let herself hope that she'd got through the door, and her determination had paid off, though she smiled when she caught herself thinking she was like Harriet. The girl who'd had tea with the King while the Battle of Britain raged all around. The smile turned into another slight laugh. Harriet had been such a mess when she'd arrived at the little hospital on the coast. A scarecrow buried in oversize flying jacket and boots, her hair straggly and matted with smoke and seawater, and her face blackened from fire. Some of her clothes had to be cut from her burned skin, and shrapnel had to be pulled from her body and face, all while she lay unconscious with a faint pulse and shallow breathing, a step away from death's door. Out of the burned and filthy uniform she looked like a schoolgirl laid in the hospital bed. Young and innocent, and a million miles away from the war. The hospital had been told she'd escaped Dunkirk, and her flying jacket and boots suggested she was with the RAF, but that's all they knew at first. It was difficult for any of them at first, all of the clinical staff, to understand how such a young girl could be anything to do with the military. Worse, they didn't understand how she was still alive. Her body was barely keeping her going, and she was in what they thought was a coma for some time, until she started screaming and crying in her sleep, and writhing as though desperate to escape something. Emily had stayed with her day and night, cleaning her wounds, bathing her, and making sure she stayed alive. Talking to her when she had the terrors, and sleeping by her bed when Harriet was settled.

Then, she finally woke up. The girl became a strong minded and mischievous young woman who knew how to get what she wanted in life, and whose intelligence had her running rings around some of the senior staff, while all the time she was desperate to get back to her unit, back to the war that by her own admission had tried to kill her time and again. Though why wouldn't she? She'd lived in France for half of her life, and the last she'd seen her parents, they were right in the path of the German advance. Everyone she'd known and loved was dead or missing, why wouldn't she fight? "Is everything OK?" O'Kara's voice cut through Emily's daydreaming, and she blinked her eyes as she looked up to his warm gaze.

"Excuse me?" she asked after taking a sip of the cooling tea, and snapping back into the present.

"You seem a little distracted?"

"Just thinking," she smiled as she noticed he'd put down the phone, and realised she hadn't seen or heard a thing, and he could have been watching her for an age. "Your idea?"

"Yes…" His smile widened, and he handed her a piece of paper.

"The Savoy?" She frowned as she read it. "I'm afraid I don't understand?"

"I would recommend that you try the tea there, it's very good. Perhaps at around three this afternoon."

"Tea…?" Her frown deepened. "Your idea is for me to have tea at a fancy hotel?"

"A table by the window, perhaps, and do ask to try the macarons, they're delightful." He bowed a little as his smile broadened.

"I still don't understand?" Her voice remained firm, but she was so bewildered she couldn't rise to any more than that. She'd got lost in the hope of him helping her join the RAF, and finding out he'd organised tea had come as such a shock that she was helpless to respond beyond confusion.

"Alas, I must return to work," he sighed as he checked his watch, before straightening his uniform.

"Yes..." She stood and collected herself, then stepped out of the door he'd opened for her, before following him back down the corridor to the waiting room she'd started in.

"It's been a pleasure to meet you, Miss Strachan. It does me well to meet a friend of Miss Cornwall's"

"I'm sure the pleasure's been all mine. Thank you, Mister O'Kara." She stood straight and confident, and offered her hand, which he shook before leaning closer and whispering close to her ear.

"Try the macarons at three..." He stepped away, then opened the door for her to walk out into the still raining misery of London's cold November. She nodded, and gave him a nurse's smile, a polite smile that didn't match the frustration inside, not to mention the confusion, then stepped outside and extended her umbrella, before marching off through London's unwelcoming autumnal darkness.

Chapter 2

Macarons

Her plans to join the RAF in tatters, Emily had returned to the house she'd stayed in the previous night, to drop off her bags and freshen up before heading out to make the most of her time in London. Despite the cold, lumpy bed, and the small portions of food, she quite liked it there. It was run by the Women's Voluntary Service as a hostel for female service personnel visiting London, and she'd been told by the Matron before she left Kent that they also accepted nurses, which was a relief considering she'd had no idea where else she could stay when she arrived in the city. Two very well spoken, and very upper middle class ladies ran the show, booking the accommodation, cleaning, cooking, and making sure their guests were safe and looked after. They wore their privately purchased grey WVS uniforms with great pride, which was no surprise, considering they were probably made at Harrods, and they fussed in the most professional way. While the large, old town house was cold, and the food restricted by the rationing, they kept a fire roaring in the living room, and provided fresh baked flat biscuits on an evening. They even took it in turns playing the piano and engaging in polite conversation with their guests, giving advice on where to visit in London, and where to avoid. There were some other women there, but not many. Two girls from the Auxiliary Territorial Service, the women's branch of the army, who were in town on a forty eight hour pass before heading north to join a Royal Artillery searchlight battery, and a WAAF clerk from RAF Uxbridge who was meeting up with her boyfriend, a Sergeant Pilot who flew Hawker Hurricanes.

By the time she got back to the hostel, Emily had decided that if she wasn't going to join the RAF and follow Harriet's footsteps, she was going to go back home to Scotland, to see her parents and stay with them while she decided what next she'd do with her life. She knew they would be happy to see her, and that they'd help her work things out. They'd begged her not to leave when she did, and every time she wrote, they replied telling her that her room was always there for her. She hadn't seen them since heading south to take her job at the hospital, and she wanted to take them a gift from England, so she decided to do some shopping while she had the time, and maybe even pick up some food to supplement her rations.

The rain had eased, and the umbrella wasn't necessary as the cloud broke a little in the afternoon, letting the barely lukewarm rays of sun bounce off the murk of the Thames as she walked along the Victoria Embankment. She stopped and looked up and down the river at the boats and ships tied up, and watched as a fire tender cut along the choppy water as it headed east, no doubt in preparation for what the night could bring. She thought as she watched the firemen cruise down the river, and looked over to the grey warship a little further down, with its sailors hard at work. Everyone was doing their bit for the country, and she thought for a moment on her own situation. Had she been hasty in leaving her job as a nurse? Somebody needed to put the wounded back together again, and stop them dying, and it wasn't something everyone could do. The country was at war. A war already seemingly as big, if not bigger than the last, and already so costly and devastating. The British Expeditionary Force in France and Belgium had been kicked out of Europe, and the continent had fallen under the might of the Nazi war machine. Britain was alone in Europe, and desperate. It was enough for her to question what she was doing even further. What did it matter if she couldn't join the RAF? It wouldn't matter at all if Hitler invaded the following Spring, as everyone was suggesting he would. Maybe she'd be better keeping people alive than she would killing them.

She continued her walk, heading to the Palace of Westminster, where all the windbag politicians argued about how to run the country, and laughed to herself as she saw the huge barrage balloon above it. She'd been told that Londoners called their local barrage balloons after politicians, with them both being full of hot air and all. It was enough to keep her smiling when she reached the seat of government and saw Churchill scurry from a car into the building, followed closely by his military aids. He didn't look like much of a great war leader. Ageing, rotund, and not particularly tall, and there were enough rumours that he drank Champagne for breakfast, and took naps in the afternoon. Still, he'd told Hitler firmly that Britain would fight on the beaches and landing grounds, and after the RAF had bloodied the Luftwaffe's nose, much of the country were inclined to agree with him. Down near her hospital in Kent she'd seen the men of the Home Guard marching around with pitchforks, shotguns, and everything else, ready to take on the Germans should they have the temerity to arrive on Britain's shores. His boldness had even contributed to nurses upping and heading to London to join the RAF... She shook her head as she continued to walk, reflecting on how ridiculous she'd been. Harriet was a one off. Nobody else was going to be like her. She even frowned a little as she saw in her mind the Matron and Doctor Goode as they tried to understand her resignation. They'd trusted her, and promoted her to Senior Sister, yet only a few months later she'd decided she was going to London to join the fight. She cringed a little inside as she thought about it, and how silly they must have thought her. She looked at her watch, and after shaking the thoughts from her mind, decided to head towards The Savoy before picking up some treats in the West End to take home. If she wasn't going to fight, she was certainly going to taste the bloody macarons! There was nothing much else pleasant to be had, as she'd quickly found with the watery soup she'd been presented at a small place she'd stopped at for lunch.

She marched down the streets, and took a breath before having the door opened for her by the concierge, and stepping into the hotel and making her way to the dining room.

"Good afternoon, madam," a well attired man with silver hair and a thin moustache said. "How may I help?"

"I'd like a table by the window, please."

"For just the one?" He looked over her shoulder, almost comically, as if searching for somebody else.

"Unless you're too busy?" Her eyes narrowed a little as her firm tone cut through the air. She wasn't desperate enough to taste French pastries that she'd put up with any nonsense.

"Oh, not at all, madam. Lunch is well behind us, and we have a few hours yet before dinner. Can I take your coat and umbrella?" After hanging them in the cloakroom and handing her a ticket, he smiled

15

as he held out his arm, gesturing towards the dining room. She glanced around as she walked, it was an impressive place, to say the least, dotted with people here and there having tea. Some in uniforms, others not, but it wasn't even half full, and the conversation was generally a dull hubbub, making it difficult to actually hear anything. "You said by the window?"

"Yes…"

"Would this table suit?" He pulled out the chair of the table furthest from the door, the last against the window, with the wall to the back of it.

"Perfect, thank you." She smiled at the offering. She could sit with her back to the wall, and look out of the window, knowing there'd be nobody sitting behind her talking loudly and ruining her peace.

"I'll have the waiter take your order directly."

"Thank you, I'm looking forward to trying the macarons."

"Excuse me?" He looked at her with curiosity, as though she'd ordered a box of frogs.

"The macarons. I'm told I should try them. With tea, obviously." She felt her own curiosity rise as she thought back to her conversation at the Air Ministry several hours earlier, and hoped she hadn't misunderstood, though the longer she thought, the more she questioned how anyone was making macarons while eggs and sugar were rationed, even at The Savoy.

"Obviously…" He forced the look from his face and smiled, then straightened up again. "I'll have the waiter take care of your order." He left, a little more hurried than he'd arrived, stopping only to mutter at a waiter as they both glanced over to her briefly, making her wonder all the more whether she'd got the wrong end of the stick that morning. She'd been disappointed when she hadn't got the answers she wanted, and the conversation had been a little confusing. She shook her head gently and looked out of the window. She rationalised that he'd said he'd give the waiter her order, which was why they were talking, and as she gazed out into the increasing gloom of London, she couldn't wait to get home to Scotland. After finishing her tea, and macarons if such a thing existed in The Savoy, she needed to get her train ticket north for the following day.

She lost herself in her thoughts of Scotland. It wasn't going to be a quick journey, but the more she thought of it, the more impatient she became. She'd have to go to Glasgow, and then take a local train to the northwest, and then buses until she got to the coast. It would be an entire day, at least, probably more. It had been a long drag the other way around, but at that time she had a mission in her mind, to get to the south coast of England, as close as she could get to France, and the war. She'd been determined, and she got her wish. This time, though, she was heading north to her family, but beyond that, she hadn't a clue. There'd be nursing jobs in Scotland, of course, but they'd be a different pace from what hers had been since the Spring.

"Your tea," a distinctly English female voice said, and she turned with a hint of curiosity as to why somebody so well spoken was working as a waitress, and looked at the strikingly beautiful woman standing before her. She was wearing a smart skirt suit, and her shoulder length brown hair was flawless, as was her makeup and dark red lipstick. She glanced down to the teapot and two cups sitting on the tray on the table.

"Thank you…" Emily replied as she looked into the woman's fierce brown eyes, wondering just how exclusive The Savoy was for them to hire such people, and pay for such exquisite clothes. "Though it's only me, so I'll only need the one cup." She let herself smile.

"The other cup's for me." The glamorous brunette took a seat without invite, then went about placing the cups and the teapot, before sliding the tray across the floor behind her.

"I..." Emily started, but quickly realised that while she was used to having an answer to everything and anything, she didn't know where to start.

"You, what?" the brunette asked as she looked Emily over.

"Asked for the Macarons," she replied as she composed herself.

"Indeed you did, why else would my otherwise quite busy day be disturbed for me to be dragged to The Savoy?"

"I..."

"Don't know, is the answer you're looking for." The brunette smiled, then turned the teapot before pouring Emily's, and then hers. "The tea can be quite nice here, but you don't want to let it stew too long, or it gets heavy. They're usually good in bringing fresh water to top it up if you're polite. So that's something."

"It is."

"Yes, it is. So?"

"So?"

"Why am I here talking to you, when I have a hundred and one other things I should be doing?"

"Maybe that's something for you to decide..." Emily remained composed as her mind spun, and she tried to work out exactly what was going on. The woman had confidence in spades, and unless a recent air raid had bombed an asylum that she'd subsequently escaped from, she was there for a reason beyond tea.

"You don't know?" the brunette frowned as she sipped on her tea.

"Why would I know your itinerary? I'm just here for tea, and it was you who joined me, in case you'd forgotten."

"And the macarons."

"Excuse me?"

"You did tell the Matre'd you wanted to try the macarons?"

"Yes… I'm told they're good."

"The delicate sweet treats beloved in Paris?"

"Unless there's another type?"

"The delicate sweet treats beloved in Paris, that you'd expect to find in a London besieged by rationing and the Luftwaffe?"

"One lives in hope." Emily took a mouthful of her tea while looking the brunette in the eyes. She knew there was rationing, yet she'd held out a small hope that a fine restaurant was somehow making them.

"It'd probably be a week's ration in sugar just for one."

"Probably…"

"At least the tea's nice."

"Indeed."

"So, why do you want to kill Germans?" the brunette asked as she put her teacup down on the table and clasped her hands together lightly.

"Excuse me?" Emily almost choked on her tea as the words shocked her to the core.

"You're not hard of hearing?"

"My hearing is perfect, thank you."

"Eyesight?"

"Equally as perfect."

"Good. So, why do you want to kill Germans?"

"Why do you want to know?" Emily put down her own cup and clasped her hands, mirroring the brunette.

"Because a friend at the Air Ministry told me that some angry Scottish nurse had kicked down his doors and demanded to be a pilot in the RAF." The corners of her mouth turned up in the faintest hint of a smile as she watched the pupils of Emily's eyes pinpoint.

"Your friend was mistaken."

"You're not a nurse?"

"I wasn't angry. Frustrated, perhaps, but not angry."

"No?"

"No, I don't get angry."

"Intriguing…"

"Quite. So, why am I really here?"

"I was worried you were going to say you weren't Scottish for a moment."

"Why would I say that?"

"I've no idea, but it would have been quite ridiculous to do so. You obviously have a Scottish twang, however soft. West coast, I think."

"Possibly, but the west coast of Scotland's longer than you'd imagine."

"It wasn't a question, Miss Emily Marion Strachan, daughter of John William Strachan, accountant and former British Army officer who served in the last war, and Elise Eléonore Strachan, née Paquin, former French Red Cross Nurse from Dijon. Though until not so long ago you were of course Mrs Emily Marion MacRae, widow of the late Lieutenant Arthur Michael MacRae of the Royal Engineers, until he was lost in a skirmish with the Germans north of the British lines on the Belgian border... Parlez vous français?" She lifted her cup to take a sip, remaining as casual as if she'd just read the shipping forecast, and not just turned Emily white with the name of her dead husband, and detailed family history.

"What...?" Emily finally managed to reply as she stared at the brunette, not able to think of anything else. "How?"

"French. Do you speak French?"

"What? Yes! Oui!"

"Tell me what the weather is like today?"

"Who are you?" Emily asked, her mind was spinning, as suddenly she felt lightheaded and cold, and wondered whether she was stuck in some strange and terrifying dream."

"No, I asked you to describe the weather."

"Rain...' Emily shook her head after looking out of the window, partly to check the weather, part to make sure London was still there, and she hadn't gone insane.

21

"In detail, and in French." The brunette smiled in a way that was a long distance from reassuring, and Emily replied, giving a detailed appreciation of the weather she'd experienced throughout the day, only pausing a few times to remember the French she'd hardly used since her last visit to Paris with her parents, though having been taught the language since she could talk, the words came quickly when she started talking again. "Perfect..." The brunette's face lit up. "With your west coast Scottish, your French sounds positively southern in regional accents, with a hint of your mother's Dijon. Bravo!"

"What's happening?!" Emily demanded, switching from confused young woman to fiery and fierce nursing sister.

"Why do you want to kill Germans?"

"Because they invaded my mother's country, and I remember what my parents told me happened the last time they did that!" she half hissed, keeping her voice low, but firm, as she felt a fire she hadn't experienced for a long time. "And because they tried to kill my friend, and because they killed my husband, and if we don't do something to stop them, they'll kill everyone else, and I'm not going to stand by and let them!" The brunette stared for a moment, the same slight mile turning up the corners of her mouth.

"First Aid Nursing Yeomanry," she said firmly after a minute or two of silence, then took another drink of her tea.

"Excuse me?" Emily was unsettled, she felt herself shaking, while inside she was furious at herself for breaking and saying the things she did. Her anger hadn't been seen by anyone for many years, it had always been kept inside, away from everyone, including her family. She even stood stoic and almost emotionless at the funeral for her husband's empty casket, yet a conversation with an unknown stranger over tea had pushed a button she didn't know she had.

"You're going to report to Wellington Barracks on Birdcage Walk, and tell them you're there to join the First Aid Nursing Yeomanry." She pulled an envelope from her bag and passed it over the table.

"I don't want to be a nurse, thank you." Emily felt herself settle and compose as she smiled a little, and left the brunette holding the envelope. "I thought I'd made that quite clear."

"I'm not recruiting nurses."

"Then why would you suggest that I join the First Aid Nursing Yeomanry?"

"Sometimes, the route to what we want isn't a straight line, and we have to take a leap of faith." She flicked the envelope in front of Emily. "It's a onetime offer. Take it now, or I leave, and we never talk again. You can head back to your hospital in Kent, or home to the safety of mummy and daddy. Or, you can take a leap of faith…" Despite her slight smile, her eyes were fierce in a way that Emily hadn't seen in anyone before. "Last chance. When I've counted to three, it's over. One… Two…"

"Three," Emily said as she snapped the envelope from the brunette's hand, feeling the corners of her own mouth turn up a little, as the brunette sat back in her chair and went back to drinking her tea, the dark fierceness gone in an instant.

"Read, consume, and report to Wellington Barracks tomorrow morning at nine. Tell them you're there to join the First Aid Nursing Yeomanry, and do as you're told. They'll be expecting you, so there shouldn't be any problems. Oh, and there's a joining fee."

"A joining fee?"

"Yes, it's a volunteer organisation. As such, you pay a subscription to join. You'll also need to pay your own expenses until such a time as you're picked up for work. It shouldn't be long, so I wouldn't worry too much. Anyway, you have a little over an hour to run your errands before everything closes for the day." She looked at her watch, then finished her tea before standing and straightening her clothes.

"Wait…"

"What is it?"

"I don't even know who you are?" The brunette simply smiled, then turned and left, marching across the dining room with graceful confidence, and drifting through the doors. Emily sighed, and after pouring herself more tea, she looked at the envelope for a moment. She wasn't poor by any means, but neither was she wealthy, and while she'd saved much of her pay from her time at the hospital, she didn't like the idea of having to pay to join an organisation she knew nothing about, to do a job she had no idea of, while paying her own way. At the same time, she'd just been offered the hope of what she'd wanted since leaving the hospital. She put down her cup and opened the envelope, then pulled out a folded letter that was paper clipped closed, which she unfastened to see that attached to it was a cheque for one hundred pounds in money, making her eyes open wide. The letter was simple, written on government headed stationary it instructed her to report to Wellington Barracks, London, on the following day's date. It was signed by a civil servant in a department she'd never heard of, the Inter Service Research Bureau, and that was it. There was a slip behind the letter, that had sat between it and the cheque, that simply said 'Something to ease the burden. Go to the bank today, before reporting tomorrow. Good luck, and do as you're told!' She looked in the envelope, but there was nothing else in there, no other surprises, then went back to looking at the cheque. It was from something of an institution in the banking world, and hardly some questionable back street organisation. It was also for a lot of money, and she couldn't quite get her head around why somebody would hand her, a stranger, so much. She checked the letter again, and the note and cheque, and made sure there was nothing else she'd missed before putting it in her handbag and waving the waiter over, noting the time, and the instruction to cash the cheque sooner rather than later.

"Yes, madam?" the waiter asked politely.

"I'd like the bill, please."

"The bill, madam?" He raised an eyebrow in casual confusion.

"For the tea…" she said firmly.

"Oh, I'm sorry, madam. Your friend already paid."

"She did? Well, thank you anyway, the tea was very nice."

"My pleasure, madam. Would there be anything else?"

"Yes… Do you serve macarons?"

"Oh, no. We wouldn't be able to get the sugar, or the egg whites for that matter. No, we haven't had anything like that since before the war. I could maybe see if chef has any sponge cake left?"

"No, that won't be necessary. Thank you."

After gathering her things, she'd headed through the darkening afternoon, and through the type of fine drizzle that soaked everything, making her shudder a little in the cold, and almost long for the uncomfortable and chilly bed she knew she was heading to that night, at least it was dry, and she knew the food would be good, despite there not being much of it. The previous night they'd served what they told her was a rabbit stew. It had meat, and it was a little salty, but it was tasty, and the thick chunks of potato and carrot weren't over cooked, so they were still reasonably firm when she bit into them. They'd even provided a small baked beef suet dumpling with the stew, much to her delight.

"Good afternoon, madam. May I help?" a pinstripe suited gentleman with gold framed wire rimmed glasses asked as she stepped into the bank. He was standing behind a small podium near the door of the dimly lit, opulent marble hall, taking her quite by surprise.

"Yes, I'd like to cash a cheque."

"Oh?" He tilted his head a little while narrowing his eyes. "I'm afraid we only cash cheques from our own customers," he explained as she walked over to him, then watched as she pulled the cheque from her bag.

"I believe it is from one of your customers," she replied firmly. A little irritable at what she perceived to be some sort of snobbery on his part. He nodded and took it from her, then studied it closely.

"I believe you're right, madam. May I ask your name?"

"Strachan. Miss Emily Strachan."

"Would you kindly wait here one moment, Miss Strachan?" She gave a smile of irritation and a firm nod, and he quickly scurried away, heading to a large wooden desk behind the cashiers. He talked quickly, yet almost silently to the bald, older man sitting behind it, and handed him the cheque. A nod was given, and the tall man returned wearing a polite smile. "This way, please." He took her to a cashier, where she stood patiently as he talked. "Miss Strachan would like some assistance with her account, would you mind, Alfred?" He handed the cashier the cheque, before nodding politely and returning to his small podium.

"Not at all," the cashier replied happily while glancing down at the cheque, and holding it against a page in his ledger. "How can I help, Miss Strachan?"

"Well, I suppose you could cash that cheque you're holding."

"You mean all of it?" he gave her a frown. "It's almost dark out, and if you don't mind me saying, a young lady may not be safe carrying such a sum around London."

"And what else would you suggest I do with it?" she asked with the slightest hint of sarcasm. It had been a long and confusing day, and she wasn't in the mood for more games.

"You could take some cash and personal cheques, and put the rest in your account, perhaps? It seems it was opened just this afternoon for you by one of our more trusted clients." He checked through his ledger again and nodded. "If you'd bear with me." He headed over to the large desk at the back of the room, and collected an envelope from the bald man before returning. "Your bank book." He said cheerily as he started scribbling in it. "And how much would you like to take?"

"Excuse me?" She had been watching, and listening, but it was all a little too surreal. Not an hour earlier, a total stranger who seemed to know far too much had given her a cheque for one hundred pounds, half a year's pay as a Senior Sister, after uniform and lodgings.

"How much cash would you like to take with you?"

"Five pounds?"

"Of course. I'll make sure you have plenty of change." He smiled as he wrote in the book, then passed it to her to sign, which she did. "Would ten cheques be enough?"

"I'm sure..." She smiled and nodded, going along with the game. When she first trained as a nurse, she had to have her father's permission to open a bank account, the same as most women. Authority that then passed to her husband when she married, he'd even had to go along with her to the bank and sign to say she could still have an account. It had irritated her, but it was normal. Everyone had the same experience. Until the moment she was given a cheque, and an account at one of England's older banks. It was hard for her to get her head around, more so when he handed her the bank book with a small envelope of cheques, before counting out the notes and coins, which she accepted with a smile, before putting them in her purse and bag.

"Will there be anything else, Miss Strachan?"

"A gold bar would be nice, if you have any?" The words fell out of her mouth before she could stop them, having thought how amusing it was to suddenly be in a world where people gave her money for no apparent reason. He simply looked at her in reply, not saying a word. "Of course not, a joke." She smiled and gathered her things. "Thank you very much for your help, goodbye."

"Good day, Miss Strachan." He gave her a polite smile, then waved to the man who'd met her by the door, and soon she was heading back into the near darkness of the afternoon. She stopped outside the bank, glancing up to the dark skies as the drizzle soaked her. She felt herself smiling, and confused enough to stop trying to answer the many questions spinning around her mind. Whatever happened, she had money in her pocket, and could go to a very nice hotel if she wanted. Somewhere much more upmarket, where she could treat herself to a hot and luxurious bath. She smiled, shook her head, then put up her umbrella and headed for her hostel. The money could disappear as quickly as it appeared, and it may be more helpful to her in the future. At least that's what she told herself, having grown up with an accountant father who espoused the importance of saving almost daily.

The food at the hostel was rabbit stew, again. Rationing was hard on everyone, and people had to do with what they had, and while there was less meat than there had been the previous night, the vegetables were tasty, as was the dumpling that had been given a sprinkling of ground pepper to liven it up a bit. It was nice all the same, and after tidying up, Emily climbed into her narrow, squeaky bed and thought about her day. She'd arrived in London with a plan to join the Royal Air Force, though she'd been unable to think of what she'd do if it actually happened. She wasn't a pilot, but part of her hoped they'd maybe teach her. She'd loved flying with Harriet on the short run

28

around the south coast, and felt she'd be able to get the hang of it. She'd been stalled, though. She wasn't a pilot, and that was seemingly the only way to open the door, and then a kind Japanese man serving as an RAF officer gave her a chance. Not with the RAF, but with a strange woman whose confidence knew no bounds, and was equally matched with what seemed to be a penchant for playing mind games. Ten hours after she'd started, she had a job to go to the following morning, at least she thought she had. The only instruction, other than where to go, was to do as she was told, and the large cheque had secured that.

An air raid siren dragged Emily from her sleep sometime before midnight, not long after she'd shivered herself warm enough to slip into her curious dreams about sweet, melt in the mouth macarons. It hummed at first, creeping into her unconscious until the ear splitting wail shook her awake, and had her sitting up startled. There hadn't been air raid sirens at her hospital, not like the deep throated roar outside that sent fear running through her body. She sat stunned for a moment, wondering what to do, but when the distant rumbles of explosions vibrated through her chest, she jumped out of bed and quickly threw her clothes on, before grabbing her overcoat and handbag and running for the door, then heading down the stairs to be met by the WVS women who were as pristinely dressed as ever, while accounting for their charges as they gathered in the hall.

"Right, ladies. Stay close together, and we'll go down the street to the Underground station, it's our nearest shelter," Mrs Harris said clearly. "I'll lead, and Mrs Jennings will bring up the rear with the flask and some biscuits. Ready?" She looked around at the wide eyed group of women, all of whom were wrapped in their greatcoats, with gas mask haversacks slung over their shoulders, and steel helmets on their heads, with the exception of Emily, who had the standard small cardboard box with a boot lace for a strap to carry her civilian issue gas mask, and not even a hat, let alone a tin one. It wasn't something that had bothered her until she was about to go out into a London street during an air raid, when suddenly the merits of a hardened steel helmet were brought home to her. She found herself frowning at the prospect, then quickly shook her head as she realised the WVS ladies were wearing their fabric uniform hats, and didn't appear to be bothered in the slightest by not having helmets. They were busy fussing like they were planning a walk to the park, which reassured Emily somewhat. "Ok, let's go!" She switched off the light, making Emily's heart race a little, then pulled open the door and stepped out, leading her small band of women into the street, where the sirens echoed so loud it was hard to think. She put her hand in the air, and an orderly line formed behind her as she marched, with Emily at the back, just in front of Mrs Jennings, who gave a polite yet slightly nervous smile as Emily looked over her shoulder at her, before they both looked up as a thundering vibration filled the air. Something that resonated so intensely that Emily could feel it in her chest.

"Get off the bloody street!" an Air Raid Precautions Warden yelled at the top of his lungs as he ran out of a building. Emily looked at him as he waved his hands at them. "Get off the bloody street!" he repeated, just as a high pitched whistle cut through the vibrations and sirens, and the group instinctively started to run, scattering in every direction and sprinting towards the cover of the nearest buildings in the face of what could only be one thing. Emily found herself running hard, following Mrs Harris who was heading towards the Warden, when the street seemed to shake like it was on a board that was being violently shoved back and forth by a giant. Her legs stopped moving properly, and she found herself staggering involuntarily, then falling to the ground as the street lit up, silhouetting those somehow still standing and running, before being filled with darkness as an ear splitting roar echoed around the buildings, and a wave of dirt and stones passed overhead. Deafening thuds followed, accompanied by bright flashes, knocking Emily flat as the air boiled, and shockwaves rattled around the street. She rolled onto her side, wrapping her hands around her head and pulling her knees to her chest while masonry and wood crashed down all around her, then screwing her eyes tightly closed while letting out a scream to try and equalise the pressure in her head and chest. Grit and dust filled her throat, making her choke as a wave of heat enveloped her, and as she opened her eyes, she found herself staring at Mrs Jennings, who was still somehow standing and looking around in horror as the world around her raged with fire and thunder. She looked at Emily briefly, her eyes full of wonder and fear, before disappearing in a flash of light that had Emily clawing at the road with her fingers, desperately trying to find a way

30

to safety before another loud explosion had her curled tight in a ball and screaming again.

The thunder had passed when Emily came around, and other than the loud ringing in her ears, all she could hear was a muffled sound in the distance. She coughed as she fought to breathe, and get the grit from her lungs, then she pushed at a wooden beam that was laid over her, and kicked her legs against the surrounding rubble while rubbing her sore and painful eyes, blinking the dust from them as much as she could. The sight above her was like something she could never have imagined. Fire filled the sky, not in sheets or waves, but tiny little dots floating in the air like burning snowflakes lighting the night sky above the layer of smoke that hid the road. She stared in wonder, her brain struggling to register what was happening, or what had happened, leaving her without a coherent thought beyond how beautiful the sky looked. She wondered if she was dead, and quickly became scared that if she was, the heat and the fire suggested she'd gone straight to hell.

"There's one…" a voice said from behind her, and she spun her head to see a pair of eyes blacker than night staring back, with glowing crosses instead of pupils, and she found herself kicking at the rubble with more urgency, panicking as she desperately tried to get away from the demon coming for her, but she could hardly move. She let out a scream as a hand reached out and grabbed her shoulder, pulling her back to face whatever it was. "I've got you..." the voice said, only this time it sounded different, less dark and sinister. She quivered nervously as she stared at the demon, its black silhouette lit by an otherworldly red glow. "You're alright, love." Its other hand reached up and pulled at a scarf to reveal red lipstick, before removing the black metal goggles to reveal a smiling young woman. "Here…" She put the goggles on her thigh as she knelt, which Emily looked at closely, noticing the narrow crosses cut into the centre of each eyepiece, before handing her a water bottle. "Just a sip to swill your mouth out, then have a drink afterwards." Emily nodded and did as she was told, rinsing and spitting the water, before taking a deep mouthful and feeling her chest open, bringing the focus back to her eyes as she stared at the young woman sitting next to her wearing the black steel helmet and dark blue overalls of an ARP warden. Emily handed the water bottle back, while switching her gaze between the woman's eyes and the goggles resting on her thigh. "Splinter goggles," she said as she noticed Emily's stares. "They let you see through the tiny slits cut into crosses, while protecting your eyes from shrapnel and debris, and some of the heat and light. That's the theory, anyway, but they're awkward when you're trying to walk through rubble!" She gave Emily a smile. "Are you hurt?" Emily looked at her a moment, then shook her head.

"I don't think so..." She coughed again, then sat up properly and looked around her. Half the street was missing, all of the buildings along one side having been blown apart and reduced to piles of rubble and timber that covered the road. She looked at the young woman again, and then up to the thousands of tiny burning snowflakes filling the sky.

"They got a fabric store a few streets away," the woman added as she joined Emily in looking up. "All that rationing, and thousands of pounds worth of material has gone in an instant. Still... Looks pretty, don't you think?" She watched for a while, then gave Emily another smile. "Come on, we'd better get you looked over. She held out her hand as she stood, and pulled Emily up with her. "I don't think I'll be needing these anymore tonight." She pushed the goggles into her haversack. "Hey, where are you going?" she called out, as Emily picked her way unsteadily through the rubble, having orientated herself. "The Warden's Post is this way." Emily held up her hand to signal that she understood, then stopped as she saw what remained of a pair of very smart shoes laying dusty and singed among the bricks. For a moment, she could see Mrs Jennings standing there, clutching the flask and biscuit tin tightly, her face one of fear and fascination in the seconds before the bomb had taken her. "A friend of yours...?" the young woman asked as she stood by Emily's side and looked down at the shoes.

"No..." Emily shook her head as she stood trying to stop herself from shaking as the shock hit her like a train. "Mrs Jennings, of the WVS. Somebody should let them know."

Chapter 3

Reporting For...

"Good morning, Ma'am. How can I help you today?" the Coldstream Guards Corporal asked in a polite bark as Emily approached the gate. He was a giant of a man, towering above her in his battle dress, his keen eyes piercing from under the shadow of his rimmed steel helmet, while his rifle hung slung over his shoulder.

"Good morning. I'm here for the First Aid Nursing Yeomanry." She handed him the orders she'd been given the previous day. She felt a degree of anticipation while he stood reading the letter with a deep and considered frown. It wasn't usually her way, but the last twenty four hours had been such a whirlwind that she was half expecting him to shrug and send her on her way, as though she'd made it all up. She hadn't, she was confident of that. If she'd been imagining things, it wouldn't have been the horror of London during what was being called the Blitz.

"Ah, another FANY." He smirked as he folded the letter and handed it to her.

"Excuse me?" She gave him a firm stare, of the type she'd used a thousand times with rowdy patients, including the many soldiers that had made their way to her hospital after Dunkirk.

"First Aid Nursing Yeomanry, Ma'am." The giant of a man suddenly looked like a chided schoolboy as the pair of Guardsmen behind him smirked. "Just the letters, Ma'am. Nothing else."

"Quite…"

"If you'd like to sign in at the Guardroom, Ma'am." He pointed to the building behind him. "I'll have one of the lads show you over." She maintained her stare for a moment, making sure he was in no doubts about her thoughts. The word 'Fanny' had been derogatory slang for many years, and not something she appreciated being called by a smirking soldier, even if it had no connection whatsoever to the reason she was there. The night had been hell, with hardly a wink of sleep when she finally returned to the hostel after the all clear was sounded, where Mrs Harris went about making sure Emily and the two ATS girls were looked after with cocoa and biscuits, not even mentioning Mrs Jennings and the WAAF who hadn't come back with them. Her stare switched to the smirking soldiers, who instantly straightened up and looked elsewhere. She nodded, thanked him, then signed in before being escorted through the seemingly huge barracks to an office in a small block, where a woman similar in age to her was sitting behind a desk and wearing the khaki green skirt and jacket of the First Aid Nursing Yeomanry, and looking every bit a soldier.

"You must be Strachan," she said while finishing off writing

"I must be," Emily replied while looking around the office. A couple of khaki green greatcoats hung from a stand in the corner, with a couple of matching hats, and a black umbrella leaning in the middle. The wall had signs, instructions mostly, and a large chalkboard with names and initials. Other than that, it was an office, smelling a little of ink and old paper, and with windows crisscrossed into diamonds with tape, to stop them doing as much damage if blown in by a bomb.

"You're early..."

"Would you rather I was late?" she bristled, and the young woman looked up at her for a moment and smiled.

"Not at all. Five minutes early is on time, and all that." She stood and walked over to Emily. "Do you have your orders?" They were handed over with a nod, and she gave them a read. "Wonderful! Another cap badge, no doubt. Do come through. Leave your coat and bags here, you won't need them." She gestured to the hatstand, and as soon as Emily was ready, she led out into the wide corridor, and through some double doors, her smart lace up shoes clicking on the polished floors. Emily glanced around the austere walls, pale green with a deep green stripe running along at waist height. It wasn't that interesting to look at, but the place was clinically clean, and reminded her in a way of her hospital. For a moment, a thought slipped into her mind to ask whether she wouldn't be better off back there, doing what she was trained to, but it didn't have time to take hold. The young woman's knock on a door pulled her back into the moment, and she was soon being shown into a bigger, less austere office that looked more lived in, where a woman somewhere in her forties sat behind a large dark wood desk. "Miss Strachan, Ma'am."

"Thank you, Williams. That'll be all." The young woman gave a sharp nod, then left the room, closing the door quietly on her way out. "You're early," the austere looking woman said as she looked Emily up and down.

"So I've been told," Emily replied without a pause, her head tilting slightly as she looked directly at the woman.

"Yes…" Her voice was firm and clipped, of the finest Home Counties. Privately educated, at least, and she had a confidence that came with moving in circles where decisions were made. "I'm Staff Commander Rose. I oversee the training of the First Aid Nursing Yeomanry, and their subsequent deployment. I'm assuming that's why you're here?"

"It is…"

"OK, well, let's start the way we intend to go on. You can call me Ma'am, or Staff Commander, and you'll be Cadet Ensign Strachan." Emily gave her the slightest of nods, not knowing whether she was nodding in agreement, compliance, or whether she was weighing the situation to see if she liked what she was being told. She didn't have a clue what she was doing there, not really. She'd told an RAF officer that she wanted to do her bit, and the next thing she knew, she was volunteering for a first aid organisation that she was assured had nothing to do with nurses, despite their name. "Good. You'll know that we're an all volunteer organisation, of course. You may volunteer to join us, and you may volunteer to leave. We, however, make the decisions on whether we want you, whether we can use you, and whether we're going to keep you. Volunteers are wonderful, but they need to have the stuff we're looking for."

"And what is that stuff... Staff Commander?"

"That depends on what we're looking for. We provide drivers and mechanics to support all three services, we have administrators, map plotters, intelligence analysts... You train with us, and we'll decide where to send you, based on what we see of you. Though, if we don't see anything we can use, we'll certainly let you know. As a volunteer organisation, it's pointless wasting your time and ours if you don't fit." She spoke as though she was talking about trying on a dress in a department store, casually and without any suggestion that Emily would fit or wouldn't. "We're not soldiers, but we're expected to carry ourselves with the same discipline, and an exemplary purpose and service. You'll hold the rank of an officer, even as a Cadet Ensign you'll be the equivalent of a Second Lieutenant under training, and you'll be expected to be both a lady and a professional at all times. Our standards are the highest, and you should know that. If you want the fun of chasing fighter pilots in the Mess, you can go and join the WAAF." Emily simply nodded, though a little firmer. She had no plans to be chasing anyone. She'd left a good job in search of more, not for games. "Good! So, that leads us to the bit that doesn't need to be awkward. Your subscription to join is twenty five pounds. You can either pay in instalments, or all at once. In addition to that, you'll have a Mess bill to keep on top of, and sundries, and your uniform to pay for. The sundries are available here, the uniform you'll have to get off into town for. There's a department store in Picadilly that supply them, Lillywhites, or I can give you the details of a tailor that will be able to get you dressed pretty quickly if you want something more bespoke."

"Will a cheque do?"

"Of course. See Lieutenant Williams on the way out, and she'll take care of it." Emily gave another nod in reply. "You'll stay here at the barracks throughout your training, where you'll be expected to abide by military law. Something we'll teach you, and you'll learn in detail. We're guests of the Guards, and standards are high, something they'll tell you if you don't meet them. Assuming you get through training, we'll get you posted to somewhere that can use whatever skills we find in you. Once you're there, you'll work out the local arrangements. Some stay in barracks, others live off camp. You'll find your way... Any questions?"

"Do I get a say in where I'm posted?"

"We exist to serve, Strachan. We go where we're needed, and when the time comes, we'll make the decisions on your deployment. The soldiers out in North Africa fighting the Italians don't get to pick and choose, and neither should we. We do our duty to the best of our abilities, whether we're driving ambulances, or training recruits. Understood?"

"Perfectly."

"Good! That said, you are a volunteer, of course, and you can give us one month's notice to end your service at any time... Though we'd hope posting preferences while the country is at war and in need wouldn't be a reason most would use for leaving us." She paused for a moment, holding Emily's firm and emotionless stare. "If there's nothing else, Williams will take care of you from now. Try and get everything you need to do squared away today, because training starts at eight tomorrow morning."

"Tomorrow?" The word came out of Emily's mouth before she could stop it. She had it in her head she'd be starting right away, now that she'd actually arrived.

"Tomorrow. Get settled in, work out where the Mess is so you don't starve while you're here, and get your uniform sorted. I'd make that a priority. If you can get to the tailor early, they may be able to squeeze you in. You won't be the first we've pulled together with belts and hair pins, but all the same..."

"Standards."

"Quite."

The day felt busy, with a quiet apprehension that followed Emily around. She'd done it. She'd got somewhere different, somewhere she could do her bit, but she still didn't know what she'd done, or what bit she'd be doing. Rose had been quite clear in outlining the possible duties she could expect, and while the thought of being an intelligence officer somewhere stirred a little, the competing thought of being a driver, or a clerk, filled her with dread. Still, she was there. Having settled into the small, otherwise empty four person room with bunk beds either side of the door, it was off into London to find the tailor that had been recommended. She was seen quickly, and her uniform was adjusted with such expert precision that it fit like it had been made especially for her from scratch, despite having come off a shelf. She watched herself smile, quite unintentionally, when she tried it on and looked at herself in the mirror. The khaki green jacket and skirt brought form to the slight build she'd hidden under her nurse's uniform, and even the stockings weren't as terrible as they'd first seemed, and the shiny brown leather Sam Browne belt and matching lace up shoes pulled it all together perfectly.

The uniform was transforming, though when she thought of the price she'd paid for it, she'd expect as much. Once the tailor had finished, she'd packed her own clothes in her bag, then made her way back to the barracks, noticing being noticed, as people's heads turned at the sight of a young woman in uniform. Her khaki green greatcoat fitted snug over her uniform, and matching cap pulled smartly onto her head. She'd always been proud to be a nurse, and she sometimes appreciated the smiles and respect her uniform brought her. This was different, and her always purposeful walk had something else when she saw herself in the department store windows. A confidence she'd always had, but hadn't ever really let it come to the surface. As a nurse, she had to present authority, competence, and maybe a little confidence, but for that moment it was different. She was taller, though she'd never been particularly short, not for a woman.

The Guardsmen at the gates to the barracks were called to attention when she returned, by the Corporal she'd faced earlier, and it took monumental self control for her not to smirk when he saluted her.

The only thing getting in the way was her desperate attempts to return it with a half delivered effort to raise her hand to her eye, mirroring him, or as close as she could while getting it terribly wrong. He didn't say anything, and hardly moved, apart from the slightest shake of his head in disappointment at the sight of a woman in uniform not because she was a woman, but because she was, in her mind at least, very quickly becoming a civilian in fancy dress, and her confidence from the streets of London quickly settled.

By the evening she'd been joined by three other women in the small bunk bed and locker filled room, all new recruits. One the daughter of a retired cavalry Colonel, one an engineer, and one who'd just finished studying mathematics at university. All were pleasant, and equally as excitable. They got on well, and quickly made Emily one of them, though she felt a little different in a way. It was hardly a class thing. Her parents were comfortable, and had given her a good education, with all the hobbies she could want. She even had regular horse riding lessons when she was young, something she quickly learned was part of the First Aid Nursing Yeomanry lore. Apparently, the organisation was created by a retired cavalryman, who had the idea of nurses riding out onto the battlefield to help the wounded while the battle raged all around, or so she was told, and until recently, part of the joining requirement was to be able to ride, and have your own horse. Something fortunately waived considering the more mechanised needs of the current war. When she lay in the darkness of the creaking bunk beds as her new roommates tossed and turned in their new home, all anticipating the day to come, she thought on their differences. She was in her twenties, and already a widow. She'd finished her education at a very nice school, and gone on to train as a nurse almost immediately. She'd quickly become accomplished in anatomy and physiology, and wound care, to the point where her seniors had suggested she return to education with the intention of becoming a doctor. Something she'd planned to do, until she'd met her husband to be, had a whirlwind romance, and in a moment of defiance to a middle class world that had given her everything, decided to get married with hardly a wait. Then, he was dead under a year, and nobody would give her a job because she was expected to either be a widow and mourn, or, if they didn't know, be at home and keep the house for her husband. The 'marriage bar' was very real. Nurses, along with other professions intending to marry, were expected to resign because the system expected them to be less committed with their minds on managing the household and having children. It was something that had infuriated her even before she met her husband. When the time came, however, she simply took off her ring and sent it home to her parents along with everything else, and changed back to her maiden name, Emily Strachan, a Scottish nurse who'd come to England looking for work. All that effort. All that determination to carry on, and then she'd gone and given it all up after a chance encounter with a patient like no other. A young woman with a broken body and tortured mind, in the way only a war can inflict, who she'd nursed from the death's door back to her larger than life self. A young woman who'd nearly died at Dunkirk, and who'd lost her family in the German advance. Who had nothing at all left in life, but had made it to the safety of England, and all she wanted to do, even when her lungs and throat were still sore from being burned while she was trapped in the cockpit of a burning aeroplane, was get back to the front lines. The young woman who, through her defiance, had got Emily noticed and promoted to Senior Sister.

The women she'd met, the new recruits, had their own stories, but they were a little different to Emily's. Having watched her patient recover, and leave the hospital with a determination to get back into the fight, to put her life on the line to keep a country of strangers safe from the cruel and determined German war machine, a switch inside her had been flicked. She still had her family, which was something, but she felt empty. She didn't feel much of anything, not really. Harriet had made her laugh, and frustrated her, and even took her flying when she returned, as she promised she would, having found her way back to the war, recovered and ready to do her duty. Other than that, the only other time she'd really felt anything when she saw herself in her new First Aid Nursing Yeomanry uniform.

It wasn't long since she'd been promoted to Senior Sister, a good job in a nice hospital, with plenty of opportunity to learn and grow. She'd even considered going back to university to study medicine. She'd saved a little from her wages, and the meagre widow's pension the army had seen fit to give her, and her parents had offered to help, but it wasn't what she wanted. The thought of sitting in lecture theatres when not being a slave to senior doctors for year after year was less than entertaining, not that she was sure she'd even get a place on a course. Doctor Goode, the senior Consultant at her hospital, had told her there were less than two thousand female doctors in the entire country, and of them, most had suffered the most horrendous discrimination to get to where they were. He'd still offered to help her, if that was what she wanted. Unfortunately, it was too late by that point, she'd lost her passion. She did her job, and she worked hard to make sure her nurses, and her patients, had the best she could provide, but her fire was almost extinguished.

The following days quickly became a routine of early starts, polishing shoes, pressing clothes, and spending hour after hour on a parade square, being shouted at by a Sergeant Major from the Coldstream Guards who had the voice of thunderous gravel, and an ability to string together eloquent phrases that threatened hell, without ever once swearing at what he frequently referred to as 'The very nice ladies who would be officers... If they can somehow learn the difference between their left and right at some time before Mister Hitler himself is walking up The Mall'. He was tall, and fierce, with a chest like a barrel, and hands like shovels. A personification of authority. When he wasn't marching them around, making sure that their salute was sharp enough to cut the wind, they were in lectures, often with Rose. The ranks and structure of each of the armed forces, how they worked, how they communicated. It was a highly intense induction to the military world, with the expectation of not only learning, but knowing. In the second week, they were comfortable marching everywhere, returning salutes, and seeming much more military in their bearing, which gave them less time being shouted at as they marched, and more time in a service pit, learning how to look after a staff car. Changing the oil and filters, de rusting the road springs, changing sparkplugs and pistons, and greasing seemingly everything, before they were finally taught to drive it. Around the barracks at first, and then into London. They were taught the army way, including how to drive fast, through traffic, and how to drive evasively. Their instructor, a Captain by the name of Bradley, was insistent that if they were sent to drive senior officers around, they needed to know how to get out of trouble fast if German paratroopers started falling from the sky. Something the entire country was on edge about, with the recruits feeling it all the more with the training they received. One of them, the engineer, Aggie MacLaren, was unsettled by it, and she sometimes wept in the night, when she hoped everyone was asleep. Not Emily, though. The only emotion she had was a fear she wouldn't get it right when the time came. Paratroopers she could deal with, and her waking thoughts were filled with how.

Emily took some time with Aggie MacLaren, when the others weren't around, and tried to comfort her a little, and help her with her fear. In return, Aggie showed her how to fix engines, taking her to the garage to strip the car in a way far in advance of what Captain Bradley had taught them. It was a fair trade, and while Emily was grateful for learning more about car engines, so she could get out of trouble if she was sent to drive, even though she hoped she wouldn't be, it was the reciprocal arrangement that was important. She'd helped Aggie, and she knew that Aggie wanted to repay her with what she had, while feeling a little less helpless into the bargain, like she had something worth trading that was a little different to the near brazen confidence of Elspeth, the Colonel's daughter, or the quiet assurance of the mathematician, Penelope. Or even the hard edged and cold nurse that was Emily, a description that had her raising an eyebrow when Aggie shared it with her while washing up after stripping an engine.

At the start of the fifth week, under the watchful eye of Staff Commander Rose, and who some of the qualified First Aid Nursing Yeomanry officers they shared the accommodation with referred to as her poodle, the ever present, and always impeccably turned out Lieutenant Williams, the four were put through their paces by the Sergeant Major, who marched them around the parade square with bellowing precision that echoed around the barracks as he barked his orders, sending them left, and right, and back where they'd come. It was the final hurdle, after a morning of tests. Bradley had them repair mechanical problems on the car, then take it through a course at speed, including controlled skids on oil and sand, and manoeuvres designed to get their passengers away from roadblocks set up by German paratroopers. The day had started early with a written exam, right after breakfast, with a paper full of questions about everything they'd learned, and some things Emily was sure they hadn't, and they hadn't stopped since.

The simulated casualties that had been supplied in the form of Guardsmen from the barracks had been a challenge for Emily, though not in the way she'd expected. Their overacting would have got them booed off the stage down the road in the West End, and she'd been very firm in telling one of them to shut up unless he was dying, and if he was dying, to do it in a quiet and orderly manner, without distracting the morale of his friends. It got a raised eyebrow from the young Medical Officer supplied by the Royal Army Medical Corps attached to the barracks, a Second Lieutenant who didn't look old enough to join the Scouts, let alone the army.

Finally, when the Sergeant Major stopped them, they were inspected by Rose, who eyed them closely, checking that uniforms were pressed in the right way, shoes were polished to a high shine, and even their ties were straight. A thread out of place, a hair on the collar, and it would be a mark against them. She'd made that abundantly clear from the first day. Standards were high, as were expectations. Officers of the First Aid Nursing Yeomanry were expected to be the best, something Emily had quickly worked out to be for life, and not just training. Their accommodation housed qualified officers on the floor above, those who'd finished their basic training and awaiting a posting, or doing more advanced training where they were, along with a few on the staff. They were all very well dressed, all of the time. All very well spoken, and all very professional. Even at night, when they were relaxing, they had something about them, an air of class that came from knowing they were good at what they did. They'd been polite and welcoming, though distant when they'd been around the trainees. Not socialising, or really mixing. Keeping their distance from those yet to prove themselves.

"Come in, Miss Strachan," Rose said as Williams closed the door behind Emily. "Take a seat, please." She pointed her pen at the chair in front of her desk, and Emily did as she was asked, not saying a thing, and sitting smartly as she'd been taught. "How do you think today went?"

"I'd like to think I did what I was asked, to the best of my ability, Ma'am."

"Yes... Well, your written exam was good, at ninety six percent. There was a navigation question you got wrong, however."

"I'm sorry, Ma'am, I must have missed the part of the class where that part was taught... Though I'd like to think that I would have the opportunity to brush up on using a theodolite in the desert before actually deploying there, and being expected to use one to help me navigate." Her posture didn't change, nor her expression, and her words were well considered and without emotion, delivered in a way that made Rose look her in the eyes for a moment. She knew all too well which question it was, and she knew all too well it wasn't taught. It was a trip up question, as were some of the others. She'd learned that the First Aid Nursing Yeomanry didn't make mistakes, the training officers didn't accidentally forget to put something in the class. If it wasn't taught, it wasn't meant to be taught, and if it was on the exam, it was meant to trip up the recruits.

"Quite... There's also the medical assessment."

"Ma'am?" Emily tilted her head slightly, feeling the surprise, but not showing it beyond the tilt.

"Yes, Lieutenant Oxtoby reported that you were particularly firm with one of the casualties, and not at all considerate in your bedside manner."

"He did, Ma'am?"

"He did. He also suggested that after being rather firm, you ignored that particular soldier, and focused on somebody else, apparently frustrated with the noise."

"Frustrated with the noise, Ma'am? He said that?"

44

"He did, while suggesting that the battlefield can be a noisy place, and you don't get a quiet moment to think. You should, in his words, get on with it and save as many as you can."

"May I ask, Ma'am, how many battles the Lieutenant has been in?"

"Excuse me?" Rose recoiled a little, taken aback by the directness of the question.

"Second Lieutenant Oxtoby, Ma'am. Do you know how many battles he's been in?" The look on her face was genuinely inquisitive, while her tone stayed just on the right side of respectful, even though Emily's entire baring, while polite, was one of a nanny demanding an answer from a child caught in the act.

"I'm not sure what difference that makes?"

"The difference is, Ma'am, that the briefing ahead of the task was that the men had been injured in an artillery barrage, and while the soldier making the noise was indeed injured, a cursory assessment suggested that his wounds, while no doubt painful, were not life threatening. The man I attended, though, the quiet man, gave all the signs of advanced trauma and shock. Perhaps internal bleeding following the shockwave from the blast, perhaps a piece of shrapnel had found its way to somewhere it shouldn't. Either way, if we're trying to save as many lives as we can, he goes first. However, if we're responding to hysteria, then I'm happy to be corrected."

"I see…" Rose said as she looked at her for a moment. Then, casually picked up the telephone. The minutes waiting in silence felt like an age to Emily, who remained confident, back straight, and shoulders square. "Yes, Major Ericson. Thank you for taking my call," she continued eventually. "I wanted to thank you again for your help with the casualty management task this morning, your soldiers were most helpful. Though, I do have a question, if you'd entertain me?" The slightest of smiles curled up the corners of her mouth. "Yes, your young Lieutenant Oxtoby. Has he been in combat? What? No, not at all. I'm just considering the task he set. Wounded soldiers as a result

45

of an artillery bombardment, and the injuries we'd expect to see…"
She listened for a while, nodding appropriately. "Thank you so much,
goodbye." She put down the phone and looked Emily in the eyes.
"And you, Miss Strachan. How many battles have you been in?"

"None, Ma'am." She shrugged casually. "Though I wouldn't need to
be, the results of the battles came to me. Men bombed on the beaches
at Dunkirk were thrown on small boats, and hours later deposited in
my hospital, after being dragged across the channel with makeshift
first aid. They turned up by the ambulance load, and as Senior Sister
I needed to support the senior doctor in triage, making sure we kept
as many alive as we could. Burns are terrible, the smell chokes you,
and the sight is something not for the weak; bullet wounds can be
miserable, and agony if they're in the wrong place, like the stomach,
for example. Internal shock, though, the trauma done by the
shockwaves of explosions rupturing organs or blood vessels, they're
the ones you really have to think about. Miss those, and the patient's
dead before you know it, often without a peep. You can dress burns,
and plug holes, but internal bleeding needs something else."

"I see…" Rose sat back in her seat as she listened, tapping her pencil
against her lips. "It seems like the Senior Medical Officer would agree
with your assessment, based on his understanding of the task set." She
let herself smile at last. "Attention to detail is vitally important in this
job, as is the confidence to hold your ground and back yourself when
you know that you're right. Congratulations, Ensign Emily Strachan.
Welcome to the First Aid Nursing Yeomanry." She stood and walked
around her desk, offering Emily her hand, which was shook firmly
when Emily had stood to meet her. "When were you last home?"

"Home, Ma'am?" Emily felt herself frown a little, as an uncomfortable
feeling squeezed inside. It wasn't something she thought about that
often. Home was her hospital. Or at least it had been after her
previous home melted away with her husband. The married quarter
they'd had near Salisbury that, when news of his death came through,
she was told in a formal, yet slightly uncomfortable way, that she was
no longer entitled to. She was no longer part of the army, and the
quarters were needed by somebody else. All she got was a collection
of pitiful smiles, a handful of memories of their brief time together,

46

and a heavily taxed war widow's pension that was half of what a person could live on.

"Yes. Up in Scotland, I assume?"

"My parents live there, Ma'am. On the west coast, up near Iona."

"Well, you'd better get packed if you're going to be home for Christmas…" Her smile broadened as she spoke. "Your posting has come through, and you're to be up near Fort William at the start of January. You may as well have a few days at home before you go." Emily's eyes opened wide at the announcement. She'd heard that it was normal to be in London a while before being posted somewhere, and many spent their time working jobs in and around London anyway. Few were posted right away. "Report to the stores, and they'll issue you with what you'll need to take with you, then you'll need to be at the train station this evening for the night train to Glasgow."

"Yes…" Her thoughts raced as she processed what she was being told. "Yes, Ma'am. Thank you."

"You're going to need that keen mind when you get where you're going, so a bit of rest at home will do you the wonders of good." She offered her hand again, which Emily shook. "Very well done on your training, you were our highest scorer, even with the trip up questions. Good luck." Emily nodded and smiled, then turned for the door. "Oh, there's one other thing?"

"Ma'am?"

"That young medical officer they sent us has just finished his training. A keen physician, apparently, but hasn't even heard a door bang. At least that's what the SMO. said." Emily smiled again, then after a nod, left the office and stepped into the wide, cool corridor. She paused for a moment, taking it all in. Home… She hadn't thought she'd go back there for a while.

Chapter 4

Sign Here

The Matron back at the hospital in Kent had once told Emily that two things can be right at the same time, and the key to understanding life laid in not only accepting that fact, but in a person learning how to use it to their advantage. It made life more tolerable, or at least that's what she'd said. It was a memory that came back to Emily as she sat in the back of the rickety truck rocking its way through the cutting cold of the Scottish Highlands in early January. She'd got home for Christmas Eve, surprising her parents who were ecstatic to see her. She'd even managed to pick up some treats for them. Not much, just some tea from Fortnum and Mason in London, and a small tin of biscuits. She'd been told of the place, and while it was frightfully expensive, it also had her feeling like a schoolgirl in a sweet shop. It was a worthwhile expense, though. She hadn't spent much since joining the First Aid Nursing Yeomanry, and she wanted to do something for her parents. They'd done so much for her in life, especially when she was widowed, so it was the least she could do. It had been an odd time, despite it being her childhood home, with her room exactly as she'd left it. She was happy to be home with her family, while secretly wishing she wasn't. Her mind couldn't settle, and deep inside it felt like there was a pressure building, like a tiny, imperceptible vibration that only she could feel, unsettling her as if preparing her for something. She smiled, and she talked, but she was only half there, and her parents knew it, despite choosing to not say anything. It was nice to be home, and not. Two things were certainly true at the same time.

The journey from her home had been long, and for the most part quite cold. It was around a hundred miles, or thereabouts, and took the entire day. A car, a train, a bus, a truck, none of them with anything resembling a working heater as she made her way from pre dawn darkness, to the mid afternoon sunset of Northwest Scotland. The only thing missing was the rain, though the wind howled across the rolling hills of woods and pale green and brown grasslands, and mile upon mile of heather. It made her think of the invasion that the government had promised. Would the Germans have got as far as the

48

Highlands had they invaded? Scotland was so huge, and sometimes remote, that even the Romans didn't bother with much of it. It was a thought that made her frown. She'd volunteered because she wanted to do her bit, but she'd been posted to the Highlands, about as far away from the front lines as it was possible to get. The frowns and thoughts were only broken when she finally climbed down from the truck with the other passengers, that had all converged at the train station before being loaded on a bus. All together there were twenty six men, and four women. A man in a smart suit and overcoat had met them at the train station, and instructed them not to engage in conversation for the duration of their trip, and after a few searching glances at the start of the journey, everyone had stayed in their own business. Some read books, others did crosswords. Emily hadn't thought to bring either, and spent the entire journey in her own mind, more so at the end when they were bundled together in the back of a truck in the dark, with no scenery to look at. She'd thought about every patient, about her hospital and her work, about her training in London, and more than a few times about Harriet Cornwall, the young woman who'd set her on the journey north in the first place. They'd written often since Harriet had been discharged, and Harriet had told of what adventures she could, within the bounds of censorship rules. Then, the letters had stopped, with just a note to say she was going away for a while for a bit of a holiday, and that was that. Holidays were hardly on anyone's agenda, not with invasion looming, so she'd deduced that Harriet had likely been posted somewhere, possibly overseas. It made her sad for a while, knowing that her friend wasn't there to talk to anymore, even if it was just in a letter every now and then.

When they finally decanted from the truck, she briefly looked around to see the shadow of a large mansion house standing against the murk of clouds, before being marched along the gravel and in through the front door, past the blackout curtains, and into the lamp lit entrance hall. It was a grand looking place. Old, and big, with high ceilings, though the need for the blackout escaped her. They were about as far away as it was possible to be from anything, at least that's what she deduced from the lack of anything seen through the tailgate of the truck. A German bomber anywhere near would have to be there for the express reason of bombing them, unless it was terribly lost, and she couldn't work out which was the least likely. Bombing a group that increasingly looked like a collection of misfits when she reviewed them again in the amber glow of the lamps seemed a waste of effort and resources. Before she had too long to think, they were ushered into a large reception room filled with rows of chairs, where they were instructed to sit, their coats still on, their bags by their sides. It was another grand looking room, with oil paintings, and dark wood furniture.

"Good evening," an officer said as he walked between them to the front of the room. She glanced to see him as he breezed past, an older man with dark brown hair, and wearing the rank of Major on his uniform. "My name is Major Sinclair." He turned to face them, and his cold green eyes rest on each of them in turn. "Your commanding officer for the duration of your stay with us, and your names will be the numbers written in the envelopes you find under your seats, and until you are told otherwise, those are the only names you will use. You do not, and will not, share your names, your ages, your date of birth, your home city, or any other personal detail with any other person here unless I give express permission to do otherwise." Emily felt something build inside her as she sat perfectly still, while others around her reached under their seats and fiddled with envelopes, it was the vibration she'd felt at home. His words were like an amplifier, specifically the suggestion that they were to remain anonymous. "You will be trained rigorously throughout your stay, and tested constantly by a team of instructors considered to be the finest in their trade, who, as such, have the highest standards and expectations. Should you fail to make the grade in any way, you'll be leaving us. There are no second chances, no go arounds. Get it wrong, and you're out. Do I make myself clear?" A few of the men among the new arrivals, many of whom were wearing the uniforms of British army regiments, snapped to attention while seated smartly and replied with a firm 'Yes, Sir'. Not all of them, though, and none of the women. Two of them WAAFs of the Women's Auxiliary Air Force, and one Wren of the Women's Royal Naval Service, all officers, all quietly observant. Sinclair's eyes found hers for a brief moment as she sat listening and taking it all in. He didn't blink, or say anything, just stared coldly, and received the same in reply. "Breakfast will be at six in the morning, and lights out is at ten each night. You'll parade in battle dress each day, and both it and your rooms will remain impeccably clean and well presented. There'll be no unruly behaviour while you're here, and no leave passes granted. Finally, the only rank here is that of your instructors, and mine. Whatever you may have worn on your sleeves or shoulders when you arrived, will be left at the door. As of this moment, you are all of equal worth. Which, until we've finished with you, is next to nothing." He paused again to look around the room. "Right, there's supper in the Mess across the hall, make the most of it. I'll see you at six." Everyone sat up smartly to attention, and he marched between them again, heading for the door, where he stopped for a moment and turned. "One final point, ladies and gentlemen..." Everyone turned and looked at him. "Everything's a test. Fall out."

The room erupted into a low mutter as thirty people who hadn't been allowed to talk all day were finally given breath. Mostly they just made comments to each other about the trip, or the introduction, with a few witty remarks here and there. Emily finally reached under her seat and unstuck the thick brown envelope marked with 'HMSO' in dull red letters, signifying it was property of His Majesty's Stationary Office, in the same way almost everything in the military was marked, or named, as property. 'Number 13, Room 3, 3rd Floor.' That's all it said. She looked on the back of the paper, and in the envelope, but that was it. She replaced the slip, then put the envelope in her pocket as she stood and took her bag, following the chattering group as they made their way out of the room.

"You're welcome to join us," a brown haired WAAF officer said as Emily looked around the Mess room, and her eyes settled on the three women sat on the far right of the long table.

"Thank you," she replied as she joined them, putting her bag down and taking off her coat, which she slung over the back of her chair.

"First Aid Nursing Yeomanry," the other WAAF, another brunette, said as she looked Emily up and down. She gave her a warm smile, then offered her hand. "I'm 3, of the WAAF, though I didn't tell you the last part, if you hadn't deduced it from my uniform."

51

"4," the other WAAF said as her hand was offered.

"And I'm 18," the blonde Wren said as she introduced herself. "I look young for my age, obviously, and I'm absolutely not from the Navy, that would be giving the game away, and I'm much better at secrets than our friends from the junior service. You'll forgive them, they don't know much better, having only been established as a service five minutes ago."

"She's quite right," 4 added. "The RAF are mere children in the grand scheme of things. Especially in such vaunted company as the Sea Scouts."

"13, nice to meet you all…" Emily let herself smile at the mischievous humour.

"We should probably get something to eat before it's all gone," 18 said as she nodded to the counter stacked with soup, bread, and tea, that was being swarmed by the men. The group nodded, and they made their way over. "I heard him say rank was excused, but he didn't say anything about manners," she muttered just loudly enough to be heard by a six footer wearing the uniform of the King's Royal Rifle Corps, and the rank of a Captain, who had been busily getting in the way each time any of them had tried to reach a bowl.

"What's that?" he asked as he looked around, deliberately over their heads, before looking down at them. "Ah, sorry. Didn't see you down there. Make way for the admin girls, chaps. Don't want them getting our pay wrong." He laughed to himself more than anyone else, with a couple of other officers joining in.

"How very clever," 4 added as she stepped past him, and started handing bowls to the others. "You'll be telling me we're junior to him, too…" She glanced at 18 with a raised eyebrow.

"Even my humour has its limits," 18 replied as she passed a bowl to Emily, and gave the Captain the most sickeningly disrespectful smile Emily had ever seen. "I can see, now, why speaking was discouraged.

Suddenly, sitting silently in the back of a cold truck seems like halcyon days."

"I didn't take a vow of silence," he laughed.

"More's the pity. Could you at least move so we can get to the bread?"

"My absolute pleasure, I'm sure." He bowed slightly, getting a laugh from those around him as he stepped back out of the way. 18 just grabbed a basket and with a nod of her head, gestured they all return to their seats. "You know, had I signed up for the Navy when the balloon went up, with an innocent hope bordering on the ignorant that they'd let me go to war on a Battleship, I'd have been bitterly disappointed, and likely hung for mutiny if I'd been stuck on a boat with hundreds just like him." She tore her bread apart, then smiled. "Fortunately, I never joined the Navy, obviously, so I don't have anything to worry about."

"It's exactly why we didn't join the Air Force," 3 added as she joined in the play on words inspired by the instruction not to talk about themselves. It all made Emily smile to herself. It was clear they were all very intelligent. Their words, their looks, their wit, they hadn't talked for long, but they were sharp, each in their own way, and each in a way different to the boorish Rifles Captain. They ate, and talked, then went up to their rooms, all four of them on the third floor, two per room. Emily and 3 went billeted together. They unpacked, and prepared their clothing and equipment for the following morning, making sure everything was hung so any creases would fall out. Then, after washing and tidying up, it was bedtime, and after a goodnight, Emily spent her time staring at the ceiling until she finally drifted into a sleep with the comfort of the vibration she'd developed deep inside.

The next morning felt rushed, even though it wasn't. They were startled awake by the playing of bagpipes at five, and quickly went about preparing themselves for their day. Emily pulled on her battle dress uniform and heavy boots, making sure she was dressed exactly as instructed before she and 3 met with the others and headed down to a breakfast of porridge and strong army tea, before returning to their rooms to scrub and tidy, and make sure everything was exactly as it should be. Then, it was down to parade on the gravel outside the front door. A wiry looking Sergeant Major was waiting for them, flanked by a pair of Corporals. All in Battledress, the Corporals each carrying a backpack and a Lee Enfield rifle.

"I am Sergeant Major Short," the Irishman said quietly and firmly. "We have five miles to complete before sunrise. Anyone not back here when the sun climbs over the horizon will be on their way home by lunch. I hope you all had a good breakfast. Right turn. By the left, quick march." The thirty three dark silhouettes crunched along the gravel drive, beyond the walls, and down the dark road. Emily's heart was racing a little at the fast marching pace, but soon settled after a few minutes as her muscles woke up, and her body accepted what was happening. Boots thudded in unison as they marched, everyone staying in step as the cold wind blasted at them from seemingly every direction as the road bumped up and down. "Breaking into double time... Double, time!" One pace, and the squad broke into an orderly run, staying smartly in step as they jogged along in the darkness. The undigested porridge sat heavily, and sloshed with the tea, making Emily feel uncomfortable as she fought to settle into a rhythm, while listening to the sighs and grunts in the darkness all around as the others went through the same. Legs and lungs burned as they switched between marching and running with a frequency just enough to let them catch their breath and steady their hearts before more exertion. They'd ran in training back in London, but not that much, and every uncomfortable seam in Emily's uniform had found a place to rub, and her boots grazed at her feet like sandpaper. Both leaving her burning and irritable, sensations that kept her mind from how heavy the boots were after a few miles, and now the hills made her heart pound and her lungs squeeze. There were moments when she questioned her choices, but she quickly reminded herself that she was out running in the dark, in full battledress, in the wilds of Scotland. It didn't feel like she was there to be a clerk. As the sky lightened, and the sun threatened to cross the horizon, the Sergeant Major shouted a loud "Stand by to race the sun! Three, two, one... Charge!" Everyone started to sprint up the road towards the manor house. Emily breathed deep and felt her heart pounding as she pushed hard, sucking in the oxygen in a controlled way to make sure she took in as much as she could, and passed a couple of the men before crossing the gates and joining everyone in staggering to a deep breathing halt. One dropped to his knee and retched, others put their hands behind their heads as they walked around gasping, while 4 raced across the line last, crossing with the Corporals close behind and screaming at her just seconds before the first rays of sun shot out across the land.

After tea and hard biscuits, they were taken into a long lecture on map reading and navigation, in a dimmed room lit only by lamps at the front where one of the Corporals from the run talked in a low and slow voice with a soft accent it was difficult to place. The fire roared in the open fireplace, and from her place in her numbered chair, Emily could see heads nod here and there in the darkness as the run, fire, tea, and monotone teaching came together in a perfect storm of tired monotony. There were some grunts every now and then, when somebody dropped off for a second as the lecture dragged for what felt like an age. When the lecture was finally over, and they turned to file out of the room, the second Corporal watched them from the shadows of the back corner of the room, across from the door, where he'd obviously been watching the entire time. Emily didn't give him any more than the briefest glance out of the corner of her eye as she left through the door, noting that nobody else seemed to have done anything other than look directly forward through tired eyes.

Everyone took the same places in the Mess room, and ate their sandwiches while talking about the day so far, though focusing on the positives, and in semi hushed tones so as not to bring attention on themselves from the Sergeant Major, who sat with a Sergeant that she hadn't been seen before, talking between themselves while eating, and hardly paying attention to anyone else in the room. 18 complained about the porridge not sitting right in her stomach when they were running first thing, starting a conversation, and the others quickly agreed. 4 reported it was all she could do not to vomit from the moment they started running.

"What about you?" 18 asked Emily. Equally as sick, I'm assuming?"

"Not terribly," Emily replied with a slight tilt of her head. "A little uncomfortable for the first few minutes, but otherwise fine."

"Constitution of a dog..."

"No more than anyone else," she shrugged, before taking a sip of tea. She looked around after a moment, and saw the other three staring at her. "What?"

"Practically everyone on that run, staff excepted, looked green, which makes you more than anyone else if you weren't. So?"

"So, what?"

"You've either got the constitution of a scrapyard dog, or there's something else that you're not telling us..." She raised her eyebrows questioningly, and Emily stared at her for a moment before looking around, and then leaning in a little, silently encouraging the others to do the same.

"Milk and cream..." She looked at them, then went back to sipping her tea.

"Yes, I think we all had those too. Cream to sweeten the tea and porridge, and a glass of milk."

"I didn't."

"I'm not sure I'm following?"

"Dairy lines the stomach, and slows down the digestion. The energy from the porridge lasts longer, but it's uncomfortable if you're running about. Have milk afterwards, it's packed full of good stuff that helps you recover, but beforehand, you want sugar and jam in your porridge, and sugar in your tea if you can. No milk, no cream, and you won't feel as sick." They all looked at her as though she was teaching them how to make fire for the first time.

56

After lunch, the Sergeant Major took them for a march down the road and back, keeping it at the quick time, not double, so nobody needed to worry about being sick. It was a brisk afternoon, and the sun was already low in the winter sky when they got back from their hour long three mile march. Emily had settled into it quite quickly, and focused on the person in front of her as the soreness worked out of her muscles and joints, and the coarse battledress uniform chafed, while the boots rubbed. It had been an intense day, and it wasn't yet over. More intense than any of her training back in London, at least. It didn't compare with the long days and nights without sleep back at the hospital, working around the clock to keep soldiers alive. Her body was used to standing for days at a time, but it was feeling something different with the intensity. It was one thing to walk up and down a ward, lifting and turning patients to prevent sores, cleaning them, dressing their wounds, even helping in the operating theatre for marathon six, eight, and even twelve hour surgeries, and something quite different to run for miles on end in the biting cold.

The afternoon was a lecture on meteorology. How the weather works, and why, and how it impacts radio transmissions. It was fascinating, though once again it was delivered in a warm room with a crackling fire and dimmed lights. Experience of fatigue aside, there were a few moments when even Emily had to pinch herself to make sure she didn't drift into sleep. After the lecture had finished, and they'd had their evening meal, they were sent to the reception room, where they sat and talked in their groups while drinking tea. It was pleasant, and the small group of women laughed with each other in one corner, left alone to the point of being ignored by everyone else, beyond the occasional glance and polite smile from those on the course that had seemed generally pleasant, and the sometimes sneering glare from the Rifles Captain and his group of four or five other officers.

One at a time, one of the Corporals would arrive and call out a number, thinning them out until finally it was Emily's turn, the first of the women to go. She was led through the house to a lounge sized room complete with logs burning on the fire, and a pair of armchairs sitting in front of it with a table in between. Waiting for her was an army Captain, who gave her a half smile as he gestured to one of the chairs, then sat in the other as she got comfortable. He poured her a glass of water, which she took a sip of as she felt the heat of the flames through her stockings.

"Your file says you speak French," he said after getting comfortable.

"Mais oui," she replied.

"Good, then from now on, our conversation will be in French only. Do you understand?" he replied in fast and well spoken French, that to her ear sounded like he was native to France.

"I understand," she replied, while engaging her brain and preparing for whatever was about to come.

"Smoke?" He opened a silver cigarette case and offered it. She smiled as she politely shook her head. "Do you mind if I do?"

"Not at all."

"Is it the smell that puts you off?" he asked as he struck a match and lit his cigarette.

"Not immediately, it's more the lingering smell it leaves on the clothes and hair the next day. Cigar smoke I like the smell of, but the taste doesn't match the smell."

"You've smoked cigars?"

"I tried one, once. That was enough."

"It's not to everyone's taste, I suppose. Smoking as a whole, I mean."

"It helps keep some awake and alert, others if helps them compose themselves, so it has its place."

"So, you don't necessarily disapprove of smoking?"

"Each to their own." Her mind was racing as fast as it had done in a while, as she reached for French words long forgotten, or hardly even learned. She paused here and there, but tried to make it sound like part of the flow.

"Just not for you…"

"It wouldn't be for you, if you knew what else it did to you beyond the immediately perceived positives."

"Oh…?" He looked at her with intrigue, as she silently kicked herself for finding a way to complicate the conversation beyond her comfort.

"I once met a doctor who invited me to watch an autopsy he was conducting as part of his research. He had two bodies laid out side by side, both men in their late fifties, one a lifelong smoker, one not. He cut the lungs out of both and showed us. One was aged with smog and the smoke of life. Pink and grey. The other, the smoker, his lungs were small and black, shrivelled almost. Thick with tar that had made it increasingly difficult to breathe, until his heart gave up with the effort of trying to pump deoxygenated blood around his body. The doctor estimated that alive, the smoker had the heart and lungs of a ninety year old compared to his friend."

"I see…" The Captain looked uncomfortably at his cigarette for a moment and frowned.

"Though his friend apparently broke his neck falling off a horse, so I suppose anything can get you when it's your time." She let the corners of her mouth turn up a little at his moment of discomfort, followed by relief.

"Quite," he laughed. "I don't ride, so my odds are looking up." He took a long drag of his cigarette, then blew out a cloud of smoke. "If you don't mind me saying, your French feels quite… Conversational. Like you've done more than learn it from a book."

"I had a good teacher."

"So it would seem. You've visited, though?"

"When I was a girl. I grew up loving art, but frustrated that I couldn't paint. I just don't have the talent. So, I went to Paris to see how it was done."

"Paris?"

"Yes..." Her heart skipped for a moment. She'd quickly relaxed into the conversation, and almost immediately forgotten the rule about not sharing personal information. "To see the Louvre. It's any artist's dream, I think, seeing all of that art in one place. The styles, the interpretations. I could get lost in it. I did, in fact, several times."

"It is a beautiful place, Paris. What is it they call it? The city of love?"

"Do they?"

"Don't they?"

"I loved the art, but beyond that, I couldn't say. Perhaps?" She shrugged casually, invoking her inner Frenchwoman. She thought of those she'd met there over her many summer holidays with her parents, and talked with in the cafes and bars by the Seine, and in the Montmartre. She could almost hear their laughing, and smell their cigarette smoke... She looked at him and tilted her head. "Gitanes..."

"Excuse me?"

"Those are French cigarettes you're smoking, aren't they...? Gitanes, the black tobacco used in them is quite distinctive"

"And that was a statement, not a question."

"Am I wrong?"

"No..." He stared at her for a moment, then let himself smirk.

"It could make a person wonder."

"What could?"

"How a man sitting by a fire, in the middle of the Scottish Highlands, had access to French cigarettes. There's not exactly a shop down the street, and France has been occupied by the Germans for over half a year, so it's unlikely you're just back from... Holiday. Though with your accent, I'm sure you'd be right at home in the Montmartre. Drinking coffee and smoking your cigarettes, while watching the artists sell their wares."

"Maybe..." He smirked again. "Though the coffee can be bitter."

"Really?"

"Oh, yes. Especially in a morning. It can be thick, and heavy, and leave a sour taste."

"In the Montmartre?"

"Everywhere..."

"I see."

"You see what?"

"Do you enjoy coffee?"

"I suppose, why do you ask?"

"More than you like tea?"

"Probably, yes."

"Then if you like coffee in the Montmartre, but don't like it bitter, you'd know exactly where they grind it a little rougher, and add a sprinkle of sea salt to soften the edges. Especially in the morning." She looked at him, her eyes not blinking, her face expressionless, with just the slightest raise of her left eyebrow. She knew she'd overplayed her hand when she mentioned going to Paris, and that she'd already crossed a line in revealing information about herself. So, once over it, she decided to let it run. She knew the Montmartre like the back of her hand. The mornings she'd sat there drinking coffee in the sun; her mind could almost taste it. Her French friends had laughed at her dislike of the bitterness of some of the coffee, so took her to a place on the corner known for its smoother offerings. It's there she'd learned that they gave the beans a slow, coarse grind, and added a pinch of sea salt to soften it, and from that moment on she'd spend every morning she could there, every summer that she returned. He stared at her for a moment, his eyes a little different, scanning her, weighing her up. "It could make a person wonder," she added with a smile, breaking the silence and shifting the intensity of his stare. "Or not."

"It's been an interesting conversation." The tension relaxed, and he gave her a warm smile. "Thank you, Miss…?"

"Thirteen."

"Miss Thirteen?"

"Just Thirteen."

"Goodnight, Thirteen." He shifted and stood, and gave her a firm nod.

"Goodnight," she replied with a half smile, then headed for the door.

"Le Consulat?" he called after her as she reached for the door handle, giving her the name of an old and well known restaurant in the Montmartre area of Paris.

"No," she replied firmly. "Not Le Consulat. Goodnight."

Chapter 5

Sunshine

The following Monday there were twenty eight remaining of those that had arrived on the truck. They'd been run every morning, and marched every afternoon, with lectures in between. The days were long, and daylight was short, almost as short as the nights that were filled with scrubbing rooms and clothing, and themselves, and making sure the sweat, mud, and sand was washed out of their uniforms, boots were polished, and everything was as it should be. On average, the women got around five hours sleep per night, more the last two nights of the week when they'd worked out a system to get everything done more efficiently. One would do the uniforms, one the bathroom, the others a room each. It got everything done quicker, so all they had to do was climb into bed and try to stay warm through the night, before being knocked and shouted up at five, with the daily accompaniment of bagpipes.

Of the two that had left, one was an infantry officer from one of the county regiments, who'd spent an evening in the lounge room talking about his unit's fighting in the retreat to Dunkirk. The other was an engineer who'd badly dislocated his knee on a run, and had to be taken off to an army medical centre in Fort William. Emily had managed to get it back in its socket, and splinted the wound, both of which were commended by the unit's Medical Officer, but it was too late for the engineer. He wouldn't be walking properly for a while, so once he'd been carried back to the mansion and examined, he was gone. On the positive side, all four of the women were able to stay close to the front in the runs, with none of them struggling with sickness or gastric issues. Unfortunately, a couple of the others still hadn't worked it out, and gulped milk at breakfast each morning, then got sick every run. Of the other officers, a couple had been watching for a few days, a pair of Irish Lieutenants, one from the Guards, the other of the Royal Inniskilling Fusiliers. On the fourth day, they came over on the evening in the lounge and introduced themselves, then got straight down to business. Specifically, why the women weren't having milk and cream at breakfast. The secret was shared, and the next day they tried. The day after, most others did, too.

The week anniversary of their first day came, and they stood in the morning darkness waiting to be run for another five miles, the previous night they'd each been issued a set of webbing, pouches attached to a belt that carried ammunition, water, and food, with straps slung over the shoulders to distribute the weight, along with a large pack. A backpack in other words, packed with a waterproof cape, spare socks, and a few other bits and pieces; and they'd been told to wear the kit for all runs and marches from that moment on. The Sergeant Major appeared in the darkness, flanked by the Corporals, and each person was issued a Lee Enfield No. 4 rifle. The general issue rifle of the British army. It was hefty at around nine pounds in weight, and forty four inches long, and was almost as big as 4 when she tried to keep it steady. Once the training staff had made sure the students, as they were referred to, were all set, they were put on the back of a waiting truck, and silently went on their way. Rocking and rattling in the cold. A couple of the soldiers smoked, but nobody talked.

"The miserable and dark looking silhouette climbing away to the front of you is Rois Bheinn, the biggest hill in these parts," the Sergeant Major said in his Irish drawl as he paced up and down in front of the assembled students, who stood in their now familiar places in the squad. "The pace will be set by Corporal Mills, and Corporal Baines will bring up the rear. You are required to stay between them at all times. No racing ahead, no falling behind!" He looked along the grey faces in the pre dawn darkness. Get it right, and you'll be at the top for sunrise. Get it wrong, and you'll be on your way home by lunch. Now, if you don't have any questions, unsling your rifles." Everyone quickly pushed their rifles between their knees and started fiddling with the brass clips on the stiff webbing rifle slings, fighting to remove them. Emily did the same, having watched the Lieutenant from the Inniskillings and copied what was doing, and felt her cold fingers fumbling with the tightness of the sling. One by one the rattle of released slings echoed in the darkness, until she finally managed to convince hers to let go, before rolling it and pushing it into her pouch. "Good. Keep your weapons in the shoulder, and at the ready. Squad! Left... Turn! Front rank lead off in single file. By the left, quick march!" It was a new experience for Emily. She'd managed so far, though the daily run had left everything sore, including her feet which she'd done her best to manage, draining blisters and treating them with iodine before dressing them, and doing the same for the other women. There were sores, too, where the coarse, wet, and sweaty material of their uniforms rubbed in groins and under arms, but it was all manageable. The added weight of the webbing and large pack took it to a whole new dimension, as did the heavy and unslung rifle. The soreness and stiffness instantly doubled, and then tripled, and they were only marching up the track. "I'm climbing up the sunshine mountain, where the four winds blow!" the Sergeant Major sang boldly from the front of the small column, followed by three large bellows, as if blowing out. "I'm climbing up the sunshine mountain, this is all I know… Turn your back on all your troubles, raise your hands up to the sky… I'm climbing up the sunshine mountain, you, and I! Number 1! You, and I!" Emily was bemused, more so when 1 joined the Sergeant Major in singing the exact same words, the exact same way, with the exact same blowing, until they called 2, and so on until it was Emily's turn, and she found herself singing along while breathing hard, forcing out her words as her muscles screamed. Then, it was onwards to everyone else.

By the time they were starting the climb proper, she could hear herself breathing harder than ever as her heart and lungs screamed, sucking in oxygen, desperate to get it to the hard working muscles that were on fire with the incline and hard pace. She thought back to her anatomy and physiology classes, and tried hard to breathe in through her nose, and out through her mouth for a while, in an attempt to use the pressure difference to open up her lungs fully, but it was hard going, and she couldn't help reverting back to gulping in huge mouthfuls of air. She stumbled every now and then in the pre dawn twilight, making her feel all the more fatigued, almost to the point of panic at times. Time passed slowly, and the incline steepened as they dragged themselves through tussocks, having left the bogs behind when the trail quickly faded to nothing. Water from ankles to knees, and higher in places, followed by slippery grass, uneven stones, and hidden holes threatening to catch a boot and turn an ankle. Corporal Mills, was like a mountain goat out front, floating over the terrain while everyone else trudged some way behind. The infantry officers were all close to the front of the group, with everyone else straggling behind, and Emily closer to the back. She glanced over her shoulders every now and then, when she dared and had the energy, to make sure Corporal Baines wasn't too close, so she could calculate and regulate her pace accordingly. The wind blasted as the darkness faded, and all the time she kept singing the sunshine mountain song over and over, like it was on repeat, until the sky turned a silvery blue. She was close to the top, though the leading group were well out of sight. She took a deep breath and composed herself, then marched on, singing under her breath and swinging her rifle a little side to side, helping her keep a rhythm. It was hard, very hard, but a thought slipped in that she was doing it. She wasn't in a hospital, or a barracks, she was dragging herself, her kit, and her rifle up a huge hill in the wilds of the Scottish Highlands. It was a thought that energised her, and soon she was nearly scrambling up the finish, leaning into the slope as she checked her footing pace after pace, before finally pulling herself up to the summit. She let herself smile as she half ran, half jogged to the group crowded around the stone cairn. She glanced behind her to see 18 pop up over the ridge and follow her, and smiled again.

Nobody talked much, everyone just stretched and gasped for breath until they could settle their hearts. They swigged sips from their water bottles as the sun slipped over the horizon, bringing the faintest hint of lukewarm rays to the bodies stood steaming in the cold. 4 was the last to join them, with Corporal Baines just a step behind. Her face was pale, and her eyes rolling a little. She joined them and forced a half smile while swaying, needing 3 and 18 to stand close either side of her to keep her upright, and stop any wandering eyes assuming she was struggling while the Sergeant Major and two Corporals stood together talking, just off from the group. 18 held Emily's rifle while she pulled 4's water bottle from her belt and handed it to her, encouraging her to sip it, then, after glancing around briefly, she stepped forward and pulled a boiled sweet from her pocket and popped it in 4's mouth. It was one of the few she'd picked up from Fortnum's while in London. Treats she'd kept, rationing them once training hand started properly, as an emergency sugar boost that 4 looked in desperate need of.

"I don't know what's wrong with me," 4 said when her breathing started to settle. "I run all the time, and swim when I can. I'm fit, I know I'm fit, I just…" Her eyes were filled with upset and frustration, close to tears, but not of sadness. Emily stepped close, and looked in each eye in turn, then frowned as she looked her over, and reached to untangle 4's hair while moving close enough the feel the heat radiating from her neck.

"Is it that time of the month?" she whispered so quiet that 4 took a moment to hear, then looked at her with a slight frown before nodding as Emily made unnecessarily complicated attempts to straighten her hair. "Thats why. It's not you, it just happens." She smiled and nodded confidently. "Deep breaths, and where you can, try and let it in through your nose and out through your mouth. Sips of water, and big controlled gulps of air if you need more oxygen, and try make that sweet last." 4 nodded at her, then Emily stepped back and took her rifle from 18.

"Right! Get yourselves fallen in!" the Sergeant Major shouted, and 4 rolled her eyes in casual resignation before pulling her rifle up and taking a deep breath, as if to suggest she was ready for whatever came next. "Make the most of the sunshine," he said with a degree of glee, while pointing at the clouds of slate grey, deep blue, and ink black rolling over the hills. "What goes up, must come down. Now, let's see if we can get down to where we started before that storm empties itself on us. Right turn, front rank lead off. Quick, march!" Corporal Mills went to the front, and Baines to the rear, and soon the group were following the ridge in an extended single file, isolated and open as the wind howled, cutting through them, and bringing the storm closer. It was a long, winding march across the undulating ridge, before finally starting down, through loose rocks and gravel at first, then tussocks, then down to the bogs that poured ice cold water into boots, and sent it up legs, chilling already cold feet until they were painful. This time, it wasn't the screaming of the heart and lungs, as the thighs and glutes dragged upwards, it was the shake of the muscles in unsure steps going downwards, trying to keep a steady pace that didn't slow the column, while not getting overtaken by gravity, and going down too fast. It was uncomfortable, and the cold cut deeper than ever.

The sunlight they'd seen what felt like hours ago had been replaced by a heavy greyness when they finally collected at the truck where they'd started. Emily felt as though she'd been marching all day, and the sunlight, and subsequent lack of it, supported that. The lung bursting pain of the climb felt forever ago, and now she was just cold, and tired, and ready to get in the truck, however cold she knew it was, and get the short journey back to the house over with so she could try and warm her feet and hands again. She checked on 4, who looked paler than before, if that were possible, and gave her another sweet, though she knew it wouldn't do much good. What was in the sweet wouldn't power a few hundred paces, but she also knew it was psychological as much as anything else, and hoped it would give 4 a chance. It was all she could do.

"Alright, listen up!" the Sergeant Major shouted. "The truck will pass through the gates of our headquarters at exactly twelve noon, and you'd better be ahead of it! Head west on the road, and keep the loch to your left. If the truck catches you at any point on the route, you'll be instructed to get on board, and you'll be heading back to your unit by dinner this evening. Any questions?" He looked around the tired faces staring back at him. "Well, what are you waiting for? A written invite?" There was a hubbub of activity as everyone seemed to come together. "Anyone I see standing still once I've counted to five will start in the wagon!" Everyone burst into life and started down the road, running and jostling to find their usual places in the squad. Boots crunched in time, and Emily soon managed to find her place, her heart racing and breathing quickening as she went from stationary to a quick march.

They marched hard, keeping the regulation army pace of, what they'd been reminded from day one, one hundred and sixteen thirty inch paces per minute, designed to move soldiers at a steady three miles per hour. It wasn't slow, and the pace had to be maintained no matter if you were a six foot tall guardsman with long legs and broad shoulders, or a five foot three inch WAAF officer like 4. Military uniformity at its best. After the first mile, the squad started to fracture. A group of infantry officers pushed the pace after discussing loudly that nobody had been told to stay at the quick march, or as a squad, and soon they were striding away, seven of them in all, naturally stepping around others not wanting, or able to keep up. Everyone tried to keep pace over the following mile, leaving a long, strung out line of filthy khaki bodies marching along the barren highland road. Emily kept her head down as the wind brought sleet into the air, blowing the mixture of snow and rain around her, and making her face ache with the cold. Her chest felt heavy, and her feet were in agony, as every step sent the sensation of a thousand needles through the flesh. She marched, trying to keep a steady pace, and found herself getting annoyed at the sunshine mountain song going around and around in her head again as the small group that had broken away disappeared into the thickening sleet. She was further irritated by them marching away, breaking everything up. In her mind, a squad could protect each other from the elements, and encourage each other to keep going, instead of making it an every man for himself moment of macho selfishness. She complained bitterly to herself as she marched, until a thought settled in the centre of her mind like a lantern being lit in the darkness. She stepped out to her right, into the road, slowed, and stopped and turned to look behind her. Another officer nodded as he marched past her, having not been far behind, then she started heading in the opposite direction, going against the flow, squinting into the intensifying storm as the sleet was replaced by a curtain of snow. She shuffled, rather than marched, looking at each approaching figure.

"Where's 4?" she asked as 18 came out of the misery right behind another officer. "Have you seen her?"

"No…" came 18's reply. "No. Let's go look…" She joined Emily, and they shuffled east, until finally, two silhouettes came through the darkness of the blizzard. 3 and 4, shuffling slowly side by side.

"Are you OK?" Emily asked as they came together. 4 nodded, though her face was frozen, and her eyes elsewhere. 3 looked at her friend, then gave Emily the slightest shake of her head as if to suggest that 4 was far from at her best. "Right, ponchos!" Emily said as she stepped forward, and went behind 4. "Get each other's ponchos out of the large packs, and a pair of socks each." It took determined irritation to get her frozen fingers to work on the metal buckle and soaked strap that made it swell and almost impossible to move. Eventually, she got

69

4's poncho out, and pulled it over her head. Then, taking the spare socks from the young woman's large pack, she put one on each of 4's hands, like an extra pair of gloves. Everyone else did the same, then, when everything was fastened up, and they were covered in their heavy ponchos, they marched together. Emily in front to shield from the blasting snow, and 4 behind her, with 3 and 18 to 4's side, close, and keeping her steady as they set a pace. 18 called out a cadence, 'one, two, three, four', getting them in step, and keeping them moving together, and at a pace that was tolerable. "Let's sing that bloody song!" Emily shouted into the blizzard, "I'm climbing up the sunshine mountain, where the four winds blow!" She shouted it, and the others did the same, keeping 4 involved, and engaged, and singing with them. They marched mile after mile, and picked up another officer that had dropped back, and a mile later, another. Both joining in the singing, and marching, and keeping the pace.

Emily felt the slightest sense of relief as she saw the familiar curve in the road that they'd run every morning, and knew they were only a mile from the house. Then, there was a clatter from behind, and she turned to see 4 face down in the snow. She went and dropped to her knee as the others lifted her. She was awake, but had stumbled at the point of exhaustion.

"I…" 4 muttered as she looked around.

"Are you done?" Emily asked. 4 nodded, then shook her head, then used her rifle as a post to try and drag herself upwards. At that, the rumble of the truck's engine came around the bend, bathing the small group in the glow from its narrow slit headlights. "Get going!" She shouted at the others. "Get going, or you'll fail!" They all stood and looked uncomfortably. "Look, it's a mile to the house. Get going, and keep a good pace, and we'll try and slow the wagon, so it doesn't catch you." She looked to 4, still struggling to her knees, and then back to them. "Go! Now! Unless you want the last week to have been for nothing! Get going, and stop being so bloody emotional!" They nodded, and after 3 gave her friend a nod, they turned as a four, and quickly marched off into the snow. "Look at me," Emily said in a low voice as she knelt close to 4. "Are you done?"

"I don't want to be…" came the reply.

"Good. Then let's not give them the satisfaction of putting a pair of weak and helpless girls in the back of the wagon." 4's eyes filled with fire, and seconds later, Emily was struggling to drag her to her feet. Then, with an arm under her poncho, and her hand grabbing 4's webbing belt tightly around the left side of her waist, they started marching, Emily using all of her strength to keep the short WAAF officer upright. She pulled 4 onto her a little, taking some of her weight, and despite her initial reluctance, 4 finally let her, and put her energy instead into moving forwards. "We've got less than a mile," Emily said as they marched, much slower than regulation pace. She glanced over her shoulder, and the truck was getting closer, much closer. It wouldn't be long until they were caught. "There's no shame in falling back. You're cold, probably hypothermic, and being in the truck will likely keep you alive."

"No…"

"Then you're going to have to be brave, and pick up the pace with me. OK?" She looked a 4, getting a weak yet defiant stare in return. "Come on. I'm climbing up the sunshine mountain…" They picked up their pace with the song, inviting each other to sing, and sing, and sing again as the chorus looped around, and the steady downhill gave them a boost. "Come on! We can do it, we're there!" The truck was almost on them, and they shouted the song with all their might, trying to drown out its rattling engine and make it less real. She glanced behind again as the truck slowed to a stop, and the passenger door started to open. "Run now, like you've never run before!" She pulled at 4, dragging her by her belt, and the WAAF responded. Every step was agony, but they kept their pace, and the truck door slammed closed again, as the engine rattle increased. Soon there were shouts and cheers, and as the gates came into sight, they saw the others stood cheering them on. It was the boost they needed, and as the truck closed on them, they ran together, arms on each other's belts, dragging each other forward until they collapsed through the gates and crashed into the snow covered gravel to a huge cheer.

"Fall in, now!" the Sergeant Major shouted in a way they hadn't heard previously. "Shut your noise, and fall in!" Hands pulled Emily and 4 up, and soon they were in their places, joined by a huddled figure that climbed from the back of the truck. 12. He shuffled and stood beside Emily, not looking her in the eyes. "I do not like games, ladies and gentlemen. We are training for war, not the playground, and if your being here is about competing with others on the course instead of yourselves, you're in for a very rude awakening. I can promise you that!" He stood in front of 12. "You failed to complete the objective, as such please remove yourself and report to the debriefing room." 12 smartly turned to the right and fell out, then made his way to the house as the Sergeant Major moved down the line and stood in front of 4, who was still swaying. "You failed to complete the objective, and as such please remove yourself and report to the debriefing room." Emily's head turned sharply as she looked to make sure she was hearing right, and seeing who he was talking to.

"With respect, Sergeant Major," Emily started. "4 crossed the gates ahead of the truck, alongside me. She completed the objective." The Sergeant Major's head snapped to look at her so quickly it almost spun. He glared at her, but she didn't back down, instead squaring her shoulders and staring right back at him.

"Not!" He barked as he moved purposefully to stand in front of Emily. "Without assistance…"

"She carried her rifle and her equipment, Sergeant Major, and nobody carried her. She met the objective." Emily's voice was firm, yet she didn't shout, or sound overly disrespectful.

"Had you not been with her, she'd have stayed face down in the snow when she collapsed."

"Yet I was with her, Sergeant Major, and together we completed the objective."

"Together, you say?"

"Together, Sergeant Major. Your instructions were to keep the loch on our left, and cross the gates ahead of the truck. You said absolutely nothing about helping each other either way. However, that said, any help I offered was purely motivational. As I said, she carried her own equipment, and she carried her own rifle. According to your own instructions, she completed the objective."

"You're telling me that you, Number 13, interpreted my instructions to suggest that as long as you crossed the gates ahead of the truck, there was no other specification as to how? No inference that you should do it alone? No implying it was an individual effort? No suggestion that it was an individual race of any kind?"

"I think that would be a reasonable interpretation, Sergeant Major. In training, I was told that the army is quite specific in its instructions when it wants something."

"Indeed it is, Number 13. Indeed it is. Right! Who else interpreted my instructions in the same way as 13?" 3, 4, 18, the two that marched with them, and a couple of others raised their hands. It was almost half and half. "How lucky the armed forces of this country aren't a democracy…" he said with a shake of his head as he looked at the hands. "Number 1!"

'Yes, Sergeant Major," the infantry officer who'd increased the pace shouted smartly. "Do you agree with 13's interpretation?"

"No, Sergeant Major. I believe we needed to achieve the objective as an orderly and effective fighting unit, and that needed everyone to be able to carry themselves."

"In that case, I have no option but to ask you to remove yourself and report to the debriefing room," the Sergeant Major said while keeping Emily in his stare. "You, that is, Number 1. Off you go." The officer turned and left, and the Sergeant Major stepped out in front of the squad, looking them over. "Bravado and egos have no place in what we do here. Splitting the squad was dangerous, and had it been a combat mission, the objective could have been compromised as a result. We work together. This isn't the Olympics, the first to cross the finish line doesn't win, and it isn't cricket, you're not out when you're caught. There's always something else you can do, and as officers, that is how you should be thinking. There's always something else you can do, right to the very end, until there's nothing else you can do. Only then, are you out. Do I make myself clear?" The entire squad shouted yes in reply. "Good. There's hot soup in the Mess. You're to have that, and tea, and then clean up and warm up for the afternoon. Dismissed." He looked at Emily and let himself smile a little. "A mouth like yours will draw attention, 13. As it is, today it's got you the job of looking after 4. Good work, and let the MO know if she needs any support."

Chapter 6

Up, Again.

The running continued the following morning, after an afternoon of shivering and cleaning, drying, and pressing uniforms. 4 had taken some warming, and permission had been given to use extra water to run a hot bath for her which, to Emily's surprise, she chilled within minutes of being in it, she was that cold. The other three women took it in turns to lay in bed snuggled against her, sharing body heat and wrapped in blankets. Tea and more soup were brought up, and as soon as she warmed enough for her shivering to ease, she was asleep for the rest of the afternoon.

The next morning, she was still tired, and weak, but managed the morning run well enough, before settling into a day of lectures about the wireless, including training in building and repairing them, and using Morse code efficiently. Everyone on the course could use Morse to varying degrees of competence, tapping out a series of dots and dashes, or dits and dahs in army speak, to construct and deliver bursts of message without too much effort. For Emily, though, it was like reading Chinese. There was a short course of training in London, where the basics were explained, but otherwise she was lost. She needed a reference guide for which dots and dashes correlated to which letters, and her words were transmitted very slow, much to the frustration of the Lieutenant training them. Her mind just wasn't processing it. She was used to clear and concise conversation. A medical standard demanded of nurses and doctors, to make sure meaning was understood. Dots and dashes, no more than a collection of long and short bleeps in a headset, meant nothing.

"Come with," 18 said after dinner, when everyone had been sent to the lounge to relax for the evening. Emily looked at her with a frown, much preferring her comfy armchair in the corner. "Quickly, I need you for something." Emily sighed, and put down her near empty tea cup, then to her embarrassment, heard herself sigh even louder when she dragged her sore and aching body from the chair. The others didn't say anything, they were all the same. Even some of the infantry types were shuffling and sighing. She followed 18 out of the room, and through the house to the lecture room where they'd spent most of their day. "Don't come out before bedtime," she said as she opened the door for Emily, who raised an eyebrow before stepping inside the dimly lit room to see 4 sitting at one of the wireless sets. 18 gave Emily a wink, then closed the door behind her, leaving them to it.

"What's this?" Emily asked.

"Payback," 4 replied as Emily walked over to join her.

"I'm not entirely sure what that means."

"It means that I get to run five miles in big heavy army boots every morning because of you. So, you're going to do the same because of me, have a seat." She nodded to the chair next to her, and Emily obliged. "I taught Morse code to WAAFs before coming here, and thought we could have a talk while dinner settles?"

"Thank you. How are you feeling?"

"Ask me again…" She nodded at the headset and Morse key in front of Emily.

"It's like that, is it?" Emily sighed as she put on the headset, then reached into her pocket and pulled out the folded piece of paper with the Morse alphabet.

"It is, and you won't be needing that." 4 snatched at the paper, holding it just far enough away to make Emily's eyes narrow. She smiled, and Emily settled. Then, she went back to the beginning, and taught Emily a whole different way to that taught throughout the day. A way that almost sang, and got Emily's mind moving with the letters, and more importantly, recognising the letters in the first place. They started with simple words at first. Cat, hat, dog, log, hen, then, when, and had Emily listen for the vowels being repeated. Then the Rs, Ss, and Ts, the most commonly used consonants in written English. Piece by piece, they built words. Not trying to remember all of the letters in the alphabet, but by teaching Emily to recognise the vowels and most

76

common consonants, which in turn allowed her brain to fill in the gaps. It wasn't perfect, and neither was her Morse, but by the time they went up to bed, she was significantly more competent than the previous day.

The week was different to the first. The lectures were delivered in a more engaging tone, and the lights weren't quite as dim. There was a lot of focus on wireless work, and sending and receiving messages, and they were taken to the ranges to fire a whole host of weapons. Rifles, revolvers, pistols, submachine guns, heavy machine guns, the lot. They fired thousands of rounds, and cleaned carbon and filth from their weapons for hours, and while it was initially a little exciting for Emily, the discomfort of kneeling and laying on the cold and sometimes wet ground, and feeling sharp stones digging into her knees, hips, pelvis, and elbows, took the shine off it. It also led to her thinking more about what she'd signed up for. Despite having been through two weeks of gruelling test after test, that pushed her both physically and mentally, she still had no idea why she was there. Nobody did. They discussed it when they could, in hushed tones when in their rooms playing cards, but nobody had anything sensible to offer. There was a suggestion by some of being posted to somewhere in North Africa as wireless operators, or as translators. They'd worked out that they all had language skills, with French being common, and 3, who'd worked at the Air Ministry, talked about how there were large swathes of North Africa, such as Algeria, under Vichy French control, which had them putting the pieces together. If they were going into the desert to relay signals by wireless, they'd need to be fit, and they'd need to know how to use weapons, just in case. It was the most logical eventuality they could agree on. The only thing they could be certain of, was that they weren't there to be clerks. They wouldn't be expected to train alongside, and achieve the same objectives as their male counterparts if they were.

At the start of week three, they were paraded outside again in the darkness of a Scottish morning in late January, wearing their webbing and large packs, and holding their rifles. It was bitterly cold, the type that gets into the bones if you stand too long, and even before the Sergeant Major came out to address them, Emily was starting to shiver as the cold got into her back and squeezed at her spine.

"Alright, listen in," the Sergeant Major shouted as he stepped through the door and out into the cold. "Today's objective is simple. You are to make your way to the sunshine mountain, that's Rois Bheinn for those who weren't paying attention the first time, then climb it, and follow the ridge, before dropping back down and getting yourselves back here before two o'clock this afternoon. There will be a check point at the bottom before the climb, at the top, and when you come back down again to rejoin the road, and the wagon will be at the base to collect any casualties, before following you in on the usual rules. If it catches you, you're finished. Any questions?" He looked along the squad. "Good. One final point… Today's objective is an individual effort. You, and you alone, must complete the objective. You may not work together; you may not help each other. Likewise, you may not hinder each other. To assist in this, you'll be set off at intervals. When your number is called, step to the gate and standby." Everyone glanced around at each other, and Emily felt a chill run down her spine. Not with the cold this time, but the anticipation. They'd been told from the start that everything was a test, but they'd never so openly been told that they were to do it on their own. Something prickled in her, and she thought back to her challenging the Sergeant Major when she'd helped 4 across the finish, and she couldn't help but think that while 4 had a reprieve, and the officer who'd led the breakaway was dismissed, she was now getting her punishment. "One final thing to remember, if you haven't already done the maths, is that you only have enough time to complete the objective if you move consistently at the quick march throughout…" The words cut through Emily's discomfort as she quickly did the arithmetic in her head, and realised, as no doubt others were doing at the same time, that it would be impossible to move consistently at that pace. Not uphill, or downhill.

One at a time, the squad disappeared into the darkness, crunching up the gravel as they were called forward and sent on their way at thirty second intervals. Waiting had felt like time was going backwards for Emily, as one after another were called. She wanted to get going, while at the same time she didn't, not really wanting to feel the pain she knew was coming. Then, about half way through the squad, she was sent on her way. The nerves were intense. She'd never felt so much like she needed the toilet, and almost asked permission to go to the bathroom as she watched the first few leave, but something nagged at her not to. She knew it was nerves, and by the time she'd made it out onto the main road that would lead her to the climb, her butterflies had settled, and the urge had passed. Instead, she counted her paces as she marched, making sure she was moving at exactly marching pace, and counting how many times she'd hit a minute. The air was cold and damp, but she warmed quickly after a mile, and the road made the going easier so she could pick the pace up a little, having taken the first twenty minutes to warm her muscles and joints, and get her heart and lungs eased into the shock of what she was doing. She kept the rifle butt on the outside of her upper arm, her hands holding it lightly as she swung it slightly across her body like a pendulum, giving her pace and rhythm as she marched, keeping her shoulders forward, and her head down a little, pushing into the wind that gusted hard into her face, catching her unawares and making it hard to breathe until she turned her head. It was hard going, but she felt comfortable, like she could keep the pace, but despite knowing there were eight in front of her, having watched them set off, she couldn't see a soul up ahead. She couldn't even hear the crunching of their boots, or of those following her. It was dark, cold, and lonely out on the road, and the only thought in her mind beyond the counting was knowing that the climb was coming.

"Heads up," a male voice said from behind, breaking through her counting. "Just so you know, it's not cheating if you keep pace once I'm ten paces ahead... Stick with me as long as you can." He gave her a wink as he passed, it was one of the officers from the Intelligence Corps. He generally kept to himself, but was pleasant enough when he talked. She'd hardly seen him break a sweat in any of the runs. He was tall, and very lean, and seemed to have an unbreakable engine. She glanced over her shoulder to see nobody else, then shrugged. She gave him a nod as he went out in front, and she tried to adjust her pace to match his. Then, he broke into double time for ten paces, and she instinctively matched him, shocking herself into more life than she'd expected. Ten paces later, he dropped back to a quick march for twenty, then off at the double again for ten. The routine was hard at first, and took some adjusting to, but once she was into it, she found that she recovered in the quick march quite quickly, while the ten double time paces relieved the tension in her legs and back that built

79

with the marching. It was hard going, but she was moving quicker than she'd planned, and feeling good for it. Buying her time that she knew she'd need if she was to get in ahead of the cutoff time. She tried to keep with her counting, to keep track of where she was, but the double time messed up her system, and she was quite sure that his regular paces were over regulation. It didn't stop her, though, and she managed to keep with him until the darkness of the sunshine mountain's slopes cut through the murk. "I'll see you at the finish!" he called as he raised his left arm and waved. "Good luck!"

"Thank you!" She shouted after him. Good luck!" She watched as she finished her ten double time places and stepped out for twenty, and he just continued running off down the road without breaking his pace. For a moment, she toyed with the idea of going after him, but she knew her limits. The ten paces at a time were enough, and by eight her heart would pound. Trying to keep it going would see her in a heap before she got to the bottom of the climb, let alone the top. She kept going, keeping the ten and twenty mix, though it quickly became more challenging without the crunch of somebody else's boots just ahead, but she didn't have time to think on it, as half a mile later she was approaching the first checkpoint, where Corporal Mills was waiting to direct her to the darkness of the sunshine mountain, that even in the murky pre dawn darkness she could make out clearly.

Having checked in, and had her number ticked off his list, she turned off the side road, and followed the slight downhill as it dipped towards where the truck had stopped the last time. She knew what was coming, and just the slightest bit of dread found its way into her stomach. Something she dealt with by having a sip of water from her canteen, shortening her pace slightly to drink, then pop a rationed boiled sweet in her mouth ahead of the climb. The rations had been strict since the first introduction to sunshine mountain, saving them for when they'd be the most useful. The last four she'd shared that morning, and she was happy she had. The snow and rain of the previous days had topped up the bogs, and as she left the track, she was soon slowed to dragging herself through murky water filled with tangled grass. It was hard work, and each pace soon had her heart and lungs pounding, and she remembered that the memories of the last climb hadn't been exaggerated. If anything, the last time had been easier in a way, being part of a snaking column marching its way up. Mills had set the path through the bog, and the line had followed him, but this time, it was all on her to find her own way. She stepped, and sank, and then found a few solid paces, before going in the water again. She stopped for a moment and looked, the best she could in the darkness, and tried to work out a path, then continued on her way and, to her relief, managed to spend more time on solid ground than not as her eyes adjusted to the surroundings, and she could see the occasional footprint, or patch of flattened grass, showing the way others had been. The song came back to her as she finally broke through the bogs, and got onto the worn, steeply inclining track to the summit, though it wasn't as annoying as it had been previously, this time it was like an old friend settling down to have a conversation with her while they climbed together. Her lungs burned, heart pounded, and thighs screamed as she climbed, her short paces carefully set as she moved around rocks and holes. She didn't stop, though. She knew that if she did, it would be hard to get going again, so she kept low, and kept pumping her legs, step after step. She felt herself smile when the sky lightened, and she looked up to see the top not too far away, and then she stumbled. Her right knee hit a rock, and her face planted into the dirt as the butt of the rifle came up and hit her in the cheek. She'd let out an involuntary yelp when she went down, that quickly turned to a desperate plea under her breath as she fought to stop herself rolling back down, and doing herself an even worse injury. She caught the toes of her left boot against a rock, then before she knew it, she was being dragged to her feet by her large pack.

"No time for a picnic," one of the Irish officers said as he steadied her without stopping, letting go the moment she was upright, then passing and heading up the track. She shook her head, and spat out the dirt. She was hurting, and her heart was racing even more with the adrenaline, but she was upright, so she quickly moved forward, following him and watching his footing, while she tried to shake the ringing from her ears. Her knee hurt with every step, and her cheek throbbed, but she kept going. Mouth wide open as she gasped in the air. The song was long gone, everything was, until she was scrambling up the last climb and up onto the ridge. She stopped briefly to look down behind her, and then headed over to the cairn of stones where the Sergeant Major was waiting. He ticked her name off, looked at her dirty face in the half light of sunrise and gave her a frown, then gestured his head along the ridge.

She followed the Irishman, keeping him in her sights, but he was some way ahead. The cold sunlight made traversing the ridge easier than it would have been in the dark, and after a while her knee settled into being more of a dull ache than the stabbing pain it had been, and she stepped out a little, upping her pace slightly to try and make up time from the climb and the fall. She thought as she went on the two who'd broken the rules to help her. One pulling her along with his pace, and one picking her up when she'd fallen, and almost headed down the side of the mountain on her face. She didn't know either of them well. People talked politely, but most nights her and the other three women had been left in their corner, and at meals, their end of the table. Nobody really mixed with them, and they didn't bother that much with anyone else. One of the infantry bores had tried it on with 18 one night, and been put back in his place, and after that, they were just the women that shouldn't be there. Or, to the decent ones like the intelligence officer, and the Irish pair, somebody to say good morning to. The four women had got on, but even then, they weren't close. They couldn't be. There were rules, nobody knew each other. So, everyone just got on.

The downhill made her knee ache again, and she found herself being more cautious with her steps, and going a little slower than she'd planned, but she got down without incident, and checked in with Corporal Baines before heading to the road. It was about a mile later that her heart squeezed when she saw a bundle sitting on the side of the road, and she thought of 4. She hadn't seen her since they'd started, and hoped she'd fare better than she had previously, but the sight of a huddled pile of clothes worried her. She slowed as she came close, and stopped to see 7, one of the infantry officers, sitting with his rifle across his lap.

"Are you OK?" she asked. He looked up at her for a moment, then back down at his rifle. "Are you hurt?" He shook his head, then looked up at her again with a forced smile. "Then what are you doing? It's only a mile to the hill. If you get going now…" Then she stopped and looked at him again. He'd set off before her. He'd already been up the hill. At least she assumed he had; she hadn't seen him on her way to it. Not that she could remember.

"I just don't want to do it anymore," he said as he watched the penny drop in her mind. "You should get going."

"Come with me," she demanded. "Follow me. I'll set a pace, you follow behind. Just follow me and we'll get back." He smiled and shook his head. "Just get up! You've already been up the bloody hill!"

"Sorry we were rotten to you, 13. I'm going to wait here for the wagon, then get myself home. Good luck, you're a good person." He gave her another pained smile, then looked back down to his rifle. She stared for a moment, then turned and started walking. Glancing back briefly to see him still sitting there.

"At least go back to the check point and get in the truck!" She shouted. He just waved her away, and went back to staring, leaving her to get on her way.

The road back felt like it went on forever, and every part of her burned and ached, but there wasn't a thought in her mind of stopping. Seeing 7 looking so resigned had made her all the more determined, and she could picture herself in his place, and how she'd feel. It was the fire that got her into double time again, ten and twenty, making her way down the road with her rifle swaying across her body to keep pace. She kept going, and going, not slowing, not speeding up, until finally she descended the gravel track to the house, where 4 was standing at the gate and waiting patiently. Her face lit up when she saw Emily, and Emily felt something unexpected. A warm flutter inside that wasn't hard, or professional. She felt herself smiling like she did when she'd spent time with Harriet the previous year, back at the hospital when the young pilot was causing mayhem, and running rings around the Senior Sister. She felt happy, and she felt herself smiling bigger than she had in a long time as she pushed on to the finish, crossing the gate and getting her number ticked off the list by the waiting Sergeant.

There was a lightness around the mansion for the rest of the day. All but one had completed the objective, the man Emily had seen sitting on the ground. Nobody knew for sure, but somebody had said he'd ran from the start, and passed most in front of him, practically flying up the hill and along the ridge like some sort of Olympian, but had blown himself out, and quickly run out of steam to the point where his mind had given up in the face of the road home. If he'd managed the run out and up, he had the time to get back, even if he'd just followed Emily as she'd offered, but he had no interest. He'd gone too far in his head.

It took some time to warm up after the morning's activity, though the absence of rain or snow for the duration had been welcome, even if the wind had been icy and cutting. After a warm lunch, and lots of tea, uniforms were cleaned and pressed, and bodies and hair were scrubbed, before afternoon lectures on navigation. Map and compass, and celestial. It was like things had taken a step backwards, and the lights were dimmed, the fire was roaring, and the monotone delivery had returned. If the others hadn't worked it out, Emily had. A long and exhausting march and run in the ice cold that dragged on for hours, followed by more than enough hot food, more than the usual at lunch, followed by a seat in a warm and dark room with no sound but a miserable drone. They were being pushed, again, to their limits. Everything was a test. She moved her muscles, shifted her weight, tensed and released, drummed her fingers on her thumbs, and even nipped herself a few times to stay awake. Heads nodded, and the occasional grunt followed by a head lifting sharply made her smile to herself. At one point, a long, deep, vibrating snore echoed around the room. It was enough to make everyone stare briefly at the poor soul who'd given in. The instructor never stopped, not even missing a beat, and just let the man sleep through, snoring louder and louder as he slumped in his chair. Emily couldn't help but glance over every now and then, the sleeping man had become a fascination, something for her to focus on outside of herself, and somehow his snoring kept her awake.

The sleeping man didn't join them for dinner. He'd only jumped awake when everyone was dismissed and leaving, and hadn't been seen, or heard of, since. There was gossip around the lounge that evening suggesting his kit had gone, and his bed and locker stripped, in the same way of the others who had gone. The absences were noticeable, and those who remained were noticeably different for their experiences, mostly. Introspective, and considered. More self aware, even. They'd been through a demanding phase of training. The runs hadn't stopped, nor the afternoon marches, and twice they'd done the sunshine mountain. They'd spent hour upon hour learning Morse code, and how to build, maintain, and repair a wireless, and just as much time on the ranges, shooting all sorts of weapons, though with increasing frequency focusing on pistols, revolvers, and the new Sten submachine guns, clunky, simply designed and built weapons that had arrived in the second week, apparently fresh off the production line, and the latest weapon in the British arsenal. It was cheap, and easy to make, something the British army needed after leaving so many weapons on the beaches of Dunkirk, and designed to empty the magazine of nineteen nine millimetre bullets that stuck out the side of the weapon quickly, and in the general direction of the enemy. The instructors had shown them how to aim, and how to fire considered shots, and then told them how the weapon was so inaccurate that they wouldn't hit a barn door at fifty yards if they tried. So, they were taught how to tuck the stock into the space between their arm and ribs, trapping it tight with the elbow to keep it from moving too much, and then 'firing from the hip'. It was demonstrated, and devastating. Much more effective than regular aiming, with the bullets going roughly where the arm was pointing. It was a crude but effective tactic, and they'd all become quite proficient at ripping into targets, confidently emptying half a magazine at a time into them, to make sure the short and less powerful bullets had a chance of causing any damage. A similar approach was taken to the pistols. While aimed shots were still preferred for more distant targets, they were taught to crouch and fire single handed at those in close range, firing instinctively to kill before they were killed. Or that was the theory, at least.

When they were so competent with their weapons that they could use them in their sleep if needed, they were taken into what were referred to as the killing houses. Barns and sheds set up as houses, and loaded with hidden targets, some that operated on a pulley system controlled by the training staff; and individuals, and then teams, would work their way through the different layouts, fighting their way through the mock environments that somehow felt very real. There were even outdoor courses, where they'd run through woods shooting at targets that rolled towards them at alarming speeds, and popped up out of nowhere, making the heart race.

In between the shooting and weapons training, they were taken up into the hills where they terrified the wildlife as they were introduced to explosives. How to use them, how to set and place them, how to use timing pencils and other fuses, and how to blow up practically everything and anything. Being stuck out in the middle of nowhere meant there was nobody to see, hear, or complain, and despite the inherent danger that came with handling explosives, a great deal of fun was had by most. To her surprise, Emily had been fascinated, and found herself conceiving ingenious plans to blow things up of all shapes and sizes, something the instructors encouraged without reservation, and she found herself excited in ways she never had been every time they went out to do explosives work. The pressure and vibrations she felt in her body when one of her creations erupted made her smile like little else, and her keen medical mind made the compositions, calculations, and timings feel like an exciting puzzle she couldn't put down.

They'd trained hard, and worked hard. Their rooms were inspected daily, as were their uniforms, and slipped standards were addressed immediately. Everyone was beyond sore, blisters had blisters, and an assortment of wounds and injuries were rife. Sleep came easy, and there was never enough of it, yet they were functioning better than at any time, and becoming ruthlessly efficient in everything they did.

Chapter 7

Don't Mention It

After the following morning's run, and after they'd drank tea, and milk, and had some time to compose themselves, they were taken through to one of the larger reception halls in the house. They'd had a few lectures in there, but otherwise they hadn't seen much of it. It was large, with high ceilings, and oil paintings of scenery and cavalry charges. Unlike previous visits, however, the chairs and tables had been removed, and standing in the centre of the polished hardwood floors was a Lieutenant with a healthy looking light tan that made the whites of his eyes sparkle as he looked each of the remaining twenty four up and down.

"Have a seat," he said with a firm yet casual air to his voice. He gestured to the ground, and after a quick look around for chairs or benches, everyone slumped down and sat cross legged. "For the last three weeks you've been run and marched daily, learned about weapons, radios, and navigation, and shown how to put your skills into practice. Starting today, however, you're going to learn how to look after yourselves." He glanced as he talked, his eyes were sharp, like he was weighing everybody up. "So, to get us started, do we have any scrappers in the group? Any boxers, or brawlers? I'll even take a rugby player if we have one." Everyone looked around, and after a few smirks, one of the infantry officers, Number 19, put up his hand. "Up you come," the Lieutenant said with a welcoming smile. He was dressed in his service dress uniform. Trousers and jacket, shirt, tie, even a Sam Browne belt and revolver holster. The creases in his trousers were razor sharp, and his shoes were so highly polished that they caught and reflected the lights from around the room. "Boxer...? Brawler...?"

"Oxford Boxing Blue," 19 smirked in reply, smug in his confidence of having been selected at some point to represent Oxford University at Boxing. "Middleweight Champion, 1939. Won the Varsity against Cambridge."

"Is that so…?" the officer raised an eyebrow, suggesting he was a little nervous. "I'm not sure we've had a boxing blue through here before." 19 shrugged, still smirking. "We'll have to see how this goes… Is it a problem if we don't use gloves?"

"No…" 19 smirked and gave his head a sharp shake.

"OK. In that case, we'd better get started." He stepped back a couple of paces and faced 19, the pair of them standing side on to the seated audience. "When I give the word, you're under orders to put me on the floor. Understood?" 19 nodded and smirked as he raised his fists, left leading, and right pulled back. "Now!" The instructor didn't raise his arms in the same way, and instead just shifted his balance a little, feet shoulder width apart, left slightly ahead of the right, and weight just behind his toes, with a sliver of space between his heels and the ground. 19 stepped forward and his right arm extended as he rolled his hips, launching his fist towards the instructor, who simply stepped back slightly, moving his head backwards, and with his open left hand pushing the back of 19's fist, guiding it gently past. 19 checked himself, and frowned, then went again with the same attack, though this time, after his right was guided past, he followed up with a left, which the instructor guided in the same way, and then again with the right. Three swings in quick succession, and the instructor glanced them away each time with the palms of his hands, while rocking back and forth gently to avoid the hits. 19's smirk had gone, replaced by the instructor's. "When you're ready?" he teased, just a little, and 19 came forward swinging again, right, then left, then right, and on the third the instructor switched it up, using his right hand to guide 19's right fist, swinging it across his body using the force of the attack, and hitting 19's shoulder hard with his left hand, spinning him so his back was to the instructor. A boot to the back of 19's left knee, the leg on which he'd put all his weight when swinging his right fist forward, and the momentum sent him crashing to the ground with a clatter and a gasp. The instructor's hair wasn't even out place. He'd done hardly anything, and 19, the university boxer, was on the ground having not landed a single punch. "Try again?" he asked as 19 got to his knees and looked up at him with a mixture of shock and fury. His voice remained steady and confident, and 19 nodded as he stood, unbuttoning his battledress blouse. He pulled it off and threw it over to the side, and paced in his vest, stretching and winding his arms up while holding the instructor in his fierce glare. Without warning, he launched himself forward, his right fist flying through the air at the instructor's head with alarming speed. The instructor quickly stepped to his left and grabbed 19's wrist with both hands, rolling it as he passed, using his thumbs to push the back of 19's hand in towards his forearm, making him yelp as his arm locked behind him. Another kick, this time to the back of 19's right knee, sent him clattering down to the ground again, and the instructor sent him on his way with a shove. "Had enough yet, or are you ready to start trying?" His voice was dry, with the hint of a mocking tease. 19 wasted no time in getting up, and came at the instructor without waiting, or posturing, just diving into the attack with swinging fists aiming for the instructor's head. Each was slipped and dodged, until the instructor stepped into the attack, and with a short, sharp thrust, drove his fist into 19's solar plexus. There was a gasp, and a wheeze, and 19 staggered a little, then tried another swing, a weak swipe that the instructor took a hold of while stepping close, and with his hip and a swerving move, launched 19 through the air, rolling him over his shoulder, before dropping him hard on the floor. He followed by dropping his knee onto 19's neck until his eyes bulged as he fought for oxygen. The instructor's eyes were briefly fierce, before he released the pressure and stood, letting 19 suck in the oxygen. "OK, that'll do for now. Are you feeling alright?" He looked down with almost fatherly concern, something opposite the violence of moments earlier. As 19 nodded, a hand was offered to pull him up, and soon he was standing and composing himself. "Queensbury Rules, ladies and gentlemen, as named for the Marquis of Queensbury, who sponsored and created the rules of modern boxing, are all well and good in the ring, but they'll get you killed when it really matters. I'm here to teach you how to fight properly, how to take any opponent apart piece by piece. Not to box for points or glory, aiming for the obvious legal targets, but by being dirty, and fighting to live. The only rules are those I tell you. I can guarantee that over the coming week you are going to get hurt, so you'd better make peace with that now. If you're too fragile, or it's not for you, now's your time to walk away. Otherwise, stay awake, pay attention, and do as you're told." He paused as he looked around everyone. "Nobody's moving, so I'm assuming you're all staying." He turned to 19, who was obviously still smarting from his fight. "Alright, get yourself sat down."

What followed was a day of training in something Emily hadn't been prepared for, and had never come close to experiencing. She'd had to restrain patients, but that was about it when it came to laying hands on people with anything other than care. They were all paired off, and after being taught the basics, right from how to stand, to flex their knees, to twist and move, which took the entire morning, they moved on to basic blocks and dodges, and avoiding common attacks, which the instructor had memorised, categorised, and ordered in degree of seriousness and likelihood of use. He knew the attacks most people would use, and he knew how to combat them, and the willing students followed. Moving, rolling, slapping, and grabbing in their pairs. After the running, and hills, and weapons, and dreadfully dull lectures, it was something different, and something quite exciting that everyone seemed to enjoy, as evidenced by the excited conversation in the Mess at lunch.

The afternoon started with a refresher from the morning, and then he had them do it properly. One pair at a time in front of everyone else, selected by him and put together for the purpose of the bout, the objective of which was to put the opponent on the floor. The only rule was that they stopped when he said, and they didn't hold back. The first pair went at it hard, and a few painful looking hits were landed by each, though to the frustration of the instructor, neither were using the skills they'd been taught. Instead, they were shifting back and forth like they were dancing, and then going in with a punch, and the occasional attempt at a headlock. They weren't stopped, he just let them keep going for long minute after long minute, until they were both sweating and breathing hard. Then, he just let them keep going. Eventually, they got themselves stuck into some sort of wrestling match, grappling and twisting each other in what looked like a long and uncomfortable hug. They were both tired, and their fight had gone.

"That's enough," the instructor said with disappointment, looking at them both with eyes that conveyed it unmistakably. "The longer you take to do what needs to be done, the more tired you get. The more tired you get, the more sloppy you become. When you're sloppy, you're weak, and when you're weak, you're vulnerable. Thank you both for demonstrating how exactly not to do everything we went through this morning, and making your being here for it a total waste of time. Sit down." They both sheepishly returned to their places on the floor, still breathing hard and sweating heavily. "You." He pointed at Emily. Her heart squeezed, but she didn't need telling twice. She was up and beside him as he scanned the others. "And you." He pointed to the Rifles Captain, who smirked as he stood, and gave one of his friends a wink. "Right, face off." He stepped between them, facing the audience, and got them in position. "Let's see if the two of you can be any less disappointing. OK, go." Emily's heart was already racing, but it almost beat out of her chest when he stepped back, and the big oaf of a Rifles Captain lunged at her full speed. His giant frame threatening to bury her. Her mind raced even faster as she tried to remember the morning, and quickly she stepped to her side, then pirouetted, rolling along his outstretched arm as he passed, leaving him to stumble as he missed her entirely and tried to steady himself while she took a couple of steps away from him, raising her hands in front of her a little, but not entirely sure why. The instructor raised an eyebrow, and watched her intently. Her opponent turned quickly, and came back at her again, managing to get a hold of her sleeve as she stepped out of his way again, staying light on her toes as she'd been shown. Then, with a duck underneath him, and a twist, he lost his grip, and she stepped out of the way again. He stopped and shook out his arms, then paced in front of her a little, changing tactics for a moment, before moving forward slowly, pushing her backwards as he inched closer, then without warning swung his right fist directly at her head. She leaned back and turned her eyes to the right, just as his fist glanced past so close she could feel the draft. Remembering the instructor's first demonstration with the boxer, she put her hand on the back of his fist and pushed, making the rifleman continue with the momentum of his swing, and turn his back to her while she stepped around him, backing into the space he'd left. Her heart was still racing, and her mind only just able to think through the fog of fear. He was furious when he turned to face her, his eyes full of rage, and he let out a deep, guttural grunt as he came at her again. This time, though, he was on her, and any turn was met. He swung his right fist, and she ducked, then quickly lifted her head and pulled it back to miss the left. Before she could do anything more, his fist hit the side of her face, connecting hard just below her left temple. It didn't hurt, not at first, it was just a huge shock that rattled her brain and made her see stars. Never in her life had she been punched, and this one had been hard enough to make her ears ring. The next thing she knew, he'd used his hip to roll her, while grabbing her tight by the shoulders, and she was tumbling through the air before crashing down on the polished wood floorboards with a clatter that knocked the air from her lungs. She half writhed, half gasped, as she fought to compose herself. The pain in her cheek suddenly arrived at the same time, and she felt like she'd been hit by a train. "That'll do," the instructor said. He appeared above her and looked at her for a moment while she tried to focus her eyes. "Are you alive?" She processed the words for a moment, then nodded, and he held out his hand. She took it, and he pulled her up, something that felt as painful as going down, and twice as embarrassing as she looked at the audience and felt herself blush. "You've got the moves, but if they're looking for a fight, you can't avoid giving them one. You can only dance so much before you have to hit them. OK, both of you sit down. Next!"

4 gave Emily a pained smile as she sat, trying to be supportive while no doubt contemplating what was coming. From the start of the course, the women had been expected to meet the same standard as the men. They were expected to run, climb hills, and handle weapons the same, and now they were expected to hurt the same. Emily's cheek throbbed, but she kept her hand from it, and tried to compose herself, giving the external appearance of somebody whose face wasn't burning from being punched. She watched as pair after pair were started, with some doing better than others. The Irish were vicious scrappers, who used every dirty trick to try and outdo each other, before shaking hands and laughing. The best of everyone was the Intelligence Corps officer who'd passed her on the solo effort up the sunshine mountain and back. He used the tactics he'd been shown, and finished his opponent with apparent ease. Every one of the women was paired with a man, and each got hit to varying degrees of hardness, before being deposited hard on the floorboards. Training continued throughout the afternoon, with the instructor teaching and demonstrating more movement and blocks. The excitement of the

day's start had faded for Emily, and there was something about the hit she'd received that she couldn't get past. It had shaken her in every sense of the word, and she wasn't sure how to process it properly. She hit the floorboards twice more before the afternoon was out, and the inside of her lip had been cut, and her shoulder bruised, to add to her painful cheek, and she was ready for the day to be over. Dinner was quite subdued, with most being a little dulled by the day's antics. Everyone had hit the floorboards at least once, and some had been quite bloodied, especially those who'd really gone at each other, and it seemed that getting some food, and then relaxing before an early night was at the fore of everyone's mind. Unfortunately, that wasn't on the cards. After retiring to the lounge, they were collected again one at a time, called by number and taken from the room. Emily hadn't been in much of a mood for conversation, and instead let 18 and 3 talk back and forth about flowers, of all things. Roses, specifically. It seemed they knew everything there was to know about them, and both had experimented with grafting to try and create new roses. It was an interesting conversation, but not fascinating. Not enough to pull Emily from her thoughts, where she was questioning her choices, and asking why she was there. She wanted to do her bit, she wanted to make a difference in a way other than being a nurse, yet all she'd achieved was joining an organisation she'd never heard of, and been on training course after training course, with no idea why, and even less idea why she'd need to march up mountains, fire machine guns, or get beaten up. The previously romantic notion of being a wireless operator in the desert was starting to feel less desirable. Not if it involved being punched and kicked.

She entered the same room after having her number called, and sat in the armchair by the fire, across from the same Captain, who gave her a warm smile, and offered her tea. She took it, and sipped, while looking into the fire and waiting for him to start, trying to clear her mind so she could focus on his words, and her answers.

"That's probably going to bruise," he said while looking at the side of her face.

"Not as much as you'd imagine," she replied.

"Oh?" He looked at her questioningly, and she looked back while considering what she'd just said, and kicking herself for saying it, inviting a conversation instead of waiting for his, risking tripping herself up.

"The side of the cheek is mostly bone and a bit of muscle, there'll be a bit of swelling, but I doubt it'll bruise as much as it could have elsewhere."

"I see... Lucky, in that case."

"Quite."

"Though better not to be hit in the first place, I'd imagine." She looked him in the eyes again, but he was giving nothing away. It was no surprise that he'd know the outcome of the day's training, she'd assumed the instructors would all come together to debrief, she just wasn't expecting such a direct reference to what she felt to be her most painful failure to date. She was used to succeeding, to finding a way, and didn't like to lose. Certainly not in such a humiliating manner. She shrugged in reply, not sure how she'd reply to such an obvious statement. Nobody wanted to get hit. "How many fights have you had in your life? Fist fights, I mean?"

"I haven't..." she shook her head.

"No, of course not. You'd be surprised how few actually have. Lads fight sometimes at school, but less than you'd imagine. It's a sad fact, though, that women can often be on the receiving end more than men, but that's a different story." She nodded, the thoughts that came with the conversation made her feel uncomfortable. She instantly remembered how her husband had got angry at her, because she liked things a certain way that was different to his. It was early in her marriage, and his rage had made her tremble. She'd always had her own unique way of doing things, it was something her parents had encouraged, despite her knowing they were frustrated at her at times, but apparently it had come as a surprise to her husband. "You know, what we're doing here isn't for everyone, and while we weed people

94

out as we go, that's not the only way…" She straightened her back a little as she listened to his words, and pulled back her shoulders, the thoughts of the past instantly put back in their box and tidied away. The day's failure was suddenly eating away at her inside and making her feel nauseous. "What I mean to say is that you can ask to leave, if it's not what you want to do."

"I don't want to," she replied with barely a pause. "Leave, I mean. I don't want to ask to leave."

"OK… So, if not leave, you're going to have to do something else."

"Such as?"

"Fight…" It was his turn to shrug. "It's not enough to move, and to dodge. You have to fight. The enemy won't be sympathetic because you're a woman, they never are. In fact, history shows us that in war it's often women that suffer the most. If you don't fight, it'll lead to one of two outcomes, because there is no running away, or escaping, from a determined enemy. You'll either be killed, or perhaps worse, you'll be captured, and wish that you had been killed." The warmth had gone from his eyes, replaced with a fierceness she hadn't seen previously. "If you don't find the fire in you that lets you fight back, it'll be over, and you won't have a say in it."

"I understand," she replied through a drying mouth.

"Our training is designed to test, as I told you at the start, and we filter people out not because we're elitist, or we set unreasonable standards, but because if we don't, and we send people who don't meet the standard into harm's way, we're as good as signing their death warrants." She returned his stare and nodded. Inside was more turmoil than she'd felt in a long time. He was telling her, in no uncertain terms, that the plan, at some point, was to put her in harm's way, whatever that meant, and being able to fight was key to her survival. It was scary, and at the same time, it lit something inside her. It wasn't just that she didn't like to fail, it was something else. She nodded firmly, to convey her understanding.

"Thank you," she eventually replied. "For explaining it to me, I mean."

"Despite the current situation our country finds itself in, fighting isn't the most natural of pastimes. It is, though, something that humanity can't quite leave alone. So, when others fight, we must be prepared to defend ourselves. It's that simple, really, however I won't labour the point." He gave her a smile, the warmth returning to his eyes. "The secret to it, is knowing that the human body can take a great deal of punishment, and ultimately we'll be fine. That hit you received today will have hurt like hell, but it's the shock that finished you off." She listened carefully, and his words were remarkably accurate. The shock of the rifleman's fist connecting with her face had alarmed her, and awakened uncomfortable memories. It hadn't actually hurt that much, not at the time. That came after, when she had time to think about it. "Some six footer from the wrong side of the trenches landed a haymaker on the side of your face, and here you are, a slip of a girl, talking to me a few hours later, and drinking tea. You're not in hospital, your head didn't cave in. You'll hardly even have a bruise in the morning, if what you say is true." She felt the slightest smile curl one corner of her lips. "The thought of it hurts more than any physical pain does in the moment. Afterwards, all bets are off, but you get my meaning."

"Yes…" She nodded again, contemplating his words, and her feelings. "May I ask you something?"

"Please do."

"Am I being dismissed?"

"No. No… Not right now. Just know that if it does happen, it's to protect you. Now, if I may return the directness?" She gave him a nod. "Do you want to be dismissed?"

"No!" Her keenness surprised her, and him. "No," she repeated, in a much more composed way. She'd been through three weeks, and while she didn't know how much longer the training would last, she'd

96

been up and down that hill, she'd ran every day, she'd been punched and knocked to the ground. She wasn't ready to give up.

"OK. In that case, I think we're about done. Goodnight." He stood, and smiled warmly. She finished the tea and put down her cup, then stood and straightened her uniform, and after saying goodnight, she headed for the door. "Oh, one other thing?"

"Yes?" She turned to look at him.

"That café in Paris, the one with the good coffee. What did you say the name of it was?"

"I didn't…" She looked him in the eyes for a moment, and he gave her a nod, sending her on her way.

The next morning, after the run, they were back in the hall with the same instructor, and to Emily's mild frustration, the session started with being taught how to fall properly, this time on coconut mats to cushion the blow. How, if you knew you were going down, you could fall in such a way that it minimised the impact and potential for damage. She muttered in her mind that it would have been more useful to start the training with that part, and with the mats, considering how many times she'd been dropped the previous day, and how each time it had rattled her head, and made her body shake. She also recognised what had happened. The first day was an opener, to test and see how people responded to violence, but now they'd had a taste of it, he was putting some more structure in. Going back beyond the start, and making the most of the inevitable. Following the falling, was throwing, and flipping, and rolling, and generally shifting and moving an opponent with their own body weight, often to the ground. It was sequential, exactly as Emily had worked out. There wasn't the violent punching and attacking of the previous day, it was all much more controlled and coordinated, and very deliberate. Pairs switched, and the instructor moved around them, correcting, demonstrating, and giving support, and she found herself smiling a little when she worked out that her slight frame could shift an attacker significantly bigger, and with the correct application of force, send him to the ground with the grab of an arm, and the swerve of a hip. The way they were taught was paced, too. In slow motion at first, walking through, before increasing speed a quarter. By the end of the afternoon, they were moving in real time, and bodies were moving quickly, and crashing to the ground with routine thunder, the vast majority landing with the taught finesse that reduced the impact. That evening there were sore bodies, with some worse than others, and most had gone to bed long before lights out.

The next couple of days were more very specific, progressive training. Movement, throwing, restraining, and handling. Striking, with fist, boot, elbow, and knee, or the side or palm of the hand. Everything demonstrated, then rectified and tweaked in slow time, before increasing the pace. They were also introduced to a group of stuffed dummies attached to frames, that they could practice their more lethal attacks on, including flows, consecutive strikes that flowed together in movement to severely incapacitate an assailant. Hard strikes with the side of the hand into the throat, followed by another hard strike to the neck, or even a knife or other object such as a pen to the neck or eye. Moves that were a little too dangerous to use on each other. The runs and marches continued, too, making the physical nature of the week draining at best, and by the end of the week, nobody stayed in the lounge for more than an hour, and the house was silent long before ten, when the lights went out.

"You," the instructor said as he pointed at Emily, "and you." He pointed to the Rifles Captain. They'd watched as the previous two pairs had been called forward in turn, not long after the breakfast run, and instructed to fight until one of them was on the ground. Both fights had been a long way from those at the start. They were cleaner, and faster, and the learning had taken. Now, it was finally Emily's turn. She stood facing her adversary, and thought for a moment about what was to come. He sneered and smirked again, in the way he had since the day they started, and when the order was given, he moved towards her like lightning. Not swinging his fists like previously, but closing the distance to grab. She rolled along the outside of his outstretched arm, having stepped to her right to avoid a lunge. It all seemed like it was happening in slow motion, and as she came level with him, she drove the knuckles of her right fist into his skull, just behind his left ear, hitting with a short, sharp punch. She stopped and watched him stagger a little, after letting out a type of yelp that she hadn't heard a man make before. He turned and looked at her, his eyes closing with pain, and his hand pressed tight to the place she'd punched. He looked at her, then staggered forward and dropped to his knees, then bent over and gasped. She watched him closely, half in amazement, half in shock. She knew from her anatomy and physiology that the bones of the skull where she hit him were thin, with a lot of nerves just underneath, and considered that the right pressure would cause intense pain and dizziness. She'd surprised herself, both in that she hit without holding back, and in how she'd hit. "Alright, that'll do," the instructor said, and after looking Emily in the eyes for a moment, put his hand on the rifleman's shoulder and got a nod, before he pulled himself to his feet, and almost drunkenly went back to where he'd been sitting. Nobody looked at him. Instead, their eyes were on her. Eyebrows were raised, and mouths open, at the lithe young woman who'd dropped a six footer with one short, sharp punch, and made him scream and go down like no other punch had throughout the training.

The other fights that followed were much the same as those that went before, but Emily didn't really watch them, instead, she replayed what had happened in her own. It had happened so fast, yet so slow, and her knuckles were driving into him almost instinctively, like she knew where to hit. She was in shock, she deduced, at how she'd managed to drop him with one hand. With one blow. It exhilarated her a little. It was counter to everything her life had been about. She was a healer, a nurse who helped put people back together again, not a fighter, or a scrapper that brawled. Her mother would have been horrified, and probably her father, too. They hadn't brought her up that way.

The sleep had seemed shorter than ever over the previous week. Emily had been going to bed earlier, as had the others, and their cleaning routines had become so efficient that they didn't need as much time to make sure everything was as it should be, but she felt as tired when she woke as when she went to sleep. None of the others looked as bright, either, with everyone in some stage of automation as they got up, cleaned up, dressed, had breakfast, and dragged themselves through a run which was at that point largely silent, with few showing signs of struggling. Everyone just locked in their own thoughts as they went about doing what they could to just get it out of the way so they could get on with whatever came next, which recently had been endless day after day of fighting. Not just physically, the being hit and flipped, kicked, and thrown, and crashing into the mats, but also psychologically thinking about applying the instructor's methods to not getting hit, or into hitting, and in the case of Emily, manoeuvring and throwing about men almost twice her size. All of it was happening around the constant knowledge of being tested, and the threat of being failed at any point. The boxer from Oxford hadn't even made it to the second day of the fighting, and while nobody was ever told why somebody had left, and those who had failed were removed in such a way as nobody even got the chance to ask them, there was usually a good idea of why amongst those who remained. In this case, she'd imagined it was his bravado. When asked if he boxed, he didn't just say yes, he told the instructor he was a boxing blue at Oxford, trying to impress, or swagger. Either way, he broke the rules about sharing. It wouldn't have taken a genius to work out his approximate age, and talk with somebody from Oxford and find out who the boxers were in that time period.

"Good morning," the instructor said as they entered the room. He gestured for them to take their usual places sitting on the floor, while he watched them closely, no doubt scanning for signs of fatigue or weakness that could be exploited, as he'd taught them to do some days earlier. "You'll be happy to know that we won't be punching and kicking each other quite as much today." His eyes sparkled as he talked, and smiled somehow, even without him physically smiling. "Today, you'll be learning how to use this." He pulled a dagger from behind his back, and pinching it between his thumb and forefinger, held it up for everyone to see. Both sides of the around six and a half inch long blade tapered to a fine point, held by a silver looking, crosshatched handle. Emily looked at it and felt herself frown. She'd just about got through punching somebody, the thought of using a blade touched something inside her that she didn't know existed. "The new issue commando knife, made from the strongest steel, and long enough to get through the estimated three inches of clothing worn by an enemy soldier in winter, greatcoat and all, while still getting into their innards and making a mess of them." This time he

100

smiled slightly as he walked forward and handed it to 18. "Have a feel, then pass it around." She did as he said, while he stepped back in front of the class. "It's well balanced, and when handled properly, it can be used to dispatch an enemy both silently and completely, or sometimes not so silently." He paced a little as the knife was passed around. Emily took it in her hand and felt the weight. It was solid, and certainly not a toy. Not dainty like the scalpels she'd used to remove dead flesh from wounds, or unwieldy like the carving knives her parents had back home. She opened her hand and felt it balance perfectly, then wrapped her hand around it again, feeling how the handle, tapered at both ends, fit perfectly in her palm, like it was designed just for her, and how the slight S bend in the guard curled against her finger while inviting her thumb to rest on the other side. There wasn't anything clumsy about it, and something else she didn't recognise surprised her deep inside, she was fascinated with it, and it took an effort to pass it on to 3. When she did, she looked up again and felt herself blush as she saw the instructor looking right at her. "Today you're going to learn how to subdue an enemy permanently. Not just somebody you can fend off with your hands, but one that is intent on killing you, and your only option is to kill him, or her, first…" His words focused Emily. The weapons ranges and killing houses were impersonal in a way, bullets fired to kill and wound, but at a distance. A knife was different. He was talking about using it to kill, up close and personal, and he was making it very clear that gender meant nothing in such a situation. Man or woman, he was talking about killing them. "Right, hand that one back. It's mine." The knife found its way back to him, and sat comfortably in his hand, like it had returned home. "You will learn how to use your knife silently, where to strike to have an immediate and irreversible effect, and how to silence your enemy forever without drawing attention to yourselves, and you'll learn how to use it in a fight with somebody very much determined to stay alive. The difference between the point being pushed into the base of the skull, or thrust into the heart, or the blade being dragged across their torso, so their guts fall out, distracting them enough to stop them getting you before you finish them off. This is where it gets real, ladies and gentlemen. This is where you get to smell the wine on a man's breath as he gasps his last. Where you'll hear him beg you to spare him, and cry for his mother as he faces the inevitable. Or, and this is something you should all make peace with, looking into a woman's eyes and tasting her perfume as your point pierces her heart..." He looked around them for a moment. Nobody was grinning, or excited by what he was saying, not even the moron from the Rifles. He'd made his point, but he reaffirmed it anyway, though it wasn't needed. "You'll do this because if you don't, it'll be your ribs being spread by their blade, your blood choking you after your throat's been cut, your guts hanging agonisingly from your abdomen as you scream in horror and agony, praying they'll finish you off quickly. You'll learn from me now, and you'll pay attention like your life depends on it, because undoubtedly, it does!" Emily felt a shiver in her spine as he talked. The shooting ranges had been deliberate and dispassionate. Load, aim, fire, hit the target. It was automatic in a way. The fighting had been something she'd got to grips with, but mostly in the frame of self defence. In being able to incapacitate somebody long enough to escape. There'd been no mention of punching or kicking somebody to death. This, though. This was intimate. Tasting somebody's fear while ending them.

The day was something both similar and different to the previous week of fighting. It started with how to hold the knife, which for the training was a wooden replica tipped and edged with rubber. The recommended way to hold it being between thumb and forefinger, just below the guard, with the handle sitting in the palm of the hand and the fingers wrapped around it. It was, they were told, a foil grip as used in fencing, and that the knife was designed to be held that way to be at its most effective. At the same time, they were encouraged, as with most other things on the course, not to be rigid. If the situation demanded that they hold it ice pick style and plunge it, they should. Once holding and handling was consistent, he revealed a chalk board diagram of the human body, front and back, similar to that he'd used when teaching them where to strike with their bodies, but instead with knife puncture and cut points. Arteries, soft spots in the skull, the guts, the heart, and the many tendons and ligaments. Anywhere that could debilitate and then kill an opponent. It was very macabre, as was the casual style in which he talked about it, while all the time he reminded them that if they missed with a stab or a cut, the person would likely be left standing, with the added intensity of pain and fear, which would make them all the more dangerous. Every aspect of killing with a knife was covered, from choosing where and how, to the twisting of the blade in the opponent to maximise damage while releasing the body's pressure that would keep the blade clamped in the opponent otherwise. It was clinical, methodical, and ice cold killing. Something that vibrated uncomfortably in Emily, not that it showed. She was as clinical and cold as the instructor throughout. She listened, she learned, and having spent more than enough time up to her elbows in blood and guts, sometimes in immediate wound care, others assisting in surgery, she was able to see in her mind exactly what was happening inside the body when she struck. She'd seen punctures and cuts from shrapnel, razor sharp shards of bomb and shell fragments, and how they'd torn muscle and organs, making each movement very real. The training progressed from silently striking sentries and other unwitting targets, to fighting with the knife and other weapons while facing a hostile opponent, and the days of rolls, and balance, and blocks suddenly kicked in as they took each other on with their training weapons. It was something that levelled the playing field somewhat, though the fighting had gone some way to doing that, letting the slighter and smaller women cope perfectly well with bigger men who'd been trained the same way. Though with the blade, all four of the women had been much more deadly. It wasn't about strength, it was about speed and precision, and they nailed it fight after fight, holding their knives the way they were taught, and thrusting upwards at ribs, necks, spines, and guts. If there was any remaining misogyny among the group, it was dispelled instantly when each of them took to the floor time and again, and simulated their kills perfectly.

Chapter 8

Culled

The rain had been so hard through much of the night that it had been difficult to sleep, even with the fatigue of days on end of running, marching, and fighting, and when everyone was gathered in the hall after breakfast instead of going on their morning run, there was a glimmer of hope that after four weeks, their training was finally over, and they'd be spared an early morning drenching.

"Alright, everyone, listen up," the Sergeant Major said in his familiar way after falling them into their depleted squad. Thirty had arrived on the truck, just less than twenty remained. Over a third culled for various reasons, from not being able to keep their mouths shut, to not being able to master Morse code, or being injured or not fit enough to compete physically. He brought them to attention, and the Captain Emily had talked with a few times joined them, along with the fighting instructor and a few other members of the teaching staff. It was a tense moment, but even Emily hoped that this was it, the end of training. It was the first time they'd been paraded inside, and the first time that all of the training team had joined them.

"Good morning," the Captain started, pulling their attention to him. "Today, you'll complete a series of objectives. Failure in any one of them will result in an immediate overall failure of the course, and subsequent return to your unit." He paused to let his words take effect. "A twenty five mile individual route march will commence in thirty minutes. You'll have seven hours to complete the march, and any tasks allocated while out. You'll carry your own food, and you'll be self sufficient for the duration. You are not to work with anyone else in the completion of this objective. Maps and compasses will be issued over the next half hour, along with your rations. Be back in this room ten minutes from now with your kit, and be ready to be called forward. Good luck!"

The house erupted into activity when the squad was dismissed, with everyone hurrying to get fully kitted with webbing, packs, and rifles, and grabbing some hot tea from the Mess while they could, before heading back to the hall. Emily was almost breathless when they finally fell into their squad, and her heart was racing a little with the activity and anticipation. One at a time they were called forward, and it was Emily's turn about half way through the squad. She followed a Lieutenant out of the hall, and into one of the lecture rooms loaded with tables stacked with kit. First, she was issued her map and compass, and shown a neatly written route card, giving her grid references and landmarks for her route. She briefly studied it and made notes, before moving along to the next table to be issued with rations. Then, finally, she was given a couple of minutes to pack and check her kit, and study her map. She pulled on the issue knitted cap comforter, expecting it to be cold outside, and made sure it was pulled down over the tops of her ears before putting on her helmet. She jumped up and down a couple of times to make sure her kit was secured properly, and then was called to leave the room.

It was miserable outside. Dark, and cold, with torrential rain. She straightened her rain cape a little, and pulled up the collar the best she could, then after checking her compass, she headed out into the misery. It took a good thirty minutes to get used to the weather, and the idea that she was going to be miserable and uncomfortable for much of the day. The rain cape was keeping the heaviest of the rain off, but it was still finding its way in, and still soaking her sleeves and trousers. She knew that as well as being uncomfortable, she'd be cold and wet before the day was out, too, so she got her head down and marched, counting paces for distance, and following the familiar road for a while, until she reached the track she knew was going to take her north and off-road into the hills. She could hardly see a thing when she turned in the pre dawn murk. The cloud was low, and the rain heavy, and the track was a mixture of sticky mud that sucked at her boots, and hard stones that made her wobble and risk turning her ankle. It slowed her down significantly, but despite the time pressure of the objective, she reasoned that it was better to be slower and risk failing, than move too fast and be assured of it. The going was hard, and despite the conditioning that had come from weeks of training, her lungs were pumping like bellows when she went up slopes, and her heart pounded while her thighs burned, and downhill her legs shook and back ached as she tried to stay upright, despite the weather's best efforts to make the difficult terrain deadly, and every now and then having her wish she was on the sunshine mountain. She made turns as planned, counting paces to judged distance, adapting for the terrain, and moving left and right, but always onwards for hour after hour, until finally she saw the checkpoint she'd been heading for. A small stone cottage came out of the gloom that was supposed to be the late morning daylight, after four hours of staggering, marching, and slipping her way up and down hills a long way past rolling. The black smoke winding its way into the grey sky had helped with her navigation, and when she came close, she saw another figure leaving, and heading off into the unrelenting rain. She marched forward, and after hammering on the door, positive she was where she needed to be, it was opened, and she was invited in by an officer. The fire was roaring, and the cottage warm, with hot tea on the table, and cream, sugar, and hard biscuits with what looked like raisins in them.

"Number 13 reporting, Sir." She stood as smartly as she could, and as close to attention as her fatigue and kit would allow. He simply pointed to the wireless in the corner and raised an eyebrow. She nodded and headed over, sitting at the desk and laying her rifle across her lap as she read the card on the table showing the message that was to be sent. She set the identifier, a code word that let whoever was listening know it was her, and then coded the message as she'd been instructed in training before transmitting. She waited a moment for a response, but there was nothing. She tried again, then rechecked the details, and tried once more. She frowned, then thought for a moment. Logic dictated that if the power was on, but she couldn't transmit, the easiest answer was a problem with the crystals that dictated the frequency, and she was right. They were present, but weren't seated properly, and a piece of something had been wound around the connector. She removed the crystals, her cold fingers and thumbs almost numb, and cleared the debris, before replacing them and transmitting again. This time, she got an acknowledgement a few moments later, and an instruction to make haste.

"You may make one drink before you leave, and have one biscuit. The water's hot." the officer said as he gestured to the table. She nodded as she hurried over, slinging her rifle over her shoulder. She poured tea from the teapot, filling the cup half way, then topping it with cream, and spooning as much sugar in as she dared, while remaining the right side of respectable. He smirked a little as he watched her stir it, then down the lot. She felt her insides thaw as the warm, thick, sweet mixture worked its way down to her stomach. She then pulled out her map and route card and checked everything, while eating a biscuit, munching it down as she followed the route with her finger. By the time the biscuit was gone, she was packed and ready to go, and turned to look at the officer. "Good luck." He gave her a simple nod, and she headed out into the rain with a renewed sense of vigour. The warmth had got to her fingertips, though her toes were beyond feeling, but most importantly, the warmth of the tea, along with the sugar and cream, had given her a near instant burst of mental clarity and energy, and she hoped that the cream would help slow the digestion as she pulled one biscuit after another from her rations and munched them while heading down the track that led away from the cottage. It was relatively smooth, compared to the cross country route she'd taken to get there, and she knew from her map that it wouldn't be too long until it merged with a road. That was the stage she needed her energy for, and the tea, biscuits, and long sips from her water bottle were all in preparation for that.

The track was hard going, especially with the torrents of rainwater running down it like a river, but Emily was able to keep a steady pace according to her plan. Then, when she turned onto the road, she knew that the hardest part was behind her, she just had to follow it to the turn off to the house. Rain or not, uphill or down, she'd have relatively sure footing, and she'd be able to pick up her pace and make up the time in the off road climbs, which she did using the intelligence officer's cadence. Ten running, twenty marching, uphill and down, not stopping, or easing off, and marching through the rain soaking down her back and chilling her to the core. The only positive to the conditions was that her feet were so numb, she'd stopped feeling the blisters and sores before she'd even got to the cottage. She just had to be careful with her foot placement to avoid a fall, because she wouldn't be able to feel any holes or uneven surface with her feet, and the first she'd know was when she was on the ground. After an hour on the road, she slowed and pulled a tin from her large pack, along with the tin opener from her pocket, and opened it as she marched. It was hard going with cold fingers, but after a while she was looking at the block of corned beef from her rations. She put the tin opener away, and then, in a move that would horrify her mother. Or even herself back in the previous summer and early autumn when she was a nurse, she bit into the meat and started chewing as she went. Eating it direct from the tin, until she'd gnawed it down, then she took her fork from her pocket and dug into what was left, finishing the lot before packing the tin away again and licking the fork clean. With a boiled sweet and some chocolate for dessert, she was off. The pace and the food gave her a new warmth, in her core at least, and a mouthful of water washed it all down. For a moment, she found herself smiling as she marched down the road, suddenly feeling light and happy with the calories, and she laughed at the ridiculousness of herself. She'd been promoted to Senior Sister the previous summer, and was a very competent nurse who the hospital wanted to train as a doctor, and her hospital was small enough, with nice enough senior staff, that she couldn't have asked for a better place to work. With Dunkirk long behind them, the glut of bad wounds from the frontline had eased a little, too, though there were still enough badly wounded pilots to keep her busy. A profession and promising career, and she turned her back on them to join an organisation she'd never heard of, then spent a month running around Scotland and learning how to kill people, leading to a moment of her skipping down a road and singing to herself about sunshine mountains, having eaten a full block of corned beef direct from the tin like an animal.

It came as a surprise to Emily that her energy hadn't crashed as she ran down the gravel towards the house. The Sergeant Major was waiting and gave her a nod as she passed through the gates and he took her name, showing her his watch to confirm that she'd made it almost an entire hour ahead of schedule. She was fighting to stop herself from smiling. It had been hard, and everything hurt, but her energy hadn't crashed once. Her muscles and mind had kept going throughout, with not even the hint of a blip. She'd got her nutrition and hydration just right, and timed her effort perfectly. She stepped into the house, and after handing in her map and compass, she was instructed to head back out to the shooting ranges down the slope, in the back of the house's extensive gardens. There wasn't time to rest, or compose herself. The most she could do was pop a boiled sweet in her mouth before being stood on the firing point and told to fire five rounds standing with her rifle, followed by five kneeling, five from the waist, and then five prone. The instruction required a reload, which was hard going with numb fingers, and the cold made propping up the rifle to aim hard on her muscles, but she completed the instruction before moving along to the next table where she was to fire the Sten gun, before finishing off with a pistol in the killing house, all before marching back to the mansion and being sent to the hall where the fighting instructor told her to put her webbing and rifle in the corner before stepping up to face him in the centre. There was nobody else in there, just the two of them. Him in his smart service uniform, her looking like a little girl dressed up in her father's army uniform. Soaked to the skin, and pale from the cold. He didn't say anything else, just positioned himself defensively and waved her on to attack him. She nodded, and got her stance right and hands up, palms open, and ready to go. She took a step and pushed her left hand forward towards his, pulling it away as he stepped in to grab her, then dropping to the ground and sweeping his legs away with her right shin, sending him crashing to the ground. She pounced as soon as he was down, landing her knee on the centre of his chest while pulling off her helmet and raising it above her, ready to swing it down with her right hand, while with her left she pushed her thumb up under his nose, making him groan in discomfort. He reached out and tapped the floor with his left hand, signalling he was done, and after a moment she released him and stood to attention while replacing her helmet. Something had happened to her, she'd both thought and hadn't at the same time. She knew she was going to tempt him into a counter, and then she'd kick his legs away, but when she did it, it was all automatic, and he'd come down quicker and harder than she was expecting. What she was truly worried about, though, was how she'd got her helmet off, ready to use as a weapon. That wasn't in the plan at all, she hadn't even considered it. It had just happened instinctively, and she wasn't keen on it at all.

She was sent from the hall, still thinking on how she'd handled the fight, but she didn't have time to dwell. Still soaked, and realising how cold and tired she was, she was taken from room to room and asked questions about all of the topics they'd studied. Navigation, communications, weapons, explosives; everything and anything from the course. The rooms blurred into each other, with her not spending much time in each, just long enough for her heart rate to settle while

109

she fought through anywhere between five and ten questions, before being moved to the next. She'd been full of herself when she finished her march, but that seemed so long ago. The physical exhaustion followed by the mental challenges was disorienting, and as she went from room to room, she started to notice how hungry she was, but there wasn't the opportunity to get to her rations, and the chocolate and sweets she'd had in her pocket were long gone. Finally, she was deposited at the front door, where the Captain was waiting for her.

"Your name?" he asked.

"13, Sir," she replied exhaustedly.

"Cigarette?" He offered his silver cigarette case, and she gave her head a slight shake. "Very well. I believe that you're aware of the sunshine mountain?" She nodded in reply, while inside her stomach was sinking hard. "The route you've done previously. Up, along the ridge, and then back here. You have until lights out. Good luck." He stared at her, his face unchanging. She nodded, despite feeling inside that she could cry, then put on her helmet and cape, tightened her equipment, then headed out of the door he was holding open for her, rifle in her hands. She took a deep breath then, putting her head down, she started marching. Along the gravel drive, past the Sergeant Major, and along the track in the direction of the road. Every step hurt, inside and out. She thought she'd done it. She thought she'd finished. She'd already done twenty five miles cross country through an unrelenting rain storm. She'd fired her weapons, fought, answered questions, even fixed a wireless. She'd done everything asked of her, but it wasn't enough. The training still hadn't ended. Her mind was getting as dark as the sky, and her body was aching and screaming at her. The sitting, the warmth, it had tricked her muscles into thinking they could rest, and now it was all starting again. Instead of numb feet, it was like knives being stuck in them with every pace, and her legs felt like somebody was hitting them repeatedly with a wooden board, stinging the surface, and painfully vibrating the muscles all the way to the bones, which felt like they'd were made of ice. Her back was painfully tight, as were her shoulders, and try as she did, she couldn't get into any sort of steady rhythm. Even the road didn't give any respite.

The oatmeal block from her rations that she tried to nibble on was as miserable as her mood, not to mention dry and tacky, coating the inside of her mouth and making it difficult to swallow. She sipped water every now and then, taking care to ration what little she had left for the coming hours. She settled, nibbling, and counting paces as she marched through the murk. A few miles in and her mood had settled a little. The oatmeal block had done its job, the compressed tablet of oats, sugar, and powdered milk had finally got into her system, and she was able to think of the positives. Specifically, that she'd saved almost an hour on the first march, which gave her a little bit longer on the second, something her body was telling her she needed. The time passed slowly, with the only saving grace being that the rain was easing, and the sky was clearing. A saving grace that brought a bitter and icy downside, as the temperature plummeted, and frost started to form on the soaked ground. Sending more painful knives into her fingers and toes. Her mind wandered for a while, only brought back to full consciousness when she turned off the road to head for the bottom of the climb, where they'd been dropped by the truck on the first time. In the distance were palls of white and grey smoke rising into the evening sky. She thought she was hallucinating at first. There'd been nothing there on the previous occasions. No house, no outbuildings, nothing. Just a clearing where the truck had parked. It kept her imagination occupied, though she started to worry about her psychological wellbeing. It had been a long day, and now she was seeing things, and if that wasn't enough, as she came closer, there was something in the air. A smell, something she knew, but couldn't place until she turned the bend and saw a couple of large tents pitched in the clearing at the foot of the trail up the hill. She frowned as she approached, catching a glimpse of a shadow in the darkness that was lit with the glow of a cigarette. The shadow moved and headed towards her as she stepped into the clearing, it was the Royal Marine Major who'd greeted them on the first night. His face picked out by the glow of his cigarette as he inhaled. He had been around for the whole course, but always in the distance, watching, but not really getting involved in anything.

"Number?" he asked almost casually, yet quite curtly.

"13, Sir," she replied.

"Well done, 13." He scribbled in a small pocket book. "Tent on the left." She looked at him for a moment, then nodded and shuffled on her way, still struggling to identify the mysterious smell hanging in the air, that was accompanied by a crackling sound and light yet muffled conversation from the tent on the right. She gave her head a shake, then opened the flap and stepped into the deep amber glow emitting from a hurricane lamp hanging from the roof of the tent. She looked around and blinked while her eyes made sense of what she was seeing. Huddled around the tent, sitting on folding wooden chairs, steam rising from the collective heat of their bodies, and the potbellied stove crackling and sparking, its black chimney pipe poking up through the roof, were the faces of others from the course. Their equipment was behind their chairs, their rifles slung on the back. Everyone looked tired, their eyes sunken, yet wide. 18 gave her a smile, and nodded at the chair next to her, and Emily nodded and shuffled over, while others went back to their muttered conversations. She hung her rifle on the back of the chair, and then her helmet, then pulled off her cape and webbing, dumping them behind it before slumping down with a sigh.

"What's going on?" she asked after composing herself while looking around again. Getting a few nods from others in the tent. Before 18 could answer, one of the Corporals stepped into the tent, looked around, then headed to Emily and handed her a tin mug filled with cocoa, and left again without a word. She looked around, and noticed empty cups on the floor, and others still being held. The warmth flowed through the cup, painfully at first, until her fingers started to feel properly, then she raised it to her face and felt the steam on her nose for a while before taking a sip. "What's going on?" she asked again, then checked herself and frowned before turning and looking at 18. "Did I already ask that?"

"Yes," 18 smiled. "And you can ask again, if you like. I still won't have an answer for you. I haven't been here long myself, and neither has anyone else. We come in, collapse, and get given cocoa." Emily nodded as she listened. She didn't have much to say. She didn't have the energy. She worked out that she'd marched between twenty five and thirty miles, soaked through and cold after the first five, and had hardly any physical or psychological rest the entire time. Food had been minimal, as had fluids, and her brain was throbbing from it.

"How are you doing?"

"Everything hurts. Parts of me hurt that I didn't even know existed, even thinking hurts, and despite that I'm furious because I didn't get up that bloody hill one last time!" She rolled her eyes and let out a smile, and Emily let out the faintest laugh, mostly because 18 had said what she was thinking. She welcomed the warmth, and the cocoa, and despite being more exhausted than she'd ever been, she regretted not getting up the sunshine mountain and finishing. She thought back to the briefing at the house, searching for cut offs for getting to the bottom of the hill, but her mind was muddled. She knew she'd been moving slow, much slower than she had earlier in the day, but she thought that as long as she was back by ten, she was safe. That was the only cut off she could remember, but despite the frustration, she was too tired to care. She couldn't do anything about it. It just upset her that she'd done four hard weeks of something that now wouldn't matter that much. Being able to stab somebody with a fighting knife wasn't the skill most staff car drivers needed. Though she thought further back, and to what she'd do next. Would she go back and be a nurse if her plans to join up and do her bit ended with her being a driver, or an administrator? Or would she stick it out, and do her small part for the war effort. Whichever it was, the ability to kill somebody with a knife wouldn't be that helpful.

They muttered quietly, not really having the energy to talk. They mentioned how much their feet hurt, and their backs, but that was about it. The tent flap opened a few more times, and others came in to have the same experience Emily did. Looking around in shock and surprise, then taking a seat before receiving a cup of cocoa, and asking the exact same question. The time dragged, and the heat was enough to make Emily's eyes heavy. It was the same around the tent, though everyone helped each other, giving a nudge here and there, and finding innocent and innocuous things to talk about, whatever it took to stay awake. 18 talked about the Scottish weather, in some detail, and asked Emily for her opinion. They both laughed far harder than either intended when Emily replied, 'It's been a terrible surprise, not having been to Scotland before.' She had a soft Scottish accent, it was undeniable, yet the denial made them laugh all the harder. They were only stopped by 4's arrival. She half staggered, then slumped into a chair, and Emily and 18 quickly went about helping her out of her kit. She was done in, totally exhausted, and they had to hold her hands to the cocoa mug when it arrived, and help her drink it. The fact that she'd walked into the tent was a miracle, or so it seemed. She was lucky to have been upright. She drank the cocoa, then bent over, and had to lean against 18 for a while. She was so exhausted she couldn't speak, and her eyes were rolling every now and then. Emily dug through her kit and found a boiled sweet she'd lost and put it in 4's mouth, then gave her the last sips from her water bottle. 4 was near hypothermic, if not already. She needed sugar and warmth, and they sat either side of her, rubbing her arms and legs to stimulate the blood flow while they used their body heat to warm her.

"Is she alright?" the Major asked as he entered the tent and looked 4.

"She will be," Emily replied. "She's just getting used to the warmth again." She forced a smile, that was mirrored by 18. Despite it being over for them all, she couldn't let go of it being a test, of everything being a test, and she didn't want to let 4 down by being honest. She hoped that the warmth they had would be enough, along with the sugar left from their rations.

"Good..." He looked around the tent, then behind as the Sergeant Major joined him. "Ladies and gentlemen, I'm here to tell you that it's over. You'll be leaving us on tomorrow morning's transport, so when you get back to the house, you'll need to make sure you're packed and ready to go first thing." His eyes were stern as he looked around the slumping shoulders and bowed heads. Emily suddenly felt unexpectedly devastated, like her heart had been ripped out. She couldn't explain it, she couldn't even rationalise is, she just felt an emptiness where all the pain had been. Instead of slumping, though, she pulled her shoulders back and raised her head defiantly. "The final lesson, which I'm sure you all learned in your own way, was the importance of managing unexpected adversity as well as we manage that we expect. Today, you knew you'd be tested, and you knew it would be hard, but once you'd completed what you thought were all of your tests, not one of you expected to be sent out to climb the Sergeant Major's sunshine mountain again, or that you'd have to do it in the cold, and at night, after an already draining day." Emily searched the emptiness for what she'd done, or said, when told she had to go out again and march more. "Right, leave your kit with your chairs, and follow me outside." He looked around again, then left.

"You heard the Major," the Sergeant Major barked. "Get up and hop to it! You're not finished yet, and if you don't want a pre dawn run up the sunshine mountain, you'd better get moving!" The tired and aching bodies sprung up from their chairs, Emily and 18 included, dragging a slightly more coherent 4 with them as she tipped her mug upside down and lapped at the last drips of hot chocolate. They joined the rush through the tent flap, and formed in a squad outside.

"This way," the Major said, and pointed at the second tent. He opened the flap, and the air filled with the most incredible smell that had Emily drooling, and 4 dragging them over to the tent without waiting for further instruction. They stepped inside, and eyes and mouths fell open. At the end of the tent were the chefs, with a roast venison hanging from a rack. Tables were loaded with bread and charred jacket potatoes. Everyone stood looking amazed. There was even a beer keg on a table, and a stack of glasses. "The deer was killed fresh today, and the chefs have been roasting it all afternoon, not to mention baking bread and potatoes, and I don't want to see a single scrap of food left on your plates." They all looked at him wide eyed. "Congratulations, ladies and gentlemen, you made it. As of now, the tests are over. However, I must ask that you maintain your numbers and personal security. Enjoy your meal, you've earned it!"

Chapter 9

Goodbye

The next day had started early, as promised, and once breakfast was out of the way, they were wished all the best by the training team in a brief, almost impersonal goodbye. The words were said, the training team left, and the Sergeant Major dismissed them to the waiting truck, which they boarded dressed in their service uniforms, bags packed, and greatcoats pulled up around their ears for the cold and bumpy journey south. Nobody talked, the same way nobody had talked on the way there at the start of January, each left with their thoughts as they sat in the dark, being jostled around, and rocking side to side as the truck made its way across the hills. Emily's mind went back to the previous night, as her body still ached and tensed with the pains of the assessment day. It had been a shock to the system thinking she'd failed, and an even bigger one to find that she hadn't. It took a while to accept it, and it was only when she'd finally fell into bed several hours later that she was able to process what she'd achieved. Though, despite having got through the journey, and the tests, that was the only part she could say with any certainty that she had achieved. She still didn't have a clue what she'd signed up for, none of them did. It wasn't discussed on the last night, not sitting in a tent with thin walls while the training team were around. Instead, they'd eaten the best meal any of them had tasted since the war and rationing has started. There was more than enough venison for seconds, and thirds for some, carved into thick slices that had been roasted with a sweet redcurrant whisky glaze. The bread was fresh baked, and meltingly soft, especially good for army bread, and the potatoes were cooked perfectly. It took several glasses of beer to wash it all down, though with the physical demands and extremes of the course, Emily had quickly felt quite tired when her belly was full of hot meat and beer. It had been a celebration, and everybody was happy, despite the whispered conversation about 3. Nobody had seen her after she'd set off, and her kit was gone when they got back that night. She'd fallen short, obviously, and despite the happiness at having made it, the three remaining women felt for her getting as far as the last day. They'd got through it all together, supporting each other from the first moment, and it was sad that they'd lost one. 3 had

116

been there for them all without fail. She was pleasant, and competent at everything they'd done, and had a way of reframing the difficult times and making them feel better when things got tough. She was the glue that held them together, and then she wasn't.

It had been a long and hard month in the mountains, without a single day of rest. Weekends quickly lost meaning, and time seemed to stand still, while simultaneously racing forward. There wasn't even a light or easier, less intense day. Every morning started at five, breakfast at six, and running at seven. Lectures at nine, lunch at twelve thirty, marching at one, lectures at two, dinner at six, lounge at seven, lights out at ten, with the exception of the nights they'd spent out in the hills learning survival and night tactics. All done under a watchful eye, with cleaning and scrubbing uniforms, rooms, and everything else in between. Emily was just thankful for the long hours of her nurse training, and the long shifts on the wards. Sitting through the night writing notes by lamplight and watching over patients surrounded by darkness had prepared her for fighting the tiredness of recent days, just about. She hadn't remembered ever feeling so tired, or so tested. Whether it was climbing ladders up sheer rock faces, dragging herself and her kit across lochs filled with ice water, or just going up and down the sunshine mountain, there had been so many opportunities to fail, and that was just the physical side. Then, the last night came, just like that. They needed to clean their uniforms, and scrub their rooms, leaving them as they'd found them. The only real highlight, other than not having to run five miles in the dark after a breakfast of porridge and jam, was knowing it was over, and she'd passed. It made her feel special, and she could see that everyone felt the same. Like they'd made it through something big. Though nobody knew what, apart from being run and bossed around the Highlands.

The truck was switched to a much more comfortable bus after a while, which eventually exchanged for a train, where the group splintered into the pairs and subgroups that they'd got on with during their training, sitting in different carriages, and chatting with each other all of a sudden. It was as though they were free as soon as they were off the bus. When they'd got on it a month earlier, they'd been told to maintain their silence, and they'd imposed the same on themselves all the way back to the train station. Emily, 13, and 4 sat together on the train, that was scattered with a few civilians, and talked about their hopes for spring and summer, and anything else that wasn't the cold and wet misery of the Highlands. A businessman rolled his eyes at them more than a few times, and at one point even suggested they were lucky to have warm clothes and offices to work in, and weren't out in all weather like the many who had to work in the Highlands. He lectured them for a while on his friends and family, farmers and other folk who worked the hills raising cattle and sheep, and supplying good meat, wool, and leather for the war effort, and how a bit of hard work out in the weather would show them the real Highlands. They all smiled politely as they listened, and not one of them mentioned having to march the best part of thirty miles through the rain carrying a rifle and kit, or having to squat in a rain soaked and wind blasted ditch to go to the toilet, as they all had at one point or another, a shared experience that united them in a strange way, something that the men on the course didn't experience in quite the same manner. To the businessman, the women were probably clerks or similar. Not the type of people who'd learned how to break an assailant's neck in a fight.

It was late in the day when they arrived in Glasgow, and they only just managed to jump onto the train south seconds before it left the station. On leaving the Highlands, the course had been instructed to stay together, and make their way to Manchester, where they arrived in the early hours of the morning thanks to an air raid that had them sitting outside the city and watching with horror as the sky glowed, and flames leapt into the air while the ice white beams of searchlights cut through the glowing sky, and anti aircraft artillery scattered the darkness with shells that from a distance looked like exploding stars, an experience that left Emily revisiting the horror of the bombing in London. It was all very different from Scotland in the starkest of ways, and each stop on their journey south had been a little more populated, villages, small towns, and then the industrial smog of Glasgow, before the burning fires of what they were assured was Manchester, the place they were heading for, and suddenly nobody wanted to get to.

The train finally arrived in the station long after midnight, where they were met by a First Aid Nursing Yeomanry Captain, who was stood smartly at ease on the platform in her sharply tailored and pressed uniform, with even her greatcoat looking a little more finely cut than most. She waited patiently and quietly until approached, and then quickly had the students lined up and heading through the station behind her like a gaggle of lost children, out to a bus waiting on the street. She stood by the door, and checked names off her list one at a time before letting the students on the single deck bus, which had another First Aid Nursing Yeomanry officer behind the steering wheel, a young looking Ensign with a big smile. The Captain looked Emily up and down after ticking her name off the list, and gave her the faintest smile and nod, recognising the uniform and insignia, before gesturing for her to get on board and join the others. Once everyone was accounted for and seated, the Captain took her place at the front of the bus, and it slowly nudged into life, moving through the dark streets lit by the flickering orange of fires. The air had tasted of smoke and chemicals when they'd stepped off the train, it was bitter and caught the throat, and was little better on the bus, especially when it was taken quite close to a large fire for a time, and the passengers got to look out at the devastation of narrow terraced houses reduced to piles of bricks, beams, and scattered possessions. Emily frowned and tried not to shudder. She'd put London out of her mind the best she could, and the intensity of Scotland had helped, though every now and then, when she was tired, she still saw Mrs Jennings looking at her with bemusement and fear before melting away into nothing but smoke and ashes. The city was filthy, and burning, and flattened, and Emily felt uncomfortable at seeing it up close. She hadn't appreciated how the fire would affect her when watching it from outside of the city, instead just thinking how mesmerising it was, but being among the destruction again just made her want to get off the bus and run, and she was relieved when the damage was left behind, and the bus wound its way through the city and out the other side, heading south and leaving the dull orange glow in the distance.

Finally, after a long and tiring drive, the bus arrived in a driveway, and the students were ushered off and into what seemed to be yet another grand looking manor house which gave Emily an uneasy twinge. The last time she'd arrived in such a place, she was hours away from morning runs, mountain climbs, weapons training, and a fight club, all of which had exhausted her. Her mind processed the thoughts as they stood in the grand entrance hall, looking around at the opulent surroundings. The previous night she was close to broken at having to go climb the sunshine mountain in the dark while already drained, then again when she thought she'd failed. A sleep, and a day and night of travelling, and there was a nagging worry that it was all about to start once again. She didn't have long to think on it, though. The Captain announced that breakfast would be at seven, then started handing out room keys and directions, and the party started to disperse, until there were just the three women left. They were told they'd be sharing, something that didn't bother them in the slightest, and then the Ensign showed them up to the top of the house and a room with four large, comfortable beds that they fell into as soon as they could get cleaned up in the ensuite bathroom, dropping into a deep and instant sleep.

The next morning was filled with anticipation. The three got up early, cleaned up, and made sure their room was immaculate and ready for inspection, before dressing in their battledress and heading down to the hall, ready for breakfast and a five mile run. The apparent new normal of their life. Emily felt something inside sigh as she walked down the wide staircase, listening to it creak under the thud of their boots. She hadn't recovered from the final day in Scotland; the long miles had taken it out of her. Despite the near euphoria of passing whatever Scotland was, she wasn't convinced she wanted to run five miles every morning for the rest of the war, and she was quite sure it wasn't something everyone in uniform did.

"Good morning," the smiling Ensign who drove the bus the previous evening greeted them politely. They smiled and returned the greeting, Emily half frowning at the unexpected lack of a stern Sergeant Major telling them to 'listen in', and making sure they'd eaten, because they'd be upping the pace on the morning's run. Something he'd said almost routinely since day one, and rarely was he lying. "Breakfast is through in the dining room, I'll show you." She marched ahead, shoulders pulled back, and her back as straight as a rod, as she took them to the large dining room, where others from their group were seated at four person tables scattered around, again quite different to Scotland. They sat, and an older woman appeared wearing a white shirt, and black tie and skirt, bringing them a pot of tea.

"I'll have breakfast out to you shortly. Toast?" She looked at each of them, who in turn sat and stared at her for a moment, eyebrows raised questioningly. Toast? Emily thought in shock as they were suddenly receiving waitress service. "I'll bring some jam for you to have with it, it's strawberry. Made local last year. We don't have any marmalade, I'm afraid." she answered for them, then wandered off, leaving them looking at each other in silence. They didn't say anything, other than 18 offering to be mother and pour the tea, which they all sipped at while looking around subtly. It was then that Emily recognised a familiar smell, and looked over her shoulders at the others in the room, they had tea and toast, but that wasn't what she was smelling. She twitched her nose a few times to make sure, frowning as she sought to find the source, until the woman arrived again carrying a tray of toast racks, and small pots of jam and butter. It was enough to distract her, and the three of them quickly went about devouring the thick, chewy warm toasted bread that tasted like it had been baked fresh that morning, spread with butter and jam that filled Emily's senses. It tasted good, and started to address the hunger she'd felt after such a long journey. She froze still as she reached for a second slice, and watched hungrily and longingly as the woman came back in pushing a trolley loaded with plates of bacon and eggs. The smell took over the entire room as everyone gazed, eyes wide open. The woman put plates in front of each of the women, leaving them staring in disbelief to go and deliver plates to other tables.

"Bacon…" Emily said as she looked at it. The smell had been real. She looked at the others, their eyes meeting, and smiles stretching onto their faces. She picked up her knife and fork, and sliced a piece off the bacon before raising it up in front of her eyes and looking at it for a moment, then popping it in her mouth. She smiled as her senses exploded at the taste of the salt and fat, and instantly she was taken back to her hospital, and Harriet. The last time she'd had bacon was when Harriet forced her to share her breakfast, and she felt herself smiling with warm memories as she chewed slowly, savouring the taste.

"I don't care if they make us run, and I vomit it all back up," 18 added as she made a start on her own. Sighing dramatically and sinking a little bit in her chair as she tasted the bacon. Emily and 4 gave her a nod, and they got on with their food almost silently. Emily chewed as slowly as she could, savouring the taste for as long as possible, while doing her best to break down the meat into small enough pieces that her stomach would be able to process it, while reducing the risk of it coming back up when the inevitable run came. It was difficult, however, and she had to fight to hold herself back, but ultimately ended up doing the same as the others, and pouring more tea to help her wash the bacon, eggs, and toast with salty butter and jam down into her increasingly full stomach. If she was going to suffer, she may as well get some pleasure first. At least that was the logic she applied to the situation after shrugging off her reservation.

Breakfast drifted on at an alarmingly slow rate, it was both leisurely and relaxing, and a little nerve inducing. Emily and the others at her table talked about how the lack of runs or anything else filled them with a sense of doom, like what was coming would be big. Others around the room said the same, quietly, while glancing around nervously, and everyone was collectively relieved and simultaneously terrified when the First Aid Nursing Yeomanry Captain appeared and asked them if they'd join her outside. She asked so politely, yet with an edge of firmness, that it was somehow more chilling than the Sergeant Major's bark back in Scotland, and the entire room jumped into action with memories of week after week of constant tests, of every movement, response, and reaction being judged, and nobody wanted to risk being failed. Not when they'd made it as far as they had. The Captain just smiled, part knowingly, part menacingly, depending on the perspective of the person looking at her as they hurried past and made their way outside to stand in their squad in the greyness of the cold February morning near Manchester. Outside, she brought them to attention, and started them marching, with the Ensign following along at the rear, and Emily started composing herself and preparing for what was coming, while only slightly regretting the breakfast she'd had. Then it occurred to her that while all of the students were in battledress and boots, the Captain and Ensign were in service dress and greatcoats. Skirts, tunics, shoes, not at all what would be appropriate for running, and while she knew that the First Aid Nursing Yeomanry were trained to be fit, having experienced the training in London, they'd never ran in service dress. It was something that gave her hope, though the weeks in Scotland had taught her to be wary of that, especially that last day, so she marched and waited, as they were led around the seemingly huge mansion house and into an even bigger garden in the rear that had eyes opening wide. There was a large and odd looking trapezium in the centre, built of poles and platforms, and ropes and pulleys, and around the perimeter were different pieces of apparatus from benches to beams to platforms, all at different heights. Standing in the centre by the trapezium was an RAF Flight Sergeant in battledress, wearing a badge showing what looked to Emily like a lightbulb surrounded by wings and a laurel wreath. The squad was halted and turned to face him, and then the Captain and Ensign simply marched away, leaving them on the cold, grey lawn and surrounded by apparatus of all types.

"Stand at ease," the Flight Sergeant said in a composed and almost jovial manner. "I'm Flight Sergeant Cross, the Senior Parachute Instructor. It's my job to teach you, in record time, how to jump out of a perfectly serviceable aircraft from five hundred feet or less, and land without making a nuisance of yourself to those around you." Emily's heart and mind raced in unison, and she felt her eyes widening with a mixture of fear and excitement. "You'll do as I say, when I say, and you won't be told twice. Any injuries will result in an automatic failure. Any refusal to comply with my instructions will result in an automatic failure. However, I'm good at this. They wouldn't let me loose on you if not. So, listen up, follow instructions, and you may get through the coming days without cracking your heads open, or breaking your legs." The corner of his mouth turned up slightly in what Emily could only assume to be a malevolent smile. "As luck would have it, Mister Newton helped us with the basics some time ago, and as such you're pretty much guaranteed of travelling in only one direction from the moment you step off something higher than yourselves courtesy of gravity. The art to it is what you do when you come into contact with the ground at approximately ten to twenty miles per hour, depending on the size of you, and how much kit you're carrying. The equivalent of a twenty foot drop, fully loaded. Get it right, and you'll be up and running minutes after you've left the confines of that shaking, noisy, stinking aeroplane and stepped into the fresh air. Get it wrong, and twisted, sprained, and dislocated ankles and knees are common. Get it worse, broken legs are waiting

123

for you. Really cock it up, and you'll break your back or your neck. Or, if it all goes wrong entirely, your parachute won't open in the first place, and instead of the equivalent of a twenty foot drop at ten to twenty miles per hour, it's a five hundred foot drop at well over one hundred miles per hour. Sprains and breaks would be the least of your problems at that time, as you can imagine." Emily's mind raced again, though this time it was as she calculated the damage such a fall could cause the human body. She'd seen falls before, and the damage they did to internal organs, not just bones.

Cross had a Sergeant who'd joined him to demonstrate falling, a man called Carlin, who sought to teach them the thing they'd done much of when learning how to fight up in Scotland, but this was different. This was keeping knees and ankles together, to stop them taking the impact individually or at an angle, and breaking or dislocating, and keeping the knees slightly bent to reduce the chances of bones shattering on contact with the ground. Then there was the collapse, falling to the side immediately after impact to relieve the force while dropping to the ground. The Sergeant made it look quite easy, if not a little ridiculous, and soon everyone was having a go, trying not to snigger at themselves as the collapsed into the ground. Some struggled with the concept a little, and couldn't quite drop to the floor properly, which had Emily raising an eyebrow. Once they'd all had a few turns, and done the best they could, their minds were focused by having to jump from a short wooden bench and practice the drop and roll, and then they went up to a table height drop. They continued for much of the morning, dropping again and again from different heights, with a few sore heads and bottoms as they progressed, but nothing much higher than table top height until everyone could land and roll in their sleep if they needed to. Then, without warning or fanfare, they were sent off for lunch. No marching, no shouting or running, and as a group they made their way into the house for soup and bread.

In the afternoon they made their way outside, ready for a casual walk to the apparatus again, but waiting for them was Flight Sergeant Cross and Sergeant Carlin, who some had nicknamed Cross' flying monkey, and both had a look in their eyes that gave Emily flashbacks to when they had been surprised with trips up the sunshine mountain. To help further the unease, an open back truck was running, the

Captain and Ensign in the cab, and the rear frame stripped of its tarpaulin. It was ominous at best, and there were a few nervous faces when they were encouraged onto the back of the truck, and told to hold on tight. Emily grabbed one of the bars of the frame and clung to it, with 4 grabbing her just in time as the truck lurched into life, sending a couple falling to the deck.

"I hope you were all paying attention this morning!" Cross shouted as they rolled along the boot high grass in the next field. He slapped his hand hard on the roof of the cab, and the truck slowed to walking pace as he made his way to the back, where the tailgate was hanging down. "OK, watch and learn! Sergeant Carlin, when you're ready." Carlin gave a nod, then jumped from the back of the truck without a second thought, hitting the ground and rolling in the way they'd been taught that morning. "We couldn't go any slower without stopping, but it'll still hurt if you get it wrong. So, remember your training. First up… You!" He pointed to Emily, who was holding onto the rear left pole of the frame. Her eyes opened a little wider, and she nodded. "Well, it only works if you actually jump," he added, "otherwise, you're just having a Sunday drive." She nodded again, then took a breath before looking down. Walking pace suddenly seemed awfully fast. 4 gave her a reassuring smile, and that was it. She jumped as the flying monkey had, knees and ankles together, and a split second later she was rolling in the grass. She didn't even have time to think, she'd dropped so quickly, and somehow, she'd managed through pure luck to land as she'd been taught. She gasped a little from the shock of the impact, then quickly got to her knees and looked in the direction of the truck to watch others following. Carlin appeared beside her and offered his hand, pulling her up so they could follow on, collecting others while watching those still to go dropping from the truck one at a time. Eventually, the truck stopped, and they were all on board again, ready for another go as it continued its way around the field. This time, Emily felt a little more confident, and jumped off making sure her knees were already bent, and elbows tucked, ready to hit the ground and roll, dissipating the energy of her fall across her body. She didn't wait to be collected once she'd landed, and was up and marching forward within seconds, the adrenaline flowing a little bit, and feeling something warm inside her at the thought of what they were doing. It was exciting, more than she expected jumping from a truck would be, and more than she'd thought it could be just a few minutes earlier when she was the first of the students off. A few more drops and Emily had made peace with the relative insanity of jumping from a moving truck, and was almost looking forward to another go when, with three taps to the cab roof, the truck sped up. "At ten miles per hour, the potential for injury increases significantly," Cross said almost excitedly over the noise of the engine. "If a limb's adrift, you're going to do yourself some damage. You've been warned." He gave Carlin a nod, and he quickly was gone, jumping and dropping with what looked like so much more intensity. Emily swallowed hard, but didn't look around or pause. Instead, she took her turn, jumping and hitting the ground with a force she wasn't prepared for, while forgetting to fall to her side, and everything else from her practice jumps, driving her knees into her chest and winding herself. She couldn't even make a noise, and simply rolled gasping and fighting for breath as her body tried to recover from the shock, and the intense pain in her chest.

"With respect, Ma'am, you probably don't want to do that," Carlin said as he appeared above her, looking down and shaking his head a little in despair at Emily's pained expression. "Come on. Up and moving's the only way." He held out his hand, which she stared at incredulously for a few moments. He hadn't even asked if she was alright, just shook his head and told her to get up. She tried to sigh, but couldn't, so took his hand and was soon up on her feet and walking beside him. He ran a little, and she joined him, feeling the air being sucked into her lungs as she did, then helped him pick up the next person, who'd managed to do the same. Almost everyone had the same experience, and there were shocked and pained faces as they ran to join the truck, and once they were onboard and going again, Emily's thoughts of enjoying falling from a truck were long behind her. Right up there with marching up mountains. The second time at speed went better, though she still wasn't recovered from the first, and felt sore as she rolled properly across the ground, and spent a moment on her hands and knees and catching her breath before standing to meet Carlin, and going to collect the others. Three more times they jumped, making it five at walking pace, and five at ten miles per hour.

To Emily's relief, there wasn't a twenty miles per hour. One of the others was already limping and holding his knee, having crashed awkwardly on his last landing, and she didn't want to push her luck going again, even at a slower speed. Instead, it was back to the benches and tables for more practice at drops and rolls, which suddenly felt a lot more relevant than they had in the morning, and on every turn, she made sure she did exactly as she'd been taught, as did everyone else. The smiles, and the laughing at themselves, were gone. They were now focused on getting it right while they had the chance to practice. Fall after fall, they went again and again, steadily increasing height until they were confident jumping off a platform about six feet high.

When the day was over, and they'd had time to eat and change into their service dress, Emily, 18, and 4 settled into the Mess bar, finding another corner with armchairs. Some of the others were scattered around the room, while a few had chosen to have an early night. It had been a demanding day in a very different way to Scotland. It was infinitely more relaxed, more even than the training back in London. Other than being marched to the training ground first thing, nobody had marched anywhere, nobody had shouted much, or attacked them with knives, and while the change in intensity was welcome, it was also exhausting. Nobody was really able to relax, something the three discussed amongst themselves quietly, a shared experience evidenced by the looks on the faces of the others, and it seemed that everyone was like a coiled spring as they waited to be told that they'd said or done something wrong, and they were disappeared off to never be seen again. Alongside that, the day had been rigorous, and while cleaning up and changing, Emily noticed she had a number of bruises, as had the others, and her knees, ankles, hips, and back were sore from dropping again and again onto the cold, hard ground. They didn't last long in the bar at all, despite their plans to stay up and relax now they had Scotland behind them, and by nine o'clock the three were in their beds. Emily had tried to read a paperback book she'd found in the room, something about a female pilot during the last war, but as intriguing as the concept was, she couldn't keep her eyes open, and after reading the same page over and over, she put it down and just about managed to say goodnight before she passed out.

The next day started with a refresher on landing, following another unexpectedly good breakfast, before they moved onto the bigger and infinitely more intimidating apparatus, the intriguing looking frames and ropes that had caught Emily's attention the previous day, but had gone totally unreferenced by the Cross and Carlin, as though they were invisible. Now, though, on the chilly February morning, they were both gleaming with happiness as they instructed on the first of their machines. A parachute harness attached to cables about six feet off the ground, that Carlin demonstrated for them, as always. The harness swung, and could be swung more with the pull of a rope, and with another pull, it was lowered to the ground at a steady rate that was fast enough to simulate landing by parachute. One by one, they took their turns, learning how to fit the harness securely, with the straps passing between the thighs, and down from the shoulders, all clicking into a metal hub at the front. Some remembered their falls, some were overwhelmed by the newness of the harness, and forgot everything, landing on the ground with a crash. When it came to Emily's turn, she slowed herself down and thought of the drills they'd been taught, then jumped off and was swung a little, before dropping and landing with a perfect collapse on the hard ground, feeling a degree of happiness that she'd got it right, and more than a little gratitude for the rubber rimmed helmets they'd been issued as her head rattled on the ground. They went again and again, until finally they were moved to the scaffolding frame that dominated the site. It was high, with what looked like winches and fans, and even Emily's usual stoic demeanour was shaken a little by the size of it. Cross briefed them, and Carlin demonstrated once again. It was similar to what they'd spent the morning doing, but on a bigger scale, and they quickly learned that swing and rate of decent could be controlled, which made for an interesting development in the training. There was something exhilarating about it when she finally jumped. Being swung, and dropped from a height, it all lasted a little bit longer, and gave her a little bit more time to think, which meant that she was more prepared for landing, and collapsed perfectly, not even rattling her head. It made her heart race again, but in a good way.

The night went much the same as the previous, though there was less pretence about sitting up talking and relaxing. They had a drink, and headed off to bed. Emily was able to read a little more, but she still only managed a few pages before her eyes got heavy again. It was like the previous month in Scotland had finally caught her, and the moment she was relaxed, she was asleep. Her brain shutting her down so her body could repair and recover, and so her mind could process all that had happened. Then, before she knew it, the night had passed in what felt like minutes, and she was getting up and getting ready for another day. It was hard, not physically as such, though her body was sore. She'd adapted to the hard work, and while her body had always been quite lean, she'd noticed muscles developing in a way they never had, and her fitness improving as a result of the training. She was tired, and recovering, but she knew that was a process she needed to go through for her body to adapt to the training. The truly difficult part was the psychological side. She'd spent over a month with people, and didn't even know their names, how old they were, or even where they were from. She'd become friends with some, certainly 4 and 18, and 3, who she wondered about every now and then, but she knew nothing about them. On top of that, she still didn't know what she'd volunteered for, or where the training was going, or even when it would end. It was just relentlessly onwards, and onwards, towards an indeterminate future. She felt at times like it'd never end, and she'd spend her life training for something, and part of her even worried that the war would be over before she even knew what she'd been training to do.

After a week of training on the frames and winches, and dropping out of a realistic mock up of an aircraft fuselage, they were still being served the same tasty home cooked breakfasts, which few could get their heads around. Some of the pre war officers talked about the rarity of bacon and eggs since the war and rationing started, and how being served them was often a Mess tradition when they were about to go off into something big, like there was a battle coming. They almost made it sound like a last meal, which didn't fill Emily with any confidence, though 4 also contributed that fighter pilots in the Battle of Britain regularly had bacon and eggs, as it was important to keep their strength up. It was an attempt to lessen the thought of it being a last meal, and at the same time, Emily remembered Harriet's stories from the hospital, and the many of those young pilots she'd had brought into her hospital burned, and broken, and next to death throughout the Battle of Britain. It took some of the edge off the bacon and eggs, but not enough to stop her eating it.

In a change from the script, after seven consecutive days of training, they were loaded onto the back of a truck, covered this time, which connected to unwelcome deep memories of being driven to the sunshine mountain as they were taken somewhere further than the back garden. At first, Emily had wondered if they'd be jumping from it while it had its canvas sides up, as some sort of disorientation exercise, but the speed they were moving soon had her hoping she was very wrong. She settled when they'd been driving more than five minutes, and she could see the road out of the back of the truck. They were actually going somewhere, rather than jumping, and after passing through a main gate with armed sentries, they wound through what looked like a barracks of some sort, before finally coming to a halt. She looked around as she jumped down from the back of the truck, instinctively keeping her knees and ankles together. There were large hangars, aircraft, and squads of soldiers here and there. It was about as real as anything had been for a while, and suddenly they were surrounded by people, and noise.

After a brief moment gazing around in awe at the busy airfield filled with marching soldiers and big, twin engine Armstrong Whitworth Whitley bombers painted in green and brown camouflage, they were hurried off to a large office inside the hangar they'd parked outside of, and issued with parachutes through a covered hatch in the wall, before being loaded back on the truck and heading off again. They'd been told in the parachute bay that every parachute was hand packed and inspected by specialists, and they were handed through a blind hatch so nobody could see who was collecting it. Apparently, it made everyone feel better if the parachute didn't work, because the packer, issuer, and parachutist hadn't seen each other. It was an explanation that hadn't made Emily feel any better, having quickly got it into her head that they were going to be given a parachute, ordered onto an aeroplane, and then thrown out of it at height, without any further training, or warning. The same way they'd been surprised with hikes across the Scottish highlands. It had been a relief in some way to be loaded back into the truck, and taken back to the mansion house to train more wearing the parachutes, possibly jumping off the truck again. At least that's what she imagined. Nobody had been told a thing, as usual, and they were all left to fill in the blanks, while still remaining respectfully quiet on their truck journey, as they'd initially been conditioned.

While sitting with her thoughts, Emily realised suddenly that unless the driver was taking the scenic route, they'd been in the truck much longer than they'd been on the drive from the mansion house, which gave her a feeling in her chest right around the solar plexus, a tension she knew was coming from the unknown. It had been weeks of the unknown, right from her conversation at the Air Ministry in London the previous autumn, and she'd developed a keen sense for recognising when something was coming, and it always sat in the same place. As the drive continued, she thought back to how the sensation had been with her for much of her life. There was no point thinking on where the truck was taking her, she knew that was well beyond her control, so she thought on the past. She'd felt it in her chest when she received a telegram telling her that her husband was missing. She couldn't quite remember, not for sure, but she was convinced she'd felt it before the telegram had even arrived. She'd felt it when patients were about to take a turn for the worse, too, before they ever did. Never as acute as she had when Harriet had arrived at her hospital, though. An army ambulance had arrived late in the evening, when all of the patients had been settled, bringing a young pilot who'd been pulled out of the Channel. The driver had said they weren't expected to live, but that wasn't unusual. The hospital had a few small individual rooms, as well as the wards, thanks to its place as a local community hospital in a relatively affluent area, where wealthy people would visit for treatment in relative privacy. Officers considered to be touch and go cases had been sent there since the Phoney War had turned very real in the May of 1940, where they could be cared for intensely and privately, and in some cases, left to die in peace. Emily had met the ambulance along with the Matron and senior Consultant, Dr Goode, and been assigned to look after the young airman. The feeling in her chest hadn't prepared her for what she saw when she set about removing the pilot's cold, wet, and filthy clothing so their wounds could be assessed. Beneath the dirt, and blood, and burns, was a grey looking young woman, something that shocked them all. Then the feeling squeezed so hard it made her nauseous. More so than when her husband's likely death had been

131

confirmed, as much as it could be without a body being found. It had taken many long hours to stabilise Harriet, and when her wounds were dressed, and the filth washed from her body, the feeling stayed tight in Emily's chest as she sat and held her hand through the night, while wondering what an innocent looking young thing had been doing wrapped in pilot's clothing, and bobbing around lost at sea. The only reason they knew for sure she was a pilot at all was because of the sailor that had travelled with her, and spent the night at the hospital drinking medicinal brandy with Doctor Goode. He and Harriet had been the only two to survive a packed mine sweeper that had been torpedoed after evacuating the beach at Dunkirk, its decks stacked with soldiers heading home, many of them wounded. Among them, Harriet, a young female pilot who'd flown a Hawker Hurricane in action against the Germans, and had been shot down and wounded defending the beaches. The pair had swum together for hours before being picked up by another ship, more by luck than design. To look at her, it would have been difficult to believe it without his eyewitness testimony. Emily had felt connected though, and nursed her carefully for days on end, refusing rest breaks, and being given dispensation to sleep in a chair by Harriet's bed, where she slumped holding the young woman's hand that had taken the best part of a night to feel any more than ice cold, something that had Emily up all night checking Harriet's pulse and respirations, just to make sure she hadn't died.

"Alright, let's go," Flight Sergeant Cross said in the same casual bark he'd had since starting their training. Enough to remind people of his authority, but there was no shouting, or faux outrage that sometimes came with Senior Non Commissioned Officers. Being a parachute instructor meant he didn't have to swagger, he was the king of the air, or so the received wisdom of the course had agreed. If he had what it took to jump out of an aeroplane enough times to become a senior instructor in it, he didn't have much to prove. The tailgate clanged, and the tarpaulin was flipped up on the roof. Emily jumped down and stared in suspicious awe. They were in a large park, or so it seemed, with clear, grassy areas among the woods, and there was even a lake in the distance that shimmered in the late winter sun. Closer to them, however, was a large barrage balloon tethered to a truck crewed by WAAFs. The feeling in her chest didn't shift as the others started to mutter quietly, and 18 and 4 joined her, and the three looked at each other nervously. "We'd better get on with it while the weather holds. First five volunteers." Emily stepped forward without hesitation, quickly followed by 18 and 4. The Rifles officer was quick to join them, and the Intelligence officer. "God loves a volunteer," Cross laughed. "The rest of you make yourselves comfortable, you five get your helmets on and check your harnesses, then join me over at the balloon." He half smirked while nodding knowingly before turning and marching away to the WAAFs. "Sergeant Carlin will check you over.

"You'll thank me," Carlin said quietly while Emily's heart started to race as she pulled on the rubber rimmed, steel parachutist's helmet, and he gave the straps of her parachute harness a tight tug, making her gasp to keep in a yelp as those between her thighs suddenly got much tighter than they had been, almost uncomfortably so. He gave her a confident wink as he tightened the shoulder straps, making her smile unintentionally. He was older than her, in his mid thirties perhaps, with a barrel chest and piercing blue eyes. He didn't say much, just demonstrated, checked, and corrected according to Cross' instructions. They were obviously used to working with each other, and things happened without debate or repetition. "Remember your training, and you'll be fine. Don't rush, or let the experience panic you. Just keep breathing." He nodded, then went on to 18 while Harriet started walking towards Cross, who was waiting the other side of the truck holding the winch cable that kept the ginormous balloon on the ground. She didn't know what to think, or what to expect, all she knew was that her mouth and throat were drying quickly, and no amount of swallowing was easing them. She found him standing by a large, gondola like covered basket attached with cables to the balloon, talking with a WAAF officer who seemed to quite like him, and simultaneously not like being disturbed in her flirting when Emily showed up.

"OK, in you get," the WAAF said firmly. She pointed Emily in through the door, then followed her and moved her to the far end. "Sit, stay, and don't move unless instructed." Emily nodded, she didn't have it in her to feel insulted at the hard tones. She was too busy looking at the large, just bigger than person sized, hole in the floor. It was a muted, dull, and musty smelling basket made of metal frames and hardboard walls and floor, with a canvas roof like that

133

covering the back of a truck. In fact, the more she looked around, the basket was little more than the back of a small truck, detached from the chassis and strung up to the bottom of a barrage balloon. It didn't look, feel, or even smell safe. 18 gave her a raised eyebrow, but said nothing after being seated in the same firm way by the WAAF, and 4 just frowned, clearly toying with the idea of challenging a fellow WAAF, but thinking better of it. All five were seated, and Carlin was the last on board, closing the small gate behind them before sitting with his back to it.

"All set," Carlin shouted. "Up to seven hundred!"

"Up to seven hundred!" a woman's voice came back from outside, and the truck holding the balloon rumbled into life. "Then back down to seven ten."

"She means you'll land ten feet further down if you cock it up, and your parachute doesn't open," Carlin added with a laugh as he looked around at the mildly terrified faces. At that, the basket shook as the winch released the balloon, and it started to drag them upwards, leaving a fluttering feeling fighting with the nausea in Emily's stomach. "If you do get it wrong, though, remember to cross your legs at the ankles, and hold your arms out to the side, parallel to the earth…" He took a moment to look each of them in the eyes. "It won't save you, but it'll make it easier for us to unscrew your body from the ground." He let out a laugh, and Emily felt her eyes roll, an automatic response she'd been highly skilled at, if her parents were to be believed, and something she'd fought to control over the years. Carlin had spent the course being quiet, doing as Cross said like his own, personal flying monkey. Now they were rolling up into the sky under a huge barrage balloon, he'd discovered his sense of humour, and his tongue, and couldn't stop himself from talking. "We'll be jumping at seven hundred feet, which will give you no more than a few seconds to think, but longer than when you jumped from the back of the truck. It'll feel like an age for your static line to deploy the parachute, but don't worry. Count. 'One thousand, two thousand, three thousand, check.' Look up and make sure your canopy's deployed, and take a good grip of the riser lines, as you've been shown. Keep your elbows in, and knees bent. If you look up and it hasn't deployed properly, give the lines a tug, and try to get it unfolded. Keep your eyes on it

134

until you've got it sorted, and only look down when you've got a full canopy." Emily listened to his words, delivered confidently with the same hint of humour, and while she could see the logic in what he was saying, they'd been briefed on it enough on the big harness swing back at the house, she also knew all too well why he was saying they should keep their eyes on the canopy until it was fully deployed. With only seconds in the air, that would be long enough to distract them from their pending doom if it hadn't deployed properly, and they were hurtling towards the ground.

"Happy to take the lead this time," the Rifles Captain said after the ascent had slowed to a halt, and the basket swayed from the not altogether gentle stop. He had a look of confidence mixed with nervousness on his face, suggesting that he was keen to get off the gently swaying fairground ride. "Unless anyone has any objections about not going first?" He looked directly at Emily, who simply shrugged in reply. She wasn't overly keen on what was coming, and at the same time, she wasn't particularly excited about staying onboard and waiting for the inevitable. She'd have volunteered to go first herself if she'd been alert enough to it being an option.

"OK, shuffle over and hang your legs through the hole." Carlin said, giving the Captain a nod. He did as he was told, though his hands were visibly shaking with nerves. "Strop up." Carlin pointed to the frame above the hole, and the officer attached the end of his static line to the frame, giving it a tug to show it was attached. "Remember what we've shown you, lift your weight, straighten your legs, then forward and down you go. Just don't ring the bloody bell!" He got another nod in reply, but no action. "Look, it's February, and it'll be dark in a few hours," Carlin started after a minute. "I'd rather not still be up here when the Germans turn up for their nightly visit to bomb Manchester, so if you wouldn't mind?" No more words needed to be said, the Captain lifted, straightened his legs, and swung forward. Too far forward, and his face hit squarely against the other side of the hole as he dropped through it, a muffled 'ugh' filling the air alongside a hum from the metal frame as he disappeared, and everyone looked around in shock. "Told him not to ring the bell…" Carlin sighed, and the crude term suddenly became more real as everyone saw for themselves what it was like when a head hit the side of the hole, like the ringer striking the inside of a bell. "Now you've seen how not to do it…" Carlin said as he leant forward and looked down through the hole. "Who wants to go next?"

"I'll go," Emily said without stopping to think. The nervous energy was making her vibrate, and she didn't want to sit and watch somebody else smash their face off the hole, it would only make it worse knowing that it was a near guaranteed prospect. Carlin gave her a nod and a smile, and gestured for her to move forward. She shuffled, feeling the same nerves shaking her own hands as had done for her predecessor. She secured the strop on the frame, then put her hands either side of her and looked down to see a parachute canopy billowing on the ground below, then looked forward again.

"Any time you're ready…" he said casually, and she pushed down and lifted her behind from the floor. Then, while keeping the previous student's fate clearly in her mind, she straightened her legs and pushed forward, pulling her shoulders back as she did. She shot out of the basket like a rocket, moving so fast she didn't even see the edge of the hole, let alone hit it. Her heart was pounding, and her stomach was in her mouth as she counted out loud 'one thousand, two thousand, three thousand,' and then her head snapped back as she felt like a giant hand had grabbed her from above and pulled her upwards. She looked up and grabbed the riser lines, and smiled in relief at the sight of a fully developed canopy. She just had time to bend her knees while looking around the serene beauty of the outstretched park, the ground pale with frost, contrasted with the smog over Manchester. It was idyllic, in a way, almost peaceful. Until she very quickly remembered where she was, and looked down to see the ground coming up very fast to meet her. The rest was a blur, and one she didn't recover from until she was laid on her back looking up at the balloon. Her head was rattled slightly, but otherwise she was fine, other than her cheeks aching at the huge smile stretching across her face.

"You can stay down there, but they might land on you." Cross appeared above her and pointed upward as the next body slipped out of the basket. She nodded and turned the release at the front of the harness, and gave it a hit with her other hand, springing all the straps loose and sitting up out of them. Cross talked her through rolling in her parachute, winding it over her arms, which she did while still smiling as 4 thundered down about ten paces away from her. She watched nervously, then smiled even more as 4's grinning face quickly popped up as she waved excitedly.

18 was on the ground by the time both had collected their parachutes and withdrawn a safe distance, and once she'd joined them, Cross sent them over to the Navy, Army, and Air Force Institute truck that had turned up, where they each got a cup of tea and bread spread with margarine, a delicacy not so lovingly referred to as a 'wad'. They talked excitedly about their experiences, and how thrilling it had been once the initial fear was out of the way, while the NAAFI girl told them in no uncertain terms that nobody would ever get her to do such a thing, especially after that poor boy had smashed his face in. She'd pointed in the direction of the ambulance, where a doctor was dealing with a bloody and bruised looking Rifles officer. Emily looked at him for a moment, catching his eye briefly as the medic cleared the blood. She gave him a polite nod, and got one in return, then turned back to the others and got involved in a conversation about whether Cross would let them go back up again for another go.

The answer had been no, as they'd half expected. The balloon was needed by other soldiers, a truck of whom had turned up and was waiting in the near distance for them to finish. Three times the balloon was winched up and back down, and all together fifteen jumped, with no refusals, and only one bell rung. It didn't matter, though, there was a different level of excitement as the truck rolled away from the park again, a place that Cross had told them was called Tatton Park, to the south of Manchester. There were silent smiles all around the truck as everyone processed what had happened, with the exception of the Rifles officer, who looked sheepish with heavily bruised eyes and nose, and a burst lip for good measure, he didn't make eye contact with anyone, and instead held a bandage close to his nose to catch the remnants of the blood still dripping out of him.

Training for the unknown, where the unexpected was sprung at a moment's notice, with the expectation that those on the receiving end would simply adapt and make do, had reached a pinnacle in Emily's eyes, when they'd been deposited from the truck in front of a balloon that they were expected to jump from some minutes later. Everything else had built up to that, and she didn't think anything could surpass it. Not until she handed in her used parachute and was given a new, packed replacement, and she knew there was more to come. At first, they'd assumed it was part of the process, handing in the parachutes after use to be checked and repacked, for no other reason than that's what they were told the process was. Being issued a replacement was a surprise, but not as much as being marched over to a pair of Armstrong Whitworth Whitley twin engine bombers that the ground crew were finishing off with. Minutes later, without time to think or change their minds, the students were inside the fuselage, sitting with their backs to the walls, one left, one right, facing each other with half at the cockpit side of the hole in the floor, and half at the tail side, their legs out in front of them. Carlin was in their aeroplane, and Cross in the other, both wearing parachutes and helmets, and Carlin was his now usual mischievous self, dropping dry comments about how crossing legs wouldn't help anything if they 'cocked it up' this time, because the fall was so high they'd just be a dark red stain on the ground. It didn't faze Emily, she knew it was just military humour, she'd heard it enough in her life, though she did wonder how much of it was standard, and how much was prompted by whoever was behind the training course she was on. A subtle nudge somewhere to remind everyone how near death they were, just to see if they could get somebody to break.

The quips and comments kept coming, shouted over the noise of the engines as the aeroplane climbed and circled. Emily was able to go somewhere else, and thought back to her first ever flight in an aeroplane, when Harriet had taken her for a spin along the white cliffs of Dover in a Tiger Moth. She'd teased Harriet as she'd started to recover from her trauma, and suggested that she'd never fly after hearing of Harriet's crashes. She'd even teased about Harriet having to parachute from an aeroplane. What she didn't share is that she'd fallen in love with flying, when she'd finally got off the ground and seen the world from above. The flip in her tummy as the wheels left the ground had made her feel like nothing else had, and it was that exact same feeling that had her smiling when the Whitley had taken off. More so when she imagined what Harriet would say if she could see her not only flying, but voluntarily choosing to jump out of an aeroplane. The smile and the thoughts kept her company as the aeroplane banked, and climbed, and circled. She didn't look at the others, instead just gazed at her own boots and smiled to herself while thinking about what was to come. The balloon had been terrifying, but in a way, for the few seconds she was in the air and hanging under her parachute she felt an incredible sense of euphoria.

She thought of what was to come, and despite loving some moments, she was still quite nervous about jumping out of a perfectly serviceable aeroplane, and the flight experience didn't make her feel any more settled, despite being in something more substantial than a musty smelling, creaking, metal framed basket. The aeroplane looked and felt safe, and at the same time, dropping through the hole was the biggest challenge, more because she didn't want to ring the bell and smash her face in than anything else. She was assured that the static line would do its job, and deploy the parachute, and if it didn't, she wouldn't have much say in what followed. If it did, she'd have time to compose herself as she floated down. A whole minute, if Carlin was to be believed, which was significantly more than the second or two it had taken to hit the ground from the balloon. The aeroplane was a luxury, at least that's what her logic told her.

While the ascent was longer than it been in the balloon, that had been winched straight up, the Whitley eventually stabilised on a straight heading after circling to gain height, and the hole in the floor was soon beckoning. The smell of oil and aviation fuel suddenly felt colder, and if fear had a smell, it quickly filled the inside of the bomber's fuselage. Carlin briefed everyone one last time, and gave them a firm reminder that a refusal to jump meant failing the course. No second chances. He also shouted, at the top of his lungs 'don't ring the bloody bell!' There was no time to hesitate as soon as the order was given, and after securing the strop of the static line, the first disappeared out of the hole, and then the second, and then the third. 18 gave Emily a nod and a half smile, then lifted herself and disappeared through the hole, and then it was Emily's turn. The ice cold blast of air hit different as her legs dangled out, and the world suddenly felt much wilder and more volatile. A split second later, she lifted and pushed, her face missing the side of the hole by a hair's breadth, and then she was out in the freezing blast of nothingness. Her heart raced, and she gasped for air, hearing herself groan and mutter as she fought to breathe while shouting 'one thousand, two thousand...' she didn't get to three. Her head snapped back, and her hands reached up instinctively to grab the risers, that reassuringly were right where they needed to be, and she quickly looked up to see a fully deployed canopy. For a moment, she felt like her heart was going to explode out of her chest with the adrenaline and fear, but then, as she looked around, the euphoria returned. She was weightless, and floating, and the view was incredible. She could see the hills in the distance, north, south, and west, and the hazy smoke over Manchester, with its menacing barrage balloons standing sentry above. Once she'd caught her breath, and got over the initial shock of jumping out of a moving aeroplane and into the cold, blustery air, she took a moment to look around. The Whitley droned off into the distance as the second came into sight, and above and below were blobs floating in the air with dots hanging below them, the others who'd jumped. She smiled, and even laughed to herself briefly. Her mind rarely stopped, it never had for as long as she could remember, but jumping, that had focused her like nothing else, and even as she swung beneath the canopy and drifted down, she didn't have much in her mind other than how much her cheeks ached from the smiling. Then, reality hit, and she glanced down to see the ground suddenly rushing up towards her like a high speed train, and she barely had time to make sure her knees were bent before she hit the ground and rolled like a badly coordinated rag doll. The landing rattled and shook her, and it took a second or two to compose herself before she could jump up and pull the parachute in before it billowed in the wind. She'd had longer to prepare than the balloon jump, maybe by as much as a minute, but she'd been so busy enjoying herself that she'd forgotten all about the landing, and she was quite sure she'd managed to give herself a dead leg with the awkward way she'd hit the ground. It made her irritated at herself, though even that couldn't keep the smile from her face, and she was soon walking over to the others and trying to disguise the slight limp that came from the throb in the outside of her right thigh. She'd done it. She'd jumped from an aeroplane. She wanted to tell everyone. She wanted to tell Harriet.

The following day they jumped from the bomber twice more, followed by an unexpected night jump that was equally exhilarating and terrifying, especially as there was every chance a German raid could turn up midway through the fun. Something everybody knew, but nobody talked about, accepting that if it happened, there wouldn't be a great deal they could do about it, with the silver lining that at least they'd be wearing parachutes if their aeroplane was shot from the sky. Somebody high up had considered the chances, though, as evidenced by the early evening drop, and not a long wait for the depths of the night.

The day after the night drop, they were paraded outside the mansion house in their service dress, and told that they'd completed their parachute training. It came as a shock to Emily. She'd expected weeks of practice jumps, but it was over in just a few days of good breakfasts and falling out of trucks. They'd hardly even settled before being thrown straight into the main event. Then they were told they were heading to London that evening, and that they'd need to pack and be ready for the transport to take them into Manchester after dinner. Suddenly, it was like Scotland again. Whatever needed to be done, had been, and they were now being sent on their way to whatever next. She imagined, for a moment while Cross talked, that they'd be going to a lake somewhere to learn how to fall out of boats. It was about the only thing they hadn't done, after all. Before being dismissed there was one last surprise, and that was Cross making his way down the two lines of students and handing each of them a badge, a woven white parachute between pale blue outstretched wings. The parachute qualification badge, the wings that Emily had seen some soldiers wearing, and seeing them in her hand made her eyes open wide. She'd turned up in London wanting to follow Harriet's example, and was disappointed when the RAF turned her away. Months later, however, she was standing on a cold drive in a Cheshire suburb wearing the uniform of an Ensign in the First Aid Nursing Yeomanry, having just been presented her very own wings after weeks of endless training. They weren't pilot's wings, but they were very special in their own way.

Chapter 10

Again

There was a tension in the air around the main train station in Manchester. People were moving about purposefully, all seemingly glancing upwards every now and then, even though there wasn't much to see in the darkness. Emily felt it the same as the others, though nobody mentioned it. Nobody wanted to be in the centre of the city if another bombing raid came in, and the general state of hurry reflected the keenness to get moving. The First Aid Nursing Yeomanry Captain and Ensign had dropped them off in good time, after a final meal and briefing they were all released for two days leave in London before reporting for duty, the details of which were in sealed envelopes issued to each, on the express orders that the contents were top secret, and not to be discussed with anyone, course colleagues included. It was more mystery, but it didn't dull the excitement at two days leave in London. Some of the men were quite boisterous, and once they'd been dropped at the train station, small groups splintered off here and there to find a place on the train.

The guard was hurrying people onboard, and doors were slamming the length of the train by the time they got to it. He shouted at them to hurry if they wanted to get to London before the following day, and they quickly ran for the nearest carriage, with Emily jumping on after 4 and 18, who'd led the way onboard. The carriage was the type with six separate compartments on one side, and a narrow corridor running along them on the other, leading to the next carriage, and the next. Every compartment in carriage after carriage was full of soldiers, and there were many wolf whistles and cat calls as the three women made their way towards the back of the train, along with quite a few offers to 'find space'. They continued on their way until things thinned out a little. One compartment was full of the less friendly officers from their training course, all of whom either smiled politely or looked away, not keen to make space, so it was on to the next carriage where they even found some civilians, and then into the next, where they finally found a compartment with space enough at the end of the carriage, occupied by a young mum and her two children. They said hello, then stowed their bags before collapsing into their seats and getting comfortable as the train pulled out of the station, and headed into the night.

It was a long and tedious train journey to London, one that had Emily questioning her choices many times, and frequently wishing she'd gone back to her parents' house in Scotland for a day or two before heading south on a less crowded train. They made good time at first, then slowed progressively as the night went on, stopping for long periods, and then starting again without explanation. When they'd first set off there was excitement about the potential to find a night club still open in London when they arrived, but those plans quickly dissolved as the train lurched and slowed its way south. It was when they were in the station at Birmingham, having waited in the darkness for what felt like hours, that the conversation about the weather, particularly that nowhere could ever be as cold and wet as Scotland in January, was silenced by a familiar sound that Emily felt resonating in her chest, tightening her nerves, and setting fear running down her spine. Air raid sirens started to wind up, starting with a deep, low hum that almost made her sick, increasing in pitch and splitting the air with their terrifying wail. They looked around at each other, not sure what to do. Her heart started to race, and while she maintained her composed exterior, everything inside was spinning. She pulled the curtain to one side and peeked out onto the platform and saw people disappearing out of sight.

"What do we do?" the woman with the children asked. She had them both pulled close to her, their hands in hers, as all three of them stared wide eyed at the uniformed women sitting opposite them.

"I'll go and find out," 18 said as she stood and walked over to the compartment door, pulling it open and sticking her head into the corridor, just as the train jerked into life and started rolling.

"Get down!" a man's voice echoed down the corridor. "Everyone, get down!" Emily instinctively launched herself across the compartment and grabbed the woman and children, pulling them to the floor between the seats and pushing the children's heads down as she laid on top of them just as the entire train lit up in a brilliant white flash of light that almost blinded her, making her squint just to see. She glanced over her shoulder at 18 just as a shockwave passed through the side of the train, shattering the windows, and sending 18 flying through the compartment and rattling her against the wall as the white light was replaced by red, and a fierce, deep, guttural clap of deafening thunder blew smoke and shrapnel in every direction. She pressed down tight on the family as she felt the heat above her, opening her mouth wide and screaming at the top of her lungs as she did, taken back to the horror of the raid in London almost instantly. The light finally dimmed, and the compartment filled with smoke. She started to cough, but just as she lifted herself a little to try and find some clear air, another flash of light had her pressing down again as a second blast hit a little further away, sending splinters and shrapnel through the air like whizzing, buzzing darts that whistled and screamed through the smoke. She felt a hard jerk as the train rocked as it sped up, and despite the noise and near delirious confusion, she felt the carriage start to roll, faster and faster, and over the ringing in her ears she could hear the train's whistle howling again and again between the thunderous roars of blast after blast. She laid flat on the family, head down, with her eyes closed tight. She'd stopped screaming, but the adrenaline flowed, and it was all she could do to stop herself crying hysterically between the coughs to get the smoke from her lungs. Minutes passed, and the air quickly started to clear, with a stream of cold running through the compartment. She looked up and behind her towards the door and the corridor. There was a gaping hole in the side of the train, and she could see the hell like burning glow outside, moving fast as the train accelerated out of immediate danger. She took in a couple of mouthfuls of cooler, yet still smoke tinged air, then lifted herself shakily from the family.

"Are you OK?" she asked, realising she could hardly hear herself talk through the intense ringing in her ears. The woman looked at her for a moment, her eyes wide with shock. She was breathing and moving, but in all likelihood, couldn't hear for the same reason as Emily. She rolled, and moved to her knees to see two pairs of eyes staring back at her from underneath, both very alive and terrified into silence. She let out a sigh of relief as her head dropped and she composed herself, before gathering her strength and dragging herself half upright, then freezing in position as she glanced across the compartment to the wall, where 18 was sat with her back flat against it having been thrown from the door by the blast. She was staring into space, her uniform smoking in the orange light filling the compartment from the blown out windows and door. Emily blinked as she composed herself more.

Curled in a ball and hidden half under the seat, 4 stared back at her, eventually giving a nod as if to answer a silent question. Emily steadied herself, then crawled over the glass and wood littering the floor and stopped in front of 18. She knew right away, even before she opened 18's greatcoat and saw the burning, smoking shrapnel holes that had ripped into her body, the biggest of which was still glowing inside 18's chest. All the training as a nurse, all the surgery, the wound care, the pulling wounded soldiers and airmen back from the brink, it didn't count for anything. 18, the tall blonde Wren officer who'd made her way confidently through the challenges of Scotland without even breaking her step, was dead. The smell of her burning flesh and clothes stinging Emily's nostrils over that of the burning that surrounded them, but not making her pull away. She'd seen death before, lots of times, maybe more than a young woman her age should in a normal world, but this hit her differently. This was a friend whose name she didn't even know. A woman who, having been stood in the doorway and looking for help, had taken the worst of the shrapnel that would have otherwise cut the compartment to pieces, along with everyone in it. Emily reached forward and pushed her fingers into 18's neck, feeling for a pulse, desperately hoping that she wouldn't find one. The wounds were so bad that they'd be fatal anyway, she knew that much, and the only relief from the pain 18 would suffer if she was alive would be a quick death. There was nothing, but her skin still felt soft and warm, like she was still there, and her eyes still stared into Emily's, but there was no sign of life in them, she'd gone.

"Is she...?" 4 asked as she pulled herself up and to Emily's side.

"Yes..." Emily replied, not breaking 18's dead stare. "Yes, I'm sorry." She shook her head and looked to 4, "are you OK?" She looked the young WAAF officer up and down, searching for wounds.

"I think so. I..." 4 looked at Emily, fighting the tears that were threatening to overtake her, then back to 18. Emily nodded, then reached forward and closed 18's eyes.

"Stay with her." She forced a hard smile. "And keep an eye on those three." She dragged herself up to her feet and looked around, the carriage was shredded from the level of the seats upwards. Seats cut, the walls half blown out, windows shattered. That only 18 died was a miracle.

"Where are you going?"

"To see if anyone needs help. Keep the children in here." She stepped through the shattered doorway and into the corridor, looking right, and then left, and trying not to look too long at the splintered side of the train that had been blown open, or the orange glow seeping in through it. The next compartment was a sight she wasn't prepared for. Sitting in the seats left and right of the shredded wall and door were three soldiers, an older couple, and a young looking woman. All of them bloody and staring into space. She stepped in and started checking for pulses, looking for signs of life, but every one of them had passed before she'd even dragged herself off the floor. Faces, necks, and torsos had been viciously ripped open by shrapnel, and the entire compartment was sprayed with blood and burned with smoke and fire. Their clothes and hair were charred, while everything below the waist looked perfectly normal. She closed their eyes once she'd checked them, then left to head to the next compartment. It took some pulling and straining, but she managed to move the three dead soldiers crowded around the far wall of the compartment, the backs of their uniforms lacerated by glass, and peppered with shrapnel holes. She checked each as she moved them, but they were as dead as those in the previous carriage. Underneath them, though, was a blackened and terrified looking WAAF. She stared up at Emily, trembling with fear and eyes wide open, and very much alive. "Are you hurt?" Emily asked gently as she knelt beside the young woman, who couldn't have been more than eighteen. The girl simply shook like a leaf, curled tight into a ball with her knees to her chest and her back to the carriage wall, where she'd been since the soldiers had obviously crowded to protect her in a moment of heroism that saw her still breathing, while their bodies absorbed the shrapnel from the blast, saving her life. Emily looked back at the bodies she'd dragged onto the seats and out of the way. They didn't look much older than the WAAF. "Can you hear me?" She moved closer and spoke clearly and loudly, enunciating her words as the girl looked at her, then slowly shook her head, having read Emily's lips. Emily nodded and smiled, then used rudimentary sign language along with exaggerated words to suggest she was going to check the girl over, receiving a nod in reply. First, she checked the cut on her hairline, it was bloody, and made things look bad, as Emily knew head wounds always did, but while the gash was deep and long, likely the result of flying glass or shrapnel, it wasn't deep enough to worry about too much. She looked around her head, but other than being filthy with smoke and grit, and her face and neck bloodied from the wound, she couldn't find any other signs of damage. A quick check of the rest of her, and she was assured that the soldiers had indeed saved the young woman's life. "Come on, let's move." She squatted in her haunches and held out her hands. "An order, not a request. Snap to it." She gave a firm stare and nod, channelling the nurse she thought she'd left behind, and the WAAF nodded and unclamped her hands from around her knees, then shakily reached for Emily. As Emily stood, she pulled the young woman with her, then instinctively pulled her close and gave her a hug, having seen the tears stream from her eyes as she lifted and saw the dead men laid out around her. She reassured her, and hushed her, then guided her out of the compartment and back to her own, where she left her with 4 before heading back into the train.

She checked the three remaining compartments in the carriage. The next was full of more dead, but the final two were a mix of crying and sobbing, and faces of shock, with a few lacerations here and there, but nothing of much note. The end compartment was full of soldiers, all of whom were getting themselves together and composing themselves, while checking out each other's scratches and superficial wounds under her instruction.

"Who's that?" a gravelly voice asked out in the narrow corridor as Emily stepped out, having checked everyone over. She looked into the darkness of the corridor connector that linked the carriages to allow movement up and down the length of the train, and saw the

Guard dragging himself along, limping and gasping his way forward. Letting out a painful sigh as he came close. She could see he was blackened, and his uniform cut up a bit, with a bloody left hand and a cut cheek.

"Are you OK?" she asked as she stepped forward to meet him, scanning him as she went.

"What's that?" He looked at her for a moment, then shook his head after looking down at his hand. "Yes. Yes, I've had worse. Don't worry about the limp, the Germans did that in the last war. They obviously came back to try and finish the job." He let out a forced, half hearted laugh as he painfully raised his arm and showed her his hand. "Looks worse than it is... Anyway, how is everyone? This carriage took the brunt of it, by the looks of things."

"Those two compartments are fine, cuts and scratches. Six dead in there, three in the next," she nodded behind her to the compartment she'd taken the WAAF from. "Another six dead in the next, and one dead, one injured, in the last."

"Dead.... You're sure?"

"You can go and check, if you like. No pulse, no signs of life. Shrapnel, by the looks of it, but I'm not a doctor, so I can't call it officially."

"No... No, of course not." He stepped around her and looked into the nearest compartment of dead. "And you?"

"There are five of us survived practically unscathed in the last compartment. Six, now, with one we've rescued."

"OK. Well, stay where you are. I'll be back shortly."

"I'm a nurse... I was, I mean. Does anyone need help?"

"I'll check and come back to you. There's a doctor in the next carriage taking care of the wounded, but it looks like you took the worst of it here. Probably best you stay put for now, until we know what's going on."

"What is going on?"

"We tried to get out of the station as the air raid came in, to give us a fighting chance. Though it looks like we didn't quite make it." He forced an awkward and apologetic smile. "I'm sorry…"

"I can't imagine what would have happened if we'd stayed. Thank you for doing your best. You wouldn't happen to have a clean handkerchief, would you?" He looked at her for a moment, a little taken aback by her hard coolness and direct manner. "For a wound."

"Yes! Yes…" he snapped out of it, then rummaged in his pocket and pulled out a large, still white and neatly folded handkerchief. "It's clean, as best it can be in here. I mean, I haven't…" He shook his head again and handed it to her. "Stay put, I'll come and tell you what's going on." He turned and shouted hoarsely "Everyone stay put in their seats, please!" He was very formal, almost like he was asking for tickets, then he headed back towards the next carriage. Emily watched him go, then made her way back to her compartment. 4 gave her a forced smile, while the WAAF sobbed near controllably on her shoulder. She looked at 18 briefly, and felt a pain deep inside as something tensed. She had to blink herself back into the moment, then sat the other side of the WAAF and pulled her upright, before folding the handkerchief and holding it against the gash in the girl's head, having moved her light and messy hair from the wound, and cleaned it the best she could with the tips of the material. She looked around the carriage, then had the girl hold the makeshift bandage before removing her tie and using it to keep the handkerchief in place. The WAAF collapsed into 4 again, being comforted by an officer of her own organisation was obviously enough for the shock to come out in floods of tears. From what Emily could see, it was helping 4, too, giving her somebody to look after. Something else to focus on beyond her own shock.

149

Emily stood after a minute of staring into space, processing what had happened, and moved to slump down beside 18, sitting between the seats with her back to the carriage wall. She looked at the dead young woman she'd come to think of as a friend. A woman who, she quickly realised, didn't even have a name that she knew. Just 18. The person that sat on the eighteenth chair in the briefing on the first night in Scotland. The woman whose confidence never waned, and who always had a smart comment to lift spirits when things got hard. The woman whose heart was cut apart by flying shrapnel. She reached over and took 18's hand. It was cool, and sooty, and gritty, but it didn't matter. Emily held it tight, pulling it into her lap and staring directly forward, out of the compartment and across the corridor, and out through the gaps in the train's side into the darkness of night.

Chapter 11

Hello...

The two days of leave in London weren't what had been hoped for when they'd excitedly boarded the train south, having survived the wilds of Scotland, and throwing themselves out of aeroplanes in Manchester. Both 18 and 4 were going to go home, after a night on the town with Emily to celebrate being back in reality. The world had turned, though, and when they finally pulled into London the next morning, Emily suggested 4 go home and spend some time with her family. There were light protests, but neither fancied celebrating much, and 4 was quickly on her way.

Blankets and cocoa had been distributed by the Guard to keep the passengers warm in the now ventilated carriage, and he'd offered to get some of the surviving soldiers to help move 18 in with the rest of the dead, but Emily declined. Choosing to stay with her friend where she'd fallen, holding her hand through the night. The next morning, while the others in the compartment slept, Emily took 18's envelope from her bag, the sealed one that everyone leaving the training course had received, with strict instructions not to open them until they reached London, and put it with her own. Then, she checked the bag further and found her dead friend's identity. Second Officer Caroline Makepeace, Women's Royal Naval Service, aged twenty six. It felt strange that 18 had a name, despite the concept being perfectly normal, and Emily got lost in all the conversations they'd had. She wondered if her friend would have been a Carol, or a Caroline, or even a Carrie, and whether she had a boyfriend, and what her parents were like. She'd spent more than a month with her, talking every day, being friends, and she didn't know a thing about her.

When the bodies were collected from the train in London, and Emily had seen Caroline Makepeace carried away on a stretcher, having made sure the attending doctor had her name for his records, she'd found herself a hotel, where she'd bathed, and scrubbed, and washed herself clean of the dirt and smoke, and the blood that had found its way into her nail beds. Then, she took herself into London to find food, and to go shopping for any treats she could get her hands on. Letting go of her usual restraint, driven by a need to live, even for a moment, for Caroline if nobody else. When she was full to bursting, and swimming with tea, the exhaustion finally hit her, and it was all she could do to fall into a taxi and make her way back to the quite respectable and pleasant hotel. She took off her uniform, with the newly sewn on parachute wings above the left chest pocked, and fell into bed, where she tossed and turned her way uncomfortably through the nightmares as her mind worked its way through all that had happened on the train journey south. All the celebration, all the excitement, snuffed out in a moment. Caroline had talked to her at some point during her tortured dreams, while they were sitting on the floor of the compartment and holding hands. She'd thanked Emily for sitting with her after she'd died, and talked about her excitement at going somewhere different. She'd been chatting away quite happily while Emily sat staring, frowning, not able to work out what was happening until it was too late, and she woke again gasping and sweating.

"Ah, Ensign Strachan," the Colonel looked up from his desk as Emily closed the door of the ornate, dark wood panelled office that flickered with a roaring fire, while a cool late winter light passed through the leaded windows and mixed with the amber glow of the green shaded banker's lamp standing over the documents he was scribbling on. "Do come in and take a seat." She saluted formally, and got a nod and half smile in return as he gestured to the chair a little way in front of his desk. Not close enough to be overly comfortable, far enough away to make the person sitting in it feel a little vulnerable and isolated. Another test, she assumed. She'd travelled by train that morning, leaving London for Southampton, then being collected by a car that brought her to the New Forest, and the stateliest of all mansions so far, and up the almost polished gravel drive, with the driver depositing her at the large, ornate, and opulent entrance hall. "You found us without any bother?"

"Yes, Sir. The driver was waiting for me at the train station." She resisted the urge to frown at the question. She found them because she was taken there, it wasn't exactly a choice. Her sealed envelope had contained her orders, telling her where to report, when, and even what time train to catch. Every movement had been orchestrated for her, and she was in no doubt that she was still as much along for the ride as she had been since the first meeting with the RAF recruitment officer.

"Good! We're a little out in the sticks, so to speak. So, how was London?"

"Cold and grey, Sir. Thank you." She felt herself being less inclined to play games, and the firm nurse was rising to the surface quite unintentionally. She'd put up with the charade, but something about seeing Caroline dead on the train had got deep inside her. Her friend from the Wrens had also played the games, keeping up the pretence right to the last, and died without having a clue what it was all for. Emily had dressed the blisters on her feet, and cleaned the sores on her shoulders and back from her equipment, she'd seen how much she'd suffered, and all so she could die on a train in Birmingham, without the first idea of what all of her suffering and hard work had been for.

"Quite..." He gave her a slight frown as he tried to work her out. "Anyway, you're here now. That's what's important." She simply gave him the slightest nod, choosing not to say anything, which seemed to make him squirm a little. "OK, well, I won't beat around the bush." He picked up the buff file and leafed through it. "I have your report here from Scotland and Manchester." He glanced at her, but her expression didn't change from the firmly neutral she'd had since getting to London. "Quiet, yet engaged. Intelligent, supportive, but always in the background, never immediately noticeable in a crowd. Hard working, no complaining that was heard, and not shy to step forward when difficult situations demand..." He looked her in the eyes as she gave the slightest twitch of feeling. All the tests, all the observations, and now it seemed she was ready for the reckoning. "Good French, with a decent and helpful regional accent, articulate and very aware, always composed, and apparently well thought of by contemporaries, despite being sometimes strong minded. Physically strong and determined, and potentially lethal." The last words made him smirk, and her frown. "The senior instructing officer has rated

153

you highly, supported by the psychologist and medical officer. It seems you passed, well done."

"Thank you, Sir." The frown had gone from her face as she returned to neutral and composed.

"Hmmm," he sighed. "Usually, such feedback would get at least a smile." She didn't react. "Are you not at least a little intrigued as to what it is you've passed? You've been hard at it with hardly a break since the New Year."

"I'm sure you'll tell me, Sir. If I need to know." She pulled her shoulders back just a little as she talked. It was a deliberate move, designed to show her resistance, and that despite the nice things he was saying, she was bristling, something intensified by the 'strong minded' comment that had slipped into the report amongst the praise. A back handed complement if ever there was one.

"OK, Ensign Strachan. OK… Can we be candid with each other?" She tilted her head slightly. "No tests, no games."

"Very well, Sir. What should we be candid about?"

"Setting Europe ablaze…" He dropped her file on his desk and leant forward, resting on his elbows as he looked her in the eyes.

"Sir?" Her frown returned as she tried to work out what he was saying.

"Midway through last year, the Prime Minister issued instructions for an organisation called the Special Operations Executive to be formed, with the express purpose of taking the war to the Germans in Europe. Specifically, to set Europe ablaze, his words, and we'd like you to join us." Her eyes opened wide, quite unintentionally, and he smiled in reply. "You'll forgive all the secrecy, and the games of course, but we have to make sure we don't reveal ourselves fully, not until we're sure we've found the right type of person."

"And what is the right type of person?" she asked quite automatically.

154

"Somebody that's resourceful and determined, relentless even, and smart enough to do what needs to be done in the most difficult of situations. Join us, and you'll be putting yourself firmly in harm's way. Somewhere that a sharp mind and a sharp knife are the only things that'll keep you alive."

"Yes," she said without pause. Her heart racing, the resonance having returned to her chest, vibrating deep inside her. "What do I need to do?"

"Just sign on the dotted line…" he pushed the file over to her, and held out his pen. She stood and walked over to the desk, not bothering to shuffle her chair, then quickly flicked through her file, and the comments on her performances in training, before stopping at the cover page. Her name, her details. Seconded to the SOE from the First Aid Nursing Yeomanry. She signed to volunteer, and then signed the Official Secrets act, before handing him the pen. There were a hundred and one competing thoughts fighting for attention, and it was a fight to push them all to the back of her mind while she tried to stay composed, and listen to what she was being told. "Welcome aboard." He stood and offered his hand, which she shook firmly before returning to her chair at his gesture to do so. "Everyone here is a volunteer, and we're all here to do a job. There's a chain of command, as you'd expect, but we're otherwise quite easy going. As long as you do your job, everything will go smoothly."

"And what is my job, Sir. Exactly…?"

"For the time being, more training, I'm afraid. You've already done the basics, but from now on things will be much more specialised. You'll learn how to recruit and train agents of your own, how to sabotage machines that shut down entire factories, even how to blow up train lines. We're going to train you to set Europe ablaze, just as the PM instructed, and when you're ready, that's where we're going to send you." Her heart squeezed tight at his words, and it was becoming difficult to keep herself composed. There were stories, and guesses, right throughout the course, but nobody had been close, and she couldn't have even imagined what it was she was training for. The closest anyone had got was parachuting behind enemy lines to rescue downed pilots, or being wireless operators in the desert. Sabotage? Blowing up trains? It was all a little too much. She'd wanted to do something to make a difference, to fight, and she'd just been recruited to do exactly that. "I'll have somebody take you to your room so you can get settled in, and then you can take it easy for the rest of the day and absorb your surroundings." He gave her a warm smile that she half returned. "While we don't expect you to continue with your full anonymity, we expect you to be sensible, and we say this to both men and women, so don't be offended, but don't be getting involved with anyone here, it won't do anyone any favours." She nodded firmly; the very idea hadn't even occurred to her. "And if we're being brutally honest, I wouldn't recommend you make any friends, either..." He fixed her in his stare until she nodded. "Good. Breakfast is at seven each morning, dinner seven each evening. You'll be fed and watered throughout, and you'll be briefed at the end of each day as to what you need to prepare for the following. We expect people to be grownups here. We don't want to shout and ball, it's not the Guards Depot, and if we find that people don't do what we're asking, they'll be removed from here as quickly as they were in Scotland, or parachute school for that matter. Do your job, and we'll do ours." She nodded again. "Right, that's about it for now, unless there are any questions?"

"Just the one, Sir?"

"Yes?"

"What would have happened if I'd said no to joining?"

"Then you'd have gone to the cooler."

"The what?" Her frown returned.

"The cooler. Think of it as a type of holiday camp, of sorts, where those who get injured or don't make the grade go to forget about everything we put them through. It's a little more difficult from this point on, I suppose, because you actually know what we're doing, so if you're removed from now, you'll be sent to other duties within the organisation. However, you should know that the document you've just signed covers a quite enhanced version of the Official Secrets Act, which leads me to the final, and most important point. Specifically, that should you tell anyone outside of our organisation what we do, or even that you're a member, you will be shot for treason, or hung, depending how we're feeling about the circumstances of your disclosure. While you're one of us, you'll wear your regular First Aid Nursing Yeomanry uniform, and should anyone ask, you're a nurse trained to parachute into remote areas to rescue downed and wounded pilots, understood?" His warmth turned to ice, somehow without him even changing his expression, and she felt a chill run down her spine.

"Understood..." she replied equally as coldly.

"In that case, welcome once again. You can get yourself a cup of tea when you're settled in, the main Mess is here in the house, and there's always a hot drink available." The warmth returned to him, and the room, as quickly as it had left. There was something deeply sinister about him.

"There is just one other thing," Emily said as she stood and straightened her uniform.

"Yes?"

"Caroline Makepeace." She handed him the envelope she'd taken from her friend's bag on the train. "Number 18 on the training course in Scotland... The train south from Manchester was bombed in an air raid, and she was killed by shrapnel. I made sure the doctor had her name, and removed the envelope."

"I see..." He frowned as he took it and thought for a moment. "We hadn't heard."

"She had her service identity papers in her bag, and I made sure the doctor who collected her body at Euston Station had her name, so I imagine her unit will have been informed. Or the Navy, at the very least." He nodded and gave her a forced smile. "I didn't think you'd want the envelope with her positing details in anyone else's hands."

"Thank you. I appreciate your collecting it for us... May I ask, were you friends?"

"We were numbers." She shrugged coldly, while feeling a flicker inside as she remembered sitting and holding Caroline's hand.

"Quite... I'm sorry either way."

The following weeks were much different to Scotland. The mansion was known as the finishing school, somewhere that the finer points of the work to come was refined. There was a hierarchy, and there was discipline, but not the shouting and barking kind. Instead, the students were expected to moderate themselves. Keep their uniforms clean and smart, and their accommodation, and apply themselves in every aspect of their training. There was still a chance that they could fail the course, but only if they couldn't make the standard with coaching and training, instead of the stark do it or fail from the start of the process. There weren't any parades, or inspections, the focus remaining on developing the skills being taught instead. There were trips to factories in Southampton, where they were shown machinery and how to sabotage it, and they spent a lot of time on the railway sidings crawling about under locomotives being serviced or repaired, or blowing up stretches of disused track with explosives, something that got Emily's heart racing every time. There were also softer skills to learn, talking to people, manipulating them, even, or building and operating printing presses. It was fascinating, and Emily's mind was filled with the many new and exciting processes every day, something she thoroughly enjoyed. The manipulation was difficult for her. It wasn't her style. She'd always been direct, a straight talker with no ambiguity, and despite being able to play games with language as she had when talking about Paris with the Captain up in Scotland, immersing herself in direct manipulation and subterfuge took a lot of effort. Along with all of the new skills, they continued to practice and refine the old. The fighting, shooting, and knife work. It all seemed so much easier, in a way, now she knew why she was learning it, and despite having had no specific army training before Scotland, she took to the drills they did in the woods with ease, running, shooting, attacking, and defending, and quite enjoying herself at times. The whole training course was exhilarating, and when she looked back more, even the hardships of Scotland had been positive, in a way, and she'd quite enjoyed throwing herself out of a perfectly serviceable aeroplane in Manchester. As the weeks wore on, she recognised how far removed she'd become from the Emily who'd trained as a nurse, or even the version of her that had been a housewife. She was always determined, and always professional, but now, instead of wound care and bed baths, she could silence a sentry twice her size with just her bare hands, and use a knife like she'd been born with it in her hand. She didn't think that much, beyond the training. She wrote to Harriet, though she wasn't able to say much other than that she was having some new adventures, and she wrote to her parents, telling them how much she was enjoying life in the First Aid Nursing Yeomanry, letting them imagine the organisation's name was even remotely related to what she was doing. Other than that, she spent her evenings with 4, who'd arrived shortly before her, and introduced herself, finally, as Eve Chambers. They got on well, and Emily found Eve's company warming, and safe somehow. She was a little younger than Emily, a school teacher before the war, specialising in all aspects of mathematics. She had a remarkable skill of being able to break any situation down into its component numbers, and use numbers to solve any problem, even when numbers weren't obviously involved. She was logical, and methodical, very similar to Emily, but she also had a mischievous side, and could put Emily well at ease and have her laughing with little effort. They could talk about most subjects, and often would on an evening, either by the roaring fire in the sometimes rowdy Mess or, if things were getting a little too loud and boisterous, they'd go back to the room they shared and sit talking for hours. Eve had been something new for Emily. She'd been quite isolated when she was young, having come from quite a small place on the west coast of Scotland. She had friends, but they weren't close. Then, in nurse school she got on with other student nurses, but they were all so busy with their training that there wasn't really that much opportunity to be social. Being a little reserved hadn't helped, and it was as much of a surprise to her as anyone else that she'd ended up married after a whirlwind fling with a dashing young officer who'd taken an interest in her. Though she hadn't really needed to talk that much right from the day they'd met, he'd talked enough for both of

159

them. The only other person she'd really felt a connection to was Harriet, and that was equally as whirlwind, though in a different way. She'd gone from a corpse to a larger than life young woman who tipped full vases of flowers over Senior Sister's heads in annoyance and frustration. A firecracker, or so the Matron had called her, and once she was awake and alive, she was a handful just desperate to get back to her squadron, and get back into the fight. She could make Emily laugh, and talking with Eve reminded her of their days on the south coast. Days that were gone in a flash when Harriet was sent home to convalesce in Yorkshire as the heavy casualties started flooding the hospital from the beaches at Dunkirk. The only thing that Emily and Eve didn't discuss, not even skirting around the edges of the subject, was Caroline. They'd both been there and seen what had happened, and neither was keen to think more on it than they needed to. Back in Kent, Harriet had told Emily that on the squadron the pilots just closed ranks and kept moving forward when they lost somebody. They didn't dwell on it, they just accepted that people would die in war, and to think on it too much, or talk about them all the time, risked destabilising themselves and others. They needed to be sharp, and looking forward, no matter how they may feel inside, and it was a philosophy that Emily had chosen to adopt. As a nurse, she'd already developed what some, her husband included, had called a cold edge. She could be dispassionate about death, it was as much a part of life as anything else, and she'd been told on day one of nursing school to detach herself from it for similar reasons as those mentioned by Harriet. She felt it, of course, regardless of the training, but it was kept inside so she could do her job. It was the same with Caroline. She'd had more than a few nightmares about seeing her friend torn apart by the bomb shrapnel, as she had Mrs Jennings in London, but she knew she would never have got through the finishing school had she let the thoughts into her conscious mind.

Chapter 12

You again...

"I thought I recognised you..." a familiar voice echoed in Emily's mind as she stood at the bar of the busy West End nightclub she'd found herself in, a place that had got increasingly noisy as the evening progressed, and even at that late hour was still bustling and ramping up as the dance band tempted more and more service personnel and their dates onto the dancefloor, in between trips to the bar. The course had been stood down after the students passed their final schemes, espionage missions that gave them the opportunity to put all of their training into practice, and everyone on it had made their way straight into London for two days leave. The nightclub had been recommended, and in an attempt to appear sociable, Emily and Eve had agreed to go along, despite them both preferring the idea of a quiet pub somewhere. It had been a fun night, though, much more fun than they'd expected, and being female officers dressed in their uniforms, they were targets of flirting, propositions, and a lot of free drinks. A group of RAF fighter pilots had adopted them for the evening, keeping them safe from advances while plying them with top class champagne that seemed to flow endlessly. She'd gone to the bar to get some water. The table was swimming with fizz, but she had a thirst for something to dilute the alcohol, and hopefully ward off a hangover the following morning. She didn't really drink that much, though on the occasions she had, she'd always felt a little delicate the following day at least. She turned and looked at the young faced, dark haired WAAF officer who'd appeared next to her, taking a moment to get her champagne addled mind to think and process.

"You're..." A smile started to turn up the corners of her mouth, and her dimples started to crease as she recognised the young woman from Scotland.

"3... Or, now we're in the real world of London, Section Officer Hermione Jones, Women's Auxiliary Air Force." She stood smartly to attention and nodded her head formally, then let herself smile as she offered her hand.

161

"I can't believe it's you... Or that you're here!" Emily blurted, quite unlike herself. She smiled and shook Hermione's hand firmly. "How?"

"I work over at the Air Ministry, and a few of us come down here at times. It's a nice club, generally frequented by officers, and as such off limits to the type that like to brawl and lower the tone." She smiled as she talked, her big brown eyes wide and full of life and excitement. "What about you?"

"Oh, nothing as exciting as the Air Ministry, I'm afraid. If you'll believe it, I was trained to be dropped into the wilds by parachute to help injured aircrew who crash on their way home, and keep them alive until an ambulance can get to them, or that's the theory, at least." She rolled her eyes at the parachute wings on her uniform. "Apparently, it was the best use of my skills, being a nurse and all... It explains all the marching around the back end of Scotland, I suppose..."

"Nothing exciting?" Hermione's eyes widened further. "That's an incredible job!"

"It would be, but I'm not convinced it actually exists! Most of my time is spent driving an old army officer who looks and sounds like he last saw action at Waterloo." She let herself laugh as she spun the line she'd been briefed on before being allowed to leave the finishing school grounds. Driving was a job many First Aid Nursing Yeomanry volunteers had been assigned to, and the smart, uniformed young women could often be seen driving officers and civil servants around. It was also a job that was suitably safe and quite unexciting to most, enough for them not to ask questions. "The Air Ministry, though. That must be something. Right at the heart of the war. You must be so proud to be doing that?"

"I fell on my feet, I suppose. Which is the opposite to what happened up in Scotland when I fell off them and dislocated my ankle!"

162

"Ouch!" Emily frowned at the thought, and for a moment cast her mind back to the miserable weather of the final assessment day.

"You could say that! I was coming down a hill and making good time, then bang! One second of not paying attention, and one foot on a wet stone, and that was it. The game was up."

"Are you OK now?"

"Fine. It gets a bit sore every now and then when it's cold and damp, but otherwise you wouldn't even know."

"I'm happy to know that, and to know you're OK. It was odd not getting to say goodbye."

"Yes... You got through without any problems?"

"Apparently, and I now have all the skills I needed to protect whoever I'm driving from German paratroopers, so here I am. Driving the aforementioned old warhorse, having not even had a sniff of a parachute. I'm not sure he even does anything, if I'm honest. Just has tea with friends, lunch sometimes, and the occasional dinner, and I get to polish the car while he does."

"You don't even get to have a cup of tea?"

"Rarely. Salute, hold the door open, look smart, and do the driving. They're my orders. And beat up any German paratroopers that should drop in, obviously." They both laughed. "Still, it's nice to do my bit." She smiled warmly, then took the ordered jug of water from the barman, and poured herself a long glass that she tried not to gulp down.

"On the hard stuff, I see?"

"I like to keep a clear head."

"Even on a night off in London's West End?" She laughed, and Emily smiled.

"Would you like some?" Emily frowned at herself for forgetting her manners. I can get you a glass?"

"No. No, thank you… If I'm in a place like this, the water can wait." She waved at the barman "gin, please." She turned back to Emily "Are you sure I can't entice you?"

"The water's fine, thank you." Emily raised the glass and smiled, then took a deep mouthful before topping it up again. She glanced back to her table and saw the officers laughing and drinking, but couldn't see Eve amongst them, and when she turned back to Hermione, she was standing and looking around the dance floor while sipping her gin, staring intently as she watched the dancers as though she was looking for someone. "Are you with somebody?"

"Not yet…" Hermione smiled. "I was just looking for my friends from the office. They said they'd meet me here, but I can't see them anywhere." She frowned as she went back to looking around the dance floor, and then the tables and booths. "Do you have the time?"

"Just after eleven," Emily replied after checking the nurse's fob watch she kept under the flap of her left breast pocket. Her parents had bought her it as a graduation gift when she'd qualified as a nurse. It wasn't new, but it was Swiss. One of the best, and they'd searched high and low to get her something not just useful, but also pretty special. She frowned for a moment at the time. She and Eve had booked a hotel room for the night, and had talked about a meal, a few drinks, and then relaxing, and neither of them had expected to be out late.

"Oh…" Hermione sighed a little as her shoulders slumped noticeably.

"Is everything OK?"

"Yes. I just. Well, they said they'd be here from ten, and I can't see them anywhere." There was a sadness in her eyes as she looked around, then glanced at Emily before turning back to the bar. "Not to worry… They probably told me the wrong place." She gave a forced smile, then drank her gin. Emily's heart squeezed a little as she watched her friend, another friend whose name she'd only just learned after knowing them and going through hell with them. Hermione was obviously deflated. She'd always been the quieter of the three women Emily had met in Scotland, though that had led her to work hard to pull everyone together, and get people through difficult times. Caroline had been full of confidence, and Eve was mind bogglingly smart. Hermione had made it work, however. She wasn't the leader out front, but she found ways of picking others up almost unnoticed.

"Maybe they were here, but got their timings wrong and left already?"

"Maybe…" Hermione smiled.

"Look, I wasn't staying late, but you're welcome to join us?" She smiled warmly as Hermione's eyes widened again, and a hint of happiness found its way back in. "Besides, there's somebody you might want to say hello to." She raised an eyebrow mischievously when she noticed Eve had returned to the group. "Come on, we're with a group of RAF pilots who order champagne like it's water, you're going to regret not taking me up on a glass of the real stuff." She held out her hand in the direction of the table, and Hermione nodded and grinned.

Hermione was quickly welcomed to the party, and champagne was poured by the pilots while she and Eve caught up like long lost friends. Nobody mentioned Scotland, just the war, and their current jobs. Hermione seemed in awe of Emily's driving, and Eve's equally as made up status of being a recruiting officer signing up new WAAF volunteers, while professing to be bored with her seemingly endless paperwork at the Air Ministry. It was a conversation that was soon swallowed by the swing band that was suddenly much louder than it had been, and Eve was dragged off to dance by one of the pilots who'd been smiling shyly at her for most of the evening. Hermione was taken next, and then Emily, despite her protests, and they were all stuck among what felt like hundreds of sweaty bodies dancing and laughing as the night rumbled onwards with an increasing crescendo.

"Have you seen Eve?" Emily asked sometime later as she returned to the table, having done a circuit of the club looking for her friend. They'd been dancing with hardly a break for over an hour, and only when Emily insisted that the numerous pilots who'd queued up to dance with her, all having taken turns with the three women, let her go to the bathroom, that she realised she hadn't seen Eve for quite some time.

"Ah…" Hermione replied with a slightly embarrassed look as Emily took a seat and sipped on some water.

"Ah, what?"

"I saw her with that tall Canadian pilot some time ago, they looked like they were heading outside… She said to tell you she'd see you tomorrow?"

"Oh…" Emily sat back as she suddenly felt a little deflated, and couldn't immediately put her finger on why. Whatever it was, though, the twinge in her solar plexus, but with a difference, made her feel awkward, as did the frown she knew she had on her face. "I didn't see her." She forced a smile, while hoping the frown was easing.

"Are you OK?" It was Hermione's turn to frown as she looked Emily in the eyes after glancing around to see that none of the pilots were heading back to them, and confirming they were all still on the dance floor, cutting in with women from all over, with some getting hard looks from their dates. "Really, I mean?"

"What? Yes! Yes, of course," Emily shook her head and let a more genuine smile come into her face while she suppressed the uneasy feeling. "I just expected her to let me know she was going outside, that's all."

166

"Maybe she was just a little swept up in the moment." Hermione poured some champagne into a glass and passed it to Emily. "You know how it can be. Champagne, handsome pilots. What's a girl going to do?"

"Quite." Emily smiled again and then took a sip of the bubbles.

"Oh well, her loss. Shall we have another dance?"

"I actually think I'm going to get off… It's been a long week, and I'm almost asleep on my feet. I think I've probably had a bit too much champagne on top of being tired." She put the glass down, then picked up her water. The excitement had gone, and all she could think of was getting out of her uniform, and into her bed.

"It is late, I suppose…"

"This place will probably keep going all night. Besides, they don't seem to be slowing down any." She nodded at the dancing pilots. "You should probably prepare yourself for a night of champagne."

"Actually, I was thinking that I'm about done, too. Where are you staying?"

"In a little hotel not far from here."

"Come on, then." She finished her drink, then stood and straightened her uniform. Emily looked up at her, eyes widening a little. "I'll walk with you. I'm back on duty tomorrow, anyway. We'd better get going before they come back and catch us, or we'll be here all night." She looked over to the dance floor half suspiciously, half comedically, and Emily felt herself laugh. She finished her water, then stood, and the two of them quickly made their way to the exit, collecting their hats and greatcoats on the way out. "That red haired one had eyes for you…"

"Which one?" Emily frowned.

"The little one with the red hair. The last one you danced with."

"I'm quite sure he was blond."

"More red."

"Either way, he can make eyes all he wants." She pulled her collar up against the cool night air as their shoes clicked in the darkness of the blackout.

"Not interested?"

"Not interested…"

"Somebody waiting loyally at home?"

"A cup of cocoa at the hotel, if I'm lucky."

"All those pilots, and all that champagne, and here we are running through the dark streets of London so you can get to bed with a cup of cocoa…" Emily fired her a look, and got a big, mischievous smile in return, melting the fierceness a little.

"I did say you could've stayed…"

"I'm teasing, and I'm sorry. I really do have to be at work in the morning, though it's been so nice seeing you again after Scotland. I didn't think we'd even bump into each other again, and it felt wrong not being able to say goodbye."

"Yes…" Emily thought of the last night, when she'd marched to the foot of the sunshine mountain and sat in the tent eating roast venison. Hermione hadn't made it, and she felt exactly the same sentiment. After all they'd been through, they didn't get to say goodbye. "It was odd to think that you'd just gone." Her mind flickered to Caroline for a moment, and how she hadn't got to say goodbye to her, either.

"What about that other girl, the Wren?" she asked, as though she'd read Emily's mind. 18, wasn't it?"

"It was…"

"Have you heard from her?"

"No." The word fell out of her mouth with much more sharpness and force she'd expected. "I mean, I only just bumped into Eve recently, and didn't imagine you'd turn up."

"Yes, it's quite a coincidence, isn't it? It's like we were meant to bump into each other again." Emily smiled at her as they walked. She had a sweet way about her, an innocence almost, she'd had it since they'd met, yet somehow blended it perfectly with knowing the right thing to say and do almost all of the time. "You know… There's a little place not far from here where they put proper whisky in the coca, and serve it with fresh baked bread and real salted butter."

"That's quite a combination," Emily laughed.

"I'm serious. It's the type of place you can only go to if they know you… The bread's made fresh, and it's always warm. Thick, white, and chewy, and the butter half melts into it… It's pure indulgence. You order a cocoa with whisky, and the bread comes free."

"And what about the rationing?"

"Like I said, it's the type of place you can only go if they know you…"

"It sounds like they know you…" she laughed.

"Want to find out?" She raised an eyebrow mischievously.

"Find out…?"

"You said you were heading back to your hotel for a cocoa. Why don't we go and have a special one and some fresh bread? It'll soak up some of that champagne, if we're lucky. Besides, it'll be nice to catch up some more. I've missed you." Emily's head tilted a little and she felt herself smiling. "I mean, not in a weird way, or anything. I just kind of thought we got on. In Scotland, I mean?" Emily found herself nodding. She had the following day off, she and Eve had planned to go and see a matinee show, but with Eve disappearing with a pilot, that was no longer guaranteed, so a sleep in could be a possibility. "Is that a yes?"

"I thought you had work in the morning?"

"We're at war. A bomb could drop on us tonight, and it'd all be over. May as well have special cocoa with a friend while we can, right?"

"Right…" Emily laughed. "Just the one, though. I really have drunk enough already. You're sure they'll let us in?"

"I know them, it'll be fine. Come on." She took Emily's hand, and pulled her along the street in an excited run that made Emily feel like she was a young schoolgirl truanting school, and filled her with an unexpected excitement. They giggled as they ran, and cut down an alley that led them to a street off the main road, away from the big building facades.

"Are you sure you know where you're going?" Emily laughed, after they turned a few corners.

"Positive, we're not far," came the reply. "There, where that van is." She pointed down the street to an old baker's van that looked like it had seen better days, and there was a faint hint of baking bread in the air, at least Emily had convinced herself as much, and instantly she had to fight a rumble in her tummy as her mouth started to water at the thought of the thick, chewy bread. Whether it was the dancing, or the drinking, she couldn't be sure, all she knew was that she'd do almost anything to get her hands on the bread. The night had been a rollercoaster. The high of the dancing, followed by the unexpected

170

low of Eve disappearing off, and then the even less expected pleasant conversation with Hermione, and the promise of fresh bread and whisky tinged cocoa. There was a brief moment where she thought of Eve, and hoped she was OK, but the bread took over again.

A large, shadowy figure stepped from behind the van as they passed, and stood facing them on the pavement. Whoever it was raised their hand, palm forward suggesting they stop, and the women slowed their pace. Emily frowned, wondering if it was somebody from the secret place she was being taken. The hand was then clenched, and a finger pointed, and a dull thud echoed through her head as something hard, but not solid, hit across the base of her skull with a sickening, deep slap, and a second later she was stumbling, then crashing to her hands and knees. Her ears rang like a bomb had exploded, and she shook her head while trying to focus as she looked forward to see Hermione turn and stare at her wide eyed. The shadowy figure swung, and Hermione took a hit to the back of the head and crashed down almost facing Emily, her eyes wide with shock and fear as the shadowy figure that had hit her leaned over and pulled a hessian sack over her terrified face. Emily reached for her, hardly able to focus through her blurred eyes, and then her senses were filled with the smell of damp hessian as a bag covered her face and loose grains of sand shot up her nostrils and into her mouth. Before she could do anything about it, her hands were being tied roughly behind her back. A rope pulled the coarse, sandy bag into her mouth, almost choking her as she tried to scream, and then a hard punch to her right kidney made her almost vomit and choke simultaneously as she tried to kick her way free.

"Schnell!" a man's voice whispered. "Hol sie in den Wagen!" Emily's mind was spinning. She could hardly concentrate, the pain in the back of her head was somehow subtle, yet debilitating at the same time, and her senses were being overwhelmed by the unexpected assault. She was close to choking as she fought for breath, and she couldn't see a thing. Her heart raced as fast as her mind as she tried to work out what was going on. The words, the voice. It was German, she was sure of it. They'd been taught German every day of their training at the finishing school, and despite not getting everything, she quickly worked out 'quick' and 'in the wagon'. She tried again to wriggle to her knees, and received another punch in the kidney, before being dragged up by her shoulders in a way that sent a searing pain through her chest and neck from how her wrists were tied. Through the ringing in her ears, she heard a muffled, desperate scream, and then the dull thud of punches, and some barely audible sobs. Then, she was dragged into the van, the doorframe hitting her knee before she was thrown face down to the hard, wooden floor. She fought hard to breathe, feeling her chest tighten as her shoulders pulled back, then there was a thud as something landed heavily next to her, making her freeze in terror. The door slammed, and she heard a gasping, rasping sob as the engine roared into life. She writhed desperately as the van started to move. She could feel her head throbbing, and her senses dulling as her chest stretched, and she realised she was in danger of suffocating. With shortening, panicked breaths, she was able to roll and release the pressure on her chest, while feeling the tension pull hard at her muscles, sending pain shooting from her shoulders into her neck. She wriggled more, and gasped, and moved towards what she assumed was Hemione, then rolled and felt for her with her bound hands, finding that her friend was laid face down, too. It took effort, and a hard, painful fight that sent pain into the centre of her brain, but she was able to use her body to help Hermione roll on her side, then pushed up against her. She wasn't sure why she moved close, maybe to reassure her terrified friend, maybe to reassure herself. She got close and lay still, feeling Hermione's trembling warmth, while starting to notice the violent shaking taking over her own body. Everything shook with a mixture of pain and fear as her head swam through waves of intense dizziness and nausea, making her worry that she'd vomit into her mouth, and then choke on it thanks to the rope pulled tight, straining her jaw, and tied around the back of her head.

It felt like both hours and seconds until the van finally stopped and fell silent. Emily had passed out more times than she could remember, before being brought around again by the searing pain, each time thinking through what had happened, and then filling with intense dread before passing out again. The doors were opened, and she was dragged out of the van. Held up between two people, she half walked, was half dragged along what felt like gravel, until an unusual yet familiar sound cut through the still ringing noise in her ears. Waves. Water. It wasn't gravel, it was the pebbles by the sea, and no sooner had she worked it out, she was picked up and bundled into what she could only imagine from the smell and movement to be a boat. Her heart had raced almost out of control from the moment she'd been hit, and each waking moment since, she'd tried to make sense of it all, but kept coming up with blanks. It was the most scared she'd been in her life, and despite all she'd drank at the nightclub, she'd never been more sober.

She was loaded onto another vessel of some sort, one with an engine that vibrated her to the core, and locked in a tiny metal compartment that bobbed and rumbled endlessly, before finally she was transferred to another vehicle after so long she'd lost track of time, and then left on the cold, concrete floor of a freezing chamber that echoed with every heartbeat. All she knew at that point was that she was scared, she'd been around numerous Germans, and she was alone. She'd exhaled, then held her breath to listen, time and time again, but there were no sobs, no sighs, not even a hint of Hermione being close. Hour after hour, she rolled to relieve the pressure on her hips, shoulders, and neck, while trying not to terrify herself further with imagined fates.

Her body had almost seized when she was finally dragged to her feet. Her muscles were rigid, and the cold from the concrete floor had seeped deep into her bones, making every movement agony as she was walked from her chamber and into a room smelling of cigarette smoke mixed with something she couldn't quite put her finger on. She let out a gasp as the pain in her neck released like a rubber band snapping as her wrists were untied, then more pain followed as she tried to move her arms in front of her. The light was brilliant and blinding when the bag was finally removed from her head, and she gasped for smoke tinged air as the rope came out of her mouth, while her jaw sent pains shooting into her temples. She blinked and looked around, and her heart almost stopped seeing German soldiers either side of her, holding the ropes and bag, then her eyes opened wide as she looked forward to see an officer sitting behind the desk wearing the black uniform of the Gestapo, the German secret police. She recognised it from her training at the finishing school. The skulls, the leather belt and cross strap, the pistol holster, the red armband with white circle and a black swastika. He was right from the pages of the books they'd been shown when learning about uniforms, and a glance to the soldiers either side showed them to be military police, in their field grey uniforms with coal scuttle helmets, and solid metal gorgets on chains around their necks. It was all so real. So very real. Yet she was in London, or had been. How could she be with the Gestapo? Her heart and mind continued to spin in unison as the officer looked her up and down, and she remembered the boat, and the van.

"Good evening," the officer said in accented, yet reasonably good English. He smiled at her while waving the military police away. She didn't reply, just stared at him and frowned a little, trying to work him out while simultaneously trying to get some moisture into her mouth that had dried with fear, and was still itchy with grains of sand from the bag. "You can hear me ok, yes?" She half nodded in reply, while still glancing around her. The room was stark concrete without any windows, and nothing much else other than the desk with some buff files and an ashtray. "Good. My name is Maier." She half nodded again in reply. "Is it not customary to introduce yourself in England?" He took a drag of his cigarette, before blowing the smoke in her direction. She looked around once more, trying to make sense of the situation, then looked behind to see the grey metal door, closed and flanked by the two military police soldiers armed with submachine guns. He looked past her at the sentries and garbled something in German, then let out a sigh before looking back to her. "My English is good, is it not? I studied in England for two years, and despite my accent, most found they could understand me quite well." She just looked at him, while trying to control the shaking she felt vibrating from her core. Shaking that was beyond the cold from the concrete floor. "No?" His voice was almost fatherly, jovial and teasing a little. She looked at him for a moment, he was in his forties, or so she estimated, with brown hair that was greying at the sides, and piercing blue eyes that seemed a little close together behind his round rimmed glasses. His face was soft looking, and his smile a little crooked. "That's OK, I'll talk for us both. For now, at least. He smiled as he stood and lit another cigarette before walking slowly around his desk. "Would you like one?" He offered her the cigarette, and she shook her head slightly, no more than a twitch. He shrugged and blew out a cloud of smoke. "No, you don't smoke." He picked up the folder from his desk and glanced through it briefly, seemingly reading while tilting his head as though he was getting into a good novel, and sighing a little excitedly. "You are Ensign Emily Strachan, of the British espionage organisation called the Special Operations Executive. A spy and saboteur, trained to come here to France and infiltrate the authorities on behalf of your government." Emily frowned while fighting hard not to recoil too obviously as a whole new wave of nausea struck deep inside her stomach. "Oh, don't be surprised, Emily. We've been watching you for quite a while. We watched you leave your big house in the New Forest, and we watched you while you were in London." He paced a little while smoking and reading more. "Unfortunately, what your handlers have failed to tell you, is that we've been on to their plans for some time. We've been watching since last year, and picking up people like you long before you even got started." He let out a laugh, as though he was talking about something particularly ridiculous. "Honestly, I feel sorry for you, Emily. You and all those that came before, and will no doubt come after. They don't tell you anything, just fill your minds with romantic ideas of taking the war to the enemy, while conveniently forgetting to tell you that the vast majority of those they train fall into our hands long before their first operation, and those that do get as far as France under their own steam are met by our well prepared welcoming committees. It's horrible, Emily. Sacrifice, no more. Performative theatre, all so Mister Churchill can tell fairy stories to your people, and say that the British are still fighting. Meanwhile, your cities are bombed, your families starved, and your armies in North Africa are defeated." He sighed again while dragging on his cigarette. "Would you care for some coffee, if not a cigarette? It's good quality, French roast beans. We even have cream, if you'd like some with it?" She half frowned, half winced, while trying to process what was happening. He looked behind her at one of the guards and barked what she understood to be a coffee order, and the door behind her opened and closed. He turned back to her and put his hand on her shoulder, making her flinch nervously, which got a warm, fatherly smile from him again. "It's OK, Emily. It's OK, I know it's a lot to take in, and I know it'll all be quite difficult to believe. Especially after all you've been through. Yet here you are in Calais. I know your name, I know about your training, and I know about the lies you've been fed. You may wrestle with the truth in your mind, and what your superiors taught you will try to overwhelm common sense, but you'll feel it in here." He tapped her on the top of her chest. "Your heart will know."

He paced again and took another drag on his cigarette while reading the file. "Would you like to know, Emily, how I can convince you that I'm telling you the truth?" He smiled again as she stood shaking while his words rattled around her tired and aching mind. "I'll tell you... Why are you here?" She half shook her head again in reply. "You're here because you were recruited. Why were you recruited? This is the important part, so pay attention..." He leaned forward and lowered his voice as though he was telling her a bedtime story. "You were recruited, Emily, because they're quite desperate..." He raised his eyebrows for a moment while looking her in the eyes. "How many on your course? Twenty? Thirty? How many people do you imagine they'd be able to send to France at once without us being suspicious? Thirty people all arriving at the same time, you may as well send a platoon of soldiers. Ridiculous. No, they needed thirty of you because maybe only two or three will get here. Only two or three, because we pick up the rest." He sighed and shook his head, then went back to pacing. "Nobody needs thirty spies, Emily. What they need is one or two, and enough of a supporting cast to manage the ten to one failure rate." The door opened behind her, then slammed again, making her jump. His eyes lit up as a small silver tray with a coffee pot and two cups was placed on the desk by the guard. "Ah, coffee." He smiled as he went over to the pot. "I'll pour you one and let it cool a little while we talk." He busied himself as though he was preparing dinner at home. "You see, Emily. Your government are more than a little desperate. Churchill himself is desperate. That's not to say they're desperate for recruiting you personally, of course. I'm sure you have many wonderful skills, and my words aren't a commentary on you. Just a system designed to lie to young boys and girls, with a hope that somebody gets through." He sipped the coffee and sighed contently. "So... Here you are. You and your little friend, the most recent travellers on what your masters call the 'Berlin Express'. London to the Kent coast in two hours, and then just thirty kilometres across the Channel in one of our fast torpedo boats. Then, well, that depends on you... The Berlin part is something of a misnomer, something else your grand paymasters got wrong. Some of you go on to Berlin, some... Don't." He gave her a very different type of smile, more forced and uncomfortable. "Generally, Berlin is better than your body being washed up at the foot of those famous white cliffs of Dover, which is where we usually tend to send the returned goods. Personally, I'm not convinced on the necessity of such pantomime.

We know that the sight of the bodies of the most recent recruits turning up on the beaches doesn't deter your government. They simply bury them in unmarked graves, and send their families a telegram saying they're missing in France. It doesn't exactly deter them from recruiting more, and sending them over here, as your presence testifies." He shook his head while frowning as though the whole business genuinely saddened him. "You don't even know that we offered terms, do you?" He sipped his coffee while looking into Emily's eyes again. "Herr Hitler offered a truce last autumn. Your Royal Air Force put up a stronger fight than anyone expected, nobody's denying that, and the Luftwaffe were given a bloody nose, and our invasion was postponed. Hitler recognised this, and not only offered a truce, but gave his word that for as long as Britain kept their end of the bargain, we'd be at peace. He even said you could keep your empire, and go on as before. We'd both go on about our business, and not bother each other. There were even trade offers, if you'd believe it?" He became much more animated as he talked, as his annoyance and frustrations boiled over. "You don't know any of this, of course, how could you? All we get is Churchill's drunk speeches, while the Americans try to talk him into seeing sense. Meanwhile, sheep like you are recruited by the wolves, taught French, and how to fire a gun, then sent out to slaughter." He shook his head and let out an angry groan while Emily's head spun, and she tried to make sense of what he was saying. "How about that coffee?" he finally asked as he turned to her again, his smile returning. She shook her head and looked down. "Very well, Emily. Perhaps later." He barked his orders in German, some of which she worked out, and the sentries appeared at her side. Heavy metal manacles were put on her wrists and ankles, the cold metal nipping tight against her skin. "Think about what I said. About Berlin. We'll have coffee later." He gave the guards a nod, and heavy hands grabbed her by the shoulders, and she was taken from the room and out into the corridor that somehow felt so warm it was hard not to feel overwhelmed by it.

Chapter 13

Breaking

She'd lost count of the hours sometime after being taken back to the cold cell she'd started in, having had an introduction to the Gestapo that had left her mind spinning as she tried to piece together everything that had happened. He'd been so casual, yet so precise in the way he'd talked to her, though he hadn't actually asked anything. Just told her what he already knew, before putting her in chains and sending her back to the cell that had become something so different to the cold and echoing prison she'd started in when bound and blindfolded. Instead of darkness, the world was a brilliant white that felt like a railway spike had been driven through the top of her head and deep into her brain after several hours. The walls, the ceiling, even the concrete floor, they were all painted bright white, lit by a pair of dazzling white spotlights that were recessed above her, bathing the cell in a glare so bright it was like being caught in a searchlight beam. It had been reassuring at first, being able to see around herself, and know she was alone. Then, as time went on, her head started to hurt, her eyes bulged, and she lost her ability to count. She buried her head in the corner to hide from the light, but it was pervasive, and her neck would eventually stiffen, forcing her to move. All the while, the lights buzzed behind the glass that diffused them, while at the same time somehow magnifying the blazing light. It was enough to exhaust her already tired mind as she thought on a loop about what he'd said. About how easy it had been to pick her up. About how the British government were recruiting hordes of volunteers in the hope that at least a handful would get as far as France. She was a nurse, after all. What were they doing sending her of all people?

It felt like days had passed when the metal bolt on the outside of the door was dragged open with a clang that made her jump. The light had been on continuously, with no sound in the thick walled cell except the buzzing of the lights, and her shivered breathing as the cold sunk deep into her bones, chilling her so much she had to move, and march around her cell, her heavy chains scraping and jangling as she did laps while watching her breath. The sentry barked at her in German while waving his hand, and she shuffled out into the dimly lit corridor, where the heat hit her like a wall, making her frozen skin and muscles itch as they reacted to the warmth while she shuffled with one guard ahead, one behind, along corridors she could hardly see through her strained eyes, until finally she was deposited in front of Maier, who was sitting reading a ratty looking board backed book.

"Ensign Strachan, would you like coffee?" he asked warmly as he read, not looking up from his reclined position behind his desk, his boots balanced on it as his eyes twitched intently at the page in front of him. He barked at the sentry, not taking his eyes from the book, or waiting for Emily to reply, just leaving her to glance around as her eyes struggled to focus. "The best of all possible worlds... Ha!" He snapped the book closed and threw it on the desk quite jovially. "Voltaire's Candide, have you read it?" His eyes were excited, and his smile twitching and spreading, like he'd just discovered gold. "The young protagonist, Candide, keeps saying that he is in the best of possible worlds, while all the time life gets more and more difficult. As though God himself is trying to say that his optimism is misplaced." He laughed again, then shook his head as if to try and move on from what had clearly entertained him. "The chateau where I live has a very well stocked library, the previous owner was obviously quite well read. Fortunately, I have good French!" He shuffled the papers on his desk, and picked up what looked like the buff file from their last conversation and leafed through it, muttering to himself as he read. "This, however, is less enjoyable..." He read intently for a moment, then let out a sigh as he put it on his desk. "So..." He stood, slapping his thighs as he did, then walked around the desk and stood in front of Emily. "Now we have been introduced, and you've had some time to rest and consider your position, we must, as you English say, get down to business." He frowned a little uncomfortably. "You've no doubt heard stories of the Gestapo. Many of your forebears had. Always they talk of psychopaths. Monsters who take pleasure in their work, but this is not true. I'm just a policeman with a job to do. I'd much rather stop spies and assassins from killing people the easy way, with a bit of conversation over coffee and a cigarette, not the other things people talk of, the stories. People always focus on the stories, not the routine, the run of the mill. The conversation." He shrugged and smiled as the door opened, and the smell of coffee wafted into the room. A coffee pot, cups, and a jug of cream were put on his desk by

179

a young woman dressed in the field grey of the German army, while the door closed. He said something to her, his words rolling fast, and she replied equally as fast, being quite short and curt. He nodded, and she stepped behind the desk, taking a seat and pulling out a pencil and paper. "I hate taking notes while I work," he explained. "I find it breaks the conversation, it's inauthentic. You know?" Emily just looked in reply. "Anyway, now she's here, we can begin." He rubbed his hands together almost gleefully. "Before we start, it's important for you to know that I simply do not care about your mission, your friends, or even your loyalty to your country. I won't ask about them, and you won't betray them. There's no need to make you a traitor that could be punished. Your government have already done enough to you, and we shouldn't give them excuse to do more. No, all I want is some details. A few names. You tell me what you know, and you go to Berlin, where you'll see out the war in a low security military prison. You'll need to be a prisoner, of course, so your side know that we see you as the enemy, but on the inside, you'll have all the comforts of home. Better, in fact. Those there have wine and cheese from France, and fresh bread every day. Better rations than in London, but then we can afford it, we control all of Europe!" He smiled at her warmly. "Anyway, I'll get to it so we can both get on. I have books to read; you have bread and cheese to eat. So, the woman who recruits spies in London. Who is she?" Emily looked him in the eyes, as she had so often when he talked, trying to read him in some way. He stared back, then talked over his shoulder in German before being handed a piece of paper and pencil. He scribbled, then held it in front of Emily's face. 'Who is the woman who recruits spies in London?' He nodded as she read. "In case you cannot hear me." She just looked, remaining silent. She knew exactly who he was asking after. She could see her as clear as day from their meeting at The Savoy. "This is why there are stories!" he sighed in frustration. "You know what I must do, don't you?" He paced a little while looking at her. "Just tell me. What harm can it do to have a name? We've literally picked up hundreds like you since last year. Hundreds sent to their death by that woman, and you won't even give us a name?" Emily just stared. She wasn't sure she could speak even if she wanted to. Inside she was filled with terror and pain. She hadn't said anything since she'd groaned when hit on the back of the head when she was taken. "Please, Emily. I don't have time for games. Everyone talks. Every single one of you who has stood there before me has talked, some sooner, some later, but everyone talks. I don't like the stories, you should know, or what's in them, but if you leave me no choice…" his voice lowered as he stepped so close she could smell the tobacco on his breath as he whispered in her ear. "Write it on the paper, fold it in half, and put it in the book. Nobody will know, and I promise you'll be on your way to Berlin." He stepped back and looked her up and down, before barking in German and then looking her in the eyes. "Think about what is coming!" He said to her sternly, then gave her the slightest wink as the female soldier joined him in heading for the door. Emily watched over her shoulder as they left along with the sentries, closing the door and leaving her all alone.

She looked around, still trembling as her sore eyes focused, part from the cold, part from the fear. Thinking had become difficult after hours in her illuminated cell. She'd tried to process all that had happened, but the light, the buzzing, the tiredness, and the fear conspired to make holding a train of thought any more than a few seconds quite difficult. She'd thought of all the training in Scotland, all the fighting, and how none of it had been a scrap of use to her. She'd been incapacitated the second she was hit on the back of her head, right at the base of her skull where it meets the neck. It had dulled her senses immediately, and sent her straight to her knees. Before she knew what was going on, she was bound and choking on sand. The same thought came to her as had done every time she'd thought of the attack. Her ringing ears and blurred vision, and still seeing Hermione's panicked face as she screamed. They'd been close in the van and the boat, but that was it, she hadn't seen her since. The horror in her eyes had somehow cut through the blurriness and looked deep into Emily's soul, and she just couldn't get past that image each time she thought of London. She shook her head to try and let it go, then stepped forward and looked at the desk. The pencil was the same French brand she'd used years ago in Paris, and the notepaper was headed with Gestapo markings. Next to it was the buff file, which after checking over her shoulder, she quickly opened and looked at. Her heart almost stopped when she saw the Abwehr document listing her name, age, height, and description, along with a photo of her in her uniform, standing outside the mansion. It sent a chill up her spine. They'd been taught about the Abwehr at finishing school, and the Gestapo. The former were considered to be second rate at best, and over reliant on being fed information by informants, but the latter, it was made clear, were brutal. They didn't need informants, they'd get the answers they wanted without them, and often did. The received wisdom was not to fall into their hands in the first place. She quickly closed the file and stepped back to where she'd been standing, looking around still, trying to focus on the grey concrete walls for something, anything, though she didn't know what. She was missing her hospital, she was scared, and cursing herself for not being happy with being a nurse, or even driving staff cars. She'd wanted to do her bit, but she'd never anticipated what was happening. She couldn't imagine what the future would hold, but being abducted in London before she even got started wouldn't have made her top ten guesses. It upset her as much as her fate. The thought of being nothing more than a number, cannon fodder to distract the Germans so somebody else may actually get as far as France, only to be picked up anyway.

She jumped a little, quite unintentionally, when the door opened behind her, and footsteps clicked on the concrete floor. She took a deep breath and waited as Maier and his female assistant returned. He glanced at her briefly with the hint of excitement in his eyes, then looked at the paper. He turned it over a couple of times, just to be sure, then sighed as he looked her in the eyes.

"I'm sorry that you've chosen to take this path," he said with genuine disappointment. "You do understand what you're choosing by not complying? I've made it quite clear that you will talk, and tell me what I want to know?" She looked him in the eyes, and felt her chin rise slightly, confidently, though it hadn't been a conscious movement. "Very well, Miss Strachan. We'll see if we can help you find your tongue." He nodded over her shoulder, and the sentries quickly appeared, standing each side and grabbing her roughly under the armpit and squeezing tight enough for her to let out a silent gasp as they almost lifted her off her feet. "Time to visit the kitchens, I think." He gave a sharp nod, and she was turned and marched to the door. She was about on her tiptoes as she tried to keep up, as the heavy chains that manacled her ankles scraped and rattled on the concrete floor. Her heart raced again, and a ball of nausea tensed deep in her guts, made all the worse by the near sweltering warmth of the corridor she was dragged out into. As they passed through a heavy, metal door

182

at the end of the corridor, the ball of nausea turned into a wave that had her struggling to breathe as the sound of desperate screams filled the next corridor. Gasping, deep, yet high pitched at the same time, and then nothing. Silence. Her eyes were wide open, and focus returned almost instantly as they moved down the corridor, and then the screams started again, gasping, more desperate than the previous time, more urgent, and much louder, followed by muffled crying and babbling, and more intense screams. A river of sweat ran down her spine as they got closer, until finally they stopped outside another heavy, metal door that was painted the same grey as everything else. The cries were coming from inside, and the hairs in the back of her neck stood on end as she heard the distinctly female voice sobbing and pleading breathlessly when Maier opened the door and stepped inside. A fast conversation was had that she couldn't keep up with, and then he reappeared and stood in front of her. "Last chance…?" he half whispered. "I don't want this any more than you, Emily. Please, tell me, so we can both get some rest and avoid this… This unpleasantness." She shook her head, though it was no more than a twitch, and tried to raise it defiantly. "Very well." She was pushed against the corridor wall and held in place by the guards as chains rattled inside the room, entwined with sobs that echoed around the hollow walls. Scraping followed, and a few cries, and a pair of guards appeared through the door, slung between them, being dragged face down, was a mop of messy, soaked brown hair on top of an RAF blue tunic and skirt, with neutral stocking legs trailing along the concrete floor. Emily almost vomited as Hermione raised her head and looked at her briefly, her red and tear filled eyes rolling in her head, her tunic and blouse unfastened and soaked dark. She looked to Maier as Hermione's sobs drifted down the corridor and through the steel door, that cut off the cries and left her in silence when it was closed. He held her stare for a brief moment, but his face was otherwise emotionless, and after a silent pause he gave the guards a nod.

It was all that Emily could do to stay conscious when she was pulled reluctantly into the room, her feet stumbling and legs locking as her body protested beyond her control. The room was as grey and austere as the one she'd left, with a surgical operating table of some sort stood in the centre instead of a desk, and strange implements hung off the walls, some with wires attached, some with chains. Standing by the table was a blond man wearing field grey trousers and smart black boots, and a white vest with the Nazi insignia. He was imposing, bronzed and muscular with ice blue eyes, and veins bulging across his arms and shoulders. He snapped smartly to attention as Maier entered the room, giving the Major a nod before glancing at Emily a little too long. Her mind was spinning with fear, and despite hearing the German words exchanged fluently between them, she'd given up understanding. It was as though her mind was trying to protect her by filtering what was being said, not that it mattered, the guards lifted her and dragged her face up onto the operating table. Leather straps were secured around her arms and legs, in addition to the manacles, and pulled tight, preventing her from moving. Something tested by the guards riving at her roughly before stepping back.

"Hallo, englische Hündin," the blond man said as he stood over her, laughing as he tried to look in her eyes while she desperately tried to look around and see what was happening. "It's time to play some games, ja?"

"One more chance?" Maier offered as he stood the other side of the table and looked down at her. He didn't look happy in any way; his eyes were pleading with her. "Once he starts, he won't stop until you give him much more than what I asked you for. Work with me now, Emily, or he'll make you denounce your own grandmother!" His voice was a half whisper, desperate, raging, demanding. "You saw what happened to your friend!" Emily looked at him, then desperately looked around before closing her eyes tight and shaking her head.

"Good! I don't like it when they give up before we have some fun," the blond said with a malevolent look in his eyes as she looked up at him, her eyes wide with a desperation that grew as he unfastened her tie, then unbuttoned her tunic before starting on her blouse. She writhed with fear as her subconscious took over and tried to get her out of the restraints, which just dug all the deeper with every move and twist. A tug at her shirt had it pulled up and out, with the collars over by her shoulders. She stopped thinking. At least any conscious thoughts. Her mind tried to protect her from what was coming by focusing her on pulling at the restraints, rather that than acknowledge the potential of what would come next. The blond stepped back and gave the guards a nod. They stood either side and put a hand each on her shoulders while the blond pinched her nose hard. As she let out a yelp, a thin, pencil shaped piece of rubber was pushed between her teeth, forced all the way back to her molars and locking her mouth open. Before she could catch her breath, a muslin scarf was pulled over her mouth and nose, and held tightly in place by the guards, pinning her head and stopping her from moving. Her eyes bulged with fear, and her heart nearly exploded out of her chest as a ratchet clunked, and the table tilted, just by a few degrees so her feet were higher than her head, and then the blond stood over her and looked her in the eyes. "It'll be over soon," he said in his strongly accented English. With that, he lifted a black rubber hose and trailed it over her face, letting the slow dribble of ice cold water splash her cheeks and make her blink, before directing it over her nose. It wasn't a powerful blast, it was no more than a trickle at the most, yet as soon as the muslin soaked, water started to drip down her nostrils and made her cough and gasp, and fight to move her head. She couldn't get her tongue to the back of her throat to get it, so she only had the force of air to try and stop it running into her lungs. It dripped slowly at first, and then as the cloth saturated, a small stream ran into the back of her throat and she instantly gagged, retching painfully as she fought to keep the water from her lungs, but each time she coughed it out into her mouth, it met the muslin and rubber pencil and dripped back down, and the air she sucked in took the water into her lungs with it, making her choke desperately. It had only been a few minutes, and already she felt like she was coughing so hard her head was going to explode, and the water was starting to accumulate. In desperation she closed her throat the best she could, when she realised her mouth was filling, and she wasn't able to eject the water. The air in her lungs burned, and her brain screamed, desperate for oxygen, as her mouth filled and the water started to flow over the muslin and down her face and neck. Her eyes bulged as she fought, but it was no use. He just kept the water trickling, and then it happened. She coughed out the remaining air from her lungs, and quickly the water ran into to replace it, slowly drowning her.

The hose quickly moved away, and the muslin and rubber pencil followed, and she instinctively turned her head and lifted it as much as she could as she gasped at the air and coughed the water from her lungs, letting out a deep and unconscious cry of fear as she did. Tears streamed from her eyes, and mixed with the water and spit foaming from her mouth and nose, as the rest of the water drained. She had to force it from her nose between coughs and sobs, and felt it running into her hair. She gasped and breathed deep, and without warning the pencil was pushed back in place, and her head pulled tight to the table with the wet muslin. She tried to shake her head, begging, pleading, but it was no use. She couldn't say anything if she wanted to, and nobody was asking anything. This time, he pushed the hose between her lips and up against the pencil, wiggling it a little so the trickle of water went straight down the back of her throat as the already drenched cloth gave immediately. It wasn't a torrent, but it felt like it, and she was quickly gasping and coughing again, and then quickly choking and drowning after once again holding her breath as long as she could. It was the most terrifying and agonising thing imaginable. She couldn't stop it, she couldn't move, she couldn't do anything except slowly drown until she was all but unconscious. Then, the cloth and gag were removed, and she was left to gasp and cry again as she fought to breathe.

He continued with the drowning again and again, switching between her nose and mouth according to how he felt, sometimes doing the same over and over, just so she couldn't work out a pattern, and sometimes speeding up the flow to a gush that almost drowned her instantly, others slowing to just drips. Each time he took her to the edge of life, and each time she coughed and cried, hearing herself and recognising the same desperation as she'd heard from Hermione. No questions were asked. She was just slowly drowned time after time while Maier smoked, and occasionally shared a few words with the blond. Her mind went after a while, and she was able to think of nothing other than breathing. She vomited up water from her stomach and lungs repeatedly. It came out of her nose, her mouth, and even her eyes, as the water was pumped into her relentlessly.

Finally, after being hit in to solar plexus to force the water from her lungs and stomach when her body had stopped responding and coughing, and she'd just laid drowning and near unresponsive, the restraints were unfastened, and she was rolled onto the hard concrete floor. She half bounced, and lay sobbing and whimpering as her eyes

186

rolled. She was what she'd seen in Hermione. The guards picked her up by her shoulders and dragged her out of the room and back to the brilliant white cell, where she was left face down, unable to move or even think as the dazzling light flooded the room and the buzz fought with the ringing in her ears for prominence. Not a question was asked. No interrogation. Maier didn't even look at her once the torture had started. Instead busying himself with his book, or talking with the blond.

She laid on the floor, unable to move, for hour after hour. Passing out every now and then, before waking thinking she was drowning, and gasping for air. She couldn't think beyond the words he'd put in her mind, about the futility of her recruitment, of her future. Finally, she was collected again, dragged to her feet and steadied, and then helped to walk along the corridor, back to through the door, and back to the desperate screams inside. Hermione was dragged out, and she was taken in, and it all started again. The third time, the involuntary fight saw her weakened body trying to push back, and resist being tied to the table, not that it helped. She even tried to clench her teeth closed, but running the hose straight at her nostrils soon had her coughing and choking, and the pencil and cloth back in place as she went through the torture of drowning once again, nobody asking any questions, just the desperation of fighting near death.

There were no screams or sobbing on her fifth visit. Each time, Hermione had got a little quieter, until it was just gentle crying when the door opened. Their eyes met occasionally, but that was all. Life had become such a cruel routine, and so quickly. She'd be drowned for what felt like hours, until she was close to death, and then deposited in her cell to go through cycles of consciousness for countless hours more, before it all started again. She didn't think, and all she felt was fear and desperation, apart from the fifth time. Maier was waiting for her at the door, his eyes full of something she couldn't place.

"Please, stop this before you join her..." he half whispered under his breath, almost trembling with his own desperation. "Please, this isn't what anyone wants. Just stop this." His eyes pleaded, and then he stepped to one side as she was pulled into the room. Laying against the wall, face up and lifeless, was Hermione. Her eyes, sunken and ringed with redness, stared up at the ceiling, her brown hair soaked and ratty around her shoulders, and her tunic and shirt open and drenched.

"No…" Emily gasped as she felt her knees give way. "No…" She was hit by a wave of nausea as she stared at the body of her young friend, the WAAF officer who'd helped get them all through training with her positivity, and who despite being failed from the course, was still doing her bit and making something of herself. She wasn't what Emily was. She hadn't been to finishing school. Emily herself hadn't learned what she was signing up for until long after leaving Scotland. She knew the risks, and she signed up knowing what could happen if she fell into enemy hands, the finishing school instructors had made it very clear. Hermione, though. She was an administrator working in an office. She'd been taken for no other reason than she'd bumped into Emily in a night club, and invited her for a drink and some good food. She'd done nothing to deserve being tortured, and left for dead on the concrete floor of some cold room in Calais. It was like a knife to Emily's heart, and hurt her more than any of the drowning. She didn't resist as she was pulled up onto the table, she just kept twisting her head to look at Hermione as they secure her arms and legs.

"I'll ask you one last time, Ensign Strachan," Maier said as he looked down at her. "Please, just tell me?" She looked him in the eyes for a moment, then laid her head back and stared up at the ceiling before opening her mouth compliantly and waiting for the rubber pencil. He frowned, then nodded at the blonde, who put the pencil in place before the guards pulled the muslin over her mouth and nose. She didn't struggle, and didn't move. Instead, she just felt a tear run from the corner of her eye as she thought of Hermione, and what was to come. The water started, but instead of fighting it, she just drank down all she could while forcing the air from her lungs and waiting for the inevitable. There were natural convulsions, the type her body was always going to go through as she let the water in, but she didn't fight. She just closed her eyes and tried not to gag as her throat filled with ice cold water, and it started to seep into her lungs. Finally, she closed her eyes as she awaited the moment when her chest would spasm as she lifted from the table and the water went down for the last time. She was ready.

It never came, despite her acceptance of her fate. Instead, the room fell into a darkness filled only with an eerie silence and her gasping coughs as she forced the pencil from her mouth and coughed the water out of her throat and lungs while gasping for air. She rolled onto her side as she coughed, and felt water, vomit, and spit draining from her between deep breaths that chased every last drop from her. It's while rolling that she realised the restraints on her arms had been released, and a kick showed the same for those on her legs. No straps, no chains, nothing. She slowly sat up, dizzy and confused. The only light came from the soft amber glow of the corridor, blinding her sensitive eyes as she sought to work out what was going on. She glanced around while coughing and rubbing the sores on her wrists, then looked at the space against the wall where Hermione had laid. She couldn't see anything, just empty concrete. She couldn't see anything, or anyone, anywhere in the room. She wiped her mouth and nose with the sleeve of her tunic, then rubbed her eyes with the other before looking around again at the deserted room. Her mind, after so long of not being able to think, started to spin. Was it playing tricks on her, or was she dead? A doctor she'd worked with in her nurse training had told her of the peace he'd seen even the most tortured souls experience in the seconds before death. His thoughts were that God takes people at the last moment, when it's certain they're going, to spare them the final suffering, and it was the only reality she could think of. Everyone had gone in an instant. Living and dead. She'd seen it in some of her patients. People who'd lived in agony were suddenly at peace, sometimes even smiling and having moments of great clarity, and able to say a few last words when all they'd managed was groans of pain.

The light flickered and made her squint as she looked to the door and the silhouette that filled it. She watched as it stepped into the room, moving closer in a confident way, gliding almost. She'd heard stories of people coming from the light when somebody died, a friend or family member come to collect them and take them to the other side. She coughed as the water still tickled her lungs, and sniffed at the drips still finding their way out.

"The real test," a well spoken woman's voice said as the silhouette came closer, "the only test that matters, isn't whether we can march for hours over the rainswept highlands, wrestle an adversary to the ground, or even jump out of an aeroplane. It's how we face our end." Emily's eyes focused as the glamorous brunette from The Savoy stopped in front of her and gave the slightest hint of a smile as she stared at Emily. "It's the strength of our minds, the ability to hold on and not break when any normal person would." She stepped closer and pulled a handkerchief from her pocket, which she used to dry Emily's eyes, and wipe around her mouth and nose before handing it to her. "Let's go for a walk. I have something to show you."

"I..."

"Come on, the air can get a bit stale down here after a while, and you could do with seeing some daylight." Her voice was upbeat and confident, as it had been when they'd first met the previous autumn. She held out her hand, and Emily took it after a moment as she slipped off the table, steadying herself against it as she fought to stay upright and not collapse. She nodded, then shuffled beside the brunette as they headed for the door, looking all the time at where Hermione's corpse had laid. They left the room, leaving the cold behind, and stepping into the searing heat again, before turning left and heading to another metal door, which when opened led to carpeted wooden stairs. Her mind was struggling with every step, and she couldn't make sense of anything. Eventually, she was invited into a small, panelled, elevator with a barrier that dropped down instead of a door closing, and then watched as floors passed while it creaked and rattled its way upwards. Finally, they stepped out, and she was shown along yet another corridor and to another metal door, though this one was painted red. The brunette gave her a smile before opening it and stepping to one side, letting Emily feel the fresh air, which she gulped in, still coughing a little as she stepped through and out onto the rooftop. The sky was blue, and the sun was shining, silhouetting the bulging barrage balloons that floated high above. She followed the cable down, then looked across London to Westminster Palace. She struggled, and felt herself overcome with emotion, and had to stand against the terrace wall while she gasped for breath and fought the tears, before dropping to one knee and coughing more.

190

"That's it, get it all out. A few deep breaths of good old London smog will have you back to normal in no time." She stood beside Emily and surveyed the city, patiently looking around and enjoying the view while Emily coughed and fought the tears. "I love the view from up here, and it's always so peaceful. People these days tend to be so caught up in the thought of air raids that I often get the place to myself, which is helpful." She looked down at Emily. "How are you doing down there?" Emily used the handkerchief to dry her eyes and mouth again, as she pulled herself upright. "It's called waterboarding. What happened down there. The Germans use it, though they're not always as restrained. Sometimes, they just go for the tried and tested holding your head under the water in an old bath tub. It gets everyone to the same destination eventually, but it's less refined. It's remarkable how the body will respond to a trickle of water…" She gave Emily a warm smile. "We humans need oxygen, as you well know, being a nurse and all. It's an instinctive process. We breathe because we must, and when we're being drowned, we'll respond just as instinctively. Regardless of what we're thinking, we'll panic, and convulse, and do anything we can to stay alive. At least most of us do…"

"Why…?" Emily gasped as she steadied herself.

"We're planning to send you into harm's way, remember? You were told at the finishing school. If the Germans get you, they'll do everything they can to break you, fair means and foul. It's a game, but not a very nice one. We've lost people… We know. They'll scare, they'll trick, they'll be friends, and they'll be the devil incarnate. They'll do whatever it takes to make you talk, and before we put you in that situation, we have to give you a taste of it, and we have to know you're not going to fold like a wet paper bag, if you'll pardon the expression. Lives depend on it." Emily half nodded in reply, still struggling to find words. "Everyone breaks on the third day, whether it's here or there. That's what we know, and that's what we try to get to in our training. We know then that if somebody's captured while we're out in the field, we have forty eight hours at the most to change everything. To move, to do things differently, to get out of town, so when the third day comes, it has minimal impact.

"I was down there three days...?" Emily asked, her throat rasping, and the cold March air suddenly chilling her more than it had when they'd first stepped out into the sunlight.

"No..." the brunette said firmly, giving her head a slight shake.

"Oh..." Her heart sank a little. She'd been through all that, and didn't make it?

"You lasted five, and in doing so redefined the meaning of stubborn. In fact, look it up in the Oxford dictionary later this year, and there'll simply be a photograph of you." She let herself smile.

"Five?" Emily's stomach squeezed tight. She didn't remember. It had all blurred.

"Five. No food, no sleep, and lots of water, and even then, you still tried to bloody well drown yourself rather than give up the game!" She rolled her eyes. "Stubborn."

"I didn't..." Emily felt her emotions getting the better of her, and a wave of sadness mixed with the fear and happiness and hit her all at once, and had her crying uncharacteristically. She hardly ever cried. She hardly ever let herself feel, but it was all too much.

"So, that's it over," the brunette continued. "Your training, that is. We have some rooms here, with warm water, soft beds, and good food. We'll have your uniform cleaned for you, then we can talk about what's next."

"Next?" Her tummy tensed at the thought of more.

"Getting you to work. You've been in training for months, and it's about time we put it into practice. Come on, straighten your uniform, and hold your head up high. Let's get you rested, then we can talk things through properly." She gave Emily a smile, and got a nod in reply as she straightened and tucked her shirt, then fastened her tie before tidying her collar and tunic. Her uniform was a mess, and so was she. She ran her fingers through her hair, and tried her best to tie it in place, before following the brunette back into the building.

The door was closed, and they took the rickety elevator down a couple of floors, then stepped off into a normal looking corridor. Her heart almost stopped as a door opened, and Maier stepped out of a smoky room with voices chatting away inside.

"Ah, Ensign Strachan. Damned good show back there! Bravo!" He offered his hand, while she tried to get her head around his very English, very well spoken accent. She took his hand, which he shook firmly. "No hard feelings, I hope? All part of the job, I'm afraid. Still, if it helps in the long run, it's all cricket." She simply nodded and half smiled, not sure what to say. "Good luck in the field!" He closed the door, then headed off down the corridor, still in his Gestapo uniform. She watched him as he marched away, humming Elgar to himself in quite an eccentric way.

"How are you feeling?" the brunette asked as Emily got comfortable sitting across the desk in the wood panelled office. She'd been gazing across the room, over the brunette's shoulder and looking out at the blue sky outside, watching the barrage balloon bob around in the distance.

"Fine," Emily eventually replied as she switched her gaze back to the woman at the other side of the desk, and reengaged. "Thank you."

"Have you managed to sleep?"

"Yes…" Emily nodded, with the slightest of frowns. She'd been exhausted when she finally settled in the room she'd been given. It was well appointed, with a soft bed as promised, and a view of the West London streets outside. Her uniform was hung on a hanger and left outside on the door handle, as instructed, and had come back pristine the next day, even her shoes had been polished to a high shine. Washing had been harder than she'd imagined. She'd filled a bath with hot water, and used the rose scented bath oil that had been delivered with the wash kit. It smelled inviting, and covered the scent of cold and damp that seemed to cling to her, but immersing herself in the water had brought the trauma of previous days to the fore of her mind, and it took willpower not to jump straight out, and hide under her bed. The thought that helped the most was going back to the previous year, when she'd helped Harriet with her own demons. The young pilot had told her of how she'd almost burned to death, and drowned, and Emily had spent many hours listening, and talking her through the trauma. It was the strength of seeing Harriet get through her nightmares, and return to herself enough to go home, that kept her in the bath, and had her scrubbing purposefully until she was clean, and then forcing herself to lay back in the bath and feel the water, and the warmth, and let it get into her bones. She knew she had to feel what had happened, and work her way through it if she was to have a chance of getting through it all in a half reasonable way.

Food had been delivered, corned beef sandwiches in thick, chewy white bread with salted butter, and a large pot of tea that tasted better than most. It had warmed her inside as she ate and drank, while listening to the music on the wireless and gazing out of the window at the sky. There'd been times when being tortured, in the moments when she was able to think, that she'd imagined never seeing the sky again. Maier's story had got to her, on reflection. She imagined being drowned on the operating table, and her lifeless body being dumped off the coast of Dover, never having seen her last sunset or sunrise. The food had been the final ingredient her body and mind had needed, and a wave of exhaustion quickly followed the last mouthful, leaving her dizzy and nauseous, and laying on her bed, where she quickly passed out, not waking again until the following day, when she'd sat up with a desperate gasp and looked around the room trying to work out where she was.

"Good. Your uniform looks like new." She gave Emily a half smile, which wasn't returned. "We're going to give you a couple of days leave. Proper leave, this time, no games. We've got what we call a safe house not far from here, in an apartment block controlled by us. The staff there report direct to us, and it's quite safe. Take some time to decompress a little, and try get into London and do some normal things. Shopping, going to the pictures, something like that. Then, report back here two days from now, and we'll talk." Emily looked her in the eyes, her slight frown always present, then gave a nod. "I know that I don't need to remind you, probably less now than ever, but it really is important that you continue to live a double life. You're about to be transferred to Wellington Barracks to teach first aid to new recruits of the First Aid Nursing Yeomanry, at least that's what anyone needs to know. You know the barracks, and the personalities there, so you can fill in the blanks as you need to." Emily nodded again. "Right, that's us. Unless there are any questions?"

"It's not the first time that somebody has told me the tests are over...?" She spoke firmly, her light Scottish twang giving her words a softness with a cutting edge, that somehow made them seem gentle while holding a threat of something dark beyond them.

"It's the first time that I've told you the tests are over, and that's what's important. I recruited you, and for all intents and purposes, I own you for the duration of your stay with us." Her words were casual and pleasant, with the same dark undertone as Emily's. "And should anyone challenge that, it's me they'll answer to." She gave a firm smile. "Beyond the obvious test, of course."

"The obvious test?"

"Doing our job. If we do that, we pass. If we don't, it won't much matter, because we'll be dead." She raised an eyebrow slightly, then picked up the phone on her desk. "Ready when you are." She put it down and gave Emily a smile. "One of the team is going to drop you off at the safe house and get you settled. Save you a walk." She stood and walked around the desk, as Emily stood to meet her. "Welcome to SOE." She offered her hand. "Cat got your tongue?" she asked as Emily's hand fell limp, and her mouth opened in surprise as door opened, and the smart young officer dressed in the uniform of the First Aid Nursing Yeomanry, parachute wings and all, entered the room. "You've met Lieutenant Jones, of course?" Her eyes stared into Emily's soul as she glanced between them. Hermione nodded politely, and gave the faintest smile. "Nine in the morning, two days from now. Make sure she's back here." She added with a nod, then released Emily's hand. "Right, I have a meeting to get to. So, if you want to have your reunion in the car to the safe house, I'd be grateful. Good day…" Emily looked at her and nodded, then followed Hermione from, the room.

"I'm sorry…" Hermione said as she started the engine, having stayed in front of Emily as she led her through the building, that had a mixture of civilians and officers of all ranks and uniforms coming and going. She didn't look at Emily, and Emily didn't look at her, choosing to keep her gaze straight forward. "I went through finishing school in the early autumn of last year, not that it matters that much, though I suppose I can tell you now you've made it through."

"I thought they'd killed you," Emily finally replied, after taking a moment to process what was happening, and consider her words. "It all looked so…"

"It was so…"

"Yet here you are."

"Yes."

"Did they actually do anything to you, or was it all an act?"

"The latter. That time, at least. Back in September last year I got the exact same treatment as you. Dragged off a London backstreet during an air raid, the van driving to Maidstone and back, the round trip to Gravesend in the boat, and three days being drowned in a cellar in central London." She glanced out of the corner of her eyes as Emily did the same. "It's curious it should all happen in the West End, it's where I trained."

"Trained?"

"As an actress, and dancer. It's all I'd ever wanted to be since I was a little girl. Ballet three times a week from the age of four, ballroom from five, contemporary from six, acting on the stage from seven."

"Why are you telling me all this?" Emily finally turned her head to look at Hermione. She could still feel the horror and nausea at seeing her cold, lifeless body on the concrete floor.

"I don't know… Because I can, I suppose. Because I want you to know that it was a job, not a choice."

"You made the choice to do the job."

"Yes… Dancing and singing on stages suddenly felt a little childish when the Germans started bombing us last summer. Especially when they flattened my lodgings, and killed half of my friends. So, I joined up to do my bit."

"I'm sorry… About your friends, I mean." She felt her stomach turn a little at the thought. Having been caught in an air raid herself, she could only imagine how terrifying it would have been for her, especially to lose friends in it, as she had Caroline.

"Thank you, me too. They weren't soldiers or anything, and hadn't done anything wrong to anyone. They just danced, and sang, and acted, the same me, yet it didn't stop the Germans killing them just the same. I wanted to do something for them, you know?" She gave Emily a thoughtful frown. "It's why I snapped her hand off when she cornered me in a bar and recruited me to the SOE."

"She?"

"M… The boss. She turned up, sat me down, and told me everything about my life, including about how the Germans had killed my friends, then asked if I wanted a chance to get my own back. A few weeks later, I was in Scotland, climbing up the sunshine mountain, and you know how the rest goes."

"So, you've done Scotland twice?"

"Three times, technically…" She smiled, and Emily found herself raising an eyebrow curiously. "When I got through finishing school, and I'd recovered from Maier's swimming class, I was told I'd be joining the training team as a Conducting Officer. We don't get many women coming through, and they wanted somebody on the course to evaluate those that go through it, so I kind of volunteered. I disappear at the end, and then turn up after finishing school to help them try and break people. Apparently, I was born for the West End, or so M tells me. I certainly can't escape the place, so it seems she must be on to something." She pulled the car in next to a new looking apartment block not far from the river, it was in the 'Jazz Moderne' style, with sleek bold lines and big curved windows. "Here we are. You can probably walk it in ten to fifteen minutes, but you've got your bags, so driving's easier."

"Emily Strachan." Emily offered her hand, which Hermione shook firmly, letting herself smile in a way that lit up her face.

"Hermione Jones, it's a pleasure to meet you formally." She gave Emily a key to the front door, after she'd unlocked it. Then, after saying hello to the man behind the desk at the entrance, she led her up two flights of wide, winding stairs to the second floor. "It's a nice enough area, and you've got everything you can possibly need here. Any problems, see whoever's on duty downstairs. They have a direct line to the office, and they're trained in pest control, so you're in safe hands." She winked theatrically, then led Emily into the room. "The tape on the windows takes something from the view, but doesn't ruin it entirely. Better that than glass flying through the air if the bombs come too close." Emily joined her looking out at the Thames. It was grander than she could have imagined. "Though the Luftwaffe hardly hit the West of the city, mostly it's the docks and the East, so you should be fine unless they get lost. If they do, though, there's a bomb shelter in the cellar, you'll be fine."

"Thanks…" Emily nodded.

"There's some tea and bits a pieces in the cupboards, all on the office account, so make yourself at home and don't be polite." She turned and faced Emily. "So, how about a show tonight?" Emily stared back as an unwelcome feeling squeezed her inside. "No games, I promise.

198

I know some of the theatre managers, and can get us tickets. My way of making it up to you."

"You've already said sorry…"

"It'll be like a fresh start?"

"If anyone hits me on the back of the head…"

"No more surprises, I promise. Well, except one." She smiled as Emily frowned. A knock on the door stopped the conversation, and Emily turned to see Eve standing in her uniform and smiling. "She's your neighbour. There, now the surprises are done. Pick you both up at seven?"

Chapter 14

M, For...

"How was your leave?" the woman Hermione had referred to as M asked. She'd never once introduced herself, and didn't seem to be interested in doing so, and Emily hadn't been bothered to ask. She was obviously intelligent, and a master at game playing, and it was assumed that if she wanted Emily to know her name, she'd tell her, and not doing so was deliberate for some reason or another, even if it was just a game she was playing because she could. Though that particular realisation left Emily frowning more than usual, when she realised that she couldn't have given her name to Maier even if she wanted to.

"Good, thank you," Emily replied, being her usual curt self.

"Room in the safe house up to scratch?"

"It's very nice, thank you."

"Good, I'm happy to know it. How was the theatre? Noel Coward has been up and down recently. Some incredible performances, some not so memorable." She looked up from her paperwork. Her face quizzical, innocent even, despite Emily knowing all too well that the puppet master sitting opposite her was likely in the audience too, probably sitting right behind her.

"Oh, it was just nice to get out and do something normal."

"Quite..." M's eyes sparkled a little as she briefly acknowledged Emily's recognition of the game she was playing. "Well, I'm happy you enjoyed it, because you're going to France tonight."

"Excuse me?" Emily's eyes opened wide as the adrenaline started to pump like a tap had been turned on.

"You didn't see that one coming, did you…?" She raised an eyebrow and smirked. "Unfortunately, I'm deadly serious. A situation has come up, and you're needed, so you're going tonight. As soon as you've been briefed, we'll get you kitted out, then you can relax in one of the rooms here until it's time to go." Emily composed herself and nodded. "Have some tea." She poured from the pot that had arrived shortly after Emily. "Our team in Paris, known as the Dancer circuit, has gone quiet. No reports, no check ins, nothing for long enough to make us nervous. We need to find out what's going on, and re establish communications, so you'll be going over to deliver a new wireless and some supplies, and act as a courier once we get things back to normal." She took a sip of her tea, and gestured for Emily to do the same, no doubt sensing that her mouth would have dried out from the shock. "It's what you've trained for. Remember what you've learned over the last few months, and you'll be fine." She gave Emily a sharp nod, which was returned. "We're hoping it's nothing more than a blip, like the wireless has given up, or something equally as mundanely irritating. If it is, you'll make yourself useful while you're there, until we can bring you out again. If it's not, you'll be setting up a new network, and picking up where they left off reporting how things are in occupied Paris, and nurturing Resistance contacts." Emily nodded again as they talked. "Good, you'll go by the field name of Geneviève Marceau while you're there, and your identity number is F13. You won't be going alone, you'll be happy to know, a senior officer will be going along with you to run the show, and they've been briefed on what needs to be done. If things have gone bad, you'll need to be on the wireless until we can get an experienced operator out there, or doing one of the many other tasks you trained for in finishing school, but it's important that you work as a team, understood?"

"Yes…" Emily replied as the tea put some moisture back in her mouth, letting her find her words. Her mind was spinning as she remembered every moment of her training, and wondered whether it was going to be enough. She'd volunteered to go into harm's way, and now it was happening, she didn't know how or what to feel.

"You'll need to write any letters, just in case. You can hand them to me before you go, and should the worst happen, I'll make sure they get to where they need to." Her words were so casual that Emily wondered for a moment how many letters she'd posted. The war had only been really raging for less than a year, but there were thirty people who started her course alone, and there were apparently more courses before she'd even got to Scotland, and it made her think on Maier's theatrics, and just how much of it was based in reality. "Not that we'll need them," she added almost too subtly, like she was reading Emily's mind. "People come and go, it's what we do, but we're in a war and anything can go wrong, so it's best to be safe. You can't give details, of course, just that you were fighting for your country. It's all rather impersonal, I know, but I will have to censor them. It comes with the job." She took another drink of tea just as there was a knock at the door. "Come," she called out, and the Rifles officer from Scotland stepped into the room. "Ah, Captain Farley. Do come in and take a seat." She nodded to the empty chair beside Emily.

"Ma'am," he replied while closing the door, then gave Emily a firm nod as he took his seat. She watched him for a moment, then looked forward.

"Captain Farley will be leading this mission," M continued. "He's been briefed, and if things are as we hope, and the team in situ just need a new wireless, you'll work with them to supplement their mission. If things are worse than that, well, you both know what to do."

"We'll do what needs to be done, Ma'am." He looked at Emily for a moment, as if waiting for her to speak, though no words came. She didn't feel she had anything to say.

"You'll do what you've been ordered to do. Appraise the situation, establish communications, and do what you can to support the restarting of our operation in Paris. We have no information coming out of the city, and can't be left in the dark like this. We need to know what's happening there, what the mood is, and what the Germans are up to…"

"Ma'am." He squared his shoulders.

"Right, we'd better get you both ready. You're both restricted to your rooms until I collect you at six. Dismissed." They both stood and nodded. "Ensign Strachan, I'd like a word if you don't mind," she added as they headed for the door. Farley gave her the briefest smirk before leaving and closing the door behind him, while Emily turned back to the desk, where M was standing, listening, with her index finger pointed into the air.

"There," she said after a minute had passed, and a door clicked closed outside. "Am I going to have a problem?"

"Problem?" Emily asked. "What sort of problem?"

"With him."

"Not from me."

"Your instructors in Scotland would suggest otherwise. He was rude and ignorant to you throughout, apparently, and rather humiliated when you beat him up…"

"If there are any problems, they won't be from me. I assure you."

"Good. He's boorish, and he's arrogant. He's also very experienced. He was cut off behind German lines during the retreat to Dunkirk, and spent time with the Resistance, so he knows how it all works over there. I've no doubt you'll need to bite your tongue at times, but I recommend you do so, you can learn from him. Besides, this mission is bigger than egos. Get the job done, that's all that matters."

"As I said, I'm not your problem."

"Good." Her eyes twinkled as she smiled. "You know, we have a country full of people desperate to do their bit. The army's fighting in North Africa, of course, and the RAF are taking the war to the Germans in Europe, while the Navy continues to rule the waves, for now at least. At the same time, there's a lot of frustration, a lot of people wanting to get their hands dirty. So many that we'd be overwhelmed if we put an advert in the newspaper and recruited conventionally. More than that, I could walk into any infantry barracks you choose, and get a battalion of volunteers overnight. Fighters, with experience and training."

"Are you telling me I can be replaced?"

"The exact opposite… I could go and get them, yet I went and got you. You're here because you have something they don't."

"Yes, I'm a woman."

"Yes. You'll be less conspicuous moving around France, less soldierly, less obvious, but you already know that. The truth is that you're here because you can march across the highlands in the rain, carrying the same as the men, in the same conditions, and the same time. You're here because despite being smaller, and supposedly weaker, you can put experienced infantry officers on their backs in a fight. You're here because after five days of torture, you choose to give your own life rather than talk. You're here because you notice things, because you pay attention to detail. You're determined in ways they don't teach in the army. You're skilled in ways they can't teach. You're smart, and you're lethal." Emily raised her nose a little and bit her tongue to stop herself from blushing. "You're also here because despite being overtly strait laced and formal, according to your file at least, something people could read as making you predictable, you're a meticulous game player."

"I am?"

"You are…"

"How so?"

"You haven't called me Ma'am once since we met. Not even just now when Farley said it half a dozen times in a handful of sentences."

"Three times."

"Proving my point."

"I don't see how."

"You noticed, you counted, you knew. He called me Ma'am, and so did Jones when she collected you to take you to the safe house. Yet you chose not to, despite your training with the First Aid Nursing Yeomanry, who we both know are sticklers for standards." She looked Emily in the eyes, getting nothing in return, not even a flinch. "You may as well have told me about how they put salt in the coffee in Montmartre cafes to take the edge off the sharpness."

"Not all of the cafes…"

"No. Not all of them. Just the one on the corner with a view of the Sacre Cœur from the tables outside on the pavement, where they serve the best croissants on a Sunday morning, as the local artists come to life and prepare to sell their wares." Emily's head tilted just a little. "Ma'am, coffee, Montmartre, it doesn't matter, and has little importance, it's your way of testing those who are testing you, seeing if they're paying as much attention as you are." Her eyes sparkled briefly as they widened for just a second.

"It also brings out the coffee's sweetness and undertones."

"I know… So, no trouble with Farley. Help, support, and keep an eye on things. Let me know how he gets on when you're back?"

"So, that's it?"

"That's what?"

"I'm your spy?"

"You know you're a spy. It's the job we've been training you for."

"I knew I was 'a' spy, I didn't realise I was 'your' spy, too."

205

"Now you do."

"How do you know you can trust me?"

"Because you'd rather drown yourself than give me away to the enemy... Oh, don't worry yourself, I'm not confusing what you did with personal loyalty. I just know that you're loyal to the mission, and the country. That's enough. That, and you refuse to call me Ma'am, just to let me know that despite everything, you know who I am, or maybe what I am." Her dimples showed as her smile softened and tightened at the same time. "Right, better get to your room. Jones will show you the way."

The rest of the day was spent being fitted for civilian clothes, the type worn in France, that had French labels sewn into them, and were tailored to fit as near as possible without looking bespoke. Emily had been given a smart skirt that buttoned up the hip, and had a few stitches here and there pulling small holes closed, some low heeled leather shoes, and a worn blouse and long navy blue wool coat. Everything was nice, and had a quality about it, though with a worn edge. Even her underwear was changed for something much more French, and everything personal that she owned was sealed in an envelope and packed away with her uniform, before being spirited away for storage. She checked the small bag she'd been told she could carry with her, it had spare socks and underwear, and a few small bits of clothing and toiletries, nothing much at all. After the tailor and seamstress had left, another man visited, an eccentric type, older, with a habit of talking to himself. He'd ask her something, then answer before she even got the chance. He'd given her French cigarettes, a half used book of matches from a Parisian bar, and a few other bits and pieces including ration books with torn out pages, bus tickets, and other French paraphernalia. He also gave her identity papers. Geneviève Marceau. Her photo was good, another she didn't know had been taken, though judging by her tiredness in it, she assumed it was sometime while she was in Scotland. He also talked her through her backstory. An orphan whose parents had died of the Spanish Flu in early 1919, leaving her to be looked after by an artist uncle who lived in the Montmartre before dying of alcoholism when she was in her early teens. Left destitute, she travelled France looking for work, picking grapes in Provençal vineyards mostly. Living in bunkhouses, and moving from vineyard to vineyard, picking in the autumn, cutting back in the winter, and doing whatever else she could to earn board between while she saved to study and train as a district nurse. Whoever had written her story had put painstaking effort into it, even listing some of the areas she'd worked, their features, and their customs, while making the most of her nursing background and trying to explain her accent. She committed it to memory, as much as she could.

The final visitor was the Chief of Codes, who at first had her thinking she was being tested again, when he turned up looking all of twelve years old at best, while smoking a cigar that looked taller than him. He was incredibly polite, though, not to mention funny and easy going, and after giving her a new poem that he'd written for her to base her secret codes on, having noticed that she'd struggled with the one she'd first chosen, he soon had her relaxed and going through her coding and decoding signals with ease, refreshing her knowledge from the finishing school in a way that brought codes alive, and actually had her enjoying them. Perhaps the biggest surprise of all.

At eight that evening, having been taken from London in the back of an unwelcome bread van that left from the deliveries loading dock of M's building just off Baker Street, she found herself in a cottage seemingly in the middle of nowhere, and sitting down to the most incredible meal imaginable. Roast beef and Yorkshire puddings, mashed and roast potatoes, glazed carrots, even some sage and onion stuffing. It was a meal fit for a king, or queen; the only downside was that she had to share Farley's company. Fortunately, M had joined them, and managed to weave a gentle and engaging conversation throughout. They were even given sticky toffee pudding and custard for afters, all of which made her eyes bulge from her head. She'd been on rations for such a long time, and the five days without food while being interrogated had left its mark, but the meal had her stomach bulging against the waistband of her trousers, she'd eaten so much. She'd worked out that it was the last supper, and wasn't about to turn it down. It had all been prepared by a pair of RAF Flight Sergeants who seemingly ran the show, making sure the cottage had everything that the guests could need, and that night she slept in a soft bed, for a few hours at least, before being gently knocked up and told it was time.

"Any questions?" M asked as she stood in the shadows of the aircraft hangar that kept them out of the moonlight, and away from the eyes of the ground crew that were busy preparing the Halifax bomber for its flight into darkness. She'd already spent time briefing Farley, before sending him to climb aboard.

"No…" Emily shook her head. She'd thought of everything, and checked everything enough times to drive her to distraction, including the poor homing pigeon hidden in its container, ready to send word of her safe arrival. Despite the nausea and fear raging inside, she wanted to get going, and get it done. All of the waiting had been hard, more so since the reality hit with being woken and driven the short journey to the hangar. "No, I don't think so."

"The training will kick in, just trust the process… Though there's still time to change your mind, if you wish? There are plenty of other ways to serve, and there'd be no shame in telling me that France isn't for you…" She smiled warmly, and Emily nodded.

"I think I'll go, all the same."

"Then you're going to need this." She took Emily's hand and placed a small, rubber pea shaped capsule in her palm.

"What is it?"

"An 'L' pill."

"A what?" She frowned as she rolled the rubber pea between her thumb and forefinger.

"Potassium cyanide. Take it out of the rubber coating, put it between the molars at the back of your mouth, and bite down. It'll slow your heart, before stopping it altogether, and you'll be dead within a minute of taking it with no way of reviving you." Emily's heart almost stopped just at hearing the words. "If you're smart, you'll put it in your hair, wrapped in a braid or bun. They won't stop if they catch you, Emily. I know that we've tried to prepare you for it, but it's not enough, not according to the reports I've read…" She paused for a moment and looked Emily in the eyes, watching her closely, assessing what her mood was. "The men they'll torture all the same. Women, though… They treat women differently. We get something… Extra." Emily nodded nervously while taking a deep breath to try and steady herself. "You're a woman, I don't need to tell you how badly men can behave even on a good day. As a prisoner, however. Well, just take the pill." She forced the most painful of smiles that got Emily nodding again as she pushed the pill into her pocket, then dusted her hands down as though she'd handled something unspeakable. "Though I'd much rather you came back, OK?"

"Yes…" Emily replied with a forced smile. She gripped her hands tight to try and stop them shaking, while breathing as deep as she could without being obvious.

"Here." M pulled a silver flask from her pocket and handed it over. Emily sniffed it, then gulped the whisky and felt it burn its way down. "Keep it," M shook her head as Emily tried to hand it back." It's made of the purest silver; about the best there is, and hallmarked for Paris."

"I couldn't…"

"You're to sell it if things go wrong, and you need the money. It should fetch enough to help get you out of trouble at least…" She half smiled, then quickly corrected herself and continued. "The bomber will drop some stores with you, food, ammunition, wireless parts. Everything you need."

"I know."

"I know you do… " She paused for a moment while looking Emily in the eyes, before giving her head a brief shake. "I won't wish you good luck. Like in the theatre, to do so is considered something of a taboo. So, in SOE tradition, I'll simply say merde alors…" She offered her hand, and they shook for a moment. "You'd better get going, they're going to start the engines any minute."

"Thank you, Ma'am. Goodbye." Emily stood smartly to attention and bowed her head slightly, then turned and marched away to the waiting bomber. She looked back to the shadows, then climbed in the hatch, dragging the weight of her parachute, kitbag, and Sten submachine gun with her, and trying not to get her kit, or the one piece camouflage jump suit she was wearing, caught on the bare metal frame inside the aeroplane. She took her place on the small, padded bench next to Farley, resting back against the fuselage, her knees half bent in front of her to brace in position and stop herself slipping forward under her load. They held a stare for a moment, then he looked out of the hatch as a member of the crew climbed on board and pulled it closed, blocking out the silver glow of the moonlight as the first of the engines rumbled into life, sending vibrations running through the airframe.

The already uncomfortable interior of the Halifax bomber's harsh metal frame became increasingly less pleasant as the flight went on. The whole fuselage seemed to shift every now and then, yawing side to side, and as they progressed, the turbulence became so frequent that it was like being in the back of a van that was being driven fast over a farmer's freshly ploughed field, with the added fun of an occasional sudden drop that had Emily desperately clutching the frame in the darkness to stop herself being thrown about. They'd had a little turbulence on her parachute jump in Manchester, the crew explained it to be a normal part of flying, rough air caused by variances in air pressure, temperature, or movement, or as they explained it afterwards, bumps in the road. Though what they were experiencing in the Halifax was more than she'd expected, and her knuckles were white as she grabbed tight to stop herself being thrown around, as flashes of light lit up the inside of the fuselage, and a sound like that of grit being thrown against the outside rattled above the noise of the engines.

"Sir!" one of the crew shouted in the darkness. Emily could just make out his silhouette as a flash of light illuminated his frame staggering towards them, and grabbing tight to the roof for his own stability. "Sir!" He shouted again as he leaned over Emily and shook Farley.

"What is it?" Farley shouted in reply.

"A storm, Sir, and a bloody big one. The pilot has told me to let you know we're going to have to turn back."

"What?!" Farley's face lit up with fury as a flash of lightning cut through the fuselage.

"We've got to turn back, Sir. It's not safe to keep pushing on."

"No, we bloody well haven't!" Farley dragged himself to his feet and steadied himself in the rocking and bumping fuselage, then pushed the crewman in the direction of the cockpit, following behind and stumbling over Emily's knees, despite her pulling her feet as far under the bench as she could. He gave her a scowl as he staggered off, bowed low in the confined space. Emily watched them go, then flinched as a drop of water landed on her nose, triggering her recent memories of interrogation. She looked up to see more drips slowly showering her shoulders and arms, and another flash of lightning showed they weren't the only ones. She held tight as the bomber bounced and rocked, then dropped so hard her stomach was left in her mouth. She never wanted to get off anything so much in her life, and at the same time, she just wanted to go home and get back to the safety of having her feet on the ground. She'd endured months of hard training, but nothing had prepared her for being stuck in a flimsy metal tube that was being bounced around the sky by a storm that was raging so hard it was raining on the inside of the aeroplane. She had no plan, other than to accept she had no say in what was going on, and being so far out of control made her feel as helpless as when she was strapped to Maier's operating table back in London. "Right, get up!" Farley shouted as he reappeared about ten minutes later. He kicked her boot as he passed.

"Sir, I must protest!" the crewman shouted as he followed close behind. "The pilot is in charge of the aeroplane, and he knows what he's doing. If you jump into a storm, you'll be killed!"

"You get forward and tell the pilot he holds course and puts us exactly where we're supposed to be, just as I told him, or I'll make sure every single one of you is in front of a court martial for cowardice in the face of the enemy! It's only five bloody minutes!" he screamed after turning and grabbing the young crewman's sheepskin flying jacket. "This mission comes all the way from the top, from Churchill himself! We go on, and we jump as planned!" The crewman shook his head before pulling away and leaving. "If I feel the aeroplane moving off course even by a single degree, I'll come up there and shoot the pilot myself, and we'll all go down!" His voice boomed so loud it drowned the engines. "What are you waiting for? I said get up!" He grabbed Emily by the shoulders and pulled her upright. "Get your strop fastened, we're going in about four minutes!" His eyes were fierce and full of rage as he stared at her angrily before heading to the hatch and securing his static line. She watched him fiddling furiously, and then tightening his parachute and kit.

"Sir," the crewman shouted as he returned. "Sir, we've had a message from HQ telling us to return home." Farley spun and looked at him. "Sir, your own CO has told you to stand down and return home! They sent the codeword Piccadilly!"

"Get hooked up!" Farley shouted at Emily, ignoring what he'd been told.

"He just said we've been ordered home!" Emily shouted in reply, while holding onto the frame above her to avoid being thrown right back down again by the intensifying storm outside.

"He's scared, and he's lying!"

"He used the codeword!" Her heart was racing with fear. It was like Farley had gone mad. She'd seen it in patients, especially some of those who'd had it bad at Dunkirk. Too much pressure in the wrong

212

environment, and suddenly it was like a switch had flipped, and they became somebody else. "It's just a storm…" she said as she stepped closer and put a hand on his arm. "We can come back tomorrow night, it's just a storm, that's all." She tried to soften her voice, while still being heard over the noise. Something inside her said he wasn't there, that he was in a battle somewhere, and the darkness and flashes of lightning were triggering something deep inside. "Please, let's just do as we've been ordered. We go back; we come back again tomorrow night." She smiled a little, her eyes pleading in desperate hope she'd get through to him.

"Get. Your. Static. Line. Hooked. Up!" He shouted firmly, his eyes filling with even more rage. "That's an order! "

"No!" She yelled in reply. "You heard the codeword; we've been called back!"

"Bloody women!" His frame expanded as he rose up like an angered bear. "Cowards, the bloody lot of you! I told them in Scotland; I told them in Manchester! Bloody women, scared by a bit of weather!"

"I'm not scared, I'm just not stupid! You jump if you like, I'll join you tomorrow." She stepped back, bumping into the crewman, and briefly looking over her shoulder into his terrified eyes. He gave her a nod and put a hand on her shoulder to stop her falling.

"Get your bloody line hooked up, or you won't be going anywhere!" He pulled his revolver from under his jump suit and put it against her chest, just below her throat. "We follow orders in war, you silly little girl, like it or not! We follow orders, or people get killed!"

"We've had orders to go back!" she replied, her voice breaking a little as she felt the muzzle of his revolver push tight against her.

"What we've had is another bloody woman panicking. She's not here, she's not making the decisions according to what's happening in real time. She's making a decision based on bad information from the pilot. Now, get hooked up before I shoot you for cowardice!" She

213

pulled her shoulders back and pushed herself against the muzzle while looking in his eyes. He'd gone. Broken. She knew that he'd shoot. He'd kill them all if that's what it took. She pushed the revolver muzzle out of the way, and took the strop of her static line in her hand. He nodded and stepped back, letting her secure it to the frame.

"Don't go!" the crewman shouted. "Please, don't go!" She looked at him and shook her head, then forced a smile as Farley pulled the hatch open to reveal the circular hole in the fuselage floor, keeping his revolver aimed at her. "You're a bloody madman!" he continued before heading forward again, as Emily followed Farley's gestures, and sat at the hatch, pushing her legs outside into the blast of wind and rain, that pulled at her so hard it almost dragged her out. A kick to her back was all it took as the green signal light flicked on, and she put her hands each side of the hatch, lifted herself, then dropped out into the night.

The wind hit her like a train, sending her tumbling through the sky as she fought to breathe, for a split second leaving her thinking of being laid on Maier's operating table again, with the hose shoved in her mouth. She felt herself making a noise, grunting almost as she tried to breathe and correct herself. Then, before she knew it, her head was pulled upwards, snapped back as the parachute deployed, and she instinctively reached up to grab the lines and check the canopy, as she'd been trained. It had felt like she was falling and tumbling through the heavy rain for minutes, though in reality, it was only a matter of seconds. A flash of lightning cut through the air above, lighting up the world around her, and she glanced below to see the ground rushing up to meet her at an alarming rate. She'd just got her legs together and bent her knees when a gust of wind collapsed her parachute canopy, and sent her hurting into the ground at a forward tilting angle. She landed half on her knees, and quickly crashed chest first into the ground, knocking the air from her lungs as her head rattled off the ground so hard that she briefly saw stars in her eyes. She gasped for air while simultaneously spitting the grass and mud from her mouth, and fighting the pain in her chest as the parachute billowed and started dragging at her. She quickly pulled herself up to her knees and started reeling in the lines, keeping low as she'd been taught in Manchester to avoid being dragged over. She breathed hard as she pulled the billowing silk down out of the wind, trying to force the air back into her lungs and shake the dizziness from her head.

"Down, you dog!" a voice called out in firm German from behind, and before she could turn to look, a boot landed square between her shoulder blades, knocking her flat on top of her gathered parachute, and pushing her face back into the soaked ground. A knee landed where the boot had kicked, pinning her flat, as a hand grabbed the rubber rim of her helmet and pulled her head back, almost snapping her neck and making her gasp as the cold steel blade of a knife was pushed tight against the side of her throat "Dogs and pigs die the same way in spring!"

"He who fears being defeated…" Emily gasped in French as she searched for the words. Her head was pulled further back, and the steel pushed tighter against her neck. "He who fears being defeated is sure of defeat!" The knife was pulled away, and her helmet released, leaving her to breathe deep and try to stop her whole body trembling.

"Welcome to France, Sport. Come on, we'd better get moving," a soft voice whispered in her ear as a shadow knelt beside her and helped unfasten her parachute harness. "Bring it with you, we could use the silk," the voice added as Emily pulled at the entrenching tool attached to her lower leg. She glanced at the shadowy figure beside her as it stood, pulling her up by the shoulder at the same time. She grabbed the parachute and her bag, and ran through the rain, heading past a raging bonfire that was being extinguished by a pair of flickering silhouettes, and into the trees at the edge of the field. A flash of lightning lit up the tree line as a roar of thunder shook the sky, sending vibrations deep into her chest as she saw more figures in the trees. She was pulled behind a thick trunk as soon as they were out of the open, and dragged downwards, where she squatted facing two others. "It's alright, she's one of us," the voice that had met her whispered, their English accented in a way she couldn't quite place. "She had the pass phrase."

"Are you bloody stupid?" a man asked as he moved close. "Jumping in this weather is suicide, it's a surprise you're not dead!" His accent was very much English. Whispered, yet firm and furious.

"I brought a wireless," she replied, lost for anything else to say. She couldn't agree any more with his point. She was still shaking from what had happened in the bomber, let alone the jump through the storm, and the terror of what waited for her when she'd landed. The whole sequence, from Farley pulling his revolver to her kneeling in a forest in a raging storm had taken five minutes at the most, and she'd almost been killed three times. Once with a bullet, once with a knife, and once by Mother Nature, and her head hadn't stopped spinning.

"Well, why didn't you say? Welcome to France, in that case." He slapped her on the shoulder. "Right, stick to her like glue." He looked to the shadow who'd met her in the field. "We'd better collect the rest of the parachutes we saw coming down, before the local garrison comes looking and finds them." He stood and disappeared into the woods. The shadow tapped her shoulder, and she quickly followed, amazed at how fast the group were moving through the trees without running into one. She slipped and staggered as she followed the shadow. A low whistle stopped them in their tracks, and then another had them changing direction and heading to a clearing, where another shadow was standing by a parachute hanging from a tree. Emily came to a halt and joined the others in looking up. It was Farley. His body hung limp, swinging silently in the wind. The shadowy figure climbed up and cut at the lines, lowering the corpse. "Broken neck…" the man said after checking Farley. "Among other things. Right, get his kit and equipment off, and put his body in the undergrowth." The shadows went into action. "I'm sorry," he said to Emily. "It's cold, I know, but we don't have time for burials, not now. I'll send somebody out tomorrow to look after him properly if I can, but for now we need to get moving. The supplies were dropped all over the place, and we need to collect them before we get out. Low flying bombers tend to pique German attention, even in a storm, and I wouldn't be surprised if they had soldiers on their way already. You understand?" Emily nodded, then looked down at Farley's broken body. His neck was twisted, and collar bones collapsed, and his left shoulder and arm were in the most unnatural position. There was nothing peaceful about him, even in death his face was contorted almost angrily with a broken jaw and cheekbone. He'd come down through the trees, clearly hitting them hard as he did. She didn't like him, and hadn't since they'd first met in Scotland, but despite his breakdown and unstable personality, he was coming to France to do a job. Seeing him dead and broken did her no good. His loss did nobody any good.

Chapter 15

Springtime in Paris

The Spring air was warm, with the occasional hint of sweet tobacco smoke drifting by every now and then, catching Emily in a not too unpleasant way. She didn't smoke, but sometimes, when there was electricity in the air, it had an aroma that almost pleased her. She twitched her nose a few times, taking in the smoke as she sat outside the Parisian cafe swirling what she was told was coffee, while simultaneously watching the young blonde weave through the street beyond, heading towards her. She wasn't particularly tall, but not overly short either, and despite having the soft glow of a hundred summers on her skin, and dusty blonde shoulder length hair that had been tied up into short braids, she somehow blended in perfectly. Her blue skirt sat on the knee, her black lace up shoes with low heels, and her long grey woollen coat that hung open and swung as she walked all helped, the colours were muted, the cut austere, she could have been one of thousands of girls coming and going in Paris. A dog barked angrily somewhere, and a man started shouting back at it in a frustrated and argumentative tone, Emily's eyes darted across the street to the altercation long enough to see the man walking away, gesturing irritably, and by the time her eyes were back on the blonde, she was brushing past a woman carrying a large, unwieldy basket, and stepping to one side to avoid being knocked over.

"Bonjour," the blonde said in a casual yet bright way as she stood in front of Emily's table. "How's the coffee?" she asked. Emily shrugged in reply as the girl took a seat opposite her, waving the waiter over as she sat. "Sometimes, they have the good stuff here, sometimes not. There's so little about, and the Germans tend to drink it all when they come." Her French was flawless Parisian with a local, middle class twang. It was fast, too, delivered with confident frustration at the coffee situation. "Lucien, how are you?" she asked the waiter who came out to see her. He was a tired looking man somewhere in his forties, with eyes that suggested life was one long disappointment.

"I'd be better if the Germans would leave."

218

"Wouldn't we all?" she half sighed, half laughed.

"You'd think so…" He frowned for a moment, then shook his head. "So, Gisele, what can I get you?"

"Do you have good coffee?" she half whispered, looking him firmly in the eyes as she did. She was strikingly beautiful, in a quirky kind of way, with a slow smile and keen light blue eyes. He looked at her for a moment, and then Emily. "This is my friend, Geneviève," she explained without being asked, watching him weigh her up. "She grew up not far from here, but went to live down in the south when she was young."

"You picked your moment to come back," he frowned, and Emily shrugged and smiled in reply. "I'll see what I can do. The Germans take everything, you know this. It'll cost more…"

"Good coffee's worth it. Besides, if we don't drink it, the Germans will, and then what? I'm sure you'd rather a pair of French girls get it before them." Emily couldn't help but smile at her casual directness, making the waiter roll his eyes at her in response.

"No promises." He threw his cloth over his shoulder and marched away purposefully.

"I hope he didn't charge you too much for that ditch water," she said as she nodded at Emily's cup.

"Enough…" she replied.

"It's because they don't know you. Strangers get the stuff they make with pinecones and whatever else they can get their hands on. They often have to serve the Germans with proper coffee, there's trouble otherwise. Though Lucien still waters it down and mixes it with, well, stuff you wouldn't want to drink…" She lowered her voice as her slow smile lit up her face.

"Wait, this isn't that…?" Emily's face gave way to revulsion.

"No," the blonde laughed eventually, quite amused with herself. "No, they save that for special guests." Emily frowned, then pushed the miserable brown water away anyway, while letting herself smile a little in reply. Tilly, the young blonde, was the circuit's courier, and she'd been tasked with bringing Emily up to speed. Showing her around Paris, getting her used to the city, and spending time with her, talking often so she could get used to conversing, thinking, and even dreaming in French, while at the same time introducing her to some of the tricks of the trade, refinements of what she'd been taught in the finishing school. Those like using a distraction to cover a hand off, as had happened when the dog barked at the man. It was only because she knew what was going on that Emily was able to shift her eyes fast enough to catch the woman with the basket dropping something into Tilly's hand as they nudged. It was lightning fast, seamless, and only noticeable to somebody who was watching for exactly that. "Here we go, the good stuff. None of the added extras." She gave Emily a mischievous wink as the coffee was delivered, each with a small, narrow slice of crusty baguette.

They'd been introduced properly the day after Emily's arrival. It was Tilly, she'd soon found out, that she had to thank for the boot between her shoulders when she'd landed in her parachute, and the knife against her throat. For somebody so young and innocent looking, the young woman had a strength about her, and she was very handy with a weapon. Something Emily learned more about in the days they'd spent in the safe house outside Paris, where they'd waited to be sent into the city for Emily's local training. Tilly was an Australian with a spirit for adventure, and while she could be quiet and contemplative, once Emily had been around for a while she'd let down her guard and talked more, sometimes excitedly, especially about Paris. A place she'd always wanted to visit, having grown up with stories about it from her grandma who'd lived there as a girl. It was her who'd taught Tilly French, and insisted she learned to the highest standard, refusing to talk to her in English right from her first words.

Tilly had been through finishing school late the previous year, and arrived in France sometime before Christmas, and she knew the city like she'd lived there since her grandmother's time. Every corner, every alley, it was like she had a map in her head that charted the places even native Parisians didn't know. She said she'd always been the same with directions. Rarely needed a compass to find her way, even in Australia's Outback, and at night when there weren't even the sun or stars to follow, she just knew where to go, and wandering around Paris was like wandering around a childhood home. For Emily, it was a little different. She recognised a few places, but there was much that looked the same, especially when they strayed away from the centre she'd visited as a girl. An apartment block was just an apartment block, and if she didn't have a river, or monument, or grand boulevard to draw reference to, it could all be a blur, not that it bothered Tilly. She just skipped along giving Emily tips and pointers to landmarks others wouldn't always think of as the most obvious. A tree with branches that hung a certain way, a street lamp in front of a red door, a boulevard with barricade marks from the Revolution. Her mind was sharp, her eyes keen, and her imagination flowed freely. She taught Emily what few could, and within a couple of weeks, Emily got around Paris without too many wrong turns.

Emily was also introduced to her job in what she was told was the Dancer circuit, the codename for the SOE network operating in Paris. It involved working with Tilly as a courier to collect information from here and there, and pass it to John, the network's organiser, who ran the show, who in turn would vet and analyse it before sending it on to London, which often involved another courier mission to deliver it to the wireless operator, Etienne, before bringing back the replies. John was calm, content, and unflappable, and he didn't stand on ceremony. His briefing to her was simple, to forget any scrap of military behaviour, and act like a normal person. Slouch, keep hands in pockets, no pretensions, no hierarchy, everyone just did their job, though ultimately, hierarchy or not, everyone knew that his decision was final. Etienne had stepped in to operate the wireless when their previous operator, somebody they didn't even name, and barely even mentioned, fell into the hands of the very real, and apparently very active, Gestapo. The wireless had gone with them, and there had been no other way to get word out of Paris and back to England before Emily arrived with a new one, some supplies, and a willing volunteer to join the cause.

221

That evening, Emily and Tilly sat at the wide open windows of the attic room of the safe house they were staying in, watching the sun set over the city, and enjoying the last of the day's warmth as the breeze brought the chill of the night. It was peaceful, and despite the nerves Emily had felt walking the streets for the first few days, she was able to relax and enjoy the calm, even smiling to herself as the accordion played at a bar down the street, its music drifting on the wind. Knowing she was in German occupied France had made her more nervous even than falling into Maier's hands. It was very real, and the Germans were everywhere. Any minute, something could go wrong. They could be followed, they could make a mistake, or a contact could betray them. The slightest little thing could lead to a visit to the real Gestapo cells, with no trips to a London rooftop afterwards. Tilly had drilled the finishing school training into Emily, how to check behind her without even looking, how to notice people noticing, how to change direction casually, while looking for watching eyes. The training in England had been first class, but there was no substitute for the real thing, and Emily had quickly grown very grateful for her young friend's patience and knowledge. "You're doing alright, you know," Tilly said, pulling Emily's gaze to her from the street outside. "You'd hardly know you weren't a local."

"Hardly?" Emily frowned in response, picking up on the detail, not the compliment, while once again being reminded that a lifetime of near obsession over detail had become an asset in the game she was now playing. Something that hadn't always been the case in life. Her parents had got used to her, and would sigh when she'd pick apart the details of stories they told her, and it was something which infuriated her husband at times. In France, however, it was a trait that seemed to serve her well.

"Yeah, you're close enough to fool any German, that goes without saying."

"But…?" She could feel the frown deepening on her face as she waited. She'd practiced her French over and over, focusing on the finest detail, and being as relaxed in demeanour as she ever had.

"Well, like I told you when you first got here, you still sound like an English girl speaking French."

"Nonsense!" Emily replied dismissively, rolling her eyes and shaking her head simultaneously. She'd been told on the first day, casually, which is why she'd practiced her French so much since. "I've worked on my accent, it's hardly perceptible."

"Look, I'm not being funny or anything, and your accent is fine. Quite rural, and from the south, which fits with your cover story. You just need to be more… Human."

"More human? What am I, some sort of automaton like in that film, Metropolis?" She raised an eyebrow enquiringly, while giving Tilly a firm look, something that got a giggle from her young friend in reply, and had done since she'd first responded to her needling and teasing. Despite having the strength of a bull, and the coldness to put a blade to Emily's throat as she laid in a rain soaked French field having fallen through a storm in her parachute, Tilly was remarkably laid back and easy going, and other than operational security, she didn't take much seriously. She was almost the opposite to Emily's firm and considered presence, and sometimes austere personality, able to relax and sleep just about anywhere, and laugh at most things, including Emily's attempted fierceness, which creased her up with the giggles in a way that made the tip of her short nose twitch like a rabbit's, and subsequently had Emily's composure easing as she smiled. She was like a little sister of sorts. Young, teasing, and easy going. The one who skipped through life in the wake of elder siblings, letting them learn the hard way.

"Here we go, whinging pom time…" Tilly sighed through her giggle. "Seriously, what I mean is, your French is a little too good. It's a compliment, if anything."

"A compliment? I'm a cold and heartless robot who needs to be more human is a compliment?" She felt herself embellishing, and enjoying the teasing. It reminded her of her time with Harriet, who was often incapable of taking things seriously when in her company, despite having lived through horrors on the beaches of Dunkirk, and over them, not to mention in the Channel. The verbal sparring had entertained her, and Tilly was quite similar in a way.

"When you put it like that, it makes more sense…" she laughed to herself. "Anyway, try be less like a robot, if you can, and remember what Alexander Pope said. 'To err is human…' Don't be so perfect in your pronunciation, or your delivery. Pause a little, search for a word, run words together, err in conversation like a local. Everyone loses words sometimes, or says the wrong thing. Make mistakes, but make them deliberately. Every err intended, every pause designed. It'll take your French to the next level. I pretend to be my grandma when I'm talking, a French girl who's lived here all her life, and is used to mixing up words, or trying new words and getting them wrong, or being frustrated when I do. It makes it more authentic… No offence meant. Y'know that, right?"

"You know, of course, that the rest of Alexander Pope's quote was 'to forgive is divine…'?" She let herself smile. "Thank you, I appreciate your constructive criticism, I'll…. Erm, try and do less worse."

"Steady on, I said be more natural. Not act like you've never even heard French before." It was Tilly's turn to frown, something she did often, but it was always deliberate and intended with meaning, then she burst into a fit of giggles again when Emily's mouth opened wide in shock at the comeback. "And yes, I'm well aware of Pope's full quote. I may have grown up on horseback, chasing beef around the bush, but mum and dad made sure I was well schooled!"

"This bush you keep mentioning, was it just the one bush? It sounds frightfully sparse, all these cows running around and around in circles around a solitary bush."

"Funny, you haven't said that one before."

"And I'm Scottish, thank you very much, not English." Emily added with a big smirk, getting an eye roll in reply. She was in Paris, at the heart of the German occupation, and at more risk than she'd ever been at any time in her life, but aside from the week with Harriet down on the Kent coast, she was also happier than she'd ever been. She was doing something she knew was worthwhile, she was really doing her bit in the war, and whatever happened, nobody could ever take that away from her. It made her feel invigorated, and the fear made her feel more alive than she'd ever been, that, and she even felt like she had a real purpose when the others in the network had been so welcoming. No hierarchy, no bowing and saluting, or standing smartly at attention. She was part of the team, and treated as an equal. Even at the best of her career as a nurse, as a Senior Sister in Kent, she was still subordinate to the Matron, and the doctors. Everything was still dusted with daily routine, and patients presented, and ordered, and disciplined. It was a life she thought she'd have forever, even when she joined the First Aid Nursing Yeomanry. Then it had started to give a little in Scotland. She was told she was an equal, and that she had to prove it. Then, in the finishing school, she had to perfect it, while earning the right to live it, and living it she was. She'd even made a friend. A proper friend. A younger sister who made her laugh, while simultaneously being incredibly smart, and able to switch in an instant to professional and serious when the moment demanded. She was in France, in Paris, a spy that was hunted and despised by the Germans, and she was loving every minute. Her feelings were a double edged sword, however. She knew the risk, and the danger, and she'd seen firsthand what the war was doing back home, not to mention the fear and deprivation that many people in Paris lived with day after day. Yet she'd never felt more alive.

The streets of Paris were different in the dark, they had an echo that somehow held onto voices and footsteps longer than they should, and it took practice to move silently with the shadows. Something Tilly had showed Emily in her first few days, and which they practiced every time they were moving around the city at night. It was a skill taught at the finishing school, and then adapted and refined by the young Australian, who'd learned at a young age how to move silently around the bush in the dark, so she didn't disturb animals, or get the attention of the rustlers who'd come onto her parents' land to steal livestock. She'd learned from the local Aborigine people, or so she said, masters of their environment, and something she was happy to show Emily how. The trick was doing it in a populated environment without people noticing, which was why they practiced whenever they went out. Sometimes walking and talking, sometimes running and laughing, and others following each other through the streets. To the casual observer they were two young women living and making the most of life under occupation, or even following each other to see who the other's lover was. They were covertly overt. The talking, the laughing, all designed to distract from the walking and the running, which quickly became near silent.

"Have a seat," John said as they joined him in the kitchen. Their walk around the Parisian night had taken them through the back streets to an apartment overlooking the River Seine. Below there were cafes popular with German officers, where music played, and laughter was commonly heard while the soldiers drank and smoked, and flirted with local women who traded conversation for supplies that couldn't be bought in the half stocked shops. They sat at the table, where Etienne was already swirling a glass of watered down wine, the same as they were poured before John sat facing them. There was a tension in the air. Etienne rarely joined them for anything, he was usually hidden away somewhere, moving around the city to transmit his messages, trying to avoid being found by the Germans who used specialist equipment to detect transmissions, and triangulate the location of the operator. Transmit for too long, stay in the same place, and they'd eventually close the net. "How's she getting on?" John asked Tilly while nodding at Emily.

"She's alright," Tilly shrugged in reply after swirling her wine and taking a sip.

"Good…" He looked to Emily, who held his stare for a moment before he half smiled, lightening the tired look on his face. "We'll soon find out, I suppose. We've got a job."

"Tonight?"

"Tonight. The Germans are moving a high value prisoner out of the city to Berlin, and London has tasked us with making sure he doesn't get there."

226

"I don't like it…" Etienne said. His demeanour was reserved to the point of being cold. Emily had met him a few times when delivering messages for him to transmit to London, or collecting the replies or other instructions, and he had always been the same. Curt, surly, dismissive, and generally disappointed with everything and everyone in life. Tilly had told her what she knew about him one evening, when they'd sat talking and looking through the window of their apartment as the Spring rain soaked the city. He was one of the hundred or so thousand French soldiers evacuated from the beaches at Dunkirk, miraculously lifted off the beaches along with the over three hundred thousand British and Commonwealth troops of what remained of the British Expeditionary Force when the Germans steamrolled their way through France and the Low Countries. Instead of joining many of his countrymen in returning to France to continue the fighting, he'd been sent to a camp in Scotland to train with the Free French commandos, and go on to serve under General de Gaulle, who'd set himself up as the commander of the Free French forces in exile when the French government surrendered. It was while he was in Scotland that he managed to bump into the SOE, and he was recruited shortly afterwards. He was mistrusting of everyone, and didn't make friends easily, and even Tilly, with her easy going personality, had struggled to get on with him when they'd worked together as couriers. He'd often drop her and disappear into the city and not be seen for hours at a time, leaving her isolated, not to mention nervous. He always returned, sometimes smelling of wine and pastis.

"Well, like it or not, London calls the shots. You shouldn't have joined if you don't have a sense of humour, you know that." John's tone was casually dismissive, as though it was all a bit of fun, and head office had sent a new instruction to do something that had already been done fifteen times before.

"I don't need a sense of humour. I need to know why our entire team is being put at risk for one person. Everything we've done here, everything we can do, put on the line for what? Many people are arrested, and it isn't the first time a prisoner is being sent to Germany, many have already gone. Why this one? Why now?"

227

"You're the one that took the message from London, you tell me?" John shrugged. He wasn't overly antagonistic in the way he talked, remaining matter of fact while the grumpy Frenchman frowned and bristled.

"That's just it, isn't it? They told us about him, not the other way around! We're here in Paris, yet we know nothing of this person. London, though, almost five hundred kilometres away, can somehow tell us about things happening right under our noses?"

"Yet we're not there, are we? In London, I mean. We're one network among how many? We know each other, and we know that we talk to London, but that's about the lot. There could be other networks scattered around the area, other people feeding them information. Hell, there could be another five circuits in Paris alone that we don't even know about. All we do know is what's in front of us, and what we're told to do, and that's the way it should be. London coordinates everything that's going on, and they get to see the bigger picture. If they tell us we need to do this, it's because they know something, and we have to trust them and give it a go. They know the risks as much as we do, don't you think? I can't imagine they'd want to risk putting an entire network out of action if it wasn't important. If for no other reason than it would be a lot of hard work replacing us, and you know as well as I do that those back in England like to knock off early on a Friday, and get down the pub. Hard work is the last thing on their minds." He gave Etienne a mischievous wink that got a disgruntled sigh in return.

"Just remember my words." He drained his wine glass, then grabbed the jug and topped it up.

"Consider them remembered." John's eyes flicked to Tilly, and then Emily. "They're going to be taking him by truck from the prison at Fort Romainville in the north east of the city, to the airfield at Vélizy-Villacoublay in the south west, about twenty kilometres as the crow flies. Based on their previous habits, it's likely they'll go straight through the centre of the city, probably sometime after curfew kicks in around nine o'clock. I'd imagine they'll give it an hour or two to make sure everyone's off the streets and in bed, then put him in one of the regular supply convoys to avoid suspicion."

"Why would they do that?" Etienne asked.

"To avoid suspicion, like I just said," John replied in his ever calm tones, like he was correcting a school pupil in class. "I know that we were taught to question everything in finishing school, Etienne, but really, you're taking the instruction a little too literally."

"Please, I am not an infant!" the Frenchman replied firmly, dragging everyone's attention to him. "Paris is under occupation, in case you hadn't noticed. What the Germans do, or don't do, doesn't really matter that much, because the local population can't do anything about it. So, whether a truck goes around the city of through it, it doesn't matter, suspicion has no relevance. The curfew matters about the same, the roads would just be quieter."

"Yet still they do it, and have done since we've been here." John's voice had the slightest hint of irritation at the questioning. "You know as well as I do, it's when they move people of interest."

"And the supply convoy?"

"Removes suspicion."

"To everyone but those watching."

"Like us… And we know their game."

"Like the Resistance…" He stared at John, sending the tension in the room up a few levels, and making the atmosphere vibrate. "They're not hiding this person from Parisians, or even from us. They're hiding whoever it is from the Resistance." He walked around the table as he talked, his slight frame growing in the candlelight, making his shadow tower menacingly. "What's going on, John? Who is this person? Why don't London want the Resistance to know about them?" His eyes were full of fire as he bristled beside John.

"The Resistance don't need to know all of our operations, old boy. You know that."

"The Resistance are our partners here. Without them, we wouldn't achieve twenty percent of what we do, old boy. You know that!"

"Yet orders are still orders, aren't they? London calls the shots. They want the prisoner in our hands."

"Fine. I won't go. You play your games with London, I resign!"

"Don't be bloody preposterous," John sighed, as though it wasn't the first time they'd had such a conversation. Emily looked out of the corner of her eye at Tilly, who shrugged casually as if to suggest it wasn't. "Look, you know the games as well as I do, and you play them just as much. Sometimes we run it our way, sometimes London tells us what to do. We don't have all the answers, and nor should we. All I do know is that if London are putting our entire team in harm's way, without asking for help from the locals, it must be important. That said, if you don't want any part of it, fine. Leave the wireless and your other equipment, and off you go… I'll tell London the Germans were onto you, and you had to leave town. Leave Paris, and don't look back. I won't tell if you won't." He smiled as he stared back at Etienne. He didn't raise his voice, or even get animated or forceful, just talked calmly.

"I walk out of here tonight, and tomorrow morning they'll find me floating in the Seine with my throat cut! I know the SOE!"

"I may work for them, Etienne, but I'm not them. I give you my word. If you want to leave, I won't stop you." He held the stare. "Just leave us what we need, and don't turn us in."

"You English…" He moved his face close to John's. "It's all games, all of the time. This is my country, these are my people. I don't have time for games; they don't have time for games."

"Yet games are what we play, old boy. You knew that on your first day in Scotland, we all did. You think the two of them are any different?" He nodded at Tilly and Emily. "Day one, everything's a test. Everything's a game. It had to be. It's only in knowing it that we know anything's real. We play the games because lives depend on it. If we're lost, if we're captured, if just one of us breaks, it undoes months of work, and sets the war effort back even longer. Those are the odds of the game, yet London chooses to gamble anyway. They know how valuable we are, they know the costs of recruiting us, of training us, and of getting us here, not to mention the thousands upon thousands they send in money, equipment, and supplies, all of it to keep us in the game, yet they roll the dice. You've been playing games as long as the rest of us, maybe even longer, so you tell me, Etienne. Do we play, or do all four of us pack up shop and go home? Tell them the game's over?"

"I'm going for a cigarette…" He shook his head and walked towards the door, clipping John's shoulder as he did, but not stopping to acknowledge him.

"We leave at eight." The door slammed as Etienne made his way outside. John waited for a moment, then looked at Tilly and gestured his head slightly towards the door in a most sinister way that left the air dark and cold. She didn't say anything, just nodded and moved silently across the room, then slipped out of the door like a shadow. "More wine?" He gave Emily a smile as he took the jug and topped up her glass, as the atmosphere softened, and the warmth returned to the room somewhat unexpectedly, and the voiceless darkness that surrounded him melted away. "Our Etienne is a good man," he said quietly as Emily swirled the glass before taking a sip. It had been a quiet yet intense exchange with so much said beyond the words. He looked at Emily for a moment as if weighing her up, then drank his own wine. "The thing is, we're not entirely sure whose side he's on." The words were delivered so casually, yet they hit Emily like a train, almost knocking the wind from her. "Not the Germans, we don't think. He's a proud Frenchman, that much is certain, but whether he's Vichy, Communist, or run of the mill Resistance is an unknown. Run of the mill we know that we can work with, of course. The Communist Resistance can leave a bitter taste in the mouth, mostly

231

because they won't do a bloody thing to help us, and answer to their masters in the east, but they're mostly benign at the moment, though they'll take their own cause over ours in a heartbeat, should the mood take them. They're quite hard to engage, let alone control. The only real worry is if he's Vichy..."

"And if he is?" She could feel her frown deepening as she processed his words. They'd been told of the Communist Resistance at the finishing school. The movement had been involved in sabotage and other acts against both the Germans and the French powers in the early days of the occupation, but they took their instructions from Moscow, whose agenda wasn't exactly aligned with that of London, not with Moscow and Berlin being allies. The communists were more of a politically and ideologically motivated group, and while they didn't want the Germans occupying their country, they didn't much favour the French government of the day either, or the patently anti communist British, which meant they were an unpredictable lot at best. The Vichy French, however, were a very different prospect altogether. Marshal Pétain, the leader of the puppet government that ran France from Vichy in the south, was nothing more than a collaborator in the eyes of most French people, and he and his government generally did whatever Hitler told them, and reportedly quite enjoyed it at times, too. Etienne working for them would be dangerous beyond words, and the thought of it made her blood run cold.

"We're all buggered," John shrugged. "It's too late for that now, though. We give him bits of information here and there, and see where it ends up. It's why he disappears every now and then, off to talk with his handlers. Tilly's followed him a few times."

"Yet you do nothing...?"

"He has a relationship with the local Resistance. The ones we actually get on with, and to a degree, we need him. We've had a lot of success, but whether that's because the Germans are playing the long game, and suckering us in, is yet to be seen. For now, however, London wants to play the game out. If he is Vichy, we can maybe flush him out before he turns us in, maybe even turn him and get him working

232

for us so we have a way into the thinking of the Abwehr and Gestapo. That's best case, of course. Worst case, we're all in a German prison before long, and London knows who the stooge is. Either way, he's right about one thing. The games are high stake; he just doesn't know which ones London are playing."

'You mean they know, yet they keep him here? They're gambling with our lives?"

"Well, yes," He gave her a frown as if trying to work out why she'd be so shocked. "Three agents is a high price to pay, four if you count the previous wireless operator, but it's a small cost to flush out a double agent that could cause untold damage in the long term. In the meantime, we're doing some good work, so everything else is a bonus, so to speak."

"And what about me?"

"What about you?"

"What makes you sure I'm not Vichy?"

"I'm not, but if you are, what does it matter? Two double agents in one team would suggest that headquarters back in London isn't just careless, it's compromised. If that's the case, the whole game's up. Wouldn't you agree?"

"Maybe…" She watched him closely. He gave nothing away, and the darkness that had filled the room when he sent Tilly after Etienne hadn't returned, but he was difficult to work out. His words were carefully crafted, expertly even, he was always smoothing any rough edges so anything that they gave away could only ever be deliberately planted. The finishing school had been intense, they'd played games, they'd interviewed each other, even interrogated each other, all with the intention of teaching them to consider every detail of what they said and did, but he was a master at it. The only other person she'd met that was similar was M. The woman who'd recruited her, and whose very persona was sinister, even when she wasn't trying to be, assuming she wasn't trying. "Besides, Tilly said you're alright, and she's a frighteningly good judge of character, not to mention loyal. If you're alright by her, you're alright by me." He gave a warming smile that melted the room a little. "Which is why I've shared this with you. Etienne may well be genuine, and he's with us for now, so don't judge. Do be aware, though, and keep your eyes and ears open, yes?" She nodded in reply, not needing to give it any thought. "Good, you need a clear head tonight. Do your job, and everything will go smoothly."

"Where did you send her? Just now, I mean, when Etienne left?"

"To watch where he was going. She's like a ghost. She could stand next to you in broad daylight without you noticing. Loyal, but terrifying."

"Do I need to worry that you'll send her to spy on me?"

"I put her with you the moment you landed here in France, and you've lived together since..." He raised an eyebrow to suggest that she could fill in any blanks in his answer. She nodded in reply. She already knew before she'd asked. Her Paris training, as it had been described, was just one of a long line of tests that she'd faced since meeting M in London the previous November. She knew all along that she was being assessed and appraised, and that as friendly and welcoming as Tilly was, she was also getting the measure of the new girl that had been dropped into France one stormy night. "As I said, she thinks you're alright, her words, not mine, and that's enough for me." He gave her a wink, then took a mouthful of wine as the door opened and Tilly returned as silently as she'd left, returning to her place by Emily, and picking up her glass to take a drink just seconds before Etienne joined them again.

"So, what do you want me to do?" Etienne asked when he eventually returned, his voice softer, yet still sharp and irritated. The smell of sulphur tinged the air slightly, the type that comes when a match is freshly struck.

Chapter 16

Stinger

"Somebody's going to hear you…" Emily whispered as she lay pressed against the side of the ditch, looking out onto the road.

"If they're close enough to hear me, we're already in trouble," Tilly whispered in reply, then went back to repeating the same, near inaudible half hum, half singing with words hardly there except in outline, just as she had for the previous fifteen or so minutes.

"They can probably hear you in Marseilles!" Emily's heart was racing, and her stomach was turning, as the adrenaline coursing through her body kept her nerves on the sharpest of edges. She was irritable, and scared, and had been since she and Tilly had slipped into the ditch that followed the dark road that ran out to the south of the city, along the Meudon forest, the site of bitter fighting the previous year when the German army approached Paris. A spring fog hung low over the road and surrounding land, spreading into the trees. The whole area had an uneasy feel to it, which is why John had chosen the stretch of road in the first place. He'd explained how the locals tended to avoid the area as much as the Germans, who would usually speed through it, especially at night. There was talk of bad things happening in the woods during the battle, things that had those on both sides feeling shivers up their spines at night, and generally giving it a wide birth. Not that the stories bothered Emily that much. She'd seen lots as a nurse, and heard lots, too. The stories, the experiences, the feelings. She'd been around death since she was seventeen, and had always felt attuned to things feeling uncomfortable, like there were things around that couldn't easily be explained. That wasn't what had her on edge, though. The bad things happening that night were something entirely different. Four agents working deep behind enemy lines were about to take on the German army, and for all of her training, experience, and confidence, and all she'd been through so far, it was her first time doing it for real. She'd been through Scotland; she'd been through the finishing school. The instructors in both places had drilled her again and again on small unit tactics, to make sure she was as comfortable and confident in a fight as any of the men who'd come from infantry regiments, and she'd practiced endlessly with a whole host of weapons. She could strip, clean, rebuild, and reload a Sten gun in her sleep, she could do the same with most common British and German weapons, yet it had all been coordinated. It had been sanitised, even when it was messy. It had been training, make believe, even when they used live bullets in the killing houses, where agents would shoot targets dressed up as enemy soldiers under the watchful eyes of their instructors. It was all designed to be as real as possible, but it never was. Finally, however, after all the training, it was about to happen. The moment had come. She was inclined against the wall of a ditch, shivering part with the damp cold that seemed to seep into her bones, and part with the very real fear of what would happen next, and all the time, all she could focus on was Tilly's song, over and over. Softly, so light an owl wouldn't hear her, but to Emily, it was as though Tilly was standing on a West End stage and belting out chorus after chorus about waltzes and billies, and it was infuriating.

"Hey…" Tilly looked at her and gave her the slow smile that Emily had come to warm to so much. "Take it easy, Sport. You've got this." Emily stared at her for a moment, then nodded nervously. "Just take a few deep breaths, in through the nose and out through the mouth, it'll settle the nerves and take the edge off." Emily nodded again and did as she was told. She didn't need to fight back, or argue, if there was one thing she knew, it was that she had to listen to Tilly and do as she said. A key tenet of what they were taught at the finishing school was to trust each other, and work together when things got tough. They'd prepared her for what was coming. "Trust the process, and the training will kick in. Alright?" Her whisper was softer than a summer breeze, and settled Emily somehow, helping her relax and breathe as she watched her friend's smile. She nodded again, then looked down the road as her heart started to steady a little, and the thud of her pulse softened. She continued her deep breathing, and Tilly went back to singing under her breath, but this time instead of it riling Emily, it comforted her like a lullaby. "Here we go, get ready with the chain." Tilly said as she lifted her head and looked down the road in the direction of the city. Emily frowned at her, and craned her neck trying to listen, but there was nothing. Not even a breath of wind on the air. She looked to Tilly again, who was still singing under her breath while focusing on the road, and a minute later the distant hum of an engine filled the air. Emily frowned for a moment. Her hearing had always been so good, but she hadn't heard a thing. "Remember, trust your training." She looked to Emily again and gave her a firm nod. "As soon as I give you the go, get that chain thrown, and then follow me in. You remember what to do?" Emily nodded and took another deep breath. Her fingers were trembling, but there wasn't a thought in her mind that she wouldn't go through with it. She'd hoped, when they'd first slipped into the ditch, that maybe the truck wouldn't come, and they'd have to go home and come back another time, but now it was happening, she was ready, she was just so scared. The lights of the German trucks came closer, illuminating the fog in an ethereal amber glow that lit up the road like a river. Two of them, just as John had suggested, separated by about five truck lengths, as was apparently standard, and racing for all they were worth through the eerie forest, making their engines scream with effort. "Ready…" Tilly's voice was a little louder, to be audible over the fast approaching engine noise. "Three… Two… One… Now!" Emily reached behind her, then swung her arm forward with all of her might, launching the coiled chain across the road, feeling the nails that were embedded in it scratching at her hand as she held it slightly too close for slightly too long, then recoiling as it scattered in front of the truck's wheels. There were loud pops and screeching hisses as the front and then back tyres rolled over the chain filled with nails of all lengths, puncturing immediately, and sending the truck skidding as the driver quickly slowed while fighting to keep control and stop it overturning.

Emily was already out of the ditch and following Tilly when the second truck ran over a second chain, the one thrown by John and Etienne, and careered off the road towards the ditch they'd been hiding in just seconds before. She ran hard with the stock of her Sten gun tucked tightly in her armpit, as she'd been taught, the safety catch already flicked off, and the muzzle pointing towards the driver's door. She squeezed the trigger as it opened, and the soldier jumped out, rifle in hand, keeping it pulled tight as she sprayed his torso with bullets that made his body shake and dance as the air filled with a fine red mist. There was no time to think, she released the trigger as he crashed against the side of the truck and spun to the ground, then she squeezed it again as she aimed into the cab, spraying the second soldier and running her bullets up his back, knocking him out of the passenger door as the inside of the cab turned red with his blood. The empty magazine was off and stuffed down her jacket, and a new one fitted within seconds, and the weapon cocked as she simultaneously checked the cab for anyone else, before moving around the front of the truck to make sure the passenger was dead. Short bursts of machine gun fire buzzed through the air, lighting up the darkness, accompanied by gasps and muffled cries. The passenger was dead, so she moved down the truck towards the back, where a pair of soldiers lay half hanging over the open tailgate, their blood pooling onto the road as Tilly climbed inside while Emily put her back to the truck and kept watch. She squinted in the amber light of the second truck's headlights, and sniffed at the smell of cordite as the gun smoke hung heavy on top of the fog. The second truck was a carbon copy of the first, with John and Etienne mirroring the moves, and the soldiers dispatched with the same cold efficiency. A filled hessian sack was put over her shoulder, making her jump briefly, until she remembered what was going on. She took it from Tilly, who disappeared into the truck again, then reappeared seconds later and jumped down to the ground carrying another sack. She gave Emily a nod, then quickly searched the two dead soldiers for anything useful, before they ran together to the driver and passenger so she could search them while Emily kept watch. Another nod, and they ran side by side to the rear of the second truck where John was lowering a tied and bagged, yet quite alive, body out of the back of the truck to Etienne, who gave the person his full attention once Tilly and Emily were in place keeping watch on the road. John followed, and after checking the bodies, he and Etienne took the person between them and ran off into the darkness, while Emily and Tilly collected both chains, wound them, and shoved them in their sacks with the weapons liberated from the dead Germans. Finally, they returned to the trucks and left prepared explosives pressed against the fuel tanks, before they headed off in the opposite direction to John, across the fields and in the direction of the city.

Emily couldn't sleep that night, despite being totally exhausted. The adrenaline refused to stop pumping, and after hours of tossing and turning, replaying every move, every breath, all remembered in vivid detail, she finally got up and poured herself a brandy, and sat looking out of the window at the city below. She'd done it. From Scotland to the ditch, everyone had told her that the training would kick in, and it had, in the most brutally effective way imaginable. She didn't stop to think once, she didn't need to. As soon as Tilly said go, it was like her body and mind knew the script, and she was just along for the ride. The entire operation had taken just a couple of minutes from beginning to end, both trucks stopped, eight German soldiers killed, supplies looted, a prisoner rescued, and explosive charges set against the fuel tanks, each with a time pencil set to blow the trucks into pieces long after the assault. They were back in Paris before the muffled explosions rumbled in the distance, and in a safe house not long after, where they dropped their weapons and other equipment to be stored before sharing out some of the supplies looted from the trucks, and melting into the night, leaving John with the prisoner. It had been efficient, to say the least, and while they couldn't know for sure, the hope was that the shooting would have been heard, or the trucks missed when they didn't show, and reinforcements would have been at the scene of the crime when the fuses that delayed the explosions finally yielded, and more of the enemy were killed or wounded in the resulting fireballs. It was murderous business. From gunning down the drivers and passengers to setting delayed explosions to kill those who came to find them, it was cold blooded in the extreme.

"You alright?" Tilly asked from her bed across the room. Emily jumped a little, then saw the moonlight on her young friend's eyes, staring at her the darkness.

"Yes…" Emily replied quietly, after giving her head a shake. "Yes, I just…" Her heat skipped, and her chest tightened, and she felt a tear roll unexpectedly onto her cheek. She quickly sniffed and rubbed it away, a little frustrated at herself. Her emotions were so close to the surface that it was difficult to contain them, and she was suddenly struggling to talk, or even think properly. "Is it always like this?" she finally asked when she could get her words out, as Tilly wandered over and sat beside her, throwing her blanket around both of them to keep out the cold.

"What's it like?" the young Australian asked as she poured herself a drink. Her voice was soft, yet direct.

"The driver wasn't so bad..." Emily explained after taking a sip of brandy that burned all the way down. "I just fired, and he went down. I hardly even saw him, if that makes sense?" She looked into Tilly's eyes as they shone in the reflected light.

"Yeah..." She nodded and gave a pained smile.

"The other one, though. The passenger. He was whimpering, crying perhaps as he tried desperately to open the cab door. I could see him scratching at it with his bare hands, like a scared animal. It was like he'd forgotten how to use a door handle in his fear, and I just ran my bullets up his back... He must have thought he'd made it when the door finally opened, but he was already a dead man. He just didn't know it yet."

"You did what you had to do."

"I know..." The forced smile was painful, and she couldn't hold it for long. "It's just that I've spent my entire adult life keeping people alive, and despite all the training we've had, and my choosing to be here, I never imagined how it would feel to do the opposite."

"Feels horrible, doesn't it?"

"Does it?" She frowned as she looked into Tilly's eyes again, having looked away in embarrassment at admitting how weak she felt at having to do her job. "For you, I mean?" Her young friend had been so matter of fact before, during, and after. Clinical and ruthless, then gone to bed and slept like a baby, or so it had seemed.

"Of course it does, dummy. What do you think I am, one of those robots out of that film Metropolis?" The moon lit the smile on her face, and the light, sarcastic delivery of her own words thrown back at her made Emily laugh unexpectedly. "You know, the Aboriginal people back home, the black fellas that lived in Australia long before us lot turned up and started turning the place on its head, don't write their history down the same way as we do, they share it through stories..." Her voice softened as she talked.

"I didn't know that…?"

"Oh, yeah. They're fascinating. There's a tribe that lives near us, and they told me some of their stories when I was a kid, some of them going back thousands of years."

"You speak their language?"

"A bit. Mum and dad said I should learn, so we could be friends with our neighbours…" She smiled, thinking of different times. "Do you want me to share one of my stories?" Emily nodded, while still drying tears from her eyes. "OK, well… Life was hard growing up. We had land, but that was about it. Not much money, or anything else for that matter." Her smile faded to a frown as she talked, and Emily nodded as she listened. "Disease took more than half of our sheep when I was young, and I had to help put those that were infected out of their misery. Lambs too, sometimes. It was necessary, you know?" She paused for a moment and gazed out of the window as her eyes went somewhere else, somewhere a long way from the attic room in Paris. "Worse was trying to keep what was left alive. The dingoes, wild dogs, that is, would come for them, sometimes getting the weak, or the young, separating them out from the herd and ripping them to pieces. Other times, they'd attack in packs, and slaughter dozens of sheep at a time. It's like they knew we were on our knees, somehow. Mum and dad did their best, but I had to do my part, and sometimes that meant fighting back… I wasn't even ten when I came up against my first dingo. I found it snooping around the back of the sheep shed where we kept all the pregnant ewes around lambing time. I was expecting to see a big ugly thing with angry eyes and teeth like razors, but when I got close, it was hardly any different from my dog, and I reckoned it was just looking for food for its family, which makes sense. Anyway, I took a shot at the ground by its feet, and it jumped, then looked at me before taking off in a ball of dust. I scared the life out of it, and made myself feel proud… The local tribe had dingoes, they'd trained them and domesticated them, and talked about how they were part of culture, and in my nine your old brain I imagined it going off to live with the tribe, away from me and my gun, and where it was guaranteed food and water, and a good life." She looked at Emily for a moment and smiled in a way that sent a message straight into

Emily's soul. "The thing about nine year olds is that they can be idealistic at times, or bloody stupid, depending on your viewpoint. Apparently, all I'd done is wind him up, and that night we were woken by screams coming from the main shed... You haven't heard anything until you've heard scared animals screaming, I can tell you that. Anyway, I hadn't scared him at all, he just went and got his mates, and the entire pack massacred most of the ewes."

"My God..." Emily gasped unintentionally as she listened to the story. "What happened?"

"Dad and me went after them, tracked them back to their lair out in the bush, and killed the entire pack, pups and all." She paused again, the hard, pained smile replaced by a frown. "Dingo packs aren't like other animals, you know? They're usually a tight family group. A breeding pair with their offspring, maybe their parents, or a few siblings. Twelve of them tops. We wiped out an entire family of them, three generations of dogs, and I didn't miss a single shot."

"And the Germans are like the dingoes to you?"

"What else?" She shrugged as though it was obvious. "There are some good ones, living peacefully with others, and there are some out killing and taking what they need. If we leave them be, they'll kill everything, and we'll have nothing left." She sighed, then took a drink and shook her head to clear the thoughts. "I'm older now, and looking back I'm pretty sure the dingoes didn't massacre our sheep out of spite, they just didn't know any better, and that's how I see the Germans. There's talk of Hitler and his mates poisoning their minds for years, telling them they're starving, and at risk, and whipping them up to go and take what they need. So, I kind of get it."

"When you put it like that, I suppose I get it too..." It was Emily's turn to frown as she thought to the news reports of Hitler and the Nazis over the years, and how her dad had told her about the state Germany was left in after the last war. In a roundabout way, Tilly's story made a lot of sense.

"Just don't get it too much, and miss when the time comes…" Her voice was low, and soft, and the moon showed the slightest turn up at the corner of her mouth. "Me telling a bunch of dingoes how it is, and hoping they'd go off to read a book and think rationally wouldn't have made a scrap of difference. The Germans, though, they're supposed to be intelligent human beings. At least that's what the history books like to tell us. The bastards should know better." She jumped up and stretched, a confident air of armour wrapping around her again, after what felt like an emotional vulnerability that Emily hadn't yet seen from her. "And get some sleep, or you'll be no good to anyone." She patted Emily on the shoulder, then returned to her bed, leaving Emily to stare out of the window for a moment while she processed the story she'd heard. It was simple, if brutal. She'd had a very different life, one where she could choose to help, and heal, and turn the other cheek. Even when she'd had difficulties with her husband, she still hadn't been in a position where life was so desperate. Not in a way that her decisions had such a profound impact. Even when she left home, she knew she could always go back, and that it would always be there. Her parents were comfortably middle class, they owned their house, they'd paid for her education, and even for her to travel. She'd never had to keep the wolves literally from the door, and when she was nine, her biggest decisions were how to line up her dolls, not whether or not she should kill a predator bent on destroying the family livelihood.

It all made her think more about what she was doing in France, and about the excitement she still felt, regardless of being conflicted about the attack on the convoy, and whether doing her bit was just a game to her. It all seemed very different for Tilly, more real perhaps, life had been hard, to the point where it was maybe preparing her for war.

"What happened after that?" Emily asked as she walked across the room and sat on Tilly's bed, then took the pillow her young friend was faffing with and fluffed it in a way she'd been trained as a nurse, a flick that settled the down and somehow made it both soft and supportive at the same time, something that could often settle restless patients.

243

"Thanks..." she said as she rested her head and snuggled a little, while Emily pulled the blankets up around her shoulders, instinctively tucking her in. "We worked hard..." She looked up at Emily, her eyes still sparkling in the moonlight. "A few years, and the disease had passed, and we were able to get on our feet again." Emily nodded and smiled.

"Were your parents forgiving of your missing the dingo the first time?"

"I don't know, I never told them..."

"Oh..." She frowned uncomfortably, feeling she'd spoken out of turn.

"It almost broke us. Other families were going under at the time, sunk by disease and the like. How does a nine year old girl tell her parents that she almost collapsed the whole lot by being sentimental?" The moonlight caught a tear on her cheek as her voice shook for the briefest of moments, making Emily's heart squeeze. She reached out and gently wiped the tear from her friend's cheek. She flinched briefly as Tilly's hand came from the covers and touched hers, thinking she'd offended her by noticing the emotion, but her hand was gentle, and held Emily's briefly. "It killed mum... She worked so hard she was near dead on her feet, and didn't have anything left to give when she got pneumonia the next year. She was dead in days." Tilly sniffed again, and moved her hand to wipe the tears from her cheek. "Dad flogged himself so hard from dawn until long after dusk after that, we both did. He worked so hard that it visibly aged him. We got there, eventually. Sheep to beef, and beef for the army. We even made enough to hire people after a few years."

"I'm so sorry. About your mum, I mean..." Emily said as she shuffled up the bed to put her back against the headboard, then put an arm around Tilly's shoulder as she snuggled against Emily and put her head on her hip.

"Dad said she was weak anyway, a heart problem or something, though that was the first I knew of it... I never told him about the dingo, as I said, but I reckon he knew. He always knew everything

244

that happened, and I reckon that was his way of trying to make me feel better, and let me know it was OK. He always was soft on me, mum told us both as much."

"Is he still…?" Emily wasn't sure how to finish her question. She knew what she was asking, yet all of a sudden it felt so cold and intrusive.

"Yeah… Just about. Though I almost killed him as well when I broke the news that I was coming to England to join up, back when the balloon went up in '39." She looked up and forced a smile, her cheeks wet with tears. "I reckon it'd be third time lucky if he knew I was playing games in France, instead of being a WAAF on an airfield back in England, like I told him when I last wrote…"

"He didn't want you to come?"

"Not really… Dad was in the last war, at Gallipoli, and then here in France. Got through the lot without a scratch, somehow. Though he didn't really talk about it much. He'd have nightmares at times, and really struggled for years, especially when he was tired, and Grandad told us the stories he'd heard about how bad it all was. Dad still tried to volunteer again when Hitler started, said he needed to come back for all his mates he left here, but they wouldn't take him. He was too old, apparently, and it broke him a bit more when he couldn't do his bit. So, I volunteered instead. Somebody needed to go, and I don't have any brothers. Besides, I wanted to do something to make it right for mum."

"Oh, Tilly…" Emily squeezed her as she snuggled tight, burying her face in Emily's leg a little, her sniffing giving away her tears. Emily ran her fingers through Tilly's hair, hoping to soothe her a little as any thoughts she had about her own suffering melted away, replaced by an ache for the pain of the young woman lying beside her. "I don't know your parents, but they made you, so they can't be half bad at all, and I can't imagine somebody like that holding anything against their daughter, least of all the compassionate actions of a nine year old."

245

"Well, let's not put the theory to the test. You need to promise me that you'll keep my being in France a secret!" She let out half a giggle, as her infectiously unserious and bubbly persona fought through the dark emotion of the moment, and Emily found herself giggling with her.

Chapter 17

Closing

Emily stopped and checked the timetable outside the Gare du Nord, one of the busiest train stations in Paris, and after reading a few lines, enough to know when the next train to the south was, she went on her way, not even looking at Etienne, who'd exited the station and put down his suitcase while he lit a cigarette with a match from a man who'd left the station after him, having searched his own pockets and found that he didn't have his own. She continued walking, glancing in windows and watching shadows in the spring sun, making sure he was following her about fifty metres behind, and that nobody else was. He'd stop sometimes to look at a street name, and then continue, he even joined with a small group of people and walked among them for a while as they crossed the boulevard, following Emily south. It was a beautiful day, not too warm, but the sky was blue, and the trees and bushes were enjoying the change in seasons, and despite the city being under occupation still, people seemed relieved that the darkness and cold of winter was behind them. Flowers were starting to bloom, too, and their scent and brightness lifted the city further, and at times, if a person didn't look too closely, things would almost seem normal.

She turned down the short residential street, lined each side with tall apartment blocks, while at the street level there were offices, cafes, and shops, all busy with people coming and going. Or, in the case of the older men who gathered at some of the cafes, just sitting and drinking ersatz coffee while smoking what they could get their hands on, and talking loudly in their groups while the world went by. It was a feature of some of the city's residential areas. There wasn't always much to do, certainly for the older generation, so they'd meet in the mornings to pass the time, especially on the weekend, and nobody really bothered them.

The areas of the city close to the train stations were often busier, with lots of transient movement as people from out of the area came to Paris to escape the war, or to find work in factories, renting rooms in the many large apartments that were put up for let by owners desperate for an income, and fitting into the community the best they could until they found somewhere else. It was the perfect place for a wireless operator to hide out. Nobody really paying attention to who was coming and going, and enough new faces for one more not to be noticed. Every now and then Etienne would be moved, from safe house to safe house. John would arrange a room in an apartment somewhere, nothing fancy, and Tilly and Emily would do the moving, collecting him from the nearest train station, and guiding him to his new home. Once there, he'd send his messages until it was thought that the Germans were getting close, and then it would be along the tracks to another busy area, mostly near a train station or the Metro. It was an established system that had worked since long before Emily had arrived, and everyone was comfortable with it. They'd got the timing down to an art, staying long enough to do what they needed to do, and moving before their position was triangulated. It was an art, but there'd been no explanation as to what had happened to Etienne's predecessor. She'd just disappeared one day, with word coming through Resistance contacts to John that she'd been seen at Fresnes prison in the south of the city, or so Emily had been told.

Emily smiled and waved excitedly as she saw Tilly standing by a lamppost, a gesture returned when Tilly finally turned and saw her approaching. "You made it!" Tilly said excitedly as they kissed each other on the cheeks as only the French can.

"Of course!" Emily replied. "I came for the terrible coffee you told me about, that's slightly better than the last place? Erm… What was it called? I don't even remember where it was now… Coffee Café something?" She babbled as she talked, rolling her eyes and gesturing a little with her hands, and being as perfectly imperfect as she'd been practicing since receiving Tilly's feedback on her linguistic skills. They both laughed, and Tilly put her arm through Emily's before leading her across the street towards a café, shortly after Etienne passed them. They laughed and joked, as any two young women would, until they were disturbed by the rumble of engines followed by shouting. They both looked to their left, to the end of street that Emily had just walked up, and at the open top German truck and the stampede of soldiers jumping from it. An MG34 machine gun was perched on the cab roof, manned by a soldier who swung it to point down the street, while the squad that had alighted spread into a line with their rifles pointed,

248

and started advancing slowly with an officer at their head. Tilly gripped Emily's arm tight as they watched, and Emily gripped right back as her heart started to race when a second truck rolled to a halt at the other end of the street, dismounting another squad with rifles at the ready, and another machine gunner keeping watch.

The chatter in the street stopped, and then voices were raised as soldiers started to coral people in the street towards the café, herding them from both directions, and refusing to let anyone leave, or pass, despite their obvious anger and annoyance. The soldiers pushed everyone back towards the café that Emily and Tilly continued to move nervously in the direction of. Emily's hand slipped down to Tilly's, and grabbed it tight. She felt sick, and warm, and even her eyes seemed sensitive to the light as she glanced around looking for a way out, while simultaneously going through every step of her journey that morning. Tilly had left long before her, slipping out while it was still dark, and heading to the new apartment via a stroll along the Seine, where she waited for Emily, marking the spot where Etienne would count the apartments to the blue door across the street, and slip inside. Emily had left after sunrise, and skipped about openly and full of life, before wandering across the city to meet her friend, picking up Etienne on the way, and guiding him in. She'd stopped, she'd checked, she'd been beyond careful, and as much as she racked her brain, she couldn't think of a single moment where she'd been remotely careless. She was positive she hadn't been followed, yet the Germans were there, advancing from both ends of the street, herding everyone towards the café, towards them. Her mind suddenly focused when she glanced back up the street and found that Etienne was nowhere to be seen. She'd seen him heading towards the apartment, and then he was gone before he even got there, beaten to the door by the advancing German squad. She looked left and right at the closing groups of soldiers, who were being followed by a black Citroen saloon car. Soon they were surrounding the café, and Emily and Tilly found themselves with others from the street being caught up with the customers and staff, including those who were being turfed out of the building and onto the street by the soldiers that had flooded inside, knocking over tables and moving anyone that didn't want to be moved. They squeezed each other's hands as the small crowd were corralled together, bumping into each other as a ring of Germans surrounded them with their rifles at the ready.

"Hush..." Emily whispered to Tilly while squeezing her hand hard, in response to the young Australian starting to lightly hum again, and sing empty words to the same tune she'd sang ahead of the ambush. Tilly paid no attention, just spun her head left and right, glancing around and studying every aspect of the situation. Emily watched her. Her eyes were sharp and bright like a hawk's, missing nothing, while she filtered out anything unimportant, including Emily's squeezing and nervous hushing. "Hey..." She gave Tilly's hand a hard pull and tight squeeze, breaking her concentration briefly as the crowd started jeering and shouting at the Germans.

"Stay here, it'll be ok," Tilly whispered, and gave Emily a wink and a barely perceptible yet reassuring nod, then released her hand and stepped away, putting a man between them and heading through the increasingly scared and irritable crowd towards the Germans.

"Silence!" a German Major dressed in the uniform of the SS shouted as he stepped out of the Citroen and walked towards the crowd, flanked by a pair of French Gendarmes that had followed him from the car. The crowd gasped and collectively ducked, taking Emily with it, as pistol shot echoed around the street, fired into the air by the Major, whose gendarmes were now joining the soldiers in pointing their weapons at the gathered French civilians.

"Sir," a voice rang out, and Emily joined everyone else in turning to see soldiers leaving the cafe with a man, woman, and two children at gunpoint, a boy and girl who were maybe in their teens. "Sir, we have them." Emily looked at the family, and the soldiers surrounding them, then quickly stepped through the crowd and grabbed Tilly's hand tight, pulling her close and shaking her head slightly, stopping her from doing what she'd imagined. They stood and watched as the crowd parted to let the family pass, until they were standing in front of the Major.

"Monsieur Roux," the Major said with a sickening smile. Emily and Tilly were stood almost next to the family as they huddled nervously together in front of the Germans, Tilly having almost made her way to the Major before Emily had grabbed her.

"Yes…" the man replied, standing in front of his family.

"Monsieur Pierre Roux, clerk for the city transport department?"

"That's correct…"

"Good." The Major looked past him to the crowd. "Ladies and gentlemen, you should know that this man, who stands among you now, and lives among you with his family, is a member of the Communist Resistance." The crowd gasped and muttered as the German spoke in remarkably good French. "More than that, last night he was one of a group that attacked a convoy of German supply trucks that were taking food and medical supplies to a hospital in the south of the city. A hospital looking after French people, your people." The crowd bristled, and Tilly reversed her previous course, taking a couple of steps backwards, and pulling Emily with her as the crowd did the same, collectively knowing what was coming, and distancing themselves to avoid being labelled as guilty by association. "This man has taken from you, as much as from us. He and his treasonous friends not only stole the food and medicine destined for the sick, they executed eight German soldiers, and blew up their trucks, killing and wounding those sent to help, including one of your doctors." Emily's mind raced as she listened. There was only one convoy attacked to the south of the city the previous night, she knew because she did it. The crowd bristled and muttered again, and this time Emily stepped back, pulling Tilly along until there was a large space between the man and his family, and everyone else. "The war is over, ladies and gentlemen. We are here at the invite of your Marshal Pétain, and your government, to help keep the streets safe from agitators like this communist, who seeks to destabilise your communities, and this is how we are treated. This is how you are treated."

"No, it's not true!" Roux protested loudly. He was scared; it was in his voice and his trembling hands. "I was here all night, with my family. I didn't do it; I didn't do anything." He turned and looked at the crowd. "I didn't do anything. You've all seen me here, you know me. You believe me, don't you? If I'd stolen food, I would have shared it with you all. If I'd stolen medicine, it would have been given to the sick. It wasn't me. I was here; I was with my family all night." His eyes were desperate, and it took a tug of the hand from Tilly for Emily to avert her eyes from his, the same as everyone else in the crowd that were quickly trying to be anywhere else. "I swear!" He turned back to the Major. "Please, take me and interrogate me, I don't mind, it'll prove that I'm telling the truth. Leave my family here, and take me to prison. I don't mind, please. I didn't do it." His words became increasingly more desperate as he negotiated, until the Major held up his hand to silence him.

"Monsieur Roux, there's really no need for that…" He smiled as he put his hand on the terrified Frenchman's shoulder. "Interrogation won't be necessary." Roux let himself smile for a moment as some of the tension dropped from his shoulders. "We've already interrogated your friends, it's why we're here. We know it was you, and we're not here to negotiate." He gave the soldiers a casual nod, and a Sergeant shouted. They formed a line, and rifles were pointed, as the crowd desperately surged backwards to get out of the firing line, with Tilly dragging Emily behind a few of the older men who'd pulled at her and stepped forward, keen to protect the young women. Roux was grabbed by the shoulders and kicked in the back of the legs, dropping him roughly to his knees, while other soldiers grabbed his family, pulling his wife and children away from him as he looked up at the Major in shock.

"A trial…" he muttered.

"You've had one, Monsieur, in absentia, and you've been found guilty of murder and theft by a French judge just this morning. The sentence for which is death." Roux trembled and turned pale, half collapsing against the soldiers standing either side of him and holding him up. "Let it be known, ladies and gentlemen," the Major continued as he paced in front of Roux, addressing the increasingly scared crowd and clearly enjoying the theatre of the moment, "that we will do all we can to support our French partners in protecting this city against the lowlifes who seek to deal in crime and evil. And, when we find those guilty of heinous crimes, we will make the hard choices not because we want to, but because we should, because we're here to support our friends." The French policemen flanking him looked confidently at the crowd as his words were delivered loudly, with the authority of the state. "You should also know that anyone who engages in such barbaric acts of cruelty not only condemns themselves, but their families, too. The evil needs to be rooted out and removed, especially when it is so insidious that it sees people such as Monsieur Roux taking his own son on his murderous raids with him."

"No!" Roux yelled while trying to stand, receiving a rifle but to the side of his head to force him back down again in response. "No…" he pleaded as his young son was grabbed.

"There are consequences, Monsieur Roux. You knew this when you killed our soldiers. You knew this when you stole from your own people. You're a communist, and a terrorist, and now you must pay." The crowd jostled and murmured, and for a moment Tilly hummed a little again.

"Wait!" Roux shouted. "Wait!"

"Yes?"

"I did it. Yes, I'm a communist, and yes, I did it. I killed your soldiers, but I didn't steal any food, or any medical supplies. I promise." He glanced over his shoulder at the crowd. "I did it because they're the enemy, not for any other reason. I'm a soldier, I served in the war, and I serve still. I'm not a terrorist, and I didn't take my son with me. I did it, not him. Look at him, he's a boy. He couldn't even carry a gun, let alone shoot anyone! Take me to prison, I confess, I'll tell you everything, just let him go. Please, let him go." The Major's smile stretched across his face in response.

"You see, ladies and gentlemen. A communist traitor living amongst you…" He let out a theatrical sigh, and then looked down at Roux, who knelt as a defeated man, knowing all too well that he'd just confessed to something he didn't do, and as a result would face agonising torture before surely losing his life. It was all Emily could

253

do not to vomit. It wasn't right. She knew it wasn't right. None of it was. "Fortunately, the German army has resolve when it comes to dealing with terrorists, and while I'm grateful for you being honest in front of your peers, it doesn't change anything." He swiped his pistol hard into Roux' face, cracking it against his mouth and making him scream out as blood and teeth fell to the floor. "I repeat, you've already been found guilty in court, and your sentence passed. As has the sentence on your family who aided and abetted your sick crimes." Roux howled out, not able to speak properly. "You'll be executed, but before you go, you'll know that your wife and daughter will be sent to a camp for… Let us say, re education." He leant closer to Roux and spoke quietly, but still loud enough for Emily to hear clearly. "Though maybe I'll send them to a soldier's brothel first…" He then stood tall and gave the soldiers a nod, and Roux' son was grabbed and tied, and a noose put around his neck. Roux was filled with rage as the crowd riled, having to be threatened at rifle point by the many soldiers. The boy cried as a sign was put around his neck explaining in French that he had stolen from French people and was a traitor to the country, and he visibly wet himself as the rope was thrown over a streetlight. Roux yelled, and his wife and daughter screamed as the boy was strung up, his face turning red, and then purple as his eyes bulged. His legs kicked, and then an older man from the cafe started singing La Marseillaise, the French national anthem, and others joined in, Emily and Tilly included, while they stood helplessly with tears in their eyes as they watched the boy slowly die. Finally, as he stopped twitching, a gunshot rang out and silenced the crowd, and Roux slumped forward, having been shot in the back of the head by the Major. Executed just seconds after watching his son die, and knowing the fate awaiting his wife and daughter. "Let this be a lesson," the Major said as he put his pistol back in its holster. "Anyone engaging in criminality will pay, as will their family. Good day." He gave a nod, and Roux's wife and daughter were taken away clinging to each other and sobbing in shock, and the soldiers retreated, rifles aimed, while the crowd watched in silence. Nobody said anything, and nobody moved. Nobody dared. They'd just watched two people executed, and two more taken away, and there wasn't a person there that believed the Major wouldn't gun them all down had they spoke out, all under the watchful gaze of two French policemen. He stepped forward and looked around the crowd, smiling as he did. "I'm sorry to have disturbed your day, and I hope sincerely that this will be the end of the matter. Please, go on with what you were doing. Good day." He snapped his heels together, and bowed his head sharply as though he'd just performed a service. Slowly, the crowd turned their backs and faced the cafe, all except Emily, who watched him turn and march away to his Citroen. Tilly pulled at her until she turned, just catching the gaze of one of the Gendarmes as she did. They held hands, and it took several squeezes for her to stop trembling so violently, while all the time feeling Tilly's vibrations coming back the other way. Finally, when the Germans were gone, the engines of their vehicles rumbling into the distance, people dispersed. Some, who'd been going elsewhere when they were corralled, wandered off down the street, others went back into the cafe.

"Here, sit," the old man who'd stood in front of them said as he pulled out a chair at one of the outside tables. Emily looked at him, frowning unwittingly as she tried with difficulty to process the most simple of invitations. He nodded at the second chair he pulled out, and Tilly led her to the table, where they both sat with the group of men who scraped the chair legs on the pavement as they made space for them. Fresh glasses were put on the table by the cafe owner, and a splash of brandy poured into each. He went around everyone, making sure all had a drink. "Vive la France," the old man muttered, and everyone did the same, Emily and Tilly included, speaking in hushed tones that were hardly a mutter between the tables. Emily gulped the brandy down to try and settle her nerves. She'd felt positive that the Major had come for them. It was all too perfect. That there'd be a family inside who was top of the list hadn't even entered her mind. She thought through what had happened while feeling the brandy burn all the way to her stomach. About how Tilly had let go of her and stepped forward, and about Etienne… She looked around again, he wasn't at the cafe, or in the street, he was nowhere to be seen. "Don't look," the old man said as he nodded to the centre of the table.

"What about them?" Emily asked as she nodded to the prone body of Roux, laying where he'd slumped having been shot in the back of the head while kneeling before the Major, and then glancing up to the sickening sight of his son, swinging slightly on the end of his rope, his eyes bulging, and his tongue hanging from his mouth.

"Leave them where they are…" He flicked his head back to the table, and she did as she was told, looking away and joining the others staring at their glasses. "The Germans will send somebody for them, eventually. Anyone moving them will be seen as a sympathiser, and they'll be next." Emily nodded, then glanced again briefly. The nurse in her wanted to go check them. She knew beyond doubt they were dead. Roux, certainly, half of his head was gone, and his brains were spread across the road. His son was still in one piece, but his face was deep purple, and had been since he was strung up. Even if he was somehow still alive, his brain would be damaged beyond repair through lack of oxygen, and death would be better for him anyway. It didn't stop her from wanting to check them, though, and lay them out with some sort of dignity. Though that was the point of the whole exercise, and she knew it well enough. The Germans could have taken the bodies with them, knowing they'd have to be collected sooner or later anyway for hygiene purposes if no other reason, even they didn't want a city overflowing with rotting corpses, but they didn't. They chose instead to leave them where they were to intimidate, and to make sure there was no dignity either for the departed or those who remained. She looked to the old man again, who gave her a nod of understanding. "We should have finished them properly in the last war…" he muttered, then waved his hand to have the drinks refilled while the other men nodded and muttered similar, and drinks were poured at other tables. This time the drinks were sipped, and the tension eased ever so slightly. "Everyone knew he was a communist, but he wasn't a bad man. He looked after his family, and worked hard…" He allowed himself the briefest of glances at the corpses. "It'll get worse before it gets better, mark my words, and you two need to be careful." He fixed Emily and then Tilly in his stare. Emily's heart squeezed and raced again as he addressed them. Did he know? How could he? Had they been so obvious? Questions spun around her mind as she thought through every moment for the hundredth time. "You heard what he said to Roux, about his wife and daughter. Young women aren't safe, not here, not from them. You need to be careful, and don't look so pretty." He gave them a warming smile as others at the table murmured, some nodding, and one even letting out a forlorn half hearted laugh. "If the Germans turn up again, be at the back, not the front. They have places, you know. Brothels. He wasn't joking about that…" His smile waned, replaced by a frown. "Ah, what do I know." He finished his drink. "I need to go home and

256

see my wife. I can't sit here looking at them." He put his glass down and said his goodbyes, as did a few others. Tilly squeezed Emily's hand and gave her a nod, and they stood and said thank you for the drinks. Tilly tried to leave a few coins, but they were waved away by the man and the owner, so she put them in the pocket and smiled painfully, then arm in arm, she and Emily walked past Roux and his son, and headed down the street.

Chapter 18

The Reckoning

"It happened all across the city..." John said in hushed tones as the jazz music drifted with a varying tempo, while people danced and the air hung heavy with cigarette smoke and perfume. It was a place they'd met every now and then, one of the many underground and quite illegal nightclubs that had sprung up around Paris when jazz was banned, and gatherings frowned on following the occupation. The Germans knew about most of them, but tended to leave them alone, theorising that the population needed some sort of release if they were to keep any sort of order. Paris had burned with resistance and revolution many times throughout its history, and while the Germans were there with a boot on the throat of the local population, it would take an entire army to subdue the city if it ignited. The clubs, the black market, they were all a pressure release valve that kept society from blowing up. Different groups frequented different clubs, and the one they were in was overseen by a friend of John's, who vetted his patrons, and was considered to be reasonably safe. "I've heard of five confirmed. All people of importance in the Communist Resistance, all executed in the street and their families taken away." He looked at Emily and Tilly, his eyes were narrowed and calculating, as though they were processing equations and balancing probabilities while he talked. The pair had spent some time in the centre of Paris after leaving the café where the executions had taken place, talking and drinking coffee, while hoping to bore anyone who could have been watching them into thinking they were no more than a pair of girls out to meet up with each other. Finally, they'd reported in to John, and he'd told them to meet him at the nightclub that evening.

"Have you heard from Etienne?" Tilly asked after taking a mouthful of wine.

"No..." John shook his head as he lit another cigarette, one of many he'd worked through since he'd been there, contributing to the blue haze that obscured the ceiling. He looked uneasy. Emily hadn't known him for long, but his demeanour had always been quite relaxed, even during the ambush, and she hadn't seen him so tense.

"We're going to have to find him, I need a monkey so I can talk with the farm. You're sure he didn't go into the hole?"

"Positive. He would have had to walk right past the pigeons to get in, they were already a door down by that point." She shrugged while swirling the wine in her glass. Emily's mind flashed back to the scene again, and she watched it all play out in crystal clear detail. One moment he was there, the next he wasn't, and there was no explaining it. "Is it the dog we picked up? That you need to get on to the farm about, I mean?" Emily watched the exchange carefully, unravelling the conversation as she did. The pigeons being the Germans, grey and everywhere, the dog being the person they'd rescued from the convoy, the hole being the safe apartment, and the farm being SOE headquarters in London, they were nonsense words that would mean nothing to anyone else, a whole language for public consumption, of which she'd been trying to learn since arriving. The one that had amused her the most was the monkey, their word for the wireless operator. Back in England they'd been called a pianist, but John had explained in his casual way that monkey was a local term he'd created, based on the statistical theory that a thousand monkeys tapping away at a thousand typewriters would eventually write the works of Shakespeare. He held that it equated to the furious tapping of a wireless operator making sense to somebody, somewhere. She didn't have much to add to the conversation, despite learning the language, she was still the new girl, so she listened and learned instead, paying attention to their cues, and tells, and their non verbal communication, along with how they used their words.

"Do you think he was picked up?" He gave Tilly a firm stare. She stared back, then looked to Emily, who shrugged in reply.

"What do you reckon?" she asked Emily, making her think for a moment. She was rarely asked her opinion, she'd delivered a few messages and packages here and there, but being invited into the conversation in that way was something new. "You were looking that way more than me."

"There wasn't a sound, so they'd have needed to move like lightning to grab him," Emily answered while considering her response. "No…

I don't think so." She shook her head, then took a sip of wine. Tilly shrugged and nodded in agreement.

"So, he was either picked up, or..." She said what everyone was thinking, and what Emily had been thinking all along.

"Or, they let him pass," John finished her sentence for her. His eyes had switched from calculating to resignation as he accepted the obvious. He'd warned Emily about Etienne, suggesting he already knew that they didn't know whose side he was on, but the day's events had practically confirmed it. There was no way that Etienne could have passed the Germans, and had they taken him, there would have been a scuffle, or at least a few minutes of him being led away that would have been clearly seen by either Emily or Tilly, or both. The only logical answer was that they let him pass, and why would they, unless they knew whose side he was on? It made Emily feel deeply uncomfortable to hear the words said out loud, and know for sure that others were thinking the same. She'd hoped there was an explanation other than the obvious, but now she knew, she didn't know what to feel.

"What do we do?" Tilly asked, her cool and calm persona finding a way of doing what Emily couldn't.

"We move. All of us move. To the clubhouse..." Emily followed the conversation intently, trying to avoid any more surprises before they happened. She'd been told about the clubhouse; an unused safe house kept in reserve for when things went wrong. A place only John knew the location of, which meant that nobody could be tortured, or otherwise encouraged to reveal its location and betray the others. A place that Etienne wouldn't know about.

"When?"

"Tomorrow... I need to check it first, and make sure it hasn't been compromised. We'll meet for lunch, and I'll give you the location."

"And if it has been?"

"We'll cross that bridge when we get to it…" He frowned as the air changed, and he looked at the source of the perfume and shadow that cast over their table in the darkest and quietest corner of the club. Emily turned to look in the same direction as Tilly's hand shot under the table, and saw the young woman staring at them, a lit cigarette in one hand, the other in the pocket of her long coat. She was young, younger than Tilly, and her eyes were fierce, full of fire and intent, and just a hint of fear. "I don't think we've met?" His tone was firm, yet playful, as he looked first at the girl, and then around the room. Emily followed his gaze, scanning the many patrons for anyone who could be with her.

"You would have remembered," she replied. Her voice was hard to read. It was both cold, while simultaneously full of enough rage to hide the nerves, and Emily struggled to work her out. "Francois wants to talk."

"I'll check my diary. How does tomorrow work for you?"

"How does right now work for you?"

"I'm not sure that's the best idea. Not here."

"No, not here. You're to follow me now, all three of you, or you'll never leave here alive." Her eyes remained the same as she lifted her hand from her pocket enough to show the grenade she was holding, the pin already pulled. John didn't look directly at the grenade, instead he just looked her in the eyes for a moment, then nodded. "That's the first sensible thing you've done in the last few days. Let's go." She gestured her head to the right and stepped to one side. John nodded and finished his wine.

"Drink up," he said casually, while nodding at Emily and Tilly. They did as he said, then joined him in standing and following the woman through the nightclub. The owner looked over, and started to move from the bar area, looking nervous and reaching into his pocket. John simply shook his head and creased his nose a little, as if to gesture not to bother, and that what was happening wasn't a problem. They followed her up the stairs, and out into the night, and another from just outside the club followed behind, tailing, no doubt armed and ready to gun the three down if they caused any trouble. They were led to a small chapel, where the young woman stood at the door and gestured them inside. Emily's heart was racing once again. It had already been a long and stressful day, from the executions to knowing they'd likely been betrayed by one of their own. Being herded from a supposedly safe nightclub on the orders of a girl armed with a live hand grenade, and led into a dark chapel in the backstreets of Paris topped it off perfectly. To make it worse, she knew that any chance of fighting their way out was practically zero. John was strict about them not carrying weapons around the city. The Parisian public were stopped and searched with monotonous frequency by both the Germans and the Gendarmes, and there was little anyone could do to explain carrying a weapon. It would just guarantee them being arrested on the spot, and taken away for interrogation. A needless risk to the operation. Tilly carried a tyre ripper on a lace around her neck, a steel ring with a claw that was used to rip open car tyres in acts of sabotage, a gift from the quartermaster's box of tricks back at the SOE in London, and something rough and innocent looking enough from a distance to be mistaken for some sort of poor girl's pendant, and Emily had taken to carrying a long leather boot lace from an old army boot, given to her by Tilly as a last line of defence, a simple and effective garrotte that she'd been taught to use back at the finishing school. A modest arsenal that wouldn't do much against a grenade. The door slammed closed behind them, and a match lit by the altar, illuminating a square looking bearded face, and the air filled with the scent of French tobacco. "Francois…" John said, his voice sounding hard in the stone chapel.

"You should know that my people surround this chapel. If there's any trouble, the three of you will be staying here permanently," the Frenchman replied in a low and gravelly voice.

"And you should know that you're overdoing the theatrics. A simple message asking to talk would suffice. Kidnapping on the threat of death by hand grenade was hardly warranted."

"I wanted to make sure I had your attention."

262

"Haven't you always had it? I thought we'd got on reasonably well when we've met previously."

"That was before eleven of my people were executed on the streets of Paris today, and their families thrown in prison, all because you and your pirates thought you'd attack a German convoy last night."

"Eleven? I'd heard it was five... Regardless, whatever we did, or didn't do last night, has nothing to do with what happened today. I'm sorry for what happened to your people and their families, but the Germans did that, not us." John's voice remained calm, though there was a firm edge to it. Emily glanced around as he talked, and saw the shadows of the sentries outside, passing the windows and making sure nobody got in, or out.

"It was a commando raid, no less, I've heard the reports. Eight German soldiers executed, their vehicles sabotaged, and explosive charges set that killed and maimed many more, and you knew the Germans would retaliate for what you did."

"We're at war, Francois, in case you hadn't noticed. There are always going to be consequences to any actions, though I suppose you'd have to actually do something to risk facing them..."

"And what's that supposed to mean?" The stocky Frenchman walked forward, blowing smoke at John. He had broad shoulders and a short beard. He looked like somebody that had done hard work all of his life.

"It means that I've been asking for your help since we arrived in Paris, for you to work with us, to do something to at least disrupt the Germans, but you haven't lifted a finger, despite them ruling over your city with an iron fist. You must have known you couldn't hide from what's happening here for ever, and the war would come to your doorstep sooner or later."

"So what? We don't get involved in your silly English games, so you betray us? What's wrong with you? We can't leave; we can't go back

263

home to England and pretend that none of this is happening. Our families our here, our lives are here. The Germans get too close to you, and what? You go, run away to safety. They get too close to us, and the people that we love, that we care about, pay the price. It's not a game! It's never been a game to us. We're not soldiers, not trained like you and your people. We're bakers, and railwaymen, and factory workers. If we get it wrong..." His voice was low, but passionate. His words resonating with a genuine tension and fear that Emily could feel in her chest over her own.

"If you get it wrong, they'll pull you from your houses and execute you in the street? Take your families to prison camps, or worse? Seize your property?" John lit a cigarette as he talked, his words staying at the same pitch they always were. Considered, casual even, without an emotion anywhere near them. "You've done nothing, Francois, yet it happened anyway. Those two got to see it up close and personal, as one of your men was forced to confess his crimes in front of his community, before watching his son hanged in front of him. What you feared the most has happened, and is happening. I told you it would, I warned you..."

"So, you had to prove it? It's happening, yes, but it's happening because of you! Because you attacked a convoy!"

"OK, fine..." John shrugged. "We attacked a convoy, and the Germans retaliated. I'm not denying it. We have orders to disrupt German activity, and to keep them on the alert, that's not a secret."

"Orders... Orders have a price."

"Yes, they do. The price on this occasion appears to have been eleven of your people, and their families."

"I wouldn't be so flippant about my people, or their families."

"You're missing my point."

"Which is?"

"That we attacked a random German convoy, something designed to rattle the enemy and let them know we're around. A commando raid, as you so accurately describe. Yet this morning, the Germans arrest your people. The bakers. The railwaymen. The factory workers you mentioned... Not soldiers. Not commandos. Just eleven members of the same Communist Resistance network." He took a long drag of his cigarette, the glow lighting the sternness of his face. "I know you, and maybe two or three of your people, let's call it four if you add the little psychopath with the grenade that we met tonight. I don't know any more, because I haven't gone looking. You made it clear that you and your people weren't interested in helping us, so we left you alone. However..." He tilted his head slightly as he looked in Francois' eyes, watching as the penny dropped. "If you haven't worked it out yet, it wouldn't have mattered if we shot one German last night, or hung a thousand of them from the Eiffel Tower, the outcome would have been the same. That is, somebody's sending you a message, old boy, and it's not us."

"What...?" Francois' demeanour changed, and in seconds he'd gone from a raging bear, poised to attack, to a dog with its tail between its legs. "What do you mean?"

"You're a member of the Communist Resistance leadership in Paris, Francois. I know that, you know that, and so do others. The fact that you're here talking to me, while eleven of your peers were publicly executed, and their families taken away, would suggest to even the most casual of observers that somebody's trying to either intimidate you and your organisation, or get rid of you. Either way, what the Germans did today wasn't about us, it was about you."

"This makes no sense at all..." The Frenchman shrugged and paced, the confidence and bravado he'd started with shaken from him in a few words. "Who?" he asked almost pleadingly as he turned back to John.

"Not us, I can assure you of that. Don't take offence, but we're a little less subtle. If we were declaring war on you, you'd know about it. Old enemies, perhaps? Old feuds? New ones...?"

265

"As you pointed out, we've kept our heads down. We attacked some factories at the start, but that was last year. We've watched, and planned, but there's been nothing. We don't even have anything in the pipeline. Official policy has been to stay quiet, and that's what we've done."

"Well, whoever it is, you've got a leak, I can tell you that much."

"I don't follow?"

"Somebody doesn't just know about you, they knew another eleven of your people, and exactly where to find them and their families. The word on the street is that there haven't been any intense sweeps by the Germans, they haven't emptied entire districts looking for you. They turned up at very specific places, and at very specific times, all in public, all with an audience. Somebody in your organisation is telling tales out of school."

The chapel fell into silence. No talking, no pacing, even the breathing was light and barely perceptible. It seemed to last for hours, as thoughts played out, and heads spun. For Emily, it had been draining. Her heart was still racing, so much that she was surprised the others couldn't hear it thudding away in her chest, but her mind had finally stopped looping through the possibilities of how they could escape, and whether Francois' mercenaries would negotiate if she had the bootlace tight enough around his throat to make his eyes bulge, like the boy's she'd seen that morning. Instead, she'd been intrigued by their conversation. John had let his adversary rant, and threaten, and walk himself down a path to a dead end there was no way out of without accepting some uncomfortable truths. Truths that hadn't even occurred to Emily. It made perfect sense, however, once John had explained it in his calm and collected manner. The truck ambush was largely inconsequential to what had happened that morning. If it wasn't that, it would have been something else to give the Germans an excuse to remove a significant part of the Communist Resistance leadership, while at the same time sending a quiet message that they likely knew everyone else, and could get to them just as easily. It was sinister at best. Francois now knew that his family, if he had one, were in danger, and anything he did would put them in harm's way.

"Please, don't do anything else…" Francois finally asked, breaking the silence in a tone that was now quite different to when he'd started. "Not right away, at least. Give me time to think, and work out what to do? Those of us that are left are obviously being watched, and I have a duty to them. You understand?"

"Unless we hear otherwise from London, we'll keep our heads down for a couple of days. You have my word."

"Thank you." He held out his hand, which John shook firmly. "Thank you, I mean that, and I'm sorry I accused you."

"We live in difficult times, Francois, and while I understand perfectly your desire to protect your people and your city, I can assure you that we're not here to play games. The Germans are your enemy as much as ours, and we're here to fight them, and let them know that Europe isn't yet finished. Every attack, every piece of information, everything we do or are involved in makes them nervous, and keeps their troops here in France looking for us, instead of fighting our soldiers in North Africa. It lets Britain keep fighting, which, like it or not, is how France is freed. The longer we last, the longer we can fortify our islands, and galvanise our empire. If we keep going, if we don't break, we can raise a force the likes of which the world has never seen, and set fire to Germany in a way unimaginable. We're not the enemy, Francois, and while there are only a handful of us here now, we will free France from the German jackboot."

"I must go… Vive la France!"

"Vive la France!" John's words were still an echo as Francois left, leaving the door open and disappearing at speed into the night. "What do you think, too theatrical?" John asked as he stood facing Emily and Tilly.

"I believed it!" Tilly replied.

"And so you should, I meant every word. Sometimes it's about getting the tone right, though, don't you think? Getting the gravity right can be a challenge, especially in French."

"What now?" Emily asked, breaking the discomfort of the irreverent conversation that had followed the tension of being abducted and taken to an abandoned chapel on threat of death by hand grenade.

"Now, we go to the clubhouse tonight. It's a risk moving around after curfew, but not as much of a risk as staying where we are. The Germans are up to something, the communists are scared, and God alone knows where Etienne is, or what he's up to, but it's not the furthest stretch of the imagination to see how he fits into all of this. I don't tend to believe in coincidences, especially not the type that involve Paris turning upside down the moment he disappears."

"Do you know that you hum when you're tense?" Emily asked Tilly as they lay in the darkness of their new room in the clubhouse, hidden away in the backstreets of Montmartre. The night was cool, and they were snuggled together for warmth under a few blankets piled on top of the old single bed that faced the window of the narrow attic space. They'd collected their things from their old place, Emily keeping watch while Tilly went in and gathered everything quickly and silently, before they both melted into the Parisian night, following alleys and passageways that looped back and switched direction, making it impossible for anyone watching to follow them to the clubhouse. Even then, they sat on sentry duty for hours after, watching and waiting, just in case. It was long after midnight when they finally climbed into bed, each with a pistol under their pillow, after John took steps to make sure they were ready for a fight, just in case.

"I what?" Tilly half laughed in reply.

"Hum. Well, it's like humming and singing at the same time, but the words are never quite there, and you'd hardly know it was a tune unless you really listened…"

"I don't know about that."

"I do. I heard it when we were waiting to ambush the trucks last night, and again today when you were trying to work out how we'd escape the Germans at the café. It's like an automatic thing that kicks in when you're thinking with intensity."

"Are you calling me a robot again?" she laughed.

"No..." Emily reassured her, frowning as she did, worrying that she was causing offence. "It's kind of a pretty tune, I think, from what I've picked up."

"Yeah, I'm not buying it. It's you hearing things when you're stressed. Why would I be humming and singing?"

"Let me try..." Emily laid back and thought, remembering each moment with her near photographic memory, something else about her that had annoyed people in the past as much as it entertained. When she was young, people were fascinated at her party trick. As she got older, they were less welcoming of a girl, and indeed a woman, that could see a person's words and remember them as clearly as a photograph. It tied people in knots. It had also made her a very good nurse, though, and contributed to why some had said she should study medicine. She remembered what she was taught, what was said, and how it was done, all with relative ease. It had also helped her through Scotland, and the finishing school. She didn't just pay attention to detail; she lived in it. She started to hum gently, until the tune matched the one in her head. "Waltzing a something, waltzing a something, you'll do something waltzing with me..."

"And he sang, as he watched, and waited 'til his billy boiled. You'll come a waltzing Matilda with me..." Tilly finished the song in the softest of voices, one that Emily hadn't heard before.

"That's it..."

"I sing that?"

"Hum... Lightly, like the breeze. A half word here and there. What is it?"

"I haven't heard that in ages..." There was an emotion in Tilly's voice that reminded Emily of the previous night, and she instinctively reached for her friend's hand and gave it a squeeze. Something that was welcomed, and a squeeze was returned, and maintained. "Dad used to sing it to me when I was a kid. He said it'd settle me when I was upset about something. He sang it to me when mum died..."

"I'm sorry." Emily's heart was squeezing as she was overwhelmed by an uncomfortable awkwardness that accompanied her thinking she'd awakened difficult memories at the end of an already difficult day. "I shouldn't have mentioned it."

"No..." Tilly squeezed her hand harder. "No. I just hadn't heard it for so long. It's where my name comes from, the name of the song, Waltzing Matilda." She half laughed, and Emily could see a smile on her tear stained face. "Dad told me that him and his mates in the ANZACS used to sing it when they were marching in the last war, to keep their spirits up and remind them of home. It reminded him of his mates, and he'd sing it, he told me, when he was wandering around the 'never never' looking for work after the war. Made sense he'd call me that, I suppose."

"It's a beautiful name."

"It's a sad song, for all he said it kept their spirits up."

"What's it about?"

"A swagman," Tilly turned on her side and looked at Emily as she sniffed at her tears, and wiped the back of her hand across her cheeks, only for Emily to reach up and dry her tears properly. "A wanderer, carrying his possessions on his back and looking for work, often in the shearing sheds out in the bush. It's what dad did after he came home from the war. They'd made him an officer after Gallipoli, and he was a Captain when he was here in France. He had to leave some of his

270

mates when they promoted him, then lost others in the fighting. Anyway, he didn't want to know when he got back home. Took the money the army owed him, sold what he had, and went looking for work. Didn't want to be around people, I suppose, not after all he'd been through. So, he was a swagman, travelling around from farm to farm, shearing, fixing fences and stuff. That's how he met mum." She smiled, and a warmth came to her voice. "In the song, the swagman catches himself a sheep down by the billabong, a bend in a river to you. It's the only real food he's had, but the landowner and police come after him, and he ends up dying…"

"That is sad…"

"Yeah… It's a song that just sticks, though. You know?"

"I do."

"Grandma said that dad could have gone that way if he hadn't found mum. She saved him, gave him somebody to love, and something to live for, and then they had me."

"Would you sing it for me?"

"No way."

"Please? I'd love to hear it properly."

"No teasing me…?"

"I promise." She gave her hand a squeeze as Tilly cleared her throat a little.

"Once a jolly swagman camped by a billabong, under the shade of a coolabah tree. And he sang, as he watched, and waited 'til his billy boiled, you'll come a waltzing Matilda with me.

271

Waltzing Matilda, waltzing Matilda, you'll come a waltzing Matilda with me, and he sang, as he watched, and waited 'til his billy boiled, you'll come a waltzing Matilda with me..." She sang through the verses, her voice soft and gentle, and at times tripping and trembling with emotion, until she got to the final verse, where she slowed a little, and the words almost disappeared.

Emily felt the tears streaming down her face as she pulled Tilly close and hugged her tight. It was instinctive, and for her every bit as much as it was for her young friend. There was something about the song that had stabbed her in the heart. It was so beautiful, yet so sad, and it had been delivered so softly by Tilly, who had such a deep connection to the words she sang, her dad's story making it all the more real to her. It both lit up the darkness and dimmed it further, and in a way she couldn't explain, it opened the door to all of the emotions she'd ever felt. Everything she had inside her that she never knew how to get out suddenly had a way into the world, and her tears came in torrents. They hugged, and they cried, until they slipped into an exhausted sleep. Whether it was the tension of the day they'd had, or the life they lived, for just one moment, two young women who'd trained to bury their emotions so they could do a job that most could never conceive, were human again. Girls with feelings, and thoughts, and a million miles away from the murderous automatons they'd been trained to be.

Chapter 19

Amen

"Good morning," John said casually as Emily walked into the kitchen. He was stood by the stove while a stranger, a man in a black shirt and priest's dog collar sat at the table staring at her through washed out light brown eyes. "Coffee?"

"Proper coffee?" Tilly asked as she followed Emily into the kitchen. They'd both slept like logs through the night, the adrenaline of the previous twenty four hours having exhausted them. "Who are you?" she asked the priest.

"This is Father Alain Moreau," John said as he poured hot water into a pot.

"Ladies," Alain added politely, while giving them an uncomfortable smile.

"Good morning," Emily replied, returning his smile with one much firmer before taking a seat opposite him at the kitchen table. She looked him over. He was old, but not. Maybe only in his thirties or forties, but he was pale and sickly looking, with thinning sandy brown hair, all of which made him look twenty years older at least, despite his frame looking quite athletic. She glanced briefly at Tilly, who sat next to her while looking him over just as warily, but choosing not to speak. They weren't used to visitors, mostly because they never had them, and waking up to a stranger in what was supposed to be the safe house nobody knew about set alarm bells ringing for them both.

"It's a beautiful day outside," he continued. "Not too cold, not too warm. The best of Spring."

"I haven't been out yet," Emily replied, maintaining the firm half smile.

"So many birds and flowers. It's enough to remind a person that God's still here, despite whatever else is happening."

"I'm not sure about that."

"Oh?"

"Coffee..." John said as he put the pot in the centre of the table, taking a seat next to the priest and stopping the conversation before it got started. "We don't have much, but we still have good coffee. Just about, anyway." He filled the four cups while Emily thought about what the priest had said, and her response. All the while, Tilly watched him, her eyes narrowed a little. She was the friendliest of people, unless she didn't know a person, and then she was instantly suspicious. "Alain is the bundle of clothes that we took out of the back of that German truck," John went on after taking a sip of coffee.

"A priest?" Tilly finally spoke.

"Yes..." Alain replied with a smile. "Surprised?" She shrugged and drank her coffee as he glanced to John.

"Not just any priest," John continued. "Alain works for the SIS, British Military Intelligence..." He smirked a little while watching Emily and Tilly for their responses, which involved looking at each other, but hardly reacting otherwise.

"Since 1938," Alain added with a smile. "I was recruited by MI6 when the storm clouds started to gather after Munich, and asked to let our English friends know what was happening here in Paris."

"Which explains why London wanted us to stop him being sent to Berlin," John added.

"I'm sorry to have put you out," Alain shrugged, looking a little awkward. "I was betrayed by a German mole in the Resistance here in Paris..." He looked to John, his awkwardness clearly growing, and got a nod of reassurance. "The same mole who betrayed your wireless

274

operator, the girl that the Germans picked up." Tilly's demeanour immediately changed, switching from cold to fire in the blink of an eye.

"Which is why London wouldn't let us reach out to the Resistance for help with the German convoy…" He looked a little conflicted as he talked. "It would appear that they have a leak."

"Unfortunately, by the time I worked out what was happening, it was too late. The Germans had me in the bag. I'd talked with London just before, and they told me to make contact with your team. It's highly irregular, of course, for us to even let you know we're in town, let alone ask for help, it's not the done thing to risk cross contamination between teams, let alone organisations, but I have something that London needs."

"What?" Emily asked. He looked to John again, who gave him another nod.

"While you've had a specific job to do here in Paris, my network has stretched a little wider, shall we say, and for the last few months I've been gathering and collating information on the German troop concentrations gathering in the Pas de Calais. Specifically, what we believe to be an invasion force preparing to attack England in the summer." Emily's tummy squeezed a little at the news, and she needed a long drink of the hot coffee to settle it. She felt herself wince at the thought of an invasion army gathering. "Six months of hard, dangerous work, gone! Photographs, unit details, even dossiers on their commanders and other officers, all painstakingly pulled together so England has at least a chance to prepare themselves for what's coming when the weather's right. Unfortunately, everything's stowed away in a place that is likely under German control these days, assuming they didn't find it when they picked me up." He shook his head with frustration before sipping at his coffee.

"I'm sorry I couldn't give you all the details when we planned the mission," John went on. "I didn't know for sure, just that there was somebody working in our area, and in a coded message to me that

275

Etienne couldn't read, London were very specific about us making sure the Germans didn't keep him."

"And I'm grateful for what you did. The local interrogators are good, but things are very different in Berlin. The Germans worked out that I was working for the English, it was practically undeniable, but they didn't know what I was working on, or who I report to. Which means we still have a chance to make something of it."

"So, you're not a priest?" Tilly asked.

"I am indeed a priest, and have been for many years. However, as the good book tells us, a shepherd sometimes needs to protect his flock, and that means keeping the wolves from the door." He gave her a mischievous smile. "I have no love for war, but what's being done, the way humans have turned on each other and become monsters... I had to do something. I had to pick a side."

"Wolves and sheep aside, this changes things," John said, "and we now need to put everything we have into getting Alain and his intelligence to England. I'm sure you can understand the urgency?" He looked at them both and got nods in reply. "However..." He paused for a moment, then gave Alain a half smile

"My time in France is at an end, I regret to say," Alain continued. "The Germans now know my face, and they took my photo and fingerprints when I was captured. So, I have no alternative but to flee to England. This is a blow to our efforts, of course, because I can no longer do my part. Though it also means that I don't have much left to lose, and I wouldn't mind one last opportunity to do something to bloody the nose of the enemy that, despite God's teachings, I confess to despising with all I am..." He frowned bitterly for a moment. "And to my eternal gratitude, John has agreed to help." He smirked again before continuing. "There is a German officer by the name of Colonel Walter Schulze of the Oberkommando des Heeres, or OKH, the strategic planning arm of the German high command. He's one of Hitler's favourites, and reports direct to Berlin. He spends much of his time with the army in the Pas de Calais, and visiting other units connected with the troop concentrations, and at our best estimation he is the single most valuable source of information regarding the coming invasion. He's with the tanks as they train, on the docks with the patrol boats and barges, and I'm told he's regularly joining the Luftwaffe for reconnaissance flights over the Channel and English coast. It's believed that he's coordinating the strategy ahead of the invasion, and I'd like to take him home with me as a gift from the French people."

"You want us to kidnap a German Colonel?" Tilly laughed, her demeanour changing noticeably once again.

"No." He frowned at her in an unfriendly way that changed the air a little. "I want you to help me kidnap a German Colonel. One who our friends back in London will have singing like a canary in a matter of hours, and will be far more valuable than all of the intelligence I could gather, even if I had another five years here."

"Should we just march into the barracks and ask him to come quietly?"

"Nothing quite as bold as that," John replied, giving her a firm stare that bordered on disapproval, the first time that Emily had seen such a reaction from him, and something that made her bristle a little as Tilly settled. "It would appear that the Colonel enjoys his weekends in Paris. We just have to be in the right place at the right time, and we can have him and Alain out of town before anyone knows he's missing."

"We've had his card marked for a while," Alain continued. "It was always the plan to try and snatch him sooner or later, if we could, so we may as well do it now while we've nothing to lose. There isn't a weekend that he isn't invited to a party somewhere, one of those that's attended by the type of society that gather whether there's a war or not, where he preys on wealthy French girls from good families, and once or twice he's been known to disappear off to hotels with them, slipping his security detail while trying to find himself a rich French wife for after the war." He frowned as he drank his coffee, clearly displeased at what he was saying. "If we introduce him to the right girl, who could lead him to the right hotel…" He stared into his cup

277

before looking up at Emily and Tilly, who both stared right back while maintaining their silence. Tilly's laughter had gone, replaced by a frown that matched Emily's. "We get him, and before we leave Paris, I promise that I'll make him tell you who the mole is in the local Resistance." He looked to John, and back to them. "You should know that Schulze was also involved in interrogating your wireless operator, he was brought in to help by the local authorities when she wouldn't talk to them."

"I'll do it," Tilly said without a pause.

"No…" Alain replied firmly, getting a scowl in return. "He likes brunettes with pale skin and light eyes. We've profiled everything about him, and that's a constant. If it's anyone, it's her." He nodded at Emily, whose heart squeezed tight as she felt the hairs on the back of her neck stand on end, then switched his gaze to Tilly. "You'll follow them to the hotel, and make sure they're not followed by anyone else; John and I will wait in the room. Once he's in there, and we know it's on, we'll subdue him." He looked to Emily. "Don't worry, you won't be left alone with him in there. Your job's to entice, to get him there, that's all. We'll do the dirty work."

"That simple?" Emily asked, finding her voice through her drying throat.

"That simple," John replied. "Alain and I have discussed it in detail, and I think we can pull it off. I'll speak with my contacts and get you on the guest list for whatever party he's invited to, and I'll sort the hotel. Somewhere that hasn't been taken over by the Germans, small, but still exclusive enough for you to be staying there. We get in, get him, and then get out. You and Alain will bring him back here, while Tilly and I go and deal with the mole." He nodded at Tilly. "Then, once it's done, you'll both escort them home by the southern route." He gave them a smile knowing that he'd just told them that their time in France was over, and they were going home to England, through Vichy France and across the Pyrenees to Spain, and then to either Gibraltar or Portugal. "Why don't you get some rest," he said to Alain after the table had been silent for a few minutes, "you must be exhausted after all you've been through over recent days."

278

"Yes... I am, as you mention it. Maybe I'll have a lay down for a while." He smiled graciously while accepting the polite request for him to leave and let John, Emily, and Tilly talk things through without him there. He finished his coffee and headed to the door, then stopped and turned before leaving, "If we're going to do it, we need to act right away... With all that's happened in the last few days, my being arrested, and the communist leadership being all but wiped out, I'm worried that your team is next. Whoever the mole is, they seem to know a lot about things they shouldn't, and time to act could be running out."

"Thank you," John gave him a smile, and he left, closing the door quietly. "So, there you have it..." he continued when he was sure Alain was gone. "You can speak freely."

"Etienne..." Tilly said. It was the name at the front of Emily's mind, too, and she found herself nodding along with John.

"It seems the obvious answer, doesn't it?"

"You really think he'd betray us?" Emily asked. "I know he was a little off, but..."

"How else did he get away from the Germans?" Tilly shrugged in reply while John raised his eyebrows questioningly. "You were there, you saw."

"I suppose..."

"It makes sense when you piece it all together," John continued. "When we lost Hannah, our wireless operator, it was the plan for Tilly to take over when we got another wireless," he explained to Emily. "She's the better candidate by far, but Etienne was adamant to the point of being insubordinate that it should be him. Made a song and dance about not putting another girl at risk, to such an extent that it was easier just to agree. With that and his erratic drinking and disappearances, it should have been obvious, and I suppose it was, really, to anyone willing to look." He frowned and swirled what

279

remained of his coffee. "The truth is, I messed up." He forced a smile as he looked at them both. "I knew Etienne was rotten, and tolerated him instead of doing something about it, and as a result we lost Hannah, MI6 almost lost a deep cover operative, a reconnaissance mission watching over the build up to the invasion has been shut down with six months of intelligence lost, and at least eleven civilians have been executed. Not to mention putting our operation at risk, knowing we'd likely be next on the list if Alain hadn't tipped us off." It was the first time that Emily had seen him show any genuine emotion. "So, if you'll indulge me one last time, and you're up for it, I'd like to at least try and rescue something from this farce, and send Schulze back to London."

"Don't talk like that," Tilly replied, her face spoke volumes about the emotions she was fighting to keep inside.

"Let's not get dramatic about it," he half laughed, without much effort behind the attempt. "It's war, things happen. It was, and always has been my job as organiser to be suspicious, to watch and ask questions, but instead I was irritated. I should've had Etienne sent back to England as soon as I got suspicious. I didn't, I waited. Wanting to keep everything going, and keep playing the game. In doing so, putting you both at risk, too, which is why you have to go back to England. Unless he's been particularly devious and got photographs, which I'm quite sure even I'd have picked up on if he had, all he will have been able to give is descriptions. Get back to England and do something else for a while, change your hair maybe, and there's no reason why you can't come back to France in the future, but maybe not here to Paris. Better than you staying, and…" He frowned as his eyes filled with so many competing thoughts and emotions. "Anyway, enough of that." He shook his head and smiled. "We'll need to get you some clothes, perhaps something more appropriate for hobnobbing with the Parisian elite. If you're up for it, that is?" He looked to Emily questioningly.

"It's what we're here for, isn't it?" She gave a smile of resignation, not entirely because she was about to put all of the skills, all of the training she'd had since arriving in Scotland, to the test in the most dangerous of ways. She was sad because she hadn't been in France long, and

280

didn't feel she'd done all that much, not compared to the others, and she was frustrated at being betrayed, not to mention being devastated on the part of everyone else who had suffered so much. Hannah, whoever she was, the communists. Alain, even. She'd known from her training that she was heading into harm's way, to a place where nothing would ever be as it seemed, and where everyone was playing a very different game of chess, but nothing could have prepared her for the reality of it. For the intense stress of not knowing if she'd be executed in the street, or be arrested and tortured, and the exhaustion that it brought. The only silver lining that she could identify, other than having made a new friend, was that she was getting to go out with a bang. She was leaving Paris, but if Alain and John's plan came off, they'd land a prize that could maybe save Britain from invasion, and prevent thousands, if not millions of deaths. She was frustrated, and annoyed, and sad, but also a little excited.

"You're sure?" Tilly asked. She was frowning, and her eyes full of fire. "If you're not, we can think of something else. Grab him in the street, or something, or break into his quarters."

"I'm sure," Emily replied with a reassuring smile that was as much for her as it was her friend. "I got through Scotland, didn't I? Not to mention finishing school, and Maier…" She let herself laugh at the memories of the mock interrogation back in London. It was good, and quite convincing, but while it had terrified her at the time with its realism, it hadn't come close to chilling her quite as much as watching what had happened to the communist and his family. It all seemed so far away from the reality of Paris.

"However…" John added. "If something isn't right when the game starts, if something about it looks wrong, or even feels wrong, we end it there and then, understood?" He fixed Emily in a firm stare. "What Alain has learned over the last six months will be enough. Schulze is the icing on the cake, that's all. If it isn't right, you make your excuses and leave. We'll see if we can recover Alain's information from its hiding place, if possible, but either way we'll get the three of you out of town. Tilly will be like a shadow, so don't think you're alone, either." Tilly nodded confidently. "Just give him the slip in the street, and if he tries to follow, or things get awkward, she'll deal with him. Understood?"

"Yes..." Emily replied, nodding in agreement.

"Good. We should probably get moving." He drained the dregs of coffee from his cup, then stood. "Any questions?"

"What about you?" Tilly asked, while Emily shook her head.

"What's that?"

"Please, don't play games... Both Plans A and B involve Emily and me leaving with Alain, either with or without Schulze, but you haven't mentioned your role beyond the hotel, and we both know that's not a mistake."

"That's because I won't be coming with you," he smiled warmly, a sadness and congruence replacing everything else that had been in his eyes. "I'll be making enough trouble around Paris for a few days to keep the Abwehr, Gestapo, SD, Gendarmes, and everyone else chasing their tails instead of chasing you. Then, I'll head north, and make a bit more, and lead them in the wrong direction before going to ground for a while. I'll give it a week, then circle back around and wait for London to send a new team in. I'll join you both back in England once I've handed over to them."

"I should stay here with you," she replied firmly. "You'll need help keeping them occupied, and two pairs of hands can do more damage than one. Emily will be fine taking Alain home."

"No." He put his cup down firmly. "Right, let's get going."

"But..." Tilly protested as she stood.

"I've always kept things pretty informal here, Tilly, don't make me give you an order. Not now." He smiled again, inviting her to step down, which she did with a sigh of frustration. "Besides, I have enough surprises left in the old toy hamper to make it rather fun, and I'm really quite looking forward to finally letting loose and putting Churchill's proclamation to the test. What is it he said? Set Europe ablaze?"

"Yeah... Something like that." She looked at Emily and gestured her head to the door. "Come on, we should get some rest while he sorts you something to wear." Emily nodded and followed her to the door. "There's one thing I don't get," she said as she stopped, and turned to look at John. "Why now...? Other than the convoy, we're hardly causing any trouble. Most of what we do is watching and intelligence gathering, and recruiting and training Resistance members. We weren't on to anyone special, or planning anything particularly big, we weren't even whipping up the Resistance into that much of a hysteria just yet. We've been careful, building networks and contacts, so why is all of this happening now?"

"I don't know..." John replied, the forced attempt at levity dropping from his face. "Maybe it's just as I said? The Germans always knew we were around, which means we're a threat they'll have been looking for. I just got sloppy, and let them find a way in, especially after they picked up poor Hannah."

"That doesn't add up, either," Tilly shook her head. "Hannah was good, you know that. The Germans wouldn't have known she was a monkey, even if she was sitting and tapping out Morse at the top of the Eiffel Tower. She was the least conspicuous, the most diligent and careful... She'd have seen them coming a mile off, even if they were tipped off."

"We have Etienne to thank for that, I suppose." He shrugged, though not casually as he usually did, his body was riddled with a remorse and guilt that filled the room. "Now I know what happened, I'm just amazed that the rest of us lasted this long. Still, never look a gift horse in the mouth, and all that. Another twenty four hours, and you'll be gone, while I get to blow things up and settle a few scores." His smile returned. "Go on, you'd both better get some rest while you can. The trip south isn't going to be an easy one, and you're going to need your energy. I'll arrange some rations to take with you, enough to keep you going. Only take what you can carry, and explain. Bring everything that you're leaving when you come down for lunch, and I'll make sure it's disposed of."

Chapter 20

Swag

"I'm told that you're in Champagne," Schulze said confidently, as though he was announcing the news. He wasn't particularly tall, but not short either, and he had a stocky build. His hair was dark, and thick, and slicked back with pomade, and his uniform was sharp and very well tailored. He'd circled the busy reception rooms several times since Emily had arrived, making polite conversation with those around her, but never actually acknowledging her in any way, until finally, after over an hour, he stopped to make his move on her. She'd watched him closely, between her polite conversations with other guests, and moments of mixed relief when she was left alone to stand in the shadows and admire the very expensive oil paintings hanging on the walls. The best of what was left after Hitler and his henchmen had looted Paris of much of its art after the surrender. She'd seen his wandering eyes in the reflections of people's glasses, and mirrors, and sometimes while looking right through the person she was talking to and seeing him in the background. He tried to be casual, but there was no mistaking his interest. Something that made her both happy and nauseous.

"No," she replied dismissively, while briefly looking him up and down, before returning her gaze to the packed room of German army officers, and very wealthy Vichy French civilians.

"My apologies, it seems I've been misinformed." He cleared his throat a little. "Or perhaps I misheard, it's easily done in such a busy place, don't you think?" She ignored him for a moment, then whipped her head around to look him in the eyes, tilting it slightly and staring as he flinched a little.

"You were asking people about me?" She frowned with distain.

"I… Only because I haven't seen or met you previously, and wanted to introduce myself."

"If you wanted to know about me, why didn't you come over and ask?"

"Touché... You have me, Mademoiselle. I wanted to make a good impression, and thought it would help strike up a conversation if I knew a little about you. A common frame of reference, if you will."

"Then you should know that my family are in wine, not champagne, and it's Madame, not Mademoiselle. I'm not an infant." She didn't shift her frown, but went back to looking past him, and then around the room. She was being deliberately antagonistic and aloof, to the point of feeding him a challenge that he wouldn't be able to resist, just as she'd been trained at the finishing school. Had she fallen at his feet, she'd have been too obvious, and too easy, had she been too harsh, she may well have scared him into the arms of one of the many other brunettes at the ostentatious party that had no business happening in an occupied city that was gripped by fear and half starved.

"My sincere apologies, Madame. I've practiced my French, almost religiously, yet still it appears that I'm clumsy."

"It would indeed. Maybe you should have practiced your geography, too, while you've been at it. Champagne is in the north; my wine is in the south. Provence, to be exact. Very different places, with different climates and soils. In the north they must make champagne, because the grapes don't get the sun as much, and to make them into anything else would be to make ditch water. In Provence we have the sun, and the warmth, and the freedom... Everything the grapes need to make very good wine. Wine not needing bubbles to make it drinkable." She talked with confidence that bordered on arrogance, sharing her knowledge of wines, and France, and its regional rivalries, in such an indirect way that gave authenticity to the character she was playing, or so she hoped.

"Alas, you have me again," he sighed a little dramatically. "I know that I like wine, but I don't know enough about wine to know why. Or where it's from, for that matter..."

"You're German, it's to be expected." She let herself giggle out loud, amused at herself, while inside there was a voice screaming and asking what the hell she was doing, and whether it would just be easier to ask him to shoot her than stand there and belittle him?

"This is true," he laughed, much to her relief. "Now, if we're talking about beer, that's a subject I am an expert on. I'm a Bavarian, after all, and we make some of the best beer in the world."

"Your family is in beer?"

"What? Ah, no. Sadly not. I drink beer, I do not make it. Which is probably for the best, it wouldn't be healthy to love your work that much, don't you agree?" He laughed out loud again, and she let herself smile in response, just a little, a turn up of the corners of her mouth and nothing more.

"Which is why I drink champagne, and not Provençal wine," she replied, while gently waving the almost empty glass in front of his face. He smirked in reply at her apparent playfulness, and some of the tension fell from his shoulders.

"I must confess that I'm not sure our hostess remembers everything as clearly as she once did," he said quietly, almost in a whisper as he leaned a little closer. "She's wonderful, of course, and very kind in organising parties like this to try and bring the German and French people together, but I think perhaps the details slip, or she enjoys the champagne too…"

"Details? Should I dare ask what else she's told you about me?" Emily feigned shock and hurt in such a way that he couldn't help but smile.

"Oh, not that much, not really. Just that your family supply wine to the French government, which makes so much more sense now that I know you're from Provence."

"Is it important what my family do?"

"Yes and no… There are many of your people, quite understandably, that, well, perhaps aren't quite as ready to see us Germans as friends and neighbours, and recognise how we're all better off without the influence of those frustrating and meddlesome English in our lives. Your family working with your government suggests that maybe you're not one of them, and as such, I can rely on you for engaging conversation, rather than a glass of champagne thrown in my face. You understand?"

"I do; things have been difficult for so many in my country… The world has changed, though. France has changed. We must make a new future, with new commerce, and new opportunities." She shrugged casually, then took a sip of her champagne. She was so immersed in her role that even her heart was steadying, and not racing as she'd expected it would be when she first saw herself in the floor length royal blue cocktail dress. She didn't ask John where it had come from, or the fine silk stockings, heeled shoes, and what she was quite sure from its weight and colour to be a solid gold necklace, bracelet, and earrings, all of which appeared to be from a matching set. She'd done her hair in a simple, yet elegant style, lifting it into a loose bun and pinning it in place, showing the long lines of her slender neck. She hadn't seen herself look like that in as long as she could remember, maybe her wedding day, but she'd been in white then, and her jewellery wasn't quite as exquisite. She'd also worn her hair down, at the request of her husband, despite her thinking she liked it better up. Her heart had raced when she'd seen herself in the mirror, and roared loud when Tilly had given her a spray of delicate yet potent Chanel perfume before sending her inside. Everything settled into place, it was as though the perfume set her in a trance, and brought out a character ready for the show. She moved with a glide, smiling seductively when she needed to, between moments of being cool and nonchalant. Her words flowed softly when she talked with guests, tripping lightly off her tongue with a delicate ease, and a purposeful inbuilt pause and reach just when she thought they were needed. It was like she'd been born for the part, and she moved around the mansion like she was at home. All the while, though, she felt like she was watching the act from outside of her body, while scanning and scoping her environment for threats, for escape routes, and for anything else that would help or hinder her mission. People who looked like they could be trouble, others like they could be manipulated, anything and everything was in the domain of her use, including Schulze, who she'd seen the moment he first entered the room, fitting John and Alain's description almost perfectly, both in his look and demeanour.

They talked for quite some time, with Schulze being the perfect gentleman throughout, conversing about anything but the war while bringing her drinks and snacks, and tending her like she was royalty. The majority of his conversation was about after the war, and looking forward to a time when he was able to hang up his uniform, and live in the Bavarian countryside raising local cattle, an apparently very traditional and noble occupation for Germans of that area. He never quite managed to sound weary of the war, however, there was always an element of not being quite ready to give it all up and live in peace, something under the surface of his words and actions that reminded Emily with frequency both of who he was, and of the game she was playing.

"I must go, I'm afraid," Emily said with the hint of a sigh as the clock struck eleven, even offering the slightest smile of resignation to convey her disappointment. "I return home to Provence early in the morning, and we're already past curfew."

"Such a shame… I feel like we could have talked all night."

"Perhaps another time, when I come to Paris again?"

"Perhaps, though it's a shame to wait. I've enjoyed your company."

"And I yours."

"Are you staying nearby?"

"Not far, a hotel only a few minutes' walk from here." She finished off what remained of her champagne, lubricating her fast drying mouth and throat as the moment of truth arrived. "I'd stay a while longer, but my father calls at midnight to make sure I'm home and safe. I

289

suppose I'll always be his little girl, which is both frustrating and warming at the same time."

"You know, Paris isn't safe at night. Despite the curfew, there are some bad types around, hiding in the shadows. Escorting you back to your hotel would be the least a gentleman should do. Besides, being with an officer, nobody will give you any trouble for being out past curfew…"

"In that case, accepting is the least a lady should do in reply to such a kind offer," she almost purred as she leant close, lingering just long enough for him to smell her perfume, and watching his hand shake and his brow perspire before she moved away again and put down her glass. "I'll get my coat…" She held his gaze for a moment, then walked away, leaving him standing and staring at her, which she acknowledged with the briefest of glances over her shoulder. She knew the game she was playing was the most dangerous dance she'd ever been part of, and she knew how high the stakes were, while at the same time, there was something deep inside that was thriving on making him lean in and squirm, and hooking him into her with carefully chosen words and glances. Part of her was enjoying it.

The night air was cool, colder than she'd anticipated, to the point where she could see her breath as she walked through the darkness of Paris at night. Schulze had continued to engage her in conversation as he walked confidently by her side, with almost a swagger as though he owned the city. He'd agreed to meet her down the street, leaving her to say her goodbyes and leave the party alone, while he slipped out the servants door at the rear of the property, and ran to meet her, having left his security detail of armed military police relaxing in the kitchens and talking with the maids. They strolled slowly, enjoying the relative silence of the streets, while all the time Emily's senses were heightening and preparing for what she knew would come next. In the reflection of a shop window, she'd caught a glance of a shadow slipping into the darkness behind her, and she felt herself smiling knowing her back was being watched. Soldiers, or police, would be too clumsy, and too loud, even the best of them. It could only be one person. The person she knew was there, and had been close to her for the entire night.

"You know, if you didn't want the night to end just yet, I have some very good cognac…" he said as they stood outside the hotel. The streets were empty, it was long past curfew, and the only sound other than their words had been their footsteps echoing around the darkness. He reached into the pocket of his overcoat and pulled out a silver flask that he held up in front of her while smiling suggestively. "The finest, Louis Tres, from a case of bottles I rescued from some uneducated soldiers who wouldn't know the difference between it and vinegar."

"How dare you?" She frowned at him furiously. "You expect me to stand in the street and drink from a flask like a common vagrant?" He looked shocked, and bristled a little. "I have glasses in my room, come on." She gave him a wink and a slow smile, and gestured her head towards the door.

"What about the concierge? You said your father calls…"

"He does call, and the concierge has been telling my mother that he's tucked up safely in bed for years when he's been here on business trips. I think perhaps the concierge can now do the same for me, if he doesn't want my mother finding out what's gone on in Paris. Come, or don't, it's up to you." She turned and walked towards the door, the heels of her shoes clicking lightly, and soon joined by the hurry of his boots, making her smirk a little to herself as he caught up. She breezed through the opulent marble and brass lobby, slightly relieved that there was nobody about, especially a concierge, and made her way to the elevator, which took them to the top floor, and along a corridor to her suite.

"What is it?" he asked as she paused at the door, moving the handle up and down, and then holding it steady. She turned slowly to look in his eyes. Her frown was deepening, and her chest rising and falling with anticipation.

"Maybe I had too much champagne…"

"No!" The word shot from his mouth with enough enthusiasm to make his excitement clear. "I mean, why? What makes you think that? You've been absolutely fine."

"Because I forgot I needed a key to get into a hotel room!" She rolled her eyes, then pulled her key from her bag and put it in the lock, rattling it loudly before pushing the door open and standing aside. "After you. Unless this is where you say goodnight."

"I don't think I want to say that just yet…" he whispered in reply, then entered the dark room, staring into her eyes as he passed her. She smiled as she watched him, then stepped in after him and flicked the light switch as she closed the door with a heavy thud, turning on the lamps that bathed the room with an amber glow.

"The glasses are in the cupboard, why don't you pour us a drink while I freshen up." She nodded across the room, then headed to the bathroom door.

"Maybe we could share the cognac while we freshen up together," he said confidently as he followed her a moment later.

"Or, maybe you can put your hands where I can see them, and stay perfectly quiet," John said as he stepped out of the darkness of the bathroom to meet him, passing Emily and putting the barrel of his German issue Walther PPK pistol against Schulze's forehead.

'What is this…" Schulze muttered as he stepped backwards, dropping his cognac and stumbling as his face drained white while John pushed him into the bedroom.

"I do believe I said silent, but if you insist on making a noise, I'm more than happy to shoot you in the knee and make it worth my while listening to you." Schulze nodded as he raised his hands. "If you wouldn't mind," John leant his head back a little, all the time keeping his eyes on Schulze. Alain followed them out of the bathroom and stepped forward, taking Schulze's Luger from its holster and keeping it pointed at him. "Sit." John pushed his pistol firmly against Schulze's

292

forehead as his knees came level with the bed, and he fell backwards, arms still in the air as he looked first at the two men holding pistols at him, and then to Emily, who stepped out of the bathroom and moved over to the window to look out of the curtain, checking outside for any movement or signs of being followed by Schulze's bodyguards. She watched for a moment, scanning the shadows and alleyways, then looked to John and shook her head. While she'd enjoyed elements of the game, she'd been on edge throughout, wondering if they could pull it off, and if they couldn't, what she'd do. Now, though, her heart was racing faster than ever, and adrenaline was coursing through her body unrestrained. It had worked like clockwork. Everything, every pace, every move, just as John had planned, and now her part was done, her body didn't know how to react. It was like all the tension needed to come out somewhere. "You are Colonel Walter Schulze of the OKH…"

"And if I am?"

"Let's dispense with the theatre, Colonel. I'm being polite. You are Colonel Schulze, if you weren't, you wouldn't be sitting here looking down the barrel of my pistol."

"So, what now? You kill me? The shot will be heard throughout the hotel, and the Gendarmes and my men will be on their way before my heart stops."

"No, that would be far too dramatic. You are, however, going to come with us, and do exactly as I say, otherwise you'll be begging through a gag for me to kill you while I take you apart piece by piece, the type of gag that makes sure nobody hears anything except for me, am I making myself clear?" Schulze looked at him defiantly, and then over to Emily, who had glanced out of the curtain again and turned back just in time to catch his gaze. His eyes were full of anger and hurt. She simply stared at him coldly, while thinking of the communist that had been executed in front of her, and his son who the Germans had hung. She had no compassion at all for the man sitting in front of her. As a nurse, she'd learned that infection needed to be cut out if a body was to survive, and she didn't see him as anything other than rotting flesh. She frowned as the door handle twitched, just slightly, and at the same time John stepped back to put some space between himself and Schulze before turning his pistol on the door. "Do his knees if he moves," he whispered to Alain, who nodded in reply. The handle clicked, and the door fell open, revealing a silhouette that only took shape and form as the person stepped forward. Emily's heart almost burst out of her chest as she stood wide eyed and stared at Etienne as he aimed his pistol ahead of himself and into the room. "Etienne..." John said as he tilted his head in surprise, eyes wide open as he tried to work out what was happening.

"Got you at last, you bastard," Etienne said, his voice trembling with rage, and his eyes red with fury. He looked like a wild beast, and a heavy air fell over the room as he stepped forward with his pistol at the ready. A shadow flitted across the room before anything else could happen, and the heavy brass pommel of a fighting knife smashed against Etienne's temple, knocking him sideways as his legs failed and he half fell. The door was kicked closed, and in seconds Tilly had his head dragged back by the hair, and her knife pushed tight against his neck as his mouth opened and closed in an attempt to talk, while his eyes rolled in pain at the sudden and intense attack.

"I don't even need an excuse," she whispered in his ear as she held him half up, half down, his throat resting on her blade while he half heartedly attempted to hold onto her hand as she held him up.

"Good timing..." John gave her a nod, which was briefly returned, before he turned his pistol back on Schulze. "Right, I think we'd better get going before there are any more surprises! Alain, get him ready to go."

"I can't..." Alain replied.

"What the hell is it now?" John blustered as quietly as he could, his frustration bubbling as he turned to look at Alain. Emily's heart almost stopped once more as the French priest's pistol switched from Schulze's chest to John's. It was like she was in the air raid again. The air had been sucked from her body, and she was rooted to the spot, unable to move.

"I'm afraid it's you that'll be coming with me..." He half smirked while glancing around the room. Emily looked to John, and then Tilly, who was looking back in horror while Etienne groaned. "We've been wanting to get our hands on you for so long, and finally, here we all are. Your entire team together in one place."

"We? What? Alain… If this is some sort of inter departmental feud, we can talk about it another time, just put that bloody gun down before you do something we'll all regret in the morning!"

"Such ignorance. Or is it innocence, perhaps?" His accent changed ever so slightly. "Allow me to introduce myself formally, while my men secure the building. I'm Hauptsturmführer Ernst Aber, from Section B of the Sicherheitsdiesnt, the counter intelligence service of the Reich, or the SD as you may know it, though many wrongly confuse us with the Gestapo. Either way, you are now my prisoners." He flashed a most menacing smile, glancing here and there to check everyone's movements and position. Emily's mind was spinning. She didn't have a gun, and she knew he'd shoot her down before she got a couple of paces if she tried to move towards him, but it was an option she was considering as all the others seemed much worse. If she tried, maybe it would buy time for John to swing around and shift his aim from Etienne to Aber. She'd be dead, she was sure of that, but maybe John and Tilly would have a chance. Her mind spun as she considered the options, she then tensed further as she heard a car screech to a halt outside, making her move her eyes involuntarily towards the curtains. "As I said, you are now my prisoners, and my men are on their way up here as we speak, so please, no heroics…" He smirked again as he glanced at Emily.

"How…?" John muttered in shock.

"We've always known you were here, but you've always been too smart, too careful. Even when we finally caught your bitch of a wireless operator, we still couldn't get you, and while she didn't say a word no matter what we did to her, it made no difference, we already had the wireless transceiver belonging to MI6, and a willing operator who would do anything we asked once we had his family in custody... We simply had the real Alain Moreau tell his handlers that he had a

295

sympathetic anti Nazi contact in the Abwehr, and then offer a prize so big it couldn't be ignored, such as a Colonel who knew all the secrets about the coming invasion of England, something we knew that London wouldn't be able to resist... It was just a matter of time."

"The real Alain?"

"Of course. Who do you think sold your superiors my cover story? Oh, don't look so surprised. You're not the only ones engaged in clandestine warfare, my friend. You play your games, we play ours. Once we'd established our story, and gained the trust of your MI6 back in London, all we had to do was get a message to your embassy in Lisbon from their friendly anti Nazi contact in Paris, letting them know that Alain had been arrested and was going to be transported to Berlin, and the job was done. Naturally, we embellished a little, about the Resistance mole, I mean, but it wasn't that much of a lie, Alain really did tell us everything once his family started to scream. Including how MI6 and the SOE hate each other so much that you don't even talk, and one didn't even know the other was here in Paris. Still, his story got your bosses back in England talking, so that's something they can thank us for." He was enjoying the theatre of the slow reveal, and seeing the colour drain from John's face. "As it is, it's all come together quite perfectly. We wipe out all of the British operatives in Paris, while removing support for the Resistance in the process, and at the same time having the perfect opportunity to eliminate the communist leadership, and put them out of business so they can't report in to their handlers in Moscow, and let them know when our troops start to march east shortly."

"East? But... England?" John's composure was gone; words were falling from his mouth as Aber pieced together the story for him.

"England is finished. Cut off and isolated. Why would we bother ourselves invading, wasting men and materiel for something of so little consequence? You're no longer in the war, and no longer a threat, which means we can now march east and get rid of the communist scum once and for all. Once that's done, and Russia is subdued, Europe is ours. Your Churchill will be replaced with somebody more amenable, and you'll do as we say. No need for an invasion at all.

That wouldn't have got you all excited though, would it? You English would have just sat back and watched Russia fall if we hadn't sold you a story about an invasion of your own green and pleasant land. Capturing a German Colonel responsible for the invasion planning would be opportunistic, but not something worth risking everything for if the target of the invasion was Russia, not England. Perhaps the English exceptionalism, the arrogance, is what has led you here?" He let out a laugh. "Of course, it helped us no end that we have such a Colonel with a penchant for rich French girls, and an inability to keep control of his pants. Something we'll talk about when all of this is over." He gave Schulze a frown of disappointment.

"But..." John looked to Etienne.

"Not one of ours, but I appreciate you bringing him along."

"I came for him... The traitor," Etienne half gasped while looking at Aber, and still only half conscious and struggling to remain upright. "I serve only France, and General de Gaulle."

"My God..." John's face was ashen. "What have I done...?" He looked to Tilly, and then Emily, his eyes lost and full of sorrow. "I'm so sorry, girls. I'm so, so sorry... If I can beg one last thing of you both, it's to do what you can with what little I have left to give." He smiled warmly, then turned with lightning speed, swinging his pistol towards Aber and firing, hitting him in the arm as the German squeezed his trigger and put a bullet in the side of John's chest that went in one side and passed right through the other, piercing his heart and lungs on its way, and sending him flailing as he fired shots into the wall before collapsing, dead before he even hit the ground. The firing continued, and more shots went across the room at Etienne and Tilly before Emily could get to Aber, and knock the gun from his hand. The shooting was deafening, and the room was quickly full of gun smoke as he turned and elbowed her in the jaw, stunning her for a moment, but not slowing her. She punched him hard in the skull, right behind his ear, knocking him to one knee. Then, as she prepared to finish him off and put him down for good, Schulze flew off the bed at her, screaming as he did, grabbing her around the throat and forcing her backwards, where he slammed her head against the wall

297

again and again, while squeezing tight around her throat. She reached out and stuck a thumb in his eye socket just as she felt the repeated impact starting to dim her senses, feeling the warm softness of his flesh as his eyeball popped from the socket and he let out a loud and piercing scream. With all his might he threw her against the wall, rattling her brain and almost knocking her unconscious. As her sight dimmed, she saw Aber running and stumbling for the door, past the bleeding and lifeless heap of limbs that were Tilly and Etienne. It was all happening in slow motion. She couldn't hear, she could hardly see, the world was turning grey as Schulze strangled the life from her. She gazed down at John who lay a few paces away, staring at her through dead eyes as his blood pooled around his corpse. It had all been so perfect, just for a moment, and then it all went so wrong. The thoughts spun around her mind. The faces of people dead and gone, Caroline, Mrs Jennings of the WVS, even her husband, and those she'd lived for, and loved, and cared about. Harriet, Eve, Hermione, Tilly… Her right hand dropped away from his wrist as she slid down the wall, dragging the hem of her dress up in a way that would have embarrassed her had she been more alive. She wasn't, though, she was all but gone. Almost, but not quite… Her hand wrapped around the brass handle of her fighting knife, and with all her remaining strength she pulled it from the scabbard on her thigh and thrust it upwards, the heavy steel blade cutting through his uniform like it was paper, and piercing his chest between the third and fourth ribs before driving straight into his heart. He didn't cry out like in the films, there was barely any noise at all, just a dull 'ugh' that was half gasp, half deep cough. His blood ran down her arm, a trickle at first, that quickly became a stream as his grip released, and the oxygen flooded into her screaming lungs. Her senses rushed back, and she saw Aber look over his shoulder before falling as a hand reached up and grabbed his leg. The slow motion world started to speed up again as she watched Aber kick free and run out into the corridor, as Tilly fought to extract herself from under Etienne and run unsteadily after him. Emily shook her head as she took in a deep breath, then ripped the knife from Schulze before digging the point in his stomach and dragging it across his body. He was already dead before his guts fell out and hit the floor just seconds before the rest of his body, and she was quickly across the room, clambering over John's corpse and taking his pistol as she went, then kneeling beside Etienne, who'd half pulled himself up against the wall while trying to stop the bleeding in his shoulder and chest.

"Downstairs… My… Stop him before…" His words were breathless, and his eyes closed tight as he fought for breath, and blood pooled at the side of his mouth. She nodded, and was on her feet and in the corridor a second later, running towards the stairs. A pair of armed men in suits and wide brim hats appeared from the elevator, their pistols half at the ready. She levelled her pistol and fired at each in turn, two shots each fired in quick succession, in what she'd been taught to be a double tap, clinical and considered shooting designed to kill not wound, just as she'd learned in the killing houses back in Scotland, taking them by surprise and dropping them both where they stood before either could get a shot off. She leapt over them and started down the stairs, descending as fast as she could while crashing off walls in her haste as gunshots rattled below, and screams cut through the air. The gun smoke stung her throat as she passed through the haze, and stepped hastily over the dead suited men in the lobby, firing at two more shadowy figures and sending them diving for cover as she emptied the magazine and dropped the pistol to the ground before she ran out into the street. She looked left, and then right, just in time to see Tilly disappear around a corner, then took off after her.

She pulled up the hem of her dress, letting her stride into her run as she gave chase. Her head was pounding, her ears were ringing, and her heart was bursting. There were a million thoughts that she had no time to think, the trap, the fight, how the training had kicked in. They'd taught her how to fight for her life, with her hands, with a knife, with a pistol, and they'd told her that she'd remember her training when the time came, but the logical side of her had always wondered. Always questioned it. She knew how to manage wounds, how to keep people alive, but she'd been a nurse for years, practicing the same skills time and again. She'd only been with the SOE for a matter of months. It didn't matter, though. However they'd learned what they had about killing didn't matter. They'd known, and they'd taught her, and despite the fear and terror that were flowing through her body along with the adrenaline, all she knew for sure was that she had to get Aber. Nothing else mattered. As long as she got him, and stopped him before he could do any more damage, tell his secrets, or kill anyone else, nothing mattered. Not John, Etienne, or any of the Resistance. She pushed harder, and ran harder, silently thanking the

SOE for pushing her to her limits in Scotland, and teaching her how to hurt through physical exertion. Without it, she wasn't sure she would have been able to push through the pain, and move like the wind through the dark Paris streets.

Her mind cleared and determination grew as she rounded another corner and saw Tilly on a bridge over the Seine, dancing in and out of the shadows cast by the moon over the nearby Notre Dame Cathedral as she fought with Aber. It was fast, violent scrapping, that saw both drop to their knees more than once, while punching, kicking, and wrestling. Emily felt her grip tightening around the handle of her knife as she got closer, feeling the crosshatches in the brass, and pushing her thumb against the guard, ready to let its do its work for a second time. There was a pause when she finally got onto the bridge, having felt like she was running towards it forever, as Tilly and Aber came together, and he slumped against her before falling and collapsing backwards against the bridge wall while grasping desperately at his neck. Emily slowed to a jog as she watched. It was done. She released her grip on her knife a little as she looked around to see if anyone was following, then back at Tilly who stumbled a couple of paces backwards, prompting her to race forward and catch her before she fell.

"I got him…" Tilly said as she looked up at Emily and smiled, nodding as she did. Her eyes wide, and chest heaving as sweat ran down her face and neck from the exertion. "I got him…" Blood dripped from her fighting knife, while it gushed from Aber's neck and soaked his clothes, and left a dark smear on the stonework as the life went from his eyes just a moment before he fell backwards and disappeared over the edge and into the river.

"And I've got you. Come on, we need to get out of here before his friends turn up." She looked in the direction they'd come from, expecting to hear boots crunching on the ground, and engines roaring, but there was nothing but an eerie silence as their hot breath formed clouds above them in the cool air. She made a move. She thought through the route in her head, and it was the long way around, but they needed to go to the cathedral, and over the bridge the far side of the island, keeping to the shadows, and getting as far away from the hotel as possible. None of the safe houses were safe anymore, least of all the most recent, where Aber had sat with them and drank their coffee, and eaten their food. He was dead, but there was no knowing who he'd told, what messages he'd dropped for his spies. Going there was too risky. "Tilly, he's dead. We've got to go." She pulled at Tilly's arm when she didn't move to follow her across the bridge, then turned back to see her swaying and her head rolling a little. "Tilly…" She looked in her friend's eyes as they rolled, and she staggered a little. "Tilly we've got to go, now!" Tilly nodded, then started to fall, and Emily ran in to catch her and hold her up, getting a half smile in return. "Hold on to me. We need to get off the bridge." She started to walk, half carrying, half dragging Tilly along with her.

"It's OK… I'm OK. I'm just a bit dizzy, that's all. He must have got a lucky hit on me."

"Then help me. Keep hold of me, and keep walking. Remember how it was in Scotland? Remember the sunshine mountain?"

"Yeah…" Tilly half laughed.

"That's all it is, just like that. "I'm climbing up the sunshine mountain, where the four winds blow!" She half sang, half talked, all the time marching and glancing over her shoulder, knowing the Germans would be on them any moment. "Sing with me, Tilly!" She demanded as loudly as she dared. "I'm climbing up the sunshine mountain!"

"Where the four winds blow!" Tilly added, and together they blew, before continuing the song as they half marched, half staggered across the bridge like a pair of drunks, stepping off it and into a park just as a figure came into view in the direction of the hotel. "I can't…" Tilly cried softly in a way Emily hadn't heard before, as her legs gave way. It took all Emily had to catch her and stop her from hitting the ground. She half carried, half dragged her over to a bench in the trees where they slumped down next to each other, and Emily wrapped her friend in a tight hug and held her for a moment, kissing her head and whispering reassurances. "I just need a minute…"

"It's OK, we're out of the way here. Let's get our breath for a few minutes, then we can push on." She breathed in through her nose and out through her mouth, trying to compose herself and slow her own breathing and heart rate while she thought through what to do next. They were in a small park that Tilly had shown her on one of their trips around Paris, it was secluded, hidden by trees, and the entrance was through an old gate overgrown by bushes. It was a memorial park of some sort, not the place many people went, hidden away near the Notre Dame with a few old rose bushes that had long been neglected, and now grew wild in the untamed undergrowth. She thought more clearly as her mind slowed, and reasoned that they could probably hide in the park for a while, moving into the overgrown bushes if needs be, and out of sight of any prying eyes. Then, when they'd both had time to catch their breath, they could move on, along the island and back into the city. Names and faces ran through her mind, people who she thought could help, but she quickly realised that she didn't really know anyone, all she'd done was run messages to and from Etienne, and move a few packages here and there, she hadn't actually met any of the network's local Resistance contacts, then she thought of the communist leader, Francois. He'd been contrite when they'd last parted, and consumed with a need to protect his family. If she could get to him, she could offer him asylum in England if he'd help get them out. She knew that the SOE would be fine with it, they'd probably recruit him and send him straight back anyway, but his family would be out. It was a reasonable plan, and better than anything else she had. Half their team were dead, they had no wireless, or weapons beyond a couple of knives, and their safe houses were compromised. All they could do was get out of town. She even considered how she could use the information about the coming attack on Russia. Maybe that would be enough to convince Francois to help them, if he needed anything else. "Right, are you ready?" she asked as she finally stopped trembling, and pulled at Tilly's arm, unintentionally sending her friend's knife clattering off the metal frame of the bench, rattling so loud it sounded like a church bell ringing through the Paris night. "Don't be throwing that away just yet, we may need it…" She half laughed as she reached down to pick up the knife, then frowned as she felt how sticky the handle was, and the ground around it. "No… No, no, no, no!" A fear so intense that she'd never felt anything like it struck deep in her heart as she let the knife drop to the grass and grabbed Tilly's hand. It was warm and sticky with blood, and she quickly reached up and ripped open her coat. "Tilly…. Tilly!" While she reached inside her jacket with her right hand, she put her left on her friend's face, turning her head to look her in the eyes. Her cheeks were wet with tears, and pupils wide. "Tilly… Say something! Where did he get you?"

"I want my dad…" Tilly said, her voice soft and sad, full of emotion.

"Oh, God. Please. Please, no." Emily's hands shot under Tilly's coat, searching through the wetness as the stench of warm blood filled the cool air, and finally she found a puncture wound in the ribs under her left arm, with blood pulsing slowly between her fingers as she pushed tight against it, making her groan a little. "Tilly… Look at me. Tilly." She moved her head to look Tilly in the eyes. "I've got you." Tilly nodded, then took a few shuddering, hard breaths before putting her head against Emily's as she started to sing.

"Once a jolly swagman, camped by a billabong… Under the shade of a coolabah tree…" Her words were weak, half there, half not, holding lightly to the tune between sharp gasps of breath and muffled sobs. "…and he sang, as he watched, and waited 'til his billy boiled… You'll come a waltzing… Matilda with me…"

"Tilly…" Emily felt tears flowing down her face as her heart almost burst with sadness. She pulled her hand tight against the wound in her friend's side, but there wasn't a flinch or gasp, she just kept singing, laying her head on Emily's shoulder as she held her tight, squeezing her for all she was worth in a desperate hope that it would make things ok. Emily cried in desperation, she was a nurse, and most of her adult life had been dedicated to helping people, and keeping them alive. She was trained, and experienced, and there wasn't a thing she could do to help. "Please don't go…" Her voice had lost the urgent edge, replaced by a forlorn hopelessness as she finally relented, and sang with her friend.

"And his ghost can be heard… As you pass by that billabong… You'll come a waltzing Matilda with me…"

The End.

Titles in the Harry's Game Series

Harry's Game – First of the Few

Published in November 2019

Harry's Game – Hell's Corner

Published in February 2020

Harry's Game – Shadows and Dust

Published in May 2020

Harry's Game – Sleeping Giants

Published in January 2021

Harry's Game – Blue Skies and Tailwinds

Published in July 2021

Harry's Game – Sands of Time

Published in November 2021

Harry's Game – Moonlight Serenade

Published in February 2022

Harry's Game – Winds of Change

Published in May 2022

Harry's Game – Last of the Few

Published in August 2022

Harry's Game – Loose Ends

Published in November 2024

Falling Shadows – A Harry's Game Story

Published in November 2025

Introducing Emily

Sometimes, characters take on a life of their own… That was certainly the case with Harriet Cornwall, who seemed to write her own story as she worked her way through over a million words across a series of ten books, with very little input from me. It was also the case for the indomitable Nicole Delacourt, who was only ever supposed to be in the first chapter of the first book, somebody to keep Harriet company as her story got underway, yet she had a very different idea when it came to her involvement. Many other characters have come and gone as Harriet made her way through the Second World War, some staying for the moments intended, others becoming more of a feature, all of them contributing something different in their own unique ways, including a young nurse named Emily Strachan, who cared for Harriet and kept her alive following the horrors of the Battle of France.

Unlike Nicole, Emily did her job without fanfare or acclaim, and once it was done, she continued with her work in relative anonymity. One of the silent millions who played their part in a brutal war, and then…

An idea kept trying to get my attention while I was writing the tenth book in the Harry's Game series, Loose Ends, and no matter how hard I tried to ignore it, or put it to the back of my mind, it kept coming back. Then, as has happened so many times through my writing journey, I decided to get the idea out of my head by writing it down. Just a chapter or two once Loose Ends was published and on its way, and that, as they say, was that! The story flowed with remarkable intensity, and a couple of chapters quickly started to feel like a story I couldn't let go, and one which I needed to see through, if for no other reason than I wanted to know how it would end. Which, if you've read this far, you'll know the answer to be 'horribly!'

With the writing came a need for a great deal of research, to make sure that as with all of the Harry's Game books, the world around the story was as accurate as it was possible to be. Emily may be a fictional character, but her adventures needed to be grounded firmly in reality. A standard set when telling Harriet Cornwall's story, when I found myself learning about the carburettors used with early Rolls Royce

Merlin engines, and wandering around the tunnels carved deep under Malta, to top up many, many years of interest and more casual research. What I found this time, however, was something very different, and the research took me down a deep and sometimes very dark rabbit hole as I learned about the SOE, and its wartime marriage of convenience with the First Aid Nursing Yeomanry.

While I'd learned a little about the SOE over the years, more so when doing research for Harriet's story, and became more acquainted with the First Aid Nursing Yeomanry (an organisation just as covert as the SOE at times, even today!), I wasn't prepared for the very real stories of those who were there, and the hardships they faced. The more I read, the more I wanted Emily's story to be for them, and writing it became even more important. My hope being, as it was with Harriet's story, that readers would be encouraged to read the real stories that that my books are based on, and that those who were really there are remembered for just a little longer, perhaps even by a new generation.

A note about the First Aid Nursing Yeomanry (FANY)

Formed in 1907, the all female voluntary unit is a civilian organisation that served with distinction in both world wars, and continues to support the British government and armed forces even today. Originally conceived as a unit of nurses who would ride onto the battlefield amid flying bullets to provide immediate care to the wounded, members were expected to be keen horsewomen with the means to support their adventures, and they had no shortage of recruits. During the First World War they drove ambulances, and supported casualty clearing stations a step back from the front lines, and provided a host of support services to keep soldiers alive, and provide assistance to the army's medical services. As you'd imagine for the time, they had to fight to be taken seriously, but by the time the war was over, they were a highly respected unit that was much in demand.

As the storm clouds of the Second World War gathered, the First Aid Nursing Yeomanry was ready once again to serve, sending around four thousand of their number to the newly formed women's branch of the British Army, the Auxiliary Territorial Service, where they formed Motor Companies of drivers and mechanics, including staffing their own driver and engineering training school. Around two thousand of their members remained independent, and became known as the 'Independent, or Free FANY', staying true to their civilian volunteer principles, and beyond the direct control of the armed forces. Of these, the vast majority were seconded to the Special Operations Executive as linguists, cryptographers, and wireless operators, in addition to staffing the SOE's training schools, and quickly became renowned for their skills as master codebreakers, with an over 90% success rate by the end of the war as they served in SOE code rooms around the world.

While attitudes of the time led to the women's branches of the armed forces, the Women's Royal Naval Service (WRNS), the Auxiliary Territorial Service (ATS) and the Women's Auxiliary Air Force (WAAF) being explicitly banned from taking up arms against the enemy directly, no such exclusion existed in the FANY's regulations. Despite wearing military uniform, and being closely aligned to the armed forces, they were a civilian organisation, and nobody had even given it a thought. So, when the SOE concluded that they needed female agents to take the war to the enemy, it was the volunteers of the First Aid Nursing Yeomanry that stepped forward.

Women who had the skills and aptitude that the SOE was looking for became 'cap badge FANYs', who wore the uniform of the First Aid Nursing Yeomanry, were commissioned as officers, and trained in the basics of being soldiers, before being sent to special training schools where they were trained as commandos, saboteurs, and military parachutists alongside their male counterparts. Skilled in languages, demolitions, guerilla warfare, and hand to hand fighting, many of them were dropped into Nazi occupied Europe, where they recruited, armed, and trained the many Resistance organisations, and sent and received secret messages containing vital military intelligence under the noses of the Germans. Some of them served as wireless operators, passing messages from the occupied territories back to England, and coordinating military operations, while others led entire battalions of Resistance fighters in combat against battle hardened German divisions. They were the very definition of what we understand these days to be special forces.

The SOE was disbanded in 1946, its mission to set Europe ablaze completed, and those with the required skills and experience were absorbed into MI6 and MI5, while the rest got to go home to their families, their service done. The organisation had the second highest combat casualty rate of any unit during the war (the average life expectancy of an SOE wireless operator in Europe was just 6 weeks), second only to Bomber Command, with agents being given a 50 / 50 chance of survival in the field.

Of those female agents who were sent into occupied Europe, three were awarded the George Cross for gallantry, while many other medals were awarded by various governments recognising the gallantry and meritorious service of women from across the SOE. The reason those three weren't awarded the Victoria Cross, which is the military equivalent of the George Cross, was that despite serving in combat, and performing acts of extreme bravery, heroism, and devotion to duty in the presence of the enemy, the women were members of the FANY, and as such, civilians…

After the war, the British Government refused a recommendation for military medals to bestowed on SOE agent Pearl Witherington, who had trained and led thousands of French Resistance fighters in combat, because she was a civilian, and instead offered her the civil honour being made a Member of the British Empire (MBE) for her work. She returned it, stating: 'There was nothing remotely civil about what I did.'

The Life That I Have

The poem 'The life that I have' was written in December 1943 by the SOE Chief of Codes, Leo Marks, on hearing that his girlfriend, a young woman training to be an aeromedical evacuation nurse, had been killed in a flying accident while training in Canada. The following year, when SOE agent Violette Szabo was preparing to parachute into occupied France ahead of the D Day landings, he noticed that she was struggling to remember her chosen poem code during her briefing, and gave her the poem as a replacement.

Poem codes were used by agents to encode their secret messages before sending them back to England, and if captured, the Gestapo would torture agents with the intention of extracting their poems, so they could send messages posing as the agents, and infiltrate the SOE's networks.

Violette was captured in August 1944, and after interrogation and torture at the hands of the Gestapo, during which she never revealed her poem code, or any other information, she was taken to Ravensbrück concentration camp in Germany, where she was executed in February 1945, just three months before the end of the war in Europe. Violette was posthumously awarded the George Cross for her valour.

So, there you have it. Emily's story, a tribute to those who lived in the shadows, so others could live in the light. I hope you've enjoyed the book, and as always, please feel free to drop me an email and say hello, if you wish.

Karl

karl@harrysgame.com

Printed in Dunstable, United Kingdom